PRAISE FOR CLAIRE WRIGHT

"Once again, the writing is lush and vivid. Claire does a fantastic job at painting the picture for you so clearly that you feel like you're right there with the characters. She expertly weaves together the plot threads from the first book whilst introducing new ones, and keeps the tension high throughout. There's many reveals and twists within, all leading to an intense climax."

—Reviewer

"Delving further into her interpretation of the realm of Irish legend, the author takes us deeper into this intricate world, further developing the lead four and cementing them as some of my favourite characters in modern fantasy fiction. Everything from the banter, character interaction, magical powers, fight scenes - all gleamed in her masterful prose. And that twist!"

—Reviewer

"Loved this one, even as much as the first. Left in suspense, cannot wait for the 3rd instalment!"

—Reviewer

"I have found myself completely immersed in the world presented by Claire Wright. Tír na nÓg is a land I've read of before - particularly as a child - but Claire's ability to describe her vision of this ancient fantasy land is outstanding. I cannot wait for the next Fair Ones book!! I'm so obsessed with these characters, I need to know what life has to offer them all."

—Reviewer

ALSO BY CLAIRE WRIGHT

Fair Ones
Realm of Lore and Lies (2022)
Realm of Trials and Trickery (2023)
Realm of Chaos and Crowns (coming soon)

REALM OF TRIALS AND TRICKERY

FAIR ONES

BOOK 2

CLAIRE WRIGHT

Realm of Trials and Trickery

Copyright © 2023 by Claire Wright

All rights reserved.

This is a work of fiction. Names, characters, places, and incidents are either a product of the author's imagination or are used fictitiously. Any resemblance to actual persons, living or dead, events or locales is entirely coincidental.

No portion of this book may be reproduced in any form without written permission from the publisher or author, except for the use of brief quotations in a book review.

Published by Leannán Press

Cover Design Art and Design by Tairelei

www.tairelei.com

Character Art by @Pangolin2b (on Instagram)

Editor: Michelle Roberts

Map Design: Rhys Davies

Identifiers

ISBN: 978-1-7397320-3-5 (eBook)

ISBN: 978-1-7397320-4-2 (Paperback)

ISBN: 978-1-7397320-5-9 (Hardback)

This is a fantasy book written for adults and therefore is unsuitable for young readers. Includes scenes depicting violence, death, sex, and strong language . . . so all the fun stuff.

authorclairewright.com

For Brendan. You looked after us all for so long. It's your time
to rest. You live on in our hearts as will all the trivia you taught
us.
And in case I didn't say it enough, I love you.

CONTENTS

Tír na nÓg	XIV
Pronunciation Guide	XVI
Encyclopaedia	XVIII
1. Chapter 1	1
2. Chapter 2	8
3. Chapter 3	16
4. Chapter 4	18
5. Chapter 5	25
6. Chapter 6	31
7. Chapter 7	39
8. Chapter 8	46
9. Chapter 9	53
10. Chapter 10	59
11. Chapter 11	67
12. Chapter 12	70

13. Chapter 13   78

14. Chapter 14   84

15. Chapter 15   89

16. Chapter 16   96

17. Chapter 17   107

18. Chapter 18   114

19. Chapter 19   118

20. Chapter 20   128

21. Chapter 21   135

22. Chapter 22   142

23. Chapter 23   151

24. Chapter 24   158

25. Chapter 25   169

26. Chapter 26   175

27. Chapter 27   185

28. Chapter 28   194

29. Chapter 29   202

30. Chapter 30   209

31. Chapter 31   213

32. Chapter 32   219

33. Chapter 33   226

34. Chapter 34   231

35. Chapter 35   242

36. Chapter 36   246

37. Chapter 37   257

38. Chapter 38   269

39. Chapter 39   278

40. Chapter 40   289

41. Chapter 41   295

42. Chapter 42   303

43. Chapter 43   310

44. Chapter 44   315

45. Chapter 45   325

46. Chapter 46   333

47. Chapter 47   340

48. Chapter 48   350

49. Chapter 49   358

50. Chapter 50   362

51. Chapter 51   370

52. Chapter 52   376

53. Chapter 53   382

54. Chapter 54   389

55. Chapter 55 — 395

56. Chapter 56 — 402

57. Chapter 57 — 411

58. Chapter 58 — 421

59. Chapter 59 — 428

60. Chapter 60 — 437

61. Chapter 61 — 444

62. Chapter 62 — 449

63. Chapter 63 — 450

64. Chapter 64 — 462

65. Chapter 65 — 468

66. Chapter 66 — 474

67. Chapter 67 — 483

68. Chapter 68 — 491

69. Chapter 69 — 501

70. Chapter 70 — 508

71. Chapter 71 — 518

72. Chapter 72 — 526

73. Chapter 73 — 533

74. Chapter 74 — 544

75. Chapter 75 — 551

76. Chapter 76 — 558

77. Chapter 77 — 567

78. Chapter 78 — 573

Acknowledgements — 577

About the Author — 579

Go Raibh Maith Agat — 580

Giant's Causeway
Grianan of Aileach
ULSTER
Lough Neagh
Beaghmore Stone Circle
Druid's Chair and Well
Cooley Mountains
Knocknarea
CONNACHT
Ratheroghan
MIDE
Knowth
Dowth
Oweynagat
Hill of Uisneach
Newgrange
Hill of Tara
Knockma Wood
River Boyne
Lough Corrib
Lough Ree

Aran Islands
Cliffs of Moher
The Burren
Lough Derg
Powerscourt Waterfall
LEINSTER
Strongbow's Tree
MUNSTER
Beara Peninsula
Drombeg Stone Circle
Tír na nÓg

PRONUNCIATION GUIDE

CHARACTERS

Aisling ASH-ling
Babd bive
Biróg ber-ogue
Caicher kaw-ker
Caoimhe Kwee-va
Ciarán keer-AWN
Cú Chulainn COO hullen
Diarmuid DEER-mid
Ethne eth-NA
Fiadh Fee-ah
Fionn Mac Cumhaill fe-UHN mack-coo-ul
Gearoid gar-owedge
Maebh maeve
Manannán mac Lir man-ann-AWN mac leer
Morrigán more-eh-GAWN
Niamh Neeve
Sinéad Shin-aid
Tiernan tier-nan
Tomás - toh-maws

PLACES

Dowth DOW-th
Hill of Tara
Knowth NOW-th

Lia Fáil lee-a F-AW-l
Teamhair cha-wur
Tír na nÓg Tier-nah-nogue
OTHER
Fianna fee-a-na
Gaeilge Gwale-geh
Rígfennid reeg-fen-ed
Samhain sow-wen
Tuatha Dé Danann tooah-day-danann

Please note there are multiple dialects within the Irish language. Readers familiar with the language should use their preference.

Want to find out more about Irish mythology? Check out the encyclopaedia.

ENCYCLOPAEDIA

An Garda Síochána an guard-a she-a-kawn-a, meaning the Guardian of the Peace. The Irish police. Also known as gardai or the guards.

Babd bive. One of three sisters that make up The Morrígan. Babd is their crow form. See also Macha and Nemain.

Banshee A female spirit in Irish folklore who heralds the death of a family member, usually by wailing, shrieking, or keening.

Bodhrán boh-rawn. An Irish frame drum consisting of a circular wooden frame covered with a goatskin head on one side. It is played by striking the skin with a small wooden stick known as a bodhrán beater, tipper or cipín.

Brehon law Laws brought in place after the Peace Treaty between Tuatha Dé Danann and humankind. Most humans are unaware of these laws except for a small group of humans with Faerie Sight, known as fianna.

Caicher Airgetlám kaw-ker AR-gid-lawm. High King of Tuatha Dé Danann. Descendant of Nuada Airgetlám, the first king of the Tuatha Dé Danann.

Caillte call-cha. Meaning 'lost' in Gaeilge (Irish language). The caillte are a group of five individuals from different clans who went missing seven years ago. Rumours circulated around the time that two of the missing persons - Gearoid McQuillan, second to Imogen McQuillan's clan, and Nessa

Cassidy, matriarch of the Cassidy clan - were having an affair. Another notable missing person during this time is Lorcan Breen, second to matriarch, Cara Breen.

Cath An important Fianna rite, where clan members may compete in a series of trials to win the High King's favour and be selected into a coveted position of highguard. If selected, warriors may live in Tír na nÓg.

Céilí kay-lee. A traditional Irish social gathering with a band of musicians and folk dancing takes place.

Changeling A baby or young child who has been secretly swapped by an ancient faerie who takes his or her place. The dying faerie tricks the infant's parents into caring for them until they die. It is unknown what happens to the human child afterwards. Some believe they are left to die, while others believe they are given as gifts to the fae in Tír na nÓg.

Clurichaun Face like a withered apple, nose red and purple and bulbous from heavy drinking. Normally haunts breweries, taverns, and wine cellars.

Cohuleen druith kaw-hool-een drew-ah. Red hat with turquoise feathers belonging to the merrow (male mermen). Magical qualities allowing the wearer to breathe underwater.

Cú Chulainn COO hullen. A legendary warrior hero and demigod in Irish mythology. Famous for single-handedly fighting an army during 'The Cattle Raid of Cooley', and for his ability to riastrád, or warp spasm, turning into a monstrous creature who knew neither friend nor foe during battle.

Dearg due dah-ruh-guh du-ah. Meaning 'red blood sucker'. The Irish version of a female vampire.

Dowth DOW-th. One of three ancient monuments situated in Boyne Valley.

Druid A mix of Fianna (humans with Faerie Sight) and wiccans (humans with the power to manipulate the elements and perform magic).

Ellén Trechend elleen trech-end. Three-headed monster from Irish mythology.

Faerie Sight The ability to see through fae glamour and therefore gaining the knowledge that fairies exist.

Fair Ones Fairies. There are two species of fae: Tuatha Dé Danann, the ruling class, and Fomorians, fae who are almost extinct in this realm, or banished to other realms.

Far liath far lee-a. Grey man. Personification of fog. Shrouds victims in its malevolent mist to disappear.

Fear Dearg far djarig. Red Man. Male Irish faerie. Solitary creature.

Fianna fee-a-na. Humans with Faerie Sight. Fianna clans are made up of families who all serve under a matriarch, who in turn answer to a provincial leader known as a rígfennid. All fianna serve under one human High King.

Fionn Mac Cumhaill fee-UHN mack-coo-ool. Also known as Finn MacCool. The first High King of Ireland and leader of Fianna warrior clans.

Fomorians Fair Ones. Thrive on chaos and destruction. Enemies to the Tuatha Dé Danann who defeated them during The Great Battle. Fomorians live in exile in the human realm.

Gardaí gar-dee. Means guardians. Irish police.

Hill of Tara A hill and ancient ceremonial and burial site.

Knowth NOW-th. One of three ancient monuments situated in Boyne Valley.

Le croí gran leh kree gran. With purity of heart.

Lia Fáil lee-a F-AW-l. Stone of Destiny. Gifted to the Fianna by the Tuatha Dé Danann. Cries out when the rightful High King touches it.

Lunantisidhe Loo-nan-tee-shee. faerie species that live in and protect blackthorn trees. As the blackthorn tree is linked to the waning moon, fairies that live within are night creatures.

Macha One of three sisters that make up The Morrígan. Macha is their female faerie form. See also Babd and Nemain.

Manannán mac Lir man-ann-AWN mac leer. Ruler of the sea, grants beings passage to the afterlife.

Medb maeve. Queen Medb is a prominent character within Irish mythology. Portrayed as both goddess and Queen of Connacht. Which she delights in.

Milesian humans who'd driven the Tuatha Dé Danann underground.

Minn óir min oi-yer . Irish crown. Translation, 'diadem of gold'.

Morrigán more-eh-GAWN. Sisters from the Tuatha Dé royal bloodline. Three female forms encompassed within their shared soul. Badb is the crow. Macha, is a female faerie and Nemain is a spirit warrior.

Mound of Hostages particular hill within Hill of Tara.

Nemain one of three sisters that make up The Morrígan. Nemain is their warrior spirit form. See also Babd and Macha.

Newgrange Ancient monument located within Boyne Valley. Part of three monuments that make up Brú na Boinne - an archaeological landscape in county Meath.

Níl sé ach ina thús. Kneel shay ach ina thus. It's only just begun.

Nuada Airgeltlám noo-ada or-geth-lawm. The silver-handed warrior god. Former High King of the Tuatha Dé Danann.

Oilliphéist all-ee-feesht. Dragon-like creatures typically associated with living in seas and lakes.

Púca pooka. Fae creature that takes different forms. Known for mischievous behaviour.

Plámás plaw mawse. Disingenuous flattery or praise to manipulate someone.

Ríastrad reea-strad. Also known as warp spasm. Taking the form of a monstrous creature.

Rígfennid reeg-fen-ed.

Samhain sow-wen. Occurs October 31st. The veil between this world and Tír na nÓg—the Otherworld—is at its thinnest. Historically, people dressed up in order to trick harmful spirits into leaving them alone. Hence the tradition of dressing up as witches and ghouls at Halloween.

Seanchai Shan-e-khee. A traditional Gaelic storyteller/historian.

Slainte slawn-chte. Means cheers in Gaeilge (Irish language).

Sluagh slew-ah. Host of the unforgiving dead. Faerie spirits.

An Taoiseach tee-shock. Head of government in Ireland.

Teamhair cha-wur. The ancient name given to the Hill of Tara.

Tír na nÓg Tier-nah-nogue. Land of Eternal Youth. Alternate realm where time moves slowly. Humans can live there almost as immortals as long as they never touch the human realm soil again. They can still die here.

Tuatha Dé Danann tooah-day-danann. Fair Ones. Known for their beauty. Children of the goddess Danu. Also known as Tuath Dé which means 'tribe of the gods'.

Uisce Beatha ish-ka bee-ha. Literally means 'Water of life'. Whiskey in Irish language.

Warp Spasm also known as ríastrad. Taking the form of a monstrous creature.

Will O' The Wisp Sprites who lead travellers through the woods at night.

CHAPTER 1
MAEBH

Maebh had always been a fighter at heart. The woodland of Tír na nÓg held its breath as she danced, not with costumes or heeled shoes, but with steel and fury. The forest was her stage, the heavy weight of her sword the only embellishment she needed. Her blade was a gleaming arc of silver, meeting its kin with a resounding clang, reverberating against her bones as the ancient trees watched.

Maebh's footwork was impeccable, her steps calculated. Her mother would have found fault somewhere. The thought had her stumble as her opponent lunged, but Maebh sidestepped in time. Sending a spray of leaves and twigs into the air with a fast pivot, her blonde curls escaped their plait and danced wildly. With each twist and turn, she felt the damp earth beneath her boots, but the clashing steel was not enough. The rattle of her bones with each hit did little to hold back the tide of her reality.

Matriarch. But not truly.

"Is that all you've got?" she asked with a wicked smirk, raising her weapon again.

Her opponent's sword was a serpent's strike, aiming for her heart. Maebh parried, her blade's path drawing a crescent moon in the air, a motion born of countless hours of practise. Every deflection and dodge brought to the surface the thoughts she'd buried.

Gritting her teeth, she lunged. Tiernan was trapped, and she couldn't rescue him. Fading back, she swung with a cry, but all she could hear was the haunting whispers of distrust. She twisted; her blade raised overhead. Setanta's disappointment filled the clearing like a fog. Maebh blocked a powerful blow. Her clan would rather he led them. She jabbed outward, blindly. Her mother had been right about her. Another parry. She was not enough.

On and on, she fought until her movements bore the weight of doubt and pain. The steel was ice, but her heart was engulfed by flames of betrayal. Each lunge was a reminder of her clan's sidelong glances. A clumsy swing brought Maebh to her knees, not from the impact, but from the force of her own thoughts. She was no longer in the forest but kneeling before the abyss of her fears. Every time she closed her eyes, she saw Tiernan's stone face and blamed herself.

Her breathing grew ragged, her strength waning as she fought against the pull of darkness urging her to jump; to fall into that depth of despair and never crawl out again. Yes, she'd always been a fighter, but her greatest enemy was her mind.

"Maebh! Breathe. It's okay."

The world came rushing back. The towering trees of Tír na nÓg, the soft, filtered sunlight. She was on her knees, blade on the leaf-strewn ground, and Ash stood nearby with concern etched in her green eyes.

Maebh blinked, gulping air as though she'd been underwater. The fog surrounding her cleared, the pain and doubt receding like a passing storm. It was just practise. Just Ash; her friend, not a foe.

"You went somewhere," Ash murmured, black hair plastered against her flushed face as she offered to help pull Maebh up.

Maebh nodded as she accepted the hand, her throat dry while her limbs ached, not from sparring, but from fighting through yet another anxiety attack. "I did," she whispered, her voice shaking as she willed her heart to steady. "I'm back now."

Ash squeezed her hand, a silent promise that she was not alone in the battles she faced. The piercing call of a trumpet echoed through the trees, instantly cutting through the haze of their combat. Both women froze. That sound was a knell, its implications clear and immediate.

Ash's eyes met Maebh's wide ones. "The coronation," she groaned, hastily sheathing her sword. "We can't be late."

Maebh nodded, looking toward the distant fortress of Tara Court. The weight of today pressed on her as she tried to breathe steadily. High King Bradan had been explicit: attendance was mandatory. The consequences of missing it were severe.

Even the high walls and imposing gates were unforgiving of those who disobeyed the new High King's orders. The gates would shut, and those left outside would be stranded indefinitely. Their welcome to this kingdom would end, and with it, any hope of saving Tiernan or freeing Ash's brother.

Ash grabbed Maebh's arm, pulling her out of her thoughts. "We shouldn't have come out here. Not today."

"We'll make it." Maebh's voice was firm, but her dread was palpable.

"Really?" Ash stuffed her hand into her combat pants' pocket, retrieving a crumpled parchment.

Maebh didn't need her to unfold it to know what it was, but she grabbed it anyway and stared down at the calligraphy.

High King Bradan Cassidy decrees all Fianna, resident, or visitor, attend his coronation for a special announcement. Failure to do so will lead to banishment from Tír na nÓg and ...

Grabbing the parchment, Ash raised it to Maebh's face, but she swatted it away. "If we're not there, we're fucked."

Maebh only nodded as she fastened her sword belt to her back harness, her fingers trembling slightly. Ash jammed the parchment back into her pocket, cursing under her breath. The two women exchanged a look before breaking into a run, leaves crunching underfoot and branches whipping past them.

Maebh's lungs burned and the weight of her sword at her back seemed to double, but she pushed on, Ash close. The trumpet was the first warning. They *could* make it.

Maebh glanced behind. "Are you always this fucking slow?"

Ash shoved her, quickening her pace through the maze of dense woodland. Towering trees with gnarled branches swayed in the sunlight, lighting up the forest ground. Ash had to take two steps for each one of Maebh's longer strides to keep up.

"He's going to share what's happening," Ash said through ragged breaths.

Lightening pierced Maebh's heart. "It's taken him long enough."

Bradan was finally going to reveal what had happened. No more avoiding questions about Tiernan and High King Aedan. Or why the Cath rules had changed, and why they no longer had to seek Fionn Mac Cumhaill. Her breath caught as she swallowed against the burning tide of apprehension. Maebh, Ash and Setanta had agreed to stay quiet about finding the first High King, and she'd fought with both over how long Bradan had let his kingdom remain ignorant to the danger they were in.

Her clan didn't know why she'd been withdrawn. They'd assumed it was because of Imogen McQuillan's death, and the burden of becoming their new matriarch. If they knew the real threat that faced them, they would understand why her focus was waylaid. That misunderstanding would finally be put to rest with this announcement. Everyone would know the peril they were truly under.

Ash stumbled on a raised tree root, her subsequent curse loud enough to disturb a nest of silver-furred lunantisidhe. The tiny moon faeries' shrill voices rose as they dislodged from the cluster of blackthorns they'd been protecting, translucent branch-patterned wings humming with ferocious speed. Maebh laughed and grabbed Ash's hand, yanking her forward as they sprinted away. Turning, she breathed a sigh of relief when the golden-eyed creatures didn't follow them. They weren't the deadliest Fair Ones, but they certainly were wicked when provoked, and waking the night faeries at this hour would invite trouble they didn't need.

They slowed to a jog when out of sight, and Maebh allowed them a moment to catch their breath before breaking into another sprint. Ash matched her quickened pace. They had no choice. Missing the coronation was not an option; not when so much was at stake.

The early morning chirp of birds accompanied the soft spring breeze, caressing the loose curls of Meabh's hair. It was always balmy springtime here, even if it was technically winter back home. Had she ever felt like she belonged in the human realm? She couldn't say she had, but here it was no better.

"What date was it for Mary and Dom last night?" Maebh asked, her voice shaky as she ran.

Ash's pale face grew pinched, her nose-ring glistening in a rare patch of sunlight in the waning trees. She was now covered in light freckles, whereas Maebh's complexion had grown darker from spending more time outdoors. Ash's face always scrunched when asked about her foster parents, but Maebh knew she wanted to talk about them. Needed to.

"It's already the twentieth of December for them."

Maebh's booted steps faltered on the uneven ground. "Winter Solstice eve."

Ash nodded gravely, her raven hair swaying with the movement. "Time is so messed up here. When I asked a local if the solstice would happen soon, they said it wasn't due to take place for another four moons."

"I still can't figure out how long a week is here, can you?"

"Nope."

They raced through the rough terrain in silence, the clock counting down to gods knew what hanging over them. There were no hours for how long the sun shone or when the moon rose in this realm. Maebh had attempted to categorise it, looking in both castle and druid libraries, but neither had offered answers.

Her studies hadn't been fruitless; learning more about different realms. There were few accounts on where scholars believed Manannán mac Lir took souls to an afterlife, but there were hundreds of scrolls on the depths of the Underworld, where the most heinous Fair Ones lived.

"Is Set still spending all his time amongst moth-eaten parchment?" Maebh probed, noting that her brother's name no longer brought a smile to Ash's lips. Instead, they turned downward as Ash stared straight ahead.

"I guess?" Ash tripped, stopping to gasp in air, so Maebh jogged back to stand beside her. Ash's cheeks were a splotchy red as she spoke. "He may as well ask for a castle room; I'm sure Bradan would allow it. He's either there or with Orla."

"You know there's nothing between them, right?" Maebh poked Ash's side, but her friend slapped her away, glaring at her. Maebh smirked before adding, "He's studying the scrolls to find out what Ethne is up to. Who she truly is."

"I know." Ash's shoulders slumped. "And I'm a selfish cow for complaining about it."

"You're not . . ."

"I'm thinking about it, and you know it."

Maebh bumped Ash's shoulder with her own as they caught their breath. "You're allowed to think about all the horrible things you want."

"No. I'm not." Ash sighed, resting her hand on the hilt of her sword. "Ethne is planning something, and we only have days to figure out what. We can only hope Bradan has a plan to stop her because we sure as the realms don't.

"We are no closer to freeing Conor from the dungeon, or Tiernan . . ." Ash's voice cracked, but she continued as if it hadn't, ". . . from the stone enchantment. We've been here for weeks, and we've accomplished fuck all about the shitshow we're in."

"We'll find out soon enough," Maebh said, casting a glance toward Tara Court, her heartbeat as erratic as her thoughts. "Bradan will have the answers."

The silver-haired female was planning something, and if Ethne's pre-show was to perform a blood sacrifice on Samhain, Maebh dreaded to think what the main event would be on Winter Solstice. Murder was high on their suspect list.

But who would be her next victim? And gods forbid, how many would there be?

The bell tolled again.

CHAPTER 2
MAEBH

Maebh and Ash were quiet as they ran toward Tara Court, but the creatures in this realm were not. Birds and winged beasts chirped and growled overhead, while the rustling of underground bushes occasionally led to a scampering of squirrels and pygmy shrews; all competing with the ringing bells in the distance. But there were other beasts in these woods.

Fair Ones.

Maebh noticed a flash of colour amongst green boughs. The fear dearg's skin was as pale as milk with thatches of orange hair peeking out from under his long red coat and cap. His legs swung idly below him like a child's, though his features had the ageless look of the Tuatha Dé as he held a wooden pipe between his lips. Wisps of fragrant smoke drifted lazily upwards in perfect circles, carrying with them the heady scent of burning heather.

Ash unsheathed her sword as Maebh unclasped a dagger on her belt. They would not make it back in time if this Fair One decided they looked like playthings, but he paid them no heed.

Maebh glanced back at the strange faerie as he faded into the greens and browns of the woodland, the encounter already taking on the half-remembered quality of a dream. She shook her head in a bid to clear the confusion attempting to grip her mind. Fae glamour was more powerful in this realm, and Fianna had to stay alert to combat its effects. They harnessed their weapons before breaking into a sprint toward the castle walls, leaving the fear dearg to his solitary vigil.

The oppressive forest finally thinned as Tara Court loomed closer. Highguard stationed at the portcullis called out warnings to stragglers as they waited for the signal to close the gate.

"Shit, come on, come on, come on!" Maebh shouted, her voice turning more shrill with every step.

They sprinted ahead as the last Fianna went through the gate and the portcullis began to lower. Maebh, her chest heaving, raced with every ounce of energy left. She heard Ash's cry from behind and she pivoted, grabbing the other matriarch's wrist, propelling her forward. If either were getting through, it had to be Ash. Conor needed her.

Maebh's fingers brushed the rough texture of the closing gate helplessly after Ash disappeared through it. She was too late. Maebh fell to her knees, a breath tearing from her lungs in a sob she couldn't hold back. A slender arm reached out, pulling her through seconds before the heavy portcullis thudded into place. The two women lay on the cobbled ground for a moment, catching their breath as Maebh stared at the iron gate inches from her face. Heart still racing, she turned to face her friend. "You could have speared me with the gate."

"But I didn't," Ash said, and the two women broke into ear-splitting grins.

A hysterical giggle escaped Maebh's lips before they both burst into torrents of laughter. She wiped tears from her eyes as a stitch burned her sides. "Stop making me laugh."

A cough sounded, and she squinted up at two imposing figures dressed in the black highguard's attire.

"You're cutting it fine today, ladies," one of the men said before leaving them to lie on the ground in another wave of laughter.

"Come on." Ash stood, wiping the last traces of amusement from her cheeks as she drew a deep, calming breath. When she reached to hoist Maebh up, a final huff of laughter broke free.

"Do I look that bad?" Maebh groaned, leaning heavily on Ash as she caught her breath.

"No. Just like you've been dragged through a ditch backwards."

"Bitch," she chuckled, letting Ash drag her by the arm through the empty, vacant streets of the market.

Not a trader, customer or child was in sight amongst the rows of deserted stalls. The town had abandoned everything to witness the new High King's coronation. Even if it hadn't been compulsory, everyone would have gone to hear his announcement. Maebh rolled her eyes as she spotted the crowds gathered at the base of the Hill of Tara, filling the open fields and buzzing with hushed anticipation. Fianna were packed shoulder to shoulder, while some milled about, trying to manoeuvre for a better view of the impending ceremony on top of the hill, an excited energy humming through the swarming masses.

Ash angled toward the warrior campsites, but Maebh pulled her back, shaking her head and tugging her toward the hill.

"Aren't you going to change?" Ash squeaked.

Maebh rotated so she walked backwards, calling out, "Are you really going to miss Bradan's coronation so you can change into a clean pair of knickers?"

"I'd settle for washing the muck off," Ash hissed as she caught up to her, scrubbing at her face, leaving her cheeks red. Maebh didn't have the heart to tell her she hadn't made things better as Ash continued her attempts at tidying up. "Do you think the Lia Fáil will cry out for him?"

Maebh only shrugged as she spotted Setanta, a head above the surrounding bodies, his hair a twin to her own like a beacon of sunlight. Navigating the heavy crowd, she directed them over to the section assigned to the visiting warrior clans. Despite mocking Ash, she swatted at her hair, pushing it away from her face as she squinted up at the ancient white stone sitting on the nearby hill.

It had been the only topic anyone could talk about for days. Would the Lia Fáil, gifted to Fianna by the Tuatha Dé Danann, finally cry out? Would the magical stone recognise their new High King as the rightful ruler of Ireland? For the Fianna, anyway. The Fair Ones had their own High King, Caicher Airgetlám, and Maebh would argue they ruled over all—humans and faerie—alike.

"Our mothers should be here," Ash murmured as she stopped, the excited murmurs of the surrounding crowd almost drowning out her voice.

Maebh squeezed her hand, glancing at Ash's sombre demeanour. She'd had a complicated relationship with her mother. As had Maebh. But Imogen McQuillan's absence had left a prism of longing Maebh hadn't expected, and she knew it was the same for Ash.

Her friend offered a weak smile. "Mary and Dom would find this fascinating."

Gathered at the hill's base was a sea of people, a blend of visitor clans and Mide residents. The warriors, distinguishable by their leather armours adorned with metal studs and emblems, stood in organised ranks, their sharp weapons catching the light and gleaming with menace.

As Maebh followed Ash through the thronged masses of the locals, she found herself engrossed by the clash of styles on display from centuries and decades past. She observed women wearing tight-fitting wool and linen dresses, adorning their long hair with wildflowers loosely held by plaits standing alongside others in flared knee-length skirts and bobbed hair, bedecked with beaded necklaces. Some men wore simple tunics and trousers, while others sported top hats, three-piece suits and used walking canes to wave merrily at the children dashing by in play.

Ash led Maebh by a small grouping of women in fitted bodices with waists pulled impossibly narrow, elaborate hairstyles towering to dizzying heights, and floor-sweeping gowns trimmed in lace trailing behind them. She had never seen the countless years so vividly condensed into one place at one time.

"Hippies, flappers and repressed Victorians, oh my," Maebh uttered, smirking when she heard Ash's chuckle.

Bards with their bodhráns and flutes moved among the crowd, playing soft tunes. Children, their faces a picture of awe and curiosity, were clustered together, held back by elder siblings or parents, but their excited whispers floated in the air.

The energy was electric. Conversations were hushed, but hopeful, the vast assembly collectively holding its breath for the arrival of the one who would lead them in these uncertain times: the High King. Ash's hand quivered in hers and Maebh noted how her lower lip trembled before Ash sucked it in.

"You'll see them again," Maebh offered, knowing Ash's mind was still with Mary and Dom and not the surrounding Fianna, but Ash shook her head.

"I need to remind them every time where I am and what I'm doing. Which, when they finally snap out of it, causes an argument between Mary and I."

"Dom always seems to calm things down," Maebh said, having witnessed exactly that on the occasions she'd joined Ash at Tiernan's satellite tree.

Her lungs spasmed as her chest grew tight, but she gritted her teeth against the wave of thoughts that would consume her. She would not think about him. Maebh hadn't spoken his name aloud in four days. Though it'd circled her mind relentlessly, she'd refused, trying desperately to convince herself that there was still hope there.

Maebh had done so little to save him and the guilt was eating her alive at night. She'd close her eyes to see his brown eyes staring back at her. She'd hear the deep timbre of his voice curl around her ear. And then she'd watch him turn to stone over and over until she couldn't sleep or even breathe. Every day, she'd felt a piece of her own heart turn to stone, too. In solidarity for a man she held a thousand what-ifs for, or in defiance; she wasn't sure. It'd been four days. And not a single one had got easier. Maebh didn't deserve to think about Tiernan Cassidy until she had more answers.

"It's becoming almost impossible to talk to them," Ash said, hugging the hems of her fitted jacket close around her petite frame, the Breen coat of arms emblazoned on her chest. "They're so confused whenever I broach the subject of time with them. It's like fae glamour is fighting to control them, and the longer we stay here, the harder it is for them to remember the truth."

"It's been nearly a month for us, Ash. Time in the human realm seemed to speed up when we first arrived, but now it's standing still. I don't know how to get my head around it, never mind Mary and Dom. They don't have Faerie Sight."

Ash bit her bottom lip before releasing it as her hushed voice broke. "I called a few days ago and Mary and I were chatting about something stupid. It was as if I were calling from uni campus, and it felt so normal. But then she froze mid-sentence, staring blankly at the screen like she didn't know who was on the other end of the call."

Maebh hugged Ash's side as she let out a sniffle, but she blinked back her unshed tears, aggressively swiping with the back of her hands. "I asked what was wrong, and she said, 'Who are you?' like I was a stranger. I had to remind her, but it took

Dom arriving home and jogging her memory, telling her about me and our lives together, for it to sink in."

"Oh, Ash," Maebh said, rubbing her arm.

"Once she remembered, Mary cried and apologised, but what if next time she can't? What if Dom forgets me, too?"

Ash met Maebh's gaze, fear darkening her emerald eyes. "I don't know how much longer they can hold on to reality with me living in this realm. And if I lose them . . ." Her thread broke off, her eyes filmed with tears.

Maebh squeezed her side before Ash led them through the clans once more. As they walked, Maebh said, "We'll find a way . . ." She trailed off, and Ash nodded sadly.

"There's nothing we can do. Time jumps here, and I will lose them. It's only a matter of when."

They stared at one another until Ash shook out her limbs, plastering a smile on her face before raising her hand in greeting to her clan. Conversation over. Maebh understood. Ash didn't want to think about what would happen when Winter Solstice actually arrived. Not for whatever Ethne would unleash, but also what it meant for the two realms and her foster parents.

Ash waved at her cousins, who had left a space for her at the front of the Breen clan. With a final nod, the women parted, and as Maebh made her way to the McQuillans, trumpets sounded from the distance along with the hooves of several horses.

Excitement coated the air as banners with the Cassidy coat of arms flew by, and their leaders arrived on horseback from the castle. The coronation had taken place within the throne room with only a select few invited, but they all would witness this next part. The part that truly mattered.

As a great white steed carried Bradan Cassidy toward the Hill of Tara, his broad shoulders draped in the rich red robes of the High King, a roaring cheer sounded.

With a shaky breath, Maebh donned her mask of indifference before turning toward the McQuillan clan. They had left no space for her at the front where Setanta stood. He glanced at her once and turned, but not before she noted disappointment mar his expression. Even the younger warriors stiffened their shoulders as she pushed past. With each cold shoulder, her icy smile widened until there was nothing gentle or weak peeking through. No. She was Maebh McQuillan. Daughter of a dead matriarch. Untouchable. They would not see her yield. She would drag them all to the Underworld before she allowed that.

Sharing emotions was a vulnerability, and she knew how dangerous that could be in a clan filled with vipers.

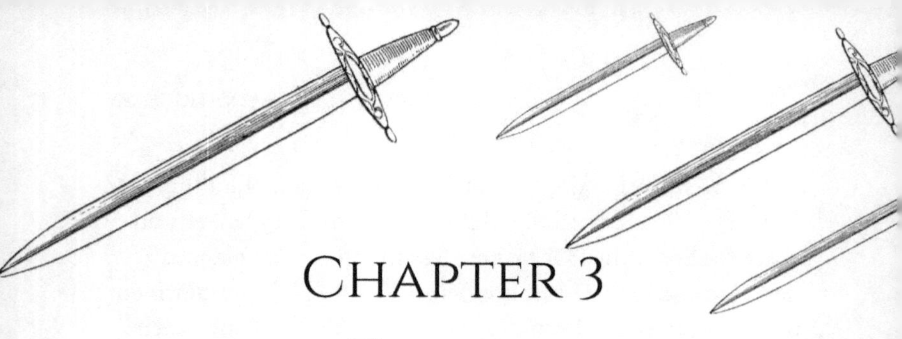

CHAPTER 3
TIERNAN

He'd once had a name.

Stay.

But now his purpose was to protect. The High King slumbered in his impenetrable bed. He was made of stone. All the guardians were.

Stay.

Sunlight hair and blue eyes flashed before him. Who was she? He used to know her name. Perhaps he once loved her?

Break. Break. Break.

No. He knew of nobody but his stone clan.

Fionn Mac Cumhaill was his kin and king.

No. His name was . . . it was . . .

Roaring from within his icy prison, he grasped for himself. Slowly, imperceptibly, he clung to the thin threads that made him different. It could have been an eternity later, but finally, he remembered. Not as much as he used to. But it was more than just being a stone guardian. He was more.

Could he have moved, he might have trembled. That had been the closest he'd been to losing himself completely. Fionn and his stone guardians had almost won.

The guardian beside him stirred. All stone guardians' consciousnesses were linked in an intricate hive mind. Nessa was her name, and she had once been his mother. Until her stone hand had punched through to his heart, turning him into this.

Stay. Protect.

Shut. Up!

Tiernan was his name.

Wasn't it?

Darkness descended before him. A suffocating blanket of midnight until a moon- white face peered up at him through a frame of silver hair.

With a too-wide smile, the alluring female purred, "Still fighting? Good boy."

Tiernan was his name.

CHAPTER 4
MAEBH

Bradan Cassidy, former Rígfénnid of Leinster, and newly-crowned High King, droned on in front of the gathered crowd at the base of the historical hill. Maebh held her arms tightly to her body, every muscle tensed and ready. For what, she wasn't sure, but she willed him to get on with it. The Lia Fáil was his backdrop, and she couldn't help noting how well he'd weaselled his way into his new role. He captivated most, his booming voice carrying on the ever-present breeze.

She squinted at his broad frame, avoiding eye contact in case he spotted her. Bradan's face was similar enough to Tiernan's that it was impossible not to think about how he stood above the ground as his son remained captured beneath. And he'd done nothing about it. He had simply built and schemed for this moment. But that was about to end.

"The Lia Fáil was gifted to Fianna at the dawn of our alliance with the Tuatha Dé Danann. The stone cried out for High King Fionn Mac Cumhaill. Regardless of the outcome, I will serve you as your king."

Applause erupted around Maebh as Bradan finally shut up, and she rolled her eyes. Even if he planned to save Tiernan and tell all Fianna about the threat looming over them, a small, selfish part of her hoped he would fail today. That everyone standing here would witness the silence of that mystical king-accepting stone.

Another figure emerged from the line-up facing them. Dancing between the white-clad druids and pompous rígfénnid, a woman with a crown woven from twigs raised a staff over her head, lamenting a melodic chant. Even from this distance, Maebh couldn't argue with how striking she was in her gold dress. Auburn plaits and twists were stacked high above her heart-shaped face, her freckled cheeks upturned to the sun as her melodious voice carried in the wind. She was like a flame flickering on the stage with her mesmerising movements.

Maebh fought against a light-headedness that threatened to pull her back into the abyss. Another druid had taken Ethne's place. What would this mean? She flashed a look at Setanta, who'd seemed to make the same connection. His jaw was set in grim acceptance.

"... and she didn't even bother to dress in clean clothes," Lorna jeered loudly from behind. "Look at the state of her. Everything handed to her, and no thanks given."

Maebh stiffened as another nasal voice joined. Her aunt's friend, Maura, and one of the McQuillan elders. The words were not a shock; the view of her clan had never wavered. They still cut.

"Put silk on a goat and it's still a goat."

Greeted with derisive laughter from a few onlookers, Maebh stood resolute on the hill, ignoring the stickiness of her training attire. She wouldn't have considered changing. The McQuillan family crest, emblazoned on the warriors' armour around her, made her grit her teeth. It haunted her, amplifying her pulse rate, igniting a painful knot in her stomach that shot tendrils of discomfort through her nerves like a virus. When she bore her own crest, the unease intensified. The nape of her neck dampened uncomfortably with sweat, a stark reminder she would never be enough. Not for any of them. Destined to never meet their expectations, she'd perfected the art of embodying her mother's disappointment.

"It's going to happen, isn't it?" whispered Caoimhe, one of the younger warriors within Maebh's clan who she hadn't bothered to spend much time with. Mostly due to the fact every time the young woman opened her mouth, Maebh experienced a migraine.

"It has to," Paul answered over Maebh's snort. "It's time."

They gripped hands as if praying. As if somehow, *they* would win a grand prize, should the stone cry out.

The flame-haired druid's lament increased in tempo, her voice solo until the other druids onstage joined her. Their sacred words wove, vibrating with power. Maebh caught the earthy scent of moss and damp grass, mingling with the lingering aroma of incense. Nature held its breath, waiting in reverence for the cry of an ancient stone. But it wasn't just nature. Nearly every person moved to the tips of their toes in anticipation. History could be witnessed today, should Bradan be the chosen one.

The air crackled with a mystical electricity. The white wand in the druid's hand seemed to glow, an extension of magic that permeated the Hill of Tara. Maebh closed her eyes, breathing in to fully experience the heady intertwining scents swirling around her on the charged morning. Fresh notes of spring blooms and zesty citrus weaved a rainbow of floral hopes not yet darkened by reality. It was a rarity to enjoy her gift, so she savoured this moment until darker notes began to sneak through like creeping ivy. She knew all too well that people never truly stayed hopeful for long.

"I think I hear something," Caoimhe muttered.

"No, he has to touch it first," Paul responded, but it was clear by his tone that's what he'd hoped for.

"What do you think the announcement is?" Caoimhe bleated for the millionth time and Maebh refrained from commenting.

"I've heard everything from an outpouring of gifts to sending everyone home," Paul murmured.

"Maybe he'll cancel the Cath."

Maebh turned to stare at Caoimhe with an arched brow. When the younger woman looked up, she blushed, mumbling an apology. Maebh didn't respond before turning. How would they react once Bradan revealed Tiernan was stuck in Fionn Mac Cumhaill's cave? Or when it was disclosed she and the others had found it, had won the first Cath, only for the leaders to decide to start again? Did the High King have a plan in place to save Tiernan? Or would he ask the clans to participate in a new Cath? A trial on breaking the spell that imprisoned the stone guardians standing sentinel over Fionn's resting place? Her heart strained, but her resolve steadied. She would win that Cath with or without the backing of her clan.

Bradan stood tall while the crowned druid continued her trance-like dance, raising her arms high to match her increased chanting. Maebh observed the scene, her pulse quickening as her mind raced with a thousand different ways he would reveal the secret eating her from within. She tasted the freedom of that unburdening just as much as the hope of the crowd.

The ticking clock on Bradan's judgement sounded loudly with each heartbeat. They wanted this. Some so badly they gripped their hands into fists and stepped forward, as if they could force their will onto fate. Maebh held herself steady, confident this would be a moment to remember.

Not because Bradan would receive acceptance from the Tuatha Dé stone— rather, he stood before everyone and would fail so publicly. A humiliation Maebh was familiar with. Bradan could not be the rightful High King; she knew it in her soul.

This was wrong. Yet she remained powerless, forced to watch and pray that when he touched that stone, the world would fall silent.

As the Gaeilge incantation echoed across the hill, Bradan dropped to his knees. The wand, now radiant as a star, met his shoulders, and he smiled broadly as he stood, revealing a minn óir on his head. The golden circlet was made of numerous slender bands that were woven and twisted together in a high point set with a large citrine gemstone, its resplendent rays catching the sunlight. It perfectly complemented Bradan's fierceness and deep mahogany skin tone, a warm hue like a chestnut's wood, rich and earthen.

A cheer erupted from the crowd, a thunderous cacophony of celebration and hope as the first part of the ritual was complete. Bradan still had to touch the stone, but Maebh was a witness to a moment that would forever be etched in the annals of Fianna. All she could think of was who stood frozen underneath layers of earth, shrouded in darkness.

Taking a fiery breath in, she held it before breathing out as subtly as she could manage. Tiernan was entombed in a magical enchantment, trapped deep within the underground caves at their feet, and she stared at his father as the druid circled him. Her fists bunched at her sides, a sting signalling she'd pierced skin, but she didn't loosen her grip.

A nudge to her shoulder had her shift her focus toward Setanta, who raised his dark blonde brows, but before she could acknowledge him, he jerked to his other side. As Maebh peered around his broad frame, Orla's cursed hand twitched again and Setanta winced. The brunette warrior remained impassive, staring straight ahead in a daze from a druid tonic.

It would mean nothing to Orla if the stone called out. Yet here she was, with Setanta steadily beside her, because this was where they were all forced to be. And for that alone, for the threat of banishment if they hadn't been within the castle walls to witness this historical moment, Maebh doubled down, knowing she might have been the only one salivating for silence.

Setanta's jaw pulsed as he was pulled again, but he remained still. Orla often drew blood, and he held her hand away so she couldn't harm herself. Nobody else could pin her down, so Orla spent most of her time either with her hand bandaged and secured by belts or with Setanta.

"Isn't my nephew so strong, Maura? Always putting the clan's needs before his own. Unlike herself."

Maebh tuned her aunt's taunts out, but her past venom burrowed in.

You may be the head, but Setanta will be the neck.

The druids' chants cut abruptly, and Maebh's attention snapped back to the present as Bradan marched up the hill toward the Lia Fáil. She bit down a snort. The Stone of Destiny was a phallic symbol if ever she saw one. The Fair Ones who gifted this penis rock to the Fianna must have had a sense of humour.

A hushed murmur buzzed as Bradan and the druid loomed over the grey-white stone, reaching only to the High King's hip. It glistened in the early morning sunshine. Even though the surrounding highwall blocked the view from outside, it was strategically positioned to catch the sunlight. Or maybe it was magic; fuck knew in this world.

All conversation cut off as the crowd collectively inhaled.

Bradan stretched out one broad, brown hand toward the stone. He hesitated, and Maebh raised her brows in surprise, but it was only for a second before his palm closed the distance. This was it; the moment they'd gathered for. Maebh clenched both hands harder until warmth pooled in her palms. She waited with every Fianna to bear witness to the unearthly roar that would declare Bradan Cassidy the rightful High King of Ireland.

The world stopped. Birds silenced and even the wind halted.
And only a glorious, vindicating silence filled the air.

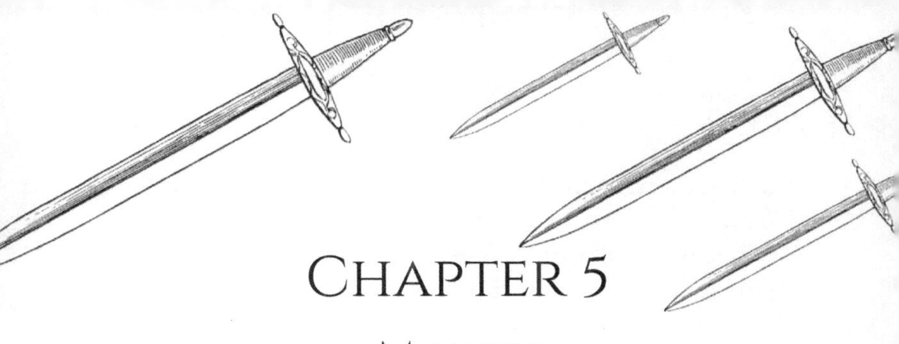

CHAPTER 5
MAEBH

Maebh swallowed her chuckle, but a hint of it bubbled up, escaping through her clamped mouth. Her surrounding clan glared at her, and even Setanta muttered a warning. Her smile was all teeth in return. The High King was a disappointment. They had more in common than she'd realised. Bradan's shoulders stiffened as the druid patted his back, partially obscuring him from view. After a few moments, he turned, a strained smile on his full lips, so like Tiernan's.

"The stone cried out for our first High King and hasn't for any king thereafter. Although the stone has not cried for me, I will serve you with all my strength and honour."

An applause sounded after a beat. Maebh's nostrils flared as the aroma of wilting flowers permeated the air. The once vibrant crowd, fresh with promise, now emitted a bitter after-scent, a harsh contrast to the intoxicating sweetness of moments ago. She smiled widely despite the rancid odour. He was not magically ordained.

"Our Fianna clansmen came here to partake in the Cath, and after unforeseen circumstances, their quest to join the highguard was . . . waylaid."

Maebh licked her dry lips, sweat gathering in her clamped palms; she ignored the pain as it mingled with her crescent moon cuts. This was it. This was the moment Bradan would reveal Ethne's involvement. Her pulse quickened as she held her breath. Hearing Tiernan's name spoken by his father would be difficult, but she would endure it, knowing it would mean they were finally closer to saving him. Maebh rose on her toes as the silence stretched throughout the quiet crowd, all waiting to hear what his announcement was.

"Ethne of the Druid Order was responsible for the murder of Cara Breen and Imogen McQuillan . . ."

Chatter and gasps erupted, and Bradan paused. Maebh ignored all the glances her way, gripping Setanta's offered hand as her eyes sought out Ash. No doubt she was receiving the same treatment and more since her brother had been imprisoned as the murderer.

The druid slammed her staff on the stage. Three loud thuds before silence fell. Bradan nodded his thanks at the auburn-haired woman and said, "Ethne is an enemy to all Fianna and will be tried once captured. My new role will start with no mercy to those who have wronged our people."

Maebh stood straight as she ground her teeth tightly together. She couldn't help being impressed by his determination. Yes, she wanted Ethne caught and retribution for her mother and Ash's, but she needed Tiernan freed more. Which made her a terrible daughter, but nobody would be surprised by that.

"This is it," Setanta breathed beside her, clutching her hand so firmly she winced. "He's going to announce the truth now."

Maebh shared a loaded glance with her twin before they both turned to the High King. Setanta was right. They were about to find a way to save Tiernan. Her nerve endings tingled as every breath heightened. A buzzing rang in her ears as if her mind could only cope with the overwhelming sense of this moment by categorising how her body worked.

"In the meantime, we will endeavour to fulfil the sacred rite of our people. Tara Court has opened its gates to welcome our visiting clans in, but for too long, those gates have shut out the rest of the Kingdom of Mide."

Everyone stirred, and Maebh stopped breathing. Her hand was a vice around her brother's, and she grasped him tightly.

"The kingdom is ours, the humans of this realm, but High King Aedan allowed Fair Ones to take it. May his soul continue."

"And his love remain," the crowd answered the Fianna blessing, but Maebh winced as the burnt garlic invaded her nostrils, highlighting their collective trepidation.

Even if they believed Aedan to be dead, it was treason to speak against a High King. They didn't know Aedan was alive. Trapped with Tiernan in stone, along with the caillte, a lost clan that included her father.

"We will use the Cath as an opportunity for fresh beginnings. Winter Solstice is imminent. After the shortest day of the year leads to the longest night, we will celebrate. Prior to that celebration, we will begin the trials."

Maebh tried but failed to keep her curse quiet, and Setanta's grip on her hand tightened once more before releasing her. When she glared at him, ready to see caution, she bit back her retort. His grey eyes were wide, his lips pressed sternly into a line. Why would Bradan not reveal they were all in grave danger and Winter Solstice was D-day?

Tiernan's father would be a good High King in many ways. If he couldn't be bothered rescuing his only son, what did that say for his honour?

Bradan knew Ethne had murdered Ash's mother in a blood sacrifice on Samhain. Conor had told them the female who'd played the role of druid had planned something for the upcoming solstice. Cara Breen's blood had been spilled on powerful stone, on a sacred night that saw both realms rubbing up against each other like two horny teenagers at a solstice bonfire. Maebh searched the crowds, but Ash was no longer standing where she'd left her.

"She's over there," Setanta whispered.

Her friend had gone from having a laughably small clan to an imposing group of warriors, and there was no subtle way to leave a gathering like this undetected. They marched past the others, who still listened to Bradan's speech, and Maebh smirked at Ash's mark of disrespect.

They'd all met with Bradan after her mother's funeral pyre weeks ago, telling him exactly what Conor had shared. He hadn't released Ash's brother from murder charges, and it was clear he didn't plan to share any plans to rescue his son.

"I was so sure he was going to do the right thing," Maebh said as other conversations broke out amongst the crowd.

Setanta tracked Ash's movements a moment longer before shaking his head. "It looks like we were wrong."

Ash met her friend's gaze as she passed and it was only then Maebh realised she'd been staring, lost in her own thoughts. The other matriarch mouthed 'Okay?' and Maebh nodded in response, swallowing down the lump that had annoyingly lodged in her throat. Moisture clouded her sight, but she wouldn't cry. Not here in front of her clan. They'd only add it to their lengthy list of annoyances against her.

Bradan mentioned in his speech that they sought to arrest Ethne, but how could you capture what lurks in between shadows? Even though Maebh wanted her caught, she hoped Bradan got burned in the process. Her days were filled with guilt and regret; yet, having a silent stone had made this one a little better.

Save your son. Bring him back to me.

No. He would not, and she didn't need him to. She'd vowed while watching helplessly as Tiernan's face turned from a healthy, glowing brown to that cold, ashen stone that she would find a way to free him.

Níl sé ach ina thús. It's only just begun.

Maebh pressed a palm to her side where their matching tattoos were. He could count on her. He deserved a friend who'd fight for him. She *would* be that friend. Tiernan had wanted Maebh to see herself as he did, and they'd left things on strained terms. She needed to make that right. She *had* to.

They'd shared a fleeting moment of passion. Even now, she could feel the whisper of his long fingers caressing her bare skin and remember marvelling at his beauty when she'd got on her knees before him. He had made her believe, if only for a moment, she was a goddess worthy of his devotion. That was before she'd inevitably messed things up. She never planned to declare undying love for Tiernan; she'd no idea if their connection could have grown beyond the undeniable attraction they'd shared. Still, she would be damned if she allowed him to remain frozen in stone.

"Remember, we travel to Newgrange on the evening before Winter Solstice to witness the sun's first light enter Newgrange. Mide residents must remain accompanied by highguard for their safety," Bradan's booming voice forced her attention back to him as he continued to address the crowds. "As for our warriors," Bradan said, waiting until Ash stopped and turned. Maebh chuckled at the look of defiance on her friend's face, but he continued without acknowledgement. "You will receive more information soon. Know this: our kingdom has been left defenceless for too long. Your Cath is to reclaim the Kingdom of Mide beyond our highwall."

A crow's cry filled the air before a set of raven wings swooped low enough for Bradan to duck. It did not attack, flying higher as a chorus of black birds joined it. A heavenly sound had come, but not from the Lia Fáil. A chorus of birds was Bradan's answer from the gods. Circling the crowd, who gasped and ducked, they rose until they were lost to the mist and walls of Tara Court.

It was clear the unrightful High King had been crowned today, and Bradan, for all his prowess, was still just a man. He'd made a show in front of the Fianna and had failed in a public way. Yet the warrior clans still accepted him. He'd been crowned regardless of his unworthiness and only time would tell how he would handle that embarrassment. Maebh took a deep, steadying breath and squared her shoulders back resolutely. Her posture remained poised yet alert, every fibre primed to face the challenge head-on. Apparently, Bradan would start his reign by throwing everyone into a war with the Tuatha Dé Danann. And none could escape.

Unless they died.

CHAPTER 6
AISLING

Firepits sparked to life as day bled into night. Warriors, Tara Court locals and courtiers were partaking in the coronation revelries, but Ash couldn't enjoy any of it. How could she when she was one of the few who knew something terrible was imminent? They'd been banned from speaking about it by order of Bradan Cassidy. Disobeying a rígfénnid would have severe consequences, but to go against her High King would ensure her a place in the dungeons beside her brother.

Shame squirmed in her gut, and she hugged her black leather jacket tighter, the weapons at her belt a heavy weight after a long and tiresome day. While part of her felt it would ease her guilt, being imprisoned beside him, how would that help Conor? Or her clan who'd finally accepted her as their matriarch? No. She was needed here.

Her warriors had dispersed after a quick meeting about Bradan's speech. They knew more than other clans, but not the full truth. She couldn't risk it, not when they didn't know enough to give real answers. The Lia Fáil had remained silent upon Bradan's touch. She'd heard Maebh's snort and had bitten hard on her lip from joining her. Although she didn't feel the same anger towards Tiernan's father, she agreed with Maebh's frustration at his passivity in saving his son. He played court politics well, but she feared it was at the cost of the Fianna's safety.

Ash sidestepped the line of revellers in front of a boar roasting on a spit and aimed for a long wooden table laden with beverages. North of where she stood, the great hall doors stood wide open, the sign overhead reading 'Teach Miodhchuarta'. The house of mead-circling was filled with elegantly dressed Fianna passing the large methers to one another, sharing honey wine. When she spotted the black hair of her grandfather, standing alongside the other rígfénnid, she pivoted in the opposite direction. They'd avoided each other for this long, and she had no intention of an awkward conversation on this night.

Warriors filled the sloping fields surrounding the Hill of Tara, but Set was easy to spot. Her breath caught at the sight of his sharp jawline and the loose unruly plaits framing his handsome face. The McQuillans congregated near a bonfire and even from this distance Ash saw who stood beside him. Whose hand he held.

A weight landed on her chest as her body grew heavy. She'd cast glances during the ceremony, tracking how attentive Set had been to Orla. Despite the tense atmosphere, he'd exuded a calm strength, his confidence evident in every breath.

Hurt burrowed deeper into her heart and it wasn't just because Set had no choice in the position he'd been given, but it felt so final. Like something between them had broken before it had started.

Set would probably deny it, but he no longer sought Ash out like he once had. His clan needed him to control Orla's cursed hand from harming herself or others. Ash had seen it break free and attack. It was as if the hand was not Orla's to command, but a predator waiting to strike, and Set was the only one who subdued it. There was no walking away from that type of commitment unattached. Even if they somehow saved

Orla from herself, she would forever feel indebted to Set and he would be obligated to look after her. Something Ash would never experience with him.

Ash had followed Set a few times, hoping to catch him before he went to the library for his obsessive research. From the lines between his brows as he walked, and the way he flexed his fists and lowered his eyes to all around him, she had not felt like there was any invitation for chit-chat.

On those occasions, she'd turned away. What could she have said? Stop taking care of your vulnerable ex? Please don't be honourable? And while you're at it, stop searching for answers about Ethne's plans, okay?

No. Set was the only one who was giving everything. Even more than she or Maebh were. How could she ask him to be or do anything other than be the perfect man he already was?

She released a long breath as a ceili band struck up their instruments in the distance. This was going to be a long night, and she needed a drink. Pushing through the closely pressed bodies, she glanced at the drinking horns, tankards, and glasses of all sizes laid out. A servant caught the emblem on her chest and ignored a woman who'd been trying to place an order.

"What can I get you, Matriarch?"

Huh. Being head of a clan had its perks, she supposed. Bowls of berry punch were interspersed between carafes of wine, black bottles of whiskey, and methers of mead. Not bothering to glance behind her, she ordered three whiskeys.

Smiling sweetly at the grumbling woman beside her, she rotated, offering out the two drinks in her hands. Sure enough, Tomás and Ciarán were the faces greeting her as she smirked. Ciarán took his, but when Tomás glowered at her offering, she pushed it against his chest.

"Relax, Tom. Nobody is going to bother me tonight."

Her burly cousins had taken on the unofficial role as her bodyguards, shadowing her this past month. She'd berated them for doing it, but they'd insisted on flanking their matriarch in large gatherings like this, whether she wanted them to or not. So she'd grown used to their company, a reassuring force of muscle and steel at her back.

At the last gathering, she hadn't known she would need her cousins to step in when the Collins warriors had accosted her. She'd been meek back then, but she was waiting for an opportunity to get her own back on those two arrogant men.

"Uisce beatha, the water of life. Good choice, Matriarch," Ciarán said with a grin, his freckled face showcasing the dimple that allowed him to get away with more than he ought to.

They clinked their glasses before raising them toward Tomás, who huffed before inclining his glass too.

"Slainte," they said in unison, drinking the fiery liquid.

They walked through the festivities. Torches lit the pathways, casting dancers and revellers in shimmering light. The air was filled with the smell of roasted meats, mulled wine, sweat, and perfume as warriors celebrated their new king's coronation.

As they moved, Ash tracked the McQuillans again. Set was nowhere in sight, and she took another sip of her drink, warring with the irrational urge to find out where he'd gone. Orla was not around either, so Ash was sure she didn't want to know.

Maebh was laughing at something Paul and Malachy were saying. With the few loyal clansfolk who respected their matriarch surrounding her, Maebh's smile lit up the festivities brighter than any torch. She chatted animatedly, blue eyes sparkling with mirth. A warmth blossomed in Ash's chest seeing her friend so at ease and she wished the others gave her a chance to show her strength, compassion and spirit shining as brilliantly as any crown.

Laughter broke out close by, and her cousins stopped to talk to some of the Breen clan. It seemed as if no one cared Bradan hadn't received the approval of the Lia Fáil when everyone had been so eager for it to happen only hours ago. Perhaps they celebrated a new king, but also mourned their own disappointment. Had no one heard Bradan's declaration? He wanted them to rid the fae from this kingdom. Maybe they were drinking away the nerves about that?

Musicians played lively reels, their feet tapping and bodhráns slapping in time with the music, taking Ash back to happier times. To home. To Mary and Dom sitting before their fire on Christmas, telling stories and breathing life into her future dreams. When dancers swirled and skipped in circles around her, she closed her eyes, wishing she could feel an ounce of that carefree nature.

Bonfires blazed as high as houses in the distance, their flames reaching for the skies in tribute to the new High King. A druid approached Ash, offering to read her future, but she declined before quickening her pace, her cousins chuckling, following. The relentless beat of drums and pipes filled the night, urging feet to move and hearts to sing. The energy of the gathering swelled around her, but she had no time to partake.

Other clans stayed close together in tight knots, whispering amongst themselves and casting wary glances at rival groups. The Cath had begun, it seemed, and warriors were already scheming and plotting how to gain the upper hand.

"What are your thoughts on the Cath, Matriarch?" Ciarán asked, his black curls so like her brother's, flopping over his forehead as he turned to face her. His brown eyes lit up with excitement, dimples showing as he grinned.

Ash sighed. "It all seems trivial compared to what we may face soon."

"True. But winning the Cath will prove our worth," Tomás demurred, with a lopsided grimace. Even the candlelight couldn't obscure the scar that puckered Tomás' lower lip and snaked down his neck, as Ash knew, to his chest. He had been attacked by a fear dearg when they were children.

The faerie had been prowling the Breen grounds, stealing nightmares to feed its insatiable appetite. Tomás had woken to a darkened figure leaning over his bed, ragged claws reaching for him. Ash remembered how Tomás had screamed—a terrifying, primal sound that had chilled her to the bone even as a child. His parents had rushed to his side, but the fear dearg had disappeared into the shadows by then.

"I don't need to 'prove myself' as matriarch," Ash said. "I have to keep our clan safe, and free Conor from his imprisonment."

"The Cath is the only thing that will keep us in this land to do those things," Ciarán said, nudging his brother as if to agree.

"True," Tomás said again, his unease evident. His black hair was far tidier than his brother's; a few unruly waves had broken free, tempering his severe countenance. "Our elders have claimed to support you as matriarch only if you win the Cath. It's utter shite, but your leadership would be uncontested if we won."

Ciarán nudged her arm with a boyish grin. "And you must admit, beating the other clans would feel pretty good."

Ash smiled reluctantly. "Defeating those Collins gobshites would."

Tomás's smile was anything but pleasant as he cracked his knuckles. "I've been waiting for an excuse to finish what they started at the first Cath opening."

"Then it's decided," Ciarán declared. "We can help you with the Cath as well as gathering the resources we need to face Ethne."

"The resources we need are standing right here." Ash gestured between the three of them, clinking her drink against theirs once more. "As long as you don't mind fighting off some clurichauns from the tavern cellars, we'll win."

Ciarán and Tomás grinned, raising their glasses in salute and her smile widened.

As they continued their perusal of the party, a melody caught Ash's attention. She followed the baritone voice until she reached a grey bearded man. Though aged, he stood tall and straight, hands clasped behind his back as his rich baritone carried powerfully over the crowd.

His eyes were screwed shut as he sang his ballad, forehead creasing in concentration while he wove lyrical tales in the old style. Simple linen tunic and trousers hinted he was a Mide resident. The singer's weathered features were slack, yet his voice conveyed wisdom and grace honed over long, richly lived years.

A group of rapt Fianna surrounding him, his voice was both soothing and melancholy; a knot formed in her throat as she listened to his lyrics.

"A brave heart had he,
true and loyal,
his clan loved him so.
A warrior born,
with cunning and skill,
more fair than any foe.
In a High King's quest,
hidden underground,
his life cut in despair,
a warrior slain,
by the wicked deeds,
of foe no longer fair.
His pyre unlit,
for no body had we to part.

Tiernan the brave
was sent to his grave,
at the ripe age of twenty-three . . ."

Tiernan. So brave and strong, yet they'd already written about his death. Her breath punched out of her lungs as the world spun faster than the tale he weaved. She couldn't save Tiernan. Despite her efforts, she couldn't save her brother either. She could hardly save herself. Pushing through sweaty bodies, she stumbled away in search of the numbing night air. Her eyes stung more than the whiskey had.

"I'll be fine," she choked, without looking at her cousins, who were only feet behind her. "Don't follow me. That's an order."

Relief flooded her when nobody followed her away from the crowd and into the quiet streets. The sensation did not last long.

CHAPTER 7
AISLING

Ash gulped in air, but her lungs only tightened further, rebelling against each short, frantic breath. She pressed a palm hard against her sternum as if she could manually open her airway. Her insides were battered; all that made her who she was tightened and compressed. Vision blurring, she staggered into a shadowed alley, one hand bracing against the rough stone wall to keep herself upright.

There was so much she didn't know. One thing she did for certain: time was not on her side.

No matter how much she'd tried, they still had no idea how to save Tiernan. If they had switched positions, she knew her second in command would already have figured out how to get her out of the stone prison.

Maybe she really wasn't the matriarch everyone hoped she could be. Something was shattered inside her, and the ragged edges stabbed without mercy. She flexed her palms against the cold stone. Each shallow breath whistled thinly through her constricted airways. Flashing lights sparked across her vision, darkness eating away at the edges.

Heart pounding, vision swimming, her eardrums filled with a thudding as her knees buckled. Strong arms caught her waist before she landed.

"Breathe, Ash." Set's voice was a quiet reassurance behind her, but she couldn't do as he said.

She wasn't sure where he'd come from or how he'd noticed her absence in the midst of all the revelry. His large, calloused hands stroked up her back, gripping her shoulders to turn her gently to face him.

"Look at me."

She blinked back tears until she could see his chest at eye level. Still no breath came. Horrible rasps wracked her body as she tried and failed to fill her damned lungs.

"Look at me, Ash." The rough tone of his voice was not a plea, but a quiet demand.

Her eyes roamed upwards until they met his unwavering storm-grey gaze. He smiled before sucking in a deep breath, holding it until she attempted the same action. After a few seconds, he released his breath, the scent of peppermint wafting toward her. She copied him. In and out, their breaths synced until finally, her mind cleared.

His smile widened as if he could see the clouds drifting away from her vision.

"There you are." He tugged on her hand, intertwining their fingers as he gestured to a wooden bench a few feet away. "Come sit with me."

Blinking at her surroundings, it was only then she realised she'd made it to the heart of the castle town. Gas lamps dotted the uneven cobblestoned footpaths, with only a few roads wide enough to allow horses and carts through. Following Set to the bench, she took in the taverns and dwellings with their pebbledash walls and thatch rooftops.

The dirt roads were unusually quiet, cloaked in twilight shadows. Hushed whispers of lovers escaping the celebration, the barely audible tunes playing in the distance, and the highguard patrolling the village wrapped the atmosphere in a blanket of haunting tranquillity.

Her jacket clung to her damp skin, and she wriggled out of it, struggling against the confining fabric until Set helped her. Welcoming the caress of the cool breeze to calm her, she fought against the words ready to spew from her mouth and ruin their moment. Until she couldn't.

"Where's Orla?"

"Asleep in her tent with her sister." He scrubbed at his face, thankfully not grasping her tone, and pulled her into his side, his fingers now trailing up and down bare skin.

She breathed him in: leather and peppermint and all-consuming man. The rich, earthy scent hung heavily in the night air. It was a balm that brought peace, twining itself among her thoughts, settling into her senses. Inhaling deeply, she allowed it to take root within her, seeping into the crevices of her very being, silencing the confusing chatter of her mind. Each breath she took was filled with him, each exhalation a silent craving for more.

The warmth of his body radiated against her back as his fingers stroked upward, each touch leaving a trail of electricity behind. She'd been waiting for a moment like this with him. To feel whatever it was she experienced whenever he was near. Everything with Set was complicated, but when it was just them, nothing else in the world mattered. Maybe that's why he'd stayed away because there were so many other things that mattered more? And Ash was selfish for wanting to escape it all with him.

Ash stared into the empty streets, the glow of various temples to worship the Tuatha Dé gods facing them. She had never visited the temples, but every week, pilgrimages of the Fianna zealots filled that district, making offerings to the various worthy Tuatha Dé Danann gods. Set's thumb moved in lazy circles in her palm, and she shivered as an unexpected wave of vulnerability swept over her. His touch was reverent, as if he were trying to soothe a bruise only he could see.

"What are you thinking about?" Set asked gently, and when she turned to him, his storm cloud eyes searched her face.

"I'm thinking about the people of *this* world and the people of our world. How none of it's fair."

Set followed her glare towards the first temple. This one dedicated to Danu, the mother goddess, came before all others. It was covered in vines that crept up the walls. Bonfires blazed in front, sending smoke and prayers up to the heavens.

"I often wondered why the Fianna built those temples to the Tuatha Dé gods," Set said, rubbing his fingertips in tantalising strokes, seemingly oblivious to her catching breath. "Lugh, Nuada, Manannán mac Lir. What have any of them done for our kind?"

Ash wrinkled her nose at the putrid air wafting toward them. No matter how much incense was lit, she could smell the decaying offerings left behind. Animal parts and rich foodstuffs were left as gifts at the temples' entrances. Bone piles grew outside from the regular rituals and ceremonies held within.

"They've forgotten us," Ash said. "Their descendants are called Fair Ones, but there is only ugliness within."

Some Fianna were born in this realm, but there were many who had won places here for Caths gone by. The human world was a playground full of easy, ignorant targets. The gods and goddesses turned a blind eye to their kin and their Fomorian enemies who they had cast into the human world.

Set leaned down and kissed the top of Ash's forehead before resting his chin on her crown.

"Do you want to tell me what's really bothering you?"

Ash stilled, debating whether to lie. With a shaky breath, she said, "Mary and Dom are forgetting more and more. I'm not brave enough to tell them our timeframes may dislodge at any moment and the next time I call, they could be long gone. And Tiernan . . ."

Words clogged in her throat like burning coals. Wiping away tears, she swallowed them down until they planted within her heart. But she didn't need to say anything else. He understood.

His large frame towered over her, but his touch was tender as he squeezed her hand. "I'm sorry I haven't been here for you more over the last few weeks. I'm so close to figuring out what Ethne is planning; I can feel it."

Ash let his words wash over her, but she couldn't deny the sting of frustration coating her tongue. As with every time Ethne was mentioned, Ash stiffened. Running through their shared investigation had become second nature. "What do we know?"

Set began their familiar speculation. "Ethne committed a blood sacrifice on Samhain, the day the veil between our realm is at its thinnest."

"And she chose Newgrange, the oldest portal connecting our worlds."

Set nodded his confirmation, rubbing his beard. It had grown since their arrival, and her fingers itched to stroke it to see if it was as silken as it looked. He continued their breakdown. "On Winter Solstice, light hits the passage in Newgrange through the roofbox, lighting up the main chamber. It's more potent than Samhain. The veil is near invisible for those few moments the sun hits the passageway. She must be planning to sacrifice more people then."

"But," Ash said, finishing off their rehearsed conversation, "we've warded Newgrange with the charms you found."

"And much like Tiernan's repellent potion, this charm should keep blood from being spilled."

"Whatever she's planning, we know one thing," Ash said, gripping the borrowed sword at her belt.

"What's that?"

"She filled the chambers with my mother's blood on Samhain; she'd better be ready for her own blood to spill on Winter Solstice."

Set gathered her closer and they sat in silence, Ash's back leaning into his solid frame. She was tired, and she still hadn't changed from her workout with Maebh. She was in bad need of a trip to the bathing tents and sleep, but she couldn't bring herself to leave the sanctuary that was Setanta McQuillan. If their moments alone were scarce, she wasn't about to lose one to hygiene and sleep deprivation.

"Do you want me to be there when you call the human realm? There's still time for you to convince the rest of your clan to join you here."

Ash wanted to say yes, but she bit on the truth about to spill. How could he promise to be there for her when his priority was to his clan and therefore Orla? Before she could answer, the sound of running footsteps had him jumping to his feet. She deflated as some of the McQuillan warriors called out to him.

"It looks like Orla needs me," Set murmured, hastening a chaste kiss on Ash's cheek. "Will you be okay?"

"Of course . . ."

He was already disappearing around a corner by the time her voice trailed off. Ash tensed, a wisp of foreboding brushing her nerves like frost down her spine as the last of Set's footsteps faded into the distance. She was alone again in the abandoned town square with only scattered lamps to hold back the encroaching darkness. The leaping flames cast dancing shadows that now seemed to lurk with ill intent. Despite how often they discussed Ethne's potential schemes, it left her jumpy.

Ash's breath caught in her throat as she scanned the empty streets and alleys surrounding her. She could have sworn she glimpsed movement from the corner of her eye. Yet each time she wheeled around, there was nothing but darkened buildings. Still, she could not escape the feeling that hidden eyes were watching her every move.

She stood abruptly, her heart hammering against her ribs. Facing the temples once more, an overwhelming urge to flee into one consumed her, to find shelter and safety there. Feet moving before her mind could tell her she was being ridiculous, Ash's attention stopped on the temple dedicated to Nuada Airgeltlám, the silver-handed warrior god.

Its smooth white marble walls glowed under the moonlight, beckoning her to enter. Ash stepped closer, tracking the intricate carvings of ancient battles and a replica of Nuada's metal hand at the top of the arched entrance, alongside his sword of light. The entire temple seemed to crackle with an energy both ancient and formidable.

Footsteps grew behind her, and she spun around, heart lurching. But it was only a couple, arm and arm, laughing as they hurried past. Ash released a shaky breath, scolding herself for overreacting. Looking back at the looming temple, she staggered back as if pushed, the sense of finding shelter there now replaced by the urge to put as much distance between her and its cold walls. Quickening her steps, she broke into a jog, desperate to escape any unseen watcher and the swelling fear that danger crept ever closer on this dark night.

CHAPTER 8
AISLING

Figuring her cousins would hunt for her soon, Ash rejoined the festival, finding them easily on the outskirts of where she'd left them, a fresh drink for her in Tomás's hand. Grateful they didn't share her ability of smelling the remnants of fear coating her, they pushed through the crowds to where the Breen clan were stationed near the ceili band. She'd have one drink with her people, and then she'd be free to crawl into bed and feel sorry for herself.

"You look like your mother," a honey-dripped voice said from behind. The druid from the ceremony stood straight-backed, like a queen of faraway lands. Her gold dress shimmered against the dancing firelight, casting a ripple of molten radiance with every graceful move she made. The imposing crown of twigs resting atop her auburn plaits seemed unusually alive under the play of shadows and flames.

"How did you know Cara?" Ash asked, voice straining over the merry crowd surrounding them.

"Come for a walk with me, matriarch," the druid said sweetly, motioning for Ash to follow to a less crowded place.

Ash handed her drink back to Tomás, ushering them toward their clan. They looked ready to protest, but she scowled until they backed away. As Ash trailed behind the druid, she found her eyes tracing over the druid's lithe form. Something about her fluid movements and the lyrical lilt of her voice was spellbinding.

"My name is Biróg," the other woman called as they weaved through the throngs of Fianna.

"I'm Aisling."

"I know who you are, Aisling Breen."

Even when she and Biróg reached the outskirts of the party, the noise was still ear-pounding.

Biróg beckoned for Ash to lean closer, fragrant incense wafting from the druid's billowing sleeves at every motion she made. As the druid smiled, the freckles on her nose scrunched and under the guttering light from the surrounding bonfires Ash couldn't help but be captivated by her. Biróg's amber eyes glowed in the star-filled night like twin beacons, catching the flames and reflecting a mirage of golds and reds.

"Cara Breen came to the Druid Order on Achill Island when she was searching for a cure for you."

Ash stilled. "A cure? For what?"

"She regretted her choices about you. She was looking for anything that would help. Sadly, what was done cannot be undone."

"And what was done?" Ash choked, her mind galloping in a thousand different directions with no clear path to understanding what the druid was talking about.

The glowing bonfires highlighted Biróg's expression as she surveyed Ash. She leaned close, her voice dropping to a murmur lost to the rest of the world, shrouding the secret she was about to share. "You are blood-blessed, child."

Goosebumps exploded along Ash's skin as she puzzled at the unfamiliar term. She stared at the druid, trying but failing to place the meaning behind it. She opened her mouth but found herself unable to speak. A dozen questions crowded on the tip of her tongue before sputtering out half-formed.

The drums of the celebration seemed muted now, as if coming from a greater distance. Ash's senses narrowed to the rich amber of Biróg's expectant stare. The persistent tug of the druid's allure slipped away and, in its place, rose a swell of doubt. Ash folded her arms, warding off a chill that hadn't been there moments earlier, fingers digging into the crook of her elbows.

"What do you mean? As in I'm lucky or is this something else?"

Biróg's expression softened as she regarded her. "Certainly, you've noticed differences between you and your kin. You read emotions."

Moments ticked by, marked only by the white noise rushing in Ash's ears. The longer she stood silent and wide-eyed before this stranger who seemed to know things she couldn't fathom, the smaller she felt. Compared to this druid she was a mere child straying too far into the forest. She nodded reluctantly.

"Can you describe that for me?"

Ash blinked slowly, licking her lips before clearing her parched throat. She couldn't see a reason to hide it from her.

"At first it was only smells, and I found it hard to distinguish what each meant, but as I've lived here, it's a bit like reading a book. Each person is a different story, and their feelings are the words. It's just . . . there, written all over their faces, their stance, their voices. There's no hiding, no pretence."

Biróg nodded. "That is part of your condition."

"Of being blood-blessed?" Ash asked sceptically.

"You are not the only one. The twin warriors, too," Biróg said. "And your stone friend."

A thundering pulse hammered in Ash's ears. Her breath escaped in a ragged exhale, her vision tunnelling as she fought to stay upright for the second time that night. Biróg's claims echoed in her mind, burning against her thoughts like an enflamed brand.

A tremor seized Ash's hands and she clamped them to still their quavering. Eyes wide and burning, she searched Biróg's face for any sign of deceit, but the druid simply tilted her chin and held Ash's questioning stare, serene yet resolute.

Swallowing around the thick knot lodged in her throat, Ash parted trembling lips, but no words emerged. A tumult roiled through her insides, an inexorable tide of disbelief, and something deeper, more dangerous. The hot pressure of foolish hope was building within her ribs, intensifying each erratic beat of her heart.

The druid seemed to notice Ash was on the brink of information overload as she patted her shoulder gently. "We have much to discuss. All of us will meet, but not while surrounded by so many."

"Can you save Tiernan?" Ash dared to allow that fragile hope to filter through her words, but the look of uncertainty on the druid's face stamped it out.

"Time will tell, young one. I waited until the Lia Fáil decided, and now silence from the stone is the answer that will spill secrets."

Another cryptic druid to contend with. How could she trust the word of a druid when all she'd dealt with was Ethne?

Biróg smiled and without speaking, she said into Ash's mind: *Ethne was no druid.*

Ash's eyes jolted to the woman's.

"You . . ."

"Use your gift."

As their eyes met, a ripple of warmth flowed down her spine. On an inhale, Ash reached out internally to brush the aura of the other woman. The air around Biróg held a distinct aroma; beyond the incense clinging to her robe was the scent of mountain air after soft rain. She could sense the core goodness of the woman. Biróg was telling the truth; or at the least, the druid believed she was.

Ash released a slow breath, sending a swirl of sparks from the nearby firepit dancing skyward. So much still lay shrouded in mystery. Biróg seemed kind, but trust took time to build. She stretched her hands to the cracking fire, letting the warmth seep into her bones as she watched the flames. She exhaled again, eyes drifting up to meet Biróg's patient expression. A half-smile settled on her lips even though a sliver of doubt lodged in her heart. Biróg's answering smile radiated sunlight.

Heavy footsteps intruded over the fire's crackle, a jarring rhythm that could only come from the highguard's synchronised march. Ash tensed before looking up to confirm Bradan's approach, flanked by his soldiers.

"Aisling," Bradan said as he strode to them. "I'm afraid I have news regarding your brother."

The world stood still as she waited. Her throat closed, but somehow, she still managed to ask, "Is he alive?"

The seconds before his answer lasted years. "He's being attended to, but he harmed himself earlier tonight."

"What happened? How badly is he hurt?" Ash's questions flowed out of her without waiting for a response, but she couldn't stop. "Can I see him?"

"He is stable, now, Aisling," Bradan said. Shadows played across his smooth, dark-skinned face, cast in flickering relief by the leaping flames. His deep-set eyes were kind but firm. "I wanted to be the one to tell you. We will tend to him, but it's best for you not to see him."

Heat flashed through Ash, a wildfire searing her veins at the High King's audacity. She stood rigid, nails biting into her palms as his refusal for her to see Conor echoed in her ears. Every fibre of her being protested the barrier she hadn't expected.

"No," Ash said, her voice laced with the steel. She fought the dark spots swimming before her vision as she bit out, "He's my brother! He's my family."

A highguard stepped forward as if to place himself between her and their king, but Bradan raised a hand, shaking his head. He didn't speak, offering only a silent look of sympathy. Her mind seethed with images of her brother lying somewhere, alone and in pain. Her eyes locked onto Bradan, but she ignored the raging storm within her as she tried to reason with him.

"I need to see him, Bradan, I need to be there. To believe he's 'stable,' as you say. Your words aren't enough, High King. Not when it's my brother we're talking about."

She almost asked how he would feel if it were Tiernan, but the words died on her tongue. He was trapped in stone, and his father had done nothing to free him. The High King might have issued a command, but Ash was the farthest thing from an obedient subject in this moment. She took a deep, steadying breath, smoothing her features into a stubborn mask.

"I'm going to see him."

Bradan pushed back a sigh, raising his eyes from Ash's resolute face to meet the flaming bonfires, his sombre demeanour casting a shadow onto the fiery backdrop. He remained quiet for a moment, as if carefully selecting his words, before eventually turning his focus back to her.

"Aisling . . ." he began, the hesitance in his voice clear. "This isn't a decision I made lightly nor an order as High King."

Ash held her breath, waiting for more revelations she wasn't ready for.

"It's Conor's wish." Bradan's voice quietened, the words meant for her alone, but he may as well have shouted them in her face.

Ash went very still. "What?"

Conor's wish . . . Conor's wish . . . The phrase skipped and repeated, taking on the rhythm of her thready pulse. Realisation crept slowly, an icy threat stealing through veins that only moments before burned with purpose. It slithered ruthless tendrils around her heart, squeezing without mercy.

"I saw to him myself. Tiernan asked me to look out for Conor and it's the least I could . . ." Bradan trailed off, his attention on the dancing flames for several moments until he met her waiting gaze once more. "Conor explicitly told me he doesn't want you visiting him. He doesn't wish to see you."

The silence that ensued was deafening. Heavy lids slid closed as she absorbed the blow. Something vital crumbled away inside her, leaving behind an expanding hollowness. Despite the vibrant energy around them, the music in the background and the distant laughter all seemed to mute into nothingness.

She pressed her lips into a thin line, fighting back the wave of emotions threatening to overtake her. The delicate balance she had been so desperately clinging to seemed like a joke in comparison to this heart-shattering revelation. She swallowed hard, the bitter taste of rejection pungently clear on her tongue.

"With your permission, High King," Biróg said, "I will visit with Aisling's brother."

"Of course, Biróg." Bradan smiled sadly at Ash, squeezing her shoulder before moving away. "I'm sorry to bring you this news, Matriarch."

Ash stared at his retreating back as every terrible scenario, each one worse than the one before, assaulted her. What had Conor done to himself? She'd feared she'd let Tiernan down, but she was also failing her brother.

CHAPTER 9
MAEBH

"You're still drunk," Lorna accused, and Maebh squinted at her aunt from behind oversized sunglasses as she plonked down on a low-lying bench.

"My best ideas come when in this state." Maebh gestured carelessly for her clan to gather around the firepit.

They had been milling around their encampment, wedged between the Breen clan, at Setanta's insistence, and the Collins clan. The latter was an imposing group that buzzed around their campsite like a stirred hive.

Maebh hugged her worn leather coat tighter, clutching the folds closer to her neck though the morning was not truly chilled. Her insides roiled queasily but she wasn't sure if it was from her hangover or something more unsettling prickling at the edge of her senses.

She found herself eyeing the Collins warriors more closely than usual as they prepared for the day, tracking their movements for any sign of how they would proceed with the Cath. Her breath clouded faintly in the air. Perhaps the temperature had dropped, or perhaps it was merely her own rising unease that made gooseflesh ripple over her skin.

Re-reading the parchment that had been left in her tent in the wee hours, she bit her lip. The Collins' had clearly decided on a plan of action for the Cath already. She stared at the map, detailing more about the kingdoms of Tír na nÓg than she'd known. High King Bradan and the other rígfénnid weren't just emissaries. They were gathering intel on the fae lands, too. With a begrudging sigh, she had to admit that was pretty badass.

As distrust wafted toward her, she wondered for the millionth time why she was even bothering. Her sunglasses cast everyone in a muted brown, and she ignored how grim her clan looked. It wasn't personal, she lied to herself. They had all enjoyed the coronation festivities well into the early hours. She certainly had, even if the poor eejits from the Cluskey clan had not.

She grinned before wincing, her tongue probing at the lump on her split lip, courtesy of a warrior who told her to smile more. When she'd told him he should breathe less things escalated.

"Fun night, sis?" Setanta mused as he offered her a large cup of steaming liquid before sitting beside her, the log sinking into the ground.

She nodded before taking a sip and gagging. "What is this?"

"Nettle tea." He shrugged before gulping from his own mug. "We don't have much else."

Maebh bit back her retort as she thrust the parchment containing the map to Setanta for him to study. She was sick of this damned place. After Bradan had taken charge, the visiting clans had been dispatched to another area of Tara Court. Apparently, they'd outstayed their welcome and had been left to fend for themselves. That meant finding food and everything else they may need through hunting or by bartering with the locals.

The term 'sing for your supper' was cast about like a joke. Some of the locals were accepting performances from the great Fianna travelling clans of the human realm, and Maebh could see the glee on the locals' faces at the insult. These Fianna had lived in this land, away from human civilisation, for far too long.

They knew little of the modern way and cared even less about it. The most recent settlers came a century ago at the last Cath.

Setanta studied the parchment with as much enthusiasm as she had. He handed it back to her and when their eyes met, she could see the worry there. Their twinship meant they often had wordless communications, and he seemed to ask, "What should we do?"

She shrugged before cocking her head. "How can he demand we play along with the Cath, knowing full well there are greater things at stake?"

He sighed but lifted a shoulder.

Maebh took another sip of the disgusting nettle tea and yacked. When she looked up, Lorna's face was a thunderous display as she glared between her and her twin.

"Care to share with your clan, Matriarch?"

Maebh ignored her mocking tone, lifting the cup toward her aunt. "Find me a wedge of lemon for this and we can begin."

Murmurs ran through her clan, and she smirked as Lorna grabbed the cup from her and stormed toward their cooling box. As her aunt rummaged loudly through the contents, Maebh retrieved a dagger from her side pocket and began picking dirt from her fingernails, frowning at the chipped pink paint. A shadow was cast as her cup was shoved under her nose, but she finished her last nail before accepting the mug with a wide smile.

Maebh felt more than heard Setanta's disapproval, but she ignored him. He didn't know what it was like to be the laughingstock of their clan. The matriarch in title, but the unwanted brat by the elders. Her mother had made sure that she would not inherit this clan with open arms.

"The High King wants us to clear his kingdom of all fae." Maebh took a sip of her tea and winced. It was still repulsive, but the lemon helped. "He sent parchment this morning to say each clan will have flagpoles to claim the territory as 'freed'. He's given us a map of Mide with zones sectioned off."

She signalled to Setanta, who passed it to Lorna. Each clan member inspected the map before circulating it to their companion, so Maebh continued. "When we clear a zone, we are to place our flagpole in that territory. It will be up to us to ensure that land remains clear, and that no other clan reclaims it."

"How are we going to do this?" Lorna queried as she turned to Setanta. The snub was not lost on Maebh, nor the others around her.

"We do it," Maebh said before Setanta could open his mouth, "by forming an alliance with Aisling Breen's clan."

Silence greeted her response. The only sound, the movement of parchment as the map continued its journey to each warrior encircling the firepit.

"Look." Maebh placed her mug by her feet and leaned forward. "I've spent the morning going through different scenarios, and this one makes the most sense. When we clear land, we'll have to leave warriors in that zone to ensure it remains ours, and that no fae come back to it. We're stronger with the alliance of another clan to ensure we can claim more zones."

"An alliance is a smart move," Diarmuid mused from a log to her right and she could have kissed her seanchaí. He smiled warmly behind his red beard before his attention drifted to Setanta in a contemplative stare, his blue eyes shining. "What would be even better is a marriage alliance."

"What?" Setanta asked flatly before Maebh could.

For good measure, she added, "What the fuck are you talking about?"

Diarmuid gestured to Setanta and the Breen encampment. "Setanta is already courting the Breen matriarch."

"My relationship with Ash is off limits." Setanta was rigid beside her, and Maebh sat back to let her twin fight this battle. He leaned on his legs, forearms straining. "It's nobody's business and I won't allow anyone to use it as some political agenda."

Maebh patted his shoulder in solidarity. For once, they could agree on something without argument. They both hated to be used as a pawn in anybody's schemes. They'd gone through that all their lives under Imogen's matriarchal reign.

"A marriage alliance is most advantageous." the seanchaí continued, ignoring her twin's furious glare. "It would only last a year and a day, the custom of this land. It is not something to shut down immediately."

"It absolutely is," Maebh said before gripping Setanta's arm to restrain him. His scent had changed. A volcanic sulphur emanated from him, a sign his monster wanted to be released. "That's not the plan I'm going for."

"How would we split the territories if we form an alliance?" Malachy queried, his closely-shaven head glistening with sweat. No doubt Imogen's former second in command had been the first one awake, training, despite the celebrations from the previous night.

"We would have to come to an agreement with Ash. I mean, Aisling," Maebh answered, focusing on Malachy's encouraging expression and ignoring everyone else. "We would split everything fifty-fifty. Every other territory would bear our coat of arms on that flagpole."

"I like your idea, Maebh, but each territory has a different weight to it." Setanta gestured for the map. His tendons were tight, but his face was impassive. As if he was still in control, or at least he was winning the battle against his monster within. "It would get too messy if we alternated wins. Can we try to do it ourselves first?"

Maebh looked at her brother as the others readily agreed. Of all her clan, she'd thought he would have had her back. She wanted to form an alliance with the woman he was clearly smitten with, but he couldn't trust her enough to try her way. It would have given them an excuse to continue working together on what was more important: stopping Ethne's mysterious plan. She looked to the fire, suddenly bone weary. A gust of wind slapped her cheeks, and she lifted the lapels of her coat to shield herself as much as possible.

"Fine."

She wouldn't look at her brother as he nudged her. The clan began making plans, their opinions and tactics drifting over her head as she stared at the torrid flames. Setanta was pulled into the conversation by her aunt, who directed all decision-making questions to him. He hesitated before answering, giving her another sideline glance, but she burrowed deeper into her coat cocoon.

She was about to fish out her dagger to continue scraping the pink polish from her nails when Eilish Corrigan stormed out of her tent. Chatter ceased as Setanta jumped up before she could reach him.

"Orla needs you," she stated, turning back with no further explanation, and disappearing through the tent flaps once more. But not before Maebh caught the dark circles and the stench of a wilting flower. Eilish was cursed the same day her sister was, but hers was with the constant worry of what might become of her sibling.

Setanta weaved through the clan, calling two warriors to come with them. When he opened the tent, cries carried out from it and Maebh jumped up, ignoring her aunt's tuts about meddling where unwanted. Orla's cursed hand must have broken free again.

CHAPTER 10
SETANTA

"Hold her down," Set demanded as he tackled Orla's hand.

Wincing, he ignored the sting of her nails as they dug into his flesh.

"Shh, it's okay. It's okay," Eilish spoke soothingly into her sister's ear as Malachy and Paul each grasped her right arm, just under her shoulder. Orla's face remained blank, brown eyes murky like pond water. She wasn't in this tent; her expression told Set she was far away, where this nightmare wasn't her reality.

The two warriors fought against her unnatural strength, but Set had the hardest job. Her cursed hand moved at odd angles, scratching, clawing, seeming to drink his blood with its nails. No matter how often Eilish filed them until they were mere stubs, Orla's nails grew faster and sharper until Set swore they were made of iron.

"I said hold her!" he ordered as the two warriors fell backward.

Orla's otherworldly strength was limited to her arm, but it was all she needed. Without even a grunt, she hurled both men across the small space, her belongings scattering across the area.

"We're trying," Paul said through gritted teeth, his face red from exertion. And probably embarrassment.

Orla had always been strong. Every Fianna warrior within the McQuillan clan was, but she'd never had the strength to sack both Malachy and Paul on their arses before. As they wrestled with her again, she remained motionless except for that cursed arm. Catching sight of her mangled face, Set bit back a curse. Four jagged lines clawed down one side, dangerously close to her eye and right to her chin. But her eyes remained glazed; the rest of her body lay limp, as if she were dead. Set hesitated, but only for a second before using his full body weight to crush her hand down as he reached for the shackles and belts beside him. They were in ribbons.

"Eilish, get me the new ones."

Eilish raced to the other side of the tent, snatching the latest restraints and throwing them to his outstretched hand. The others grunted at a violent spasm of Orla's arm but thank the gods they held firm. With practised skill, Set hoisted himself swiftly in time, weaving the belts through her fingers and wrapping them tightly around her wrist. There was no time to think or feel or even sympathise with Orla and her demon. Set was everyone's tool. A machine before a person. But if it meant helping someone battle their beast, he would press on.

He nodded at the others to keep pressure on her arm as he unlocked the iron manacle. It was specifically made by the best blacksmith of Tara Court. Shaped like a bowling ball, and roughly the same size and dimension, he worked Orla's bandaged hand into the assigned segments, using the extra strap to secure her hand in place before finally shutting and locking the ball. As with every other time, once Orla's cursed hand was trapped and out of sight, her arm went limp like the rest of her.

Paul and Malachy sagged in relief, hoisting away from the comatose woman.

Eilish leaned close to her sister, kissing her cheek. "You're safe, now, sis."

Even without Set's ability to sense emotions, the sisters' shared devastation hung in the air. The scent of damp, rotting logs permeated his nostrils, settling on his tongue. Despair coated every surface of the small tent.

"Cut it off."

If he hadn't seen Orla's lips move, he wouldn't have heard her words.

His insides bunched into a mass of knots as memories assaulted him of his time spent strapped to a bed. After a warp spasm episode, he'd ask for death, a cure, even a gods-damned mirror. All requests were rejected by his mother. *Because you didn't truly mean it.* Set froze, his back rigid at the internal whisper through his mind. He would not acknowledge that voice.

"Orla, don't say things like that," Eilish sobbed.

Set looked away, ready to follow his men, who'd already exited the tent to leave the sisters alone when his twin's figure appeared outside.

"Here." Maebh handed him a bowl of steaming water and fresh bandages.

Before he could thank her, she left. Neither woman had seen her offering, just the way his sister wanted. He gave the bandages to Orla, keeping one for himself. Leaving the tent, he cleaned himself up with a careless haste, making his way toward the firepit again.

Perhaps he could squeeze in some time in the library, but his shoulders sagged at the thought. Casting a longing glance at his unused tent, every muscle in his body spasmed, as if begging him to fall on top of his bedroll. The library was begrudgingly his second home at this rate, but he *would* find the answers he needed through the tomes, which were probably younger than Ethne.

He rotated his neck, easing the pent-up tension that was never too far away. She would not murder anyone else nor hex a limb to kill. Ethne had placed that curse on Orla because of him. Because Orla had lifted a hand to strike him through jealousy. Why Ethne had felt the need to retaliate on his behalf was something he couldn't help pondering on.

She'd provided him with answers and had helped him with his own cursed ríastrad. She could reverse Orla's malediction, and she could help him figure out how to stop his warp spasm for good. But he wasn't the only monster. She was one too. Wrapped in the veil of an angelic-faced druid.

As he searched the neighbouring camp once more, his chest tightened. All he truly wanted was to spend time with Ash. She'd been pulling away from him lately, and it was his fault. Her safety was at stake. His ríastrad had liked the idea of a marriage alliance too much so he'd immediately shut down the suggestion. Besides that, Ash deserved to be seen as a matriarch in her own right, not some bride to be allied to.

Before he could make it back to his tent, a messenger, dressed entirely in cream, interrupted his journey, handing him a folded parchment. The man wore a crisp linen tunic, his hair neatly combed, face freshly scrubbed. His boots were polished to a spotless sheen, marking him as a servant of the inner castle.

"What's this?" Set asked, but the young man ignored him, staring straight ahead.

He stood, waiting silently as Set opened the parchment and read its contents.

"When?" he sighed, at which the messenger turned on his heels and marched toward the castle.

As Set followed, he searched for his sister again, but she wasn't by the fire, nor could he see her in the surrounding McQuillan camp.

"Do I have time to change?" he called, but again the servant ignored him.

He swiped the dirt off the legs of his black cargo trousers. He'd left his sword in his tent, but he held his axe in his belt. It had been his father's. The iron head was intricately engraved with swirling Celtic knotwork, the blade honed to a mirror polish that glinted in the torchlight. The worn oak shaft fit smoothly in Set's hand, shaped by generations of McQuillans. Decorative as it was sharp, it was the one piece he'd insisted was his after their father disappeared.

Maebh normally won their battles and had claimed most of their father's belongings, including his phone, which she'd since lost. His conscience pricked at him like thorns embedded under skin, impossible to dig out. Set hated disagreeing with her in front of their clan when he knew how little they respected her. But he also wouldn't agree with Maebh blindly. The leaders for clans were historically women and he never questioned the fact she'd be matriarch. But a small part of him wondered if it would be easier if he were allowed to lead their clan. He wasn't sure if his twin genuinely wanted the role.

He clutched the axe handle as he frowned at his appearance. There was no hope for his muddied black laced-up boots, but at least his blue shirt was clean enough, so he trudged on after the servant. As he passed Ash's camp, he swallowed his disappointment.

Hoping to catch sight of Aisling Breen was one of his daily, and sometimes hourly, indulgences. It hadn't taken him long to realise she was a balm to his ravaged mind, beautiful in soul and body. He couldn't get enough of her blushes or smiles, or the way her green eyes sparkled when they caught him staring. In so many ways, Ash was his perfect escape. But allowing himself to indulge was dangerous. He could lose himself in her eyes until his last day, but being in this realm festered its own brand of problems. People had died, a powerful druid was missing, and the whims of his heart felt small in comparison.

As Set dodged another puddle of bird droppings on the once gleaming castle steps, he glanced skyward. Flocks of black birds drifted overhead, their cawing echoing back and forth, and he noticed nests within the high walls of the castle as he followed the servant through the imposing wooden doors.

Their footsteps echoed down the wide hallways and Set tried to hide his bloodied bandage as they passed nobles and courtiers. Perhaps Orla's nails had dug deeper than he'd realised. He pulled down his shirt sleeve, thankful that the light blue material didn't soak up the blood.

"Through there," the servant finally said, and Set realised he hadn't taken note of how many corridors they'd walked down to get there.

It wasn't the throne room as he'd expected, but a small room with a roaring fire and low-slung couches. Floor to ceiling curtains were tied with gold ropes, and from his position at the door, Set could make out the manicured lawns sprawled around Castle Tara. Bradan smiled up at him from the couch closest to the open fire and as Set entered, he gestured for him to take a seat opposite him.

"You wanted to see me, High King?" Set thumped his fist across his chest and bowed before taking the offered seat.

He bit the inside of his lip as he eyed the High King. What could this meeting be about? Set had been spending a lot of time in the castle library. Perhaps the scribes had informed Bradan that he'd outstayed his welcome? Tapping his heel, he stuffed his hands under his legs as he watched the king's face closely for any sign he was in trouble.

Bradan handed a tumbler of amber liquid to Set. "I thought it best to meet in private without all the fuss of the throne room and other rígfénnid."

Set took a sip, realising it was whiskey, and a fine one. It burned blissfully on the way down, and Bradan's brows rose as Set took another slug.

"I'm aware it's barely noon, but it's been a rough day," he explained before setting his tumbler on the table between them.

"I can see," Bradan said, looking pointedly at Set's sleeve. They both stared as the once blue fabric blotted with his blood, the spots spreading into one large stain across his forearm. The High King didn't look for an explanation, and Set was too tired to offer one.

"Your parchment said you had something you wanted to discuss?"

Bradan took a sip of his own drink. "Are you happy with how Maebh is behaving as a matriarch?"

Set's shoulders stiffened as he watched the High King warily.

Bradan continued, "You're her second, so you have some power over your clan. But you shouldn't wield it all. If your sister isn't taking her role seriously, something must be done."

"Has my aunt already bent your ear? I thought you would have more important things to worry about than a vicious aunt and vapid elders."

Silence filled the room as Bradan leaned back against the plush couch. A log crackled and spit, coal tumbling out of the fireplace. Bradan rose to his feet as Set moved too, but the High King shook his head. Poking the log until it splintered with orange cracks, he picked up the burning coal with his barrel-sized hand. Not flinching at the hiss of his flesh, he tossed it before catching it and eventually threw it casually back into the open fire.

"I'm working on many tasks, along with ruling a kingdom, Setanta McQuillan." Bradan stood facing the fireplace, his broad shoulders cast in shadow from the flames. "I've inherited a band of rígfénnid that I wouldn't have selected myself. As

Rígfénnid of Leinster, I know each of the others. Fintan Breen was appointed over forty years before me. The other leaders are well into a century of being in the role, and as for Aedan O'Dwyer, he'd ruled Leinster for one hundred and fifty years before he was ordained High King."

Set remained rooted to his seat. He was unsure of where Bradan was going with this, but his words weighed heavier than just an informal conversation.

"I want to free my son, make no mistake." Bradan turned to him then. "But how do I free Tiernan without freeing Aedan? Without awakening Fionn Mac Cumhaill?"

It hit Set, then. The reason Bradan hadn't told everyone about what truly happened.

"You'd rather rule as king than free your son?"

CHAPTER 11
TIERNAN

She had soft skin, and her eyes crinkled when she smiled. There was more to that smile from the woman with sunshine hair. As if the wearer did so despite the world. Whatever had been done or said to her had not defeated her. She smiled, not because she had never hurt, but because she'd lived through pain.

He wished he could remember her name. *Stay.* Shutting out the stone guardians and the slumbering king, he willed her face before him. The feel of warmth was a memory hard to cling to under layers of unforgiving stone, but when he thought of her touch, of her smile, he *could* remember.

She'd come alive under his touch. *Protect.* They'd kissed under the stars. Her creamy skin had glowed under his . . . he'd had brown skin. *Break.* Within this dark cave, the only colours were blue gems embedded in grey earth and white stone. But he'd had brown skin, and she'd had sun-kissed cream. He remembered his hands roaming over her body, and the warmth of her plump mouth against his. How he'd thought that stolen moment between them had been everything, and it had only just begun.

It's only just begun.

That had once been engraved on his skin. *Protect.* And hers. He wondered if he still had skin under the white stone. If his was still brown, or if he had organs or blood or a human heart. Hers had beaten as wildly as his own when he'd touched her. She'd looked at him as if he'd held the answers to the world. She'd smiled at him as if they'd shared secrets. *Break*. She'd walked away.

He'd sworn to show her how he saw her. But now he couldn't even remember his name.

Shadows formed before the black expanse writhed and swarmed in a flurry and another ivory-skinned woman stood before him. Her smile was too wide and wicked. Hers was not the face he wanted to see.

"Hello," she crooned, lifting a milk-white hand to stroke his face.

He felt nothing.

He did not want her here. The surrounding stone guardians quietened upon her arrival, as if by shutting up with their incessant chant, she would not approach *them*. She was a predator. Ramming against his prison, he swore and cried and raged. But outwardly, nothing happened.

"I have a gift for you," the cruel female said, circling before standing before him once more, a triumphant twinkle in her cold eyes. "I shall tell you one name. You choose. Yours or hers."

He didn't need to know his name. He didn't know how she knew, but she stepped closer, whispering in his ear, a name to which he would cling.

"Maebh."

As if life began with that name, his body spasmed, and she stepped back, surprise marring her porcelain face. And then she smiled before folding into the creases of midnight she'd come from.

Maebh. Break. Maebh. Stay. Maebh. The others tried to shout into his consciousness, to claim him as theirs once more, but he had her name. They'd had so little time together; he'd had hoped for more. He'd thought he'd had time to win her favour.

He'd wanted Maebh so badly it hurt. Glorious pain filled his insides. Whether he had a heart or lungs or any other organs, he did not know. But whatever was inside yearned for her.

Maebh. Maebh. Maebh. He wanted to see her one more time. That, he would settle for, more than the life he couldn't remember.

CHAPTER 12
SETANTA

S et hadn't intended for the accusation in his tone, but it was there, and he didn't bother trying to take it back. The two men stared at one another before Bradan sat down again. A servant knocked lightly before entering the room with a silver tray bearing cold meats, cheeses, and grapes. She placed it on the table, re-filled their glasses and left. Neither had spoken while she was present, and neither broke eye contact.

"Do you believe now is the time Fionn Mac Cumhaill should awaken? Do you think Ireland is crying out for him to return?"

"You believed it once. When High King Aedan ordered you and my parents to find him."

"I did not." Bradan slammed his glass back on the table and it was the first time Set had seen a chink in the king's tight restraint. How he envied the control he seemed to have; even if he slipped, it was only for a second. "My wife . . . Tiernan's mother . . . was a reverent believer and would have flown to the moon on a twig for Aedan if he'd said the first High King slumbered there. She was a fool and look where she ended up."

"Ethne is planning something on Winter Solstice," Set hedged. "Whatever it is, if we don't stop it, certainly Ireland will cry for Fionn then."

"That is why I want you to take on my vacant role." Bradan waited, but when it was clear Set wasn't following, he leaned forward, his thick arms resting on his legs. "As Rígfénnid of

Leinster, you will have more power and resources. Don't think I haven't been informed of how many late nights you spend in the library. There are tomes and advisors I can expose you to. You will be the leader of not only a full clatter of clans, but your sister, too. Matriarchs have always ruled over the clans, but rígfénnid rule over all."

"You want me to become a rígfénnid?" Set lifted his whiskey and drained it, swallowing with it the absurdity of Bradan's statement. What could Set bring to the table that one hundred others couldn't? He narrowed his eyes as he rotated his empty glass between his palms, attempting to come up with any possible explanation Bradan would choose him. He couldn't think of one. "I have no idea how to do that job. I'm too young, too unskilled."

He didn't add, too monstrous.

"You've shown you are willing to learn. You're a face the modern warriors will respect. Together we can stop Ethne. There will be no cry out from Ireland. Fionn can continue to slumber. If we find a way to free my son and your father . . . and a few others, we will."

A delicate breath tickled Set's ear, and he flinched, turning to face whoever stood behind him. Blinking, he frowned as he studied the bookcase by the sofa. Bradan continued to speak, but Set didn't hear his words as a familiar figure caught his attention. His glass shattered in his hand.

"What's wrong?" the High King asked, but Set couldn't speak as his mother sauntered toward him, her pallid arms stretched outwards, beckoning him closer, much like she'd done when he was a child. Her icy grey eyes pierced straight through him, freezing his blood in his veins.

His vision tinted to a hazy red. *She wants you to join her.* Set shot to his feet, the shattered glass crunching under his boots.

"Setanta?" Bradan stood, frowning at him before coming to his side. "What's the matter?"

"I . . . nothing." Set watched his mother, horror stricken as his monster crooned in his ear.

Let me out to play.

Imogen's silhouette shimmered in her pale blouse and black riding pants as she walked through the furniture to stand directly in front of him. A drumming pounded in his ears as he jerked away from her outstretched hand, raised as if to stroke his cheek. Her smile was sad as she looked down at the darkening stain spreading from her abdomen.

Bradan continued to look in askance at him, and Set's eyes widened as his mother coughed up blood. This had to be a vision. His mother was dead.

"I'm sorry for the mess I've made," he mumbled. "Can I be excused? I don't feel very well."

"Of course," Bradan said, quietly. "Consider my offer."

Set only nodded before stumbling toward the closed door. He needed to leave before he shredded the new king into pieces.

Blindly crashing into the opposite wall of the wide hallway, Set was consumed by the sense of dread that always ate his insides before his warp spasm took hold. Which way was out? He couldn't remember, not in this state, so he chose a path blindly, hoping he could calm before he met anyone. Sift. He could try to sift. Taking a shaking breath as he heard footsteps approach, he willed the power within to swell. He found nothing but fire.

The footsteps drew closer. Their pace quickened, but he couldn't see. One eye turned inward, its retreat a blazing trail as his eye socket shrank. It would lodge in his throat soon. He turned to sprint in the other direction when he spotted the curtained alcove with his remaining good eye. Ripping apart the heavy fabric, he made out a large window.

With his vision blinking in and out of focus, he could only make out a blurry view of where the window led to. It made no difference in that moment; his only aim was getting far away before his transformation took hold. He was prepared to throw himself through that window if it meant he wouldn't hurt anyone in his warped state.

Why? his monster purred in his mind. *Let us play.*

"Set?" The sound of Ash's soft concerned voice pierced through the red haze of anger consuming him. "Look at me. It's fine. Breathe."

He felt Ash before he saw her. Gentle fingers gripped his arm as she moved closer. Her touch was unexpectedly firm for such a delicate hand, grounding him. As he blinked, focusing on her face, an achingly familiar scent filled his nostrils: lavender mixed with amber and something uniquely Ash. It soothed even the rage of his monster, who settled into a contented purr.

He blinked. Once. Twice. Until he looked down at Ash. She smiled. She did not baulk at the monster he was turning into. Stepping dangerously close, she placed a hand over his erratic heart.

"Breathe."

Her soothing voice melted the tension from his body. He sank to his knees against the cold windowpane, welcoming the sharp pain anchoring him to the present.

Ash knelt before him, her black hair falling like silk around her shoulders. Her leather jacket stretched across her lithe frame, hinting at the warrior she was beneath her beauty.

"You can do this." Ash's calming voice filled the space, hints of lavender floating to him. She was using her mood gift on him. He breathed deeper. "Don't fight him. Acknowledge him and breathe through it."

Set's brows furrowed, pinning her with a look as he choked on a deep breath.

"Your ríastrad," she explained, meeting his confused gaze.

Her hands drifted up his neck and into his hair, before stroking his cheeks. Her touch was the only thing he could focus on, her warmth enveloping him, easing the taut cords of tension within him. They stared at one another, his spasms abating within the sanctuary of Ash's presence. For the first time, Set felt the monster inside him submit—not to rage or fear, but something far stronger.

Every monstrous part of him was falling for Aisling Breen, and there was nothing he could do to stop it.

"You're okay."

But he wasn't. Not really. The High King wanted him to take on the role of rígfénnid. How could he rule over the clans when he couldn't control himself? How could he be trusted when he was having visions of his dead mother?

As if sensing how far into a spiral he was going, Ash rose to her feet and even though nobody was in the hallway, she drew the curtain, enclosing them in the alcove space between the window and the rest of the castle. When she knelt again, he widened his legs, grasping her waist and pulling her closer. He just needed to feel her. To anchor him to the present. To her.

Ash's eyes widened, but she didn't protest. As she gestured for him to lower his legs, Set's pulse quickened. Her closeness was electric, every point of contact tingling as she straddled him, her long legs encircling around his back. He drank in her face, relaxed yet resolute before him. Meeting her emerald eyes, he saw the depth of her care.

He brushed a loose tendril of hair from her cheek, causing a shiver he pretended not to notice. He let his forehead meet hers, their contact a balm, easing the ragged tension of battles against his ríastrad hard fought and barely won. He let himself melt into her steadfast strength, remembering he didn't have to be invincible. No words passed between them, just the warmth of her body seeping into him. For a moment, he let the rest of the world fade away with the comforting silence they shared.

"Why were you in the castle?" he eventually asked, her body stiffening at his words before her shoulders slumped.

"I was trying to visit Conor." A thickness filled her voice, the threat of unshed tears brimming beneath her words and his arms instinctively tightened around her. The stinging surge of empathy reverberated within him, its piercing intensity resonating like an endless hymn within the Tuatha Dé Danann temples.

"What happened?" Set asked, but he had a feeling he already knew the answer.

The scent of her distress was a mixture of damp earth and fallen leaves, the beginning of nature's death before winter. He wasn't the only one who needed comfort from their embrace. Ash was just like him, shackled by her own internal struggles.

"I was denied, of course. And apparently, it's my brother who is refusing to see me."

"Any word on his condition?"

"Yes," she admitted, but her lips were pressed so thin, they'd lost their pink hue. "But it's not enough. I need to see him for myself."

Set opened his mouth to offer help, but hesitated. If he agreed to becoming rígfénnid he would surely have the power to guarantee interference. But not now. All he could offer was his arms, and although not offering everything he could went against his nature, it would have to do for now.

"Do you miss your mother?" Ash's question broke through his thoughts, and he pulled away just enough to look into her face.

"Of course. You?"

Her smile was wistful as she stroked his bearded jaw, her fingers rising to entwine in his hair. He pressed in closer to her, feeling the rumble of her words as his ear pressed against her chest. "Every day. Which is weird because we'd been separated for so long before."

"I get that," he murmured.

"I'm assaulted by regret," Ash admitted, continuing her delicate strokes. "I should have come home sooner. There's wisdom I missed out on and quality time I should have had instead of being consumed by trivial shite."

They sat in silence until Set spoke. "Everywhere I go, I'm reminded that she's not here. In old places she's been, and new places she'll never be. Are all my experiences going to have this taint to them? The absences of something in the newest adventures? The reminder that I get to do these things and she never will?"

Ash took a deep breath before answering. "I believe we all carry some measure of regret with us, some absence that shapes us. But we can't let it define us. We must forge new experiences, find new joys to fill those spaces left behind. Our mothers would want that for us."

She reached down to lift Set's chin, meeting his mournful eyes. "Your mother would be proud to see how far you've come, the good you strive to do. She lives on in your kindness, your strength, your determination."

Set clung to her waist, his head resting against her chest once more and she held him close.

"You're not alone in this," she breathed. "We carry each other's burdens now."

He held her tightly, listening to her beating heart as she stroked his hair. In this moment, they were two souls bound together by grief. She understood him in ways nobody else would and, for now, he could simply be. In their hidden nook within an ancient castle, there was just the two of them. There were no dead mothers. No elusive murderous druids. He was safe in her arms. So he wept.

CHAPTER 13
AISLING

Predawn mist cloaked the sweeping emerald hills, muting Ash's steps towards Newgrange. Set and Maebh strode alongside her, slowing their pace to match hers as they crested the ridge, bringing the mound into view, white carved stone emerging eerily from vapours swirling about its base.

Ash suppressed a shudder. The narrow passage within that monument had fed on her mother's blood not long ago, the starting point to Ethne's unknown plan. Beside the clinging mist, only grass and weathered granite surrounded the powerful site, with no lingering corruption to hint at the darkness it had witnessed. They'd come here unknown to anyone, hoping to form protection from what may come.

"I can't go in there," Ash whispered, and Set simply nodded before disappearing into the tomb with his supplies.

When they'd met at the highgate, neither had acknowledged their last encounter except for a lingering hug that Maebh had cut short by pointedly clearing her throat. Ash had stepped back from Set's embrace, her cheeks flushed. His piercing eyes promised they would revisit their moment another time when duty, obligations and a meddling sister wouldn't tear them apart so swiftly. Now was not the moment to savour the feel of his strong arms around her. There would be time later to explore what blossomed between them, if they all survived Winter Solstice and Bradan's Cath.

Maebh hugged Ash's shoulders while they waited, until finally Set emerged from Newgrange, the satchel he carried somewhat lighter. "All done, but let's place charms along the outside too."

Their boots crunched lightly on the stony earth as they circled the mound, unspooling silver twine at Set's instructions.

As he retrieved a leather wrap holding crystals, stones, and glass vials, Maebh outstretched her hand at his offering. "Is now a good time to enlighten us as to what mystical concoction you've assembled?"

Set carefully lined several items along the flat of Maebh's palm before repeating the process on Ash. "These are charms and tokens I learned from a tome in the castle library. Infused correctly, their magic can prevent blood from being spilt." When both women stared at him sceptically, he shrugged. "A druid helped me."

He held up a jagged red crystal. "Bloodstone, to create a barrier against malevolent deeds." Next, he indicated small wooden rods tied with braided grass. "Spells of protection woven into the rowan and earth elements." Finally, he showed them a vial filled with amber liquid, flecks of gold glittering within. "And blessed oil, consecrated beneath the full moon."

Maebh snorted. "And does his lordship wish to explain how he got these precious ingredients?"

Set rolled his eyes but a grin teased his mouth, the evidence they were twins never as clear as in this moment. "A couple of kitchen maids donated."

When he shot Ash an apologetic look, she laughed. "Ever the charmer."

Maebh shoved her brother, muttering he was an idiot as they moved around the mound. A smile tugged at Ash's mouth as she observed her friends' antics. Maebh lost no opportunity to poke and prod at her brother. Yet for all her sniping commentary, Maebh meticulously laid each charm and token along the stone just as Set directed.

As they walked the circumference for the third round, Ash felt the power of their spells thrumming in harmony with the site's existing magic. No blood would spill here again if their charms held true.

Watching Set's confident movements brought an ache beneath her breastbone as she recalled finding him nearly broken in that abandoned castle corridor. She could admit now that part of her was glad her request to visit Conor had been refused, simply because it allowed her to fold Set in her arms when he needed comfort—the way he so often did for her.

Ash had come close to kissing him then, her body thrumming with need to comfort him with her lips as well as her arms. But though the moment felt right emotionally, sadness clung too heavily about them both. So she held back, letting her hands channel support instead, saving their first kiss for a sweeter time unburdened by grief. Because she would kiss Setanta McQuillan, that much was certain.

As she affixed the final charm, Ash cleared her throat. "You're not the only one to talk to a druid. The High King's advisor, Biróg, cornered me at the coronation to tell me something strange. She said I'm blood-blessed."

The twins jolted toward her, surprise flashing across their identical features. Maebh broke the silence first. "And what does that mean?"

"I tried asking but she spoke in riddles." Worry drew Ash's mouth into a tense line as she considered. "She said my empathy, the way I can read emotions, is part of this condition. And . . ." she faltered, almost afraid to voice the next part. "She claimed you two are blood- blessed as well. And Tiernan."

Maebh strode closer, inches from Ash's face, urgency radiating from her tight frame. "What exactly did she say about Tiernan?"

Set placed a gentle hand on Maebh's shoulder, easing her back before turning troubled eyes on Ash. "Why didn't you tell me last night?"

Ash flushed. "It didn't feel appropriate considering . . ."

". . . I was a blubbering mess?" Set finished with a wry twist to his lips, but grabbed her hand, giving a playful squeeze.

Ash covered his hand with her own, leaning gratefully into his solid warmth. "Biróg wants to meet with all of us. She knew my mother, said Cara had tried to find a cure for whatever being blood-blessed means."

Set enfolded her close and Ash clung to his anchoring strength, meeting Maebh's fierce expression over his shoulder. Her friend vibrated with barely contained tension. The acrid scent of woodsmoke and burning metal filled Ash's nostrils, and she winced.

"You still haven't answered my question," Maebh bit out. "Did this druid say anything useful about freeing Tiernan?"

Ash pulled back, shaking her head helplessly. "Only that his fate will be revealed when the stone's silence breaks. More mystical nonsense."

Ash's heart clenched at the desperation cracking Maebh's glare. She gazed helplessly at the rigid set of her friend's shoulders as Maebh stared unseeing at the lightening sky.

Ash pictured Tiernan's gentle smile, heard his deep chuckle. Her chest constricted at his absence, not just missing the way he carried responsibility as her second, but also his steadiness and wisdom which they could all use now.

Despite his best efforts, Set could never fully replace Tiernan's reassuring presence. With every decision, every plan of action, Tiernan's level-headed input was the silent counsel she yearned for. Ash worried her nails into her palms, equal parts frustrated and sorrowful.

Maebh had lost even more. Her usual vigour was but a shell concealing how deeply the loss of Tiernan ravaged her. And they still had not found the path to restoring him, their hands grasping only shadows and dead ends.

Ash could make no promises now to lift Maebh's anguish. But they would find a way to free their friend.

"We aren't doing enough." Maebh spewed a harsh curse before pacing away.

Ash moved to go after her but Set held her fast. "Let the storm pass." He touched Ash's shoulder, eyes dark with concern. "Can this druid be trusted?"

"I could sense a goodness in her. She offered to check on Conor for me."

"I'll research the term 'blood-blessed'." He brushed a wind-tousled lock of hair from Ash's cheek, sending a shiver through her. "But for now, let's concentrate on Winter Solstice and getting back to Tara Court for the Cath announcements."

She simply nodded, peering around his frame to say goodbye to Maebh, but the other woman didn't turn, her hair glowing like a halo as the sun crested the horizon, the first fragile light gilding the grassy mound. Set drew her wordlessly into his arms. Strong hands came up to cradle the back of her head, guiding it gently to rest against the steady drum of his heart. The clean, woodsy scent of him enveloped her.

She splayed her fingers across the hard planes of his back, holding him closer, wishing to freeze this moment beyond duty's reach. Darkness engulfed them as the tugging sensation took hold. In a matter of seconds, they were suspended into nothing before reappearing outside her tent. As her legs shook, his crushing strength lingered, almost reluctant to release her. But the trumpet was already sounding.

"Go," she said, pushing him away, already regretting the loss of his warmth.

With a searing glance, he spun away to retrieve Maebh.

Ash's boots sank into hard earth as she wove between her warriors. Their breath plumed white amidst the bustle; fastening belts and weaponry, faces set with quiet focus. Woodsmoke threaded the air from freshly-kindled fires, failing to dispel the lingering night-time bite. Tomás and Ciarán stood from the firepit logs upon her appearance, charging forward.

"We've been called," Ciarán greeted her, cracking his knuckles with a dimpled smile.

Ash's shoulders slumped before nodding silently. They'd gone unnoticed for too long, and it was now their turn to partake in Bradan's agenda. Clearly the High King aimed to distract her from further efforts to see Conor by forcing the Breens to prove themselves worthy to remain in Tír na nÓg.

Ash rubbed her hands briskly as she approached the makeshift strategy table. Their map was weighted with stones against the wind's tug. She traced the outlines of Mide, picturing the zones they would soon fight to claim.

In the distance the other Fianna clans prepared for the same task. Ash surveyed the sprawling camp, the din of preparations blending into a fevered chorus of warrior strength. Unfamiliar faces mixed alongside friends and adversaries, foreign sigils on armour and banners. Fellow Fianna, called here for shared purpose, yet ultimately adversaries in the contest for land and station within the highguard.

She squared her shoulders, lifting her chin. The Breens would face this trial head-on regardless. She wished for her second and third - one trapped in stone, the other refusing her presence.

Ash smiled despite all the obstacles in her path. "Time to show these Fianna how it's done."

CHAPTER 14
AISLING

Ash surveyed her clan as they herded the last of the faeries out of the gates of Tara Court. The solitary fae came to waist height as they marched between her warriors. Although the other clans on duty had ventured outside the highwall, hers had stayed to clear the enclosed town. An idea that she'd quickly concocted when she'd heard locals complaining about their homes and taverns being infested with the small creatures.

Now, the Breen banner, the red hand underneath two moons and one star, stood tall in the centre of the square, two of her warriors standing guard under it. Their first territory was claimed, and a big one. There was a risk in claiming Tara Court, but she'd figured they spent most of their time here, and it hadn't been against the rules to claim the heart of the kingdom.

Once the other clans competing had left the gates, she'd hesitated. The plan was a good one, and she knew it, but those who were selected watched her and the rest of Breen clan carefully. Looking for weaknesses, no doubt. Today was an initiation for her, an evaluation beneath every scrupulous eye, and she couldn't help the worry that settled in her gut. The choice was not hers of course, but the cards had now been dealt and it wouldn't take long until all the Fair Ones in this land learned of Bradan's move against them. This land was his to rule by right alone, but that privilege had been granted by the same creatures he now turned away.

Marching alongside her clanspeople, she eyed the small, tricky faeries they'd caught. Clurichauns, pixies and púca—but no royal Tuatha Dé. She was thankful the weight of points only reflected territories, and not actual categories of Fair Ones. With the sad lot walking with her clan, they would surely not have bothered.

A troupe of five clurichauns huddled together, short legs fighting to keep up. Their wizened features downturned, long, hooked noses and drooping eyes red-rimmed from being corralled out of the tavern cellars they'd been squatting in. With stained clothes haphazardly kept together by patches, they grumbled in rasping voices about being woken up so early.

The pixies had been easier to spot, lurking in alleyways and under door stoops, devouring any scraps of food they could find. Their pointed teeth gleamed against leathery skin, their sharp nails clawing at her and her clan's skins when they'd first approached them. Their attempt was half-hearted though, and soon the faeries had found themselves among the line being herded out of the Fianna territory.

"Ouch," Ciarán grumbled, jerking the netted bag he'd been carrying away from his side. "One of the little feckers bit me."

Tomás chuckled before his brother threw the bag at him, the pixies screeching as they floated on translucent wings, zigzagging frantically, trying to find a way to escape. The air vibrated with an inharmonious symphony of their angry, high-pitched tones, layered with violence. Tiny, iridescent bodies twisted and surged, barely visible but for their glowing trails, sparks bouncing off their prison as if balls of lightning were entrapped. Although their collective effort shook the net, they were unable to break through iron-laden mesh.

"Hey!" Ash ran up to her cousins. "Be careful with them. We're only escorting them out of our territory. Don't hurt them."

"Sorry, Matriarch," Tomás replied solemnly.

"Try telling them that," Ciarán countered, but took the bag carefully from his brother.

The púca were the least troublesome of the group, and once they reached the woodland, they shifted from goats into horses and galloped into the woods. Ash hoped they would heed her warning. They were no longer welcome within the highwall.

She surveyed the troupe of solitary fae with a weary sigh. They had made a nuisance of themselves in Tara Court, and Bradan's orders were clear: they had to go. These fae were certainly mischievous, but they hadn't truly bothered anyone until Bradan had declared them exiled from his lands. After his coronation celebrations, clurichauns had ransacked precious ale and mead that had been in barrels for centuries. The tavern owners were furious.

"How far are we . . . escorting our little friends, Matriarch?" Ciarán asked as the group kept a steady pace through the dense trees.

As they crested a hill, the thick forest spread, welcoming them into their haven. The moss draping the branches waved like scarves in the breeze. Narrow pathways wound their way between the trees; old hunting trails and herders' tracks, the only clear routes through the wilderness.

But despite the tranquil, rural beauty of the land, an air of wildness and danger still lingered. The Tuatha Dé Danann ruled this realm beyond the safety of Tara Court's walls. And they did not welcome trespassers into their domain.

"Take them to the river, and then return to Tara Court," Ash ordered. "I'm going to the oak tree."

"We'll come with you." Tomás strode towards her, ignoring her glare. "The clan can take care of this lot. We're not leaving you alone out here, Matriarch."

"Don't be ridiculous," Ash huffed. "I've gone to the satellite tree by myself countless times."

"That was before," Ciarán said, handing the bag of pixies to a younger warrior, who looked in askance at him but accepted. Before she could ask what he meant, Ciarán continued. "The High King has taken a stand against Fair Ones by declaring them unwelcome in his kingdom. We weren't safe before, and we're less so now. The other clans are our competition, too. They won't hesitate, Ash."

"Fine," she conceded, knowing it wasn't worth the effort of winning this battle.

After informing her people of what to do, the three set off toward Tiernan's tree. Falling into the familiar route, her thoughts wandered. Despite performing her duties as matriarch, a weariness settled deep within her bones.

Yet as each day slipped away, an undercurrent of dread washed over her, the impending confrontation with Ethne casting long, foreboding shadows on her heart.

"Any word on Conor?" Tomás asked quietly.

Ash drew in a lengthy breath, looking out into the maze of the forest. Conor's confession about Ethne not truly being a druid ricocheted through the chambers of her mind, amplifying with each echo. What harm had her brother done to himself?

"Biróg sent a scroll to say he was well," she said, kicking at loose branches on the forest ground. "I wish he'd let me visit so I could see for myself."

A pang of hurt reverberated through her core every time she allowed her thoughts to hover around Conor's name. His condition remained shrouded in layers of uncertainty. Although she hoped Biróg was honest, she didn't know the woman and wouldn't be fooled into trusting anyone lightly. Was Conor afraid, hurting, or simply did not desire her company any longer?

"Con will come around," Ciarán said, bumping her shoulder. "We'll get him out of there and everything will be fine."

Ash nodded stiffly, not trusting her voice. The brothers seemed to sense her need for space and let her walk on, talking quietly as they followed.

Her thoughts drifted to Set and the moment they'd shared hidden in the castle alcove. Despite his harried mind, she longed to be there with him again, his strong hands tender as he held her close, his cheek resting against her chest. His stormy eyes always captivated her, seeing the man instead of the monster he claimed to be.

In those quiet moments they had shared, she had felt truly seen by him. Set accepted all parts of her—the warrior, the leader, her fierceness and vulnerability.

When he'd confided in her about Bradan's offer, she couldn't help but think of the greater distance it would put between them. But of course, she hadn't said that. Becoming a rígfénnid was a great honour, and to become one at his age even more so. If he held the title, he might be able to get Conor released. Biting her lip, she forced that thought away. She wouldn't hint at that thought, not when he'd been so broken and ready to warp spasm. Even if Set became a rígfénnid, it was too late for anything to be done before Winter Solstice.

Ash gritted her teeth and tightened her grip on the sword she'd borrowed from Ciarán, using the bite of its pommel into her palm to anchor her. Though outmatched, they would not back down without a fight. They would give Ethne the fiercest resistance she had seen in her long lifetime.

CHAPTER 15
AISLING

Striding through the forest, followed closely by Ciarán and Tomás, Ash scanned the oak trees as they walked, searching for the pulse of Tiernan's protective wards. As they got closer, an invisible force pushed against her. Despite her best attempts to push through, she slowed her steps as she breathed in the thick, foul-smelling air.

"I forgot how awful this part is," Ciarán spluttered.

Ash pushed on, ignoring the tightness in her chest, and grabbing each of their hands. They were ten feet from the oak when their progress halted to a standstill. The feeling of being unwelcome, of not belonging, pressed in on Ash from every side. Out of the corner of her eye, she saw Ciarán take a single step back before stumbling to a halt. Tomás was already retreating.

"No," she groaned, determination locking her limbs.

She took one step. And then another. Pulling her cousins with each agonising movement. Her vision swam as she pushed against Tiernan's ward. Halfway to the oak, she fell to her knees, gasping for breath. The feeling of wrongness coursed through her veins, every part of her screaming to flee.

With a grimace, she crawled the last few feet to the base of the ancient oak. As soon as she crossed the invisible barrier, the repellent force vanished. Gasping, she leaned against the rough bark, feeling the magic thrum within the tree.

"It never gets easier," Tomás panted beside her.

She rolled to her side in time to see Ciarán vomit. While Tomás tended to his brother, she loaded up the laptop, every keystroke reminding her of her second in command. Gods, she missed Tiernan.

As her call connected to her foster parents, she took a steadying breath. Connecting calls had become increasingly glitchy and often required multiple attempts as the weakening link strained to hold. As always, the camera was grainy, but it was better than the black screen at their end.

She fiddled with valves and dials, heart sinking as the initial flashes of connectivity gave way to static on the flickering screen. But then ghostly shapes emerged from the white noise. After the fourth try, the fuzzy video stabilised, though the visuals remained blurry.

She drank in their familiar features—Mary's cloud of silver-streaked hair, Dom's kind eyes crinkling. How long since she'd seen them in person? The screen still jumped and pixelated, struggling and failing to sharpen the image.

"I wish I could see you. You sound tired; so I'm sure you look it," Mary said through the laptop speaker. Her soft voice held a teasing warmth layered with the barest edge of rebuke. Ash refrained from rolling her eyes, sure Mary would somehow know she'd done it.

"I'm fine, honestly," Ash replied, her eyes travelling to where her cousins sat at the rim of the enchantment.

She *was* tired.

Their voices drifted as if down an endless tunnel, often fading to indecipherable murmurs. Ash's chest fractured with each snapped fragment of conversation, knowing the precious remaining time was bleeding away. Who could say how many more calls this decomposing channel might allow before scattering their connection like leaves? She ached listening to the growing holes of silence, every lost word piercing her soul. Soon only fading echoes would remain of the family she still grasped for across the void.

"Where are you?" Dom's deep voice broke through the crackling speaker. "On your uni placement?"

Before she could answer, Mary cut in. "No, silly. She's staying over at Brian's. Right?"

Ash swallowed around the tightness in her throat. "No. Remember, I'm with my Breen clan now? We're in Tír na nÓg. That's why you can't see me on the screen."

Silence greeted her and she waited to see if they'd remember. Agonising seconds passed. It was getting worse. The closer they came to Winter Solstice, the harder she found it to remind them of where she was and why.

"Your mother . . ." Mary trailed off, as if the memory of Cara's murder had only just sprung to her mind. "Aisling, you're a suspect. The gardaí searching for you."

Her words were rushed, face flushed as if she was out of breath. Dom held her hand firmly, stroking her knuckles with his broad thumb on their wooden kitchen table.

"The detective came round again after your last call," Dom said. "I told him if he showed his face again without a warrant, I'd sort him out."

Ash laughed despite herself, relief flooding her as clarity sparked on their faces again.

"Hold on, I'll get the notebook," Mary said, releasing Dom's hand and disappearing off camera.

Not before wiping at her eyes, Ash noted. She stared at Dom as he looked to where his wife had gone, and her stomach dropped. She missed them so much. They had done more for her than she could ever repay. Would she see them again in person? She knew the answer and buried it deep down. Mary came back into view, a brown leather notebook in one hand,

and two pairs of reading glasses in the other. She offered one pair to Dom and the two opened to a page and read.

While noting the contents, Dom explained. "After the last call, we could sense the fuzziness coming back on us, so we quickly jotted notes to ourselves to remind us of everything. We're not going to forget you, kid, you have my word."

Ash choked on a sob as they read whatever they'd written down. She was grateful they couldn't see her as she cried silently. She shook her head when Ciarán rose to come over but accepted a tissue from Tomás before he retreated silently. When she knew her voice was stable enough to speak, she said, "That was a clever idea. No doubt Mary came up with it."

Dom chuckled as he lowered the specs on his nose and stared into the camera with his clear blue eyes glistening. "Careful, now."

She could have sworn he could see her, even though the magical barrier didn't allow it. Tiernan was a genius. Carving a signal between the worlds with his laptop, satellite, and druid potion. There were limitations to everyone's genius she supposed, but she was grateful she could see her foster parents even if they couldn't see her.

"Ah yes," Mary said, pointing to something on her notebook before removing her own glasses to look up at the camera. "We are to tell you that Newgrange is still closed after . . ."

She knew Mary couldn't bring herself to say the words and Ash was grateful. Her mother's murder still was as raw as the first day when she'd discovered her mutilated body. A tight band snapped around her chest. She'd been distracted in finding out who her killer was. She knew that now, and even though Ethne was still at large, a mystery had been solved, and it left a gaping hole that was filled by a grief that overflowed; she didn't know what to do with it.

"Yes, okay, go on," Ash managed to get out through a shaking breath.

"No matter what specialist they call, the cleaning methods they've used won't clean the . . . damage."

Her mother's blood.

"They were cautious before, only using warm water and steam cleaning, but now they're discussing the options of more invasive treatments."

"They're debating whether to re-open," Dom interjected, his face showing exactly what he thought of that. With a tight fist, he slammed it on the table, the screen jumping in and out of focus.

Mary tutted before fixing the laptop.

"The Winter Solstice lottery should have happened by now. The public are demanding it re-open so the select few can still witness the chamber filling at first light."

"You have to insist it doesn't re-open," Ash all but shouted. "Do you remember what I told you? About Ethne . . ." She took a sharp breath but forced herself to continue. "She has something planned for that day. I don't know what, but she used Newgrange to do it. No realm is safe until we figure out what she has planned."

Even as the words tumbled out, Ash knew it was too late. They were running out of time.

"We'll barricade the chamber ourselves if we have to," Dom promised.

"No! You must get as far away as possible," Ash pleaded. Your cottage is too close to Newgrange."

The air solidified in Ash's lungs as she caught the grim resolution framing both their faces.

"Wait . . ." she licked her dry lips, her breath emerging in thin, helpless whistles. Surely she could make them see reason? Her hands wouldn't stop shaking. She clasped them tightly as she searched for ways to convince them to leave.

"We have lived here for thirty years. We've loved and we've lost . . ." Dom's voice cracked, and it had little to do with the signal.

That look of grief always appeared when either of the older couple hinted at their loss from over twenty years ago. Neither had truly recovered from having their newborn snatched away by a changeling.

When Ash had walked into their lives, a stubborn Fianna reject, they'd taken her in, and told her to do all that she could for the innocent. To the humans who had no chance against the cruel and wicked faeries that lived in their realm.

"We're staying put," Mary said simply.

Dom grabbed his wife's hand again, and Ash knew she couldn't argue. Acid crept up the back of her throat while her mind scrambled vainly for persuasive words to get them to leave. But she knew the couple she saw through tear-streaked eyes. They would not back down.

"One of your clan has called by several times," Mary added, looking down at her notebook, her glasses wedged onto the bridge of her nose once more. "Niamh."

Ash sat back on the cold ground, her cousin the last one she'd thought would check in on her foster parents. "What does she say when she comes?"

"She asks after you, and she and her wife bring us groceries, even though I told them we are quite capable," Dom said gruffly, but he smiled, and she could tell he liked Niamh and Emer. "Niamh had some stories to share about you when you were growing up."

Ash groaned, but she couldn't deny the warmth spreading in her chest.

They talked for another thirty minutes while Mary furiously scrawled down notes. Ash knew she should tell them about the shift in realms. How could she say this may be the last time they spoke? That the solstice was the one thing that had kept their time zones in sync? Afterward, they could leap apart. One day in Tír na nÓg could equate to fifty human years.

With one last look at the couple who'd saved her humanity, she said, "I'll see you soon," and ended their connection.

Glancing around, she was surprised at how dark it had grown. Tomás and Ciarán stood.

"What now, Ash?" Tomás asked quietly.

She looked into the shadowed treeline and hoped her clan were already on their way back. It would have taken too long to lead the faeries to the Mide border. She didn't truly care about winning the Cath when Ethne's games were a far higher stake.

Winter Solstice loomed over her like a malevolent vigil, a predatory eye watching her every move. She was exposed under its ominous regard, a foreboding sense of impending menace sending shivers down her spine.

With an unsteady breath, she scanned through the contacts Tiernan had coded into the laptop. She dialled a number she never thought she would, and after three rings, bright auburn hair filled the screen.

Niamh squinted at the camera, unable to see Ash through whatever magical barrier kept the realms apart. She wasn't sure what Tiernan had typed as their contact details, but her cousin knew who had called.

"Aisling?"

With a steadying breath, Ash leaned toward the screen. "Niamh, we have a lot to talk about."

CHAPTER 16

MAEBH

"Who's next?" Paul slurred, taking a large gulp from his tankard as Maebh rolled her eyes.

The McQuillan warrior motioned for the next contender to sit opposite him for another arm wrestle. The drinks had flowed freely at The Raven on Solstice Eve and Maebh's clan had decided this was where they would celebrate their first Cath win.

No thanks to her, of course. Lorna had made sure of that. The warriors had left before dawn without telling her and had cleared a section of woodland near the highwall by noon.

None of it mattered. Truly. Tensing her jaw, she drummed her now badly-chipped nails against the full tankard on the high table, her stomach hollow. If she ate or drank anything, she was sure she'd see it again.

The tavern door swung open, and Setanta strode through the threshold like an avenging angel. His imposing frame filled the space, and Maebh's stomach knotted further. Mud spattered his black cargo trousers, the worn leather of his axe handle hanging from his belt. Along with the array of blades strapped to his body, a steely glint shone in his eyes.

Although Gearoid McQuillan had been tall and broad, his son was another level of impressive. Blood-blessed. That's what the twig-crowned druid had told Ash. Maebh knew there was something special about herself and her brother. She had known no one other than Ash to share their ability to sense emotion; but to have a powerful druid hint at something to do with their blood? Her mother's dying words whispered in her ear. *Of my blood but more.*

Setanta's movements were perfectly controlled, graceful yet purposeful. Strands of his unruly blonde hair, so like hers, had escaped the leather tie at the nape of his neck. No sign of his ríastrad, Maebh noted with relief, as she watched her brother scan the room, taking in the state of their drunken clan with a stern look.

When his focus landed on Maebh, his expression shifted. Warmth flooded his eyes as he made a beeline for her, long strides eating up the distance between them. The gentle giant, fearsome in form yet kind at heart.

"You missed it, Set!" Paul called out to him, another tankard raised as the warrior he'd just defeated left with his hand pressed close to his chest. "You should have come with us instead of going to the library."

Most of the clan laughed and called after him, but her brother barely acknowledged them as he stormed over to Maebh.

"What are they doing?" he demanded. "They should be sober and ready for the Solstice."

Maebh shrugged, flexing and releasing her hand around her tankard. "They showed up half-drunk. Lorna bought this for me."

"That was . . . nice of her," Setanta said, his full lips downturned.

"As a celebratory drink over their win." She handed the mead to Setanta. "Theirs, not ours."

Setanta pushed the tankard away, mead spilling onto the wooden bar. She stared at the spreading mess, a waste of a good drink, but she didn't care. Lorna had seemed surprised Maebh hadn't dumped the contents over her head when she'd handed it to her, something she would have normally done. But the Solstice was imminent, and her aunt's pettiness was nothing compared to what they were bound to face.

"Hey." Rían glowered at the twins, the tavern owner's ever-present towel over one shoulder. He snatched the tankard away. "If you're not going to drink my mead, feck off and go to Newgrange. We're closing soon anyway."

Before either could answer, Rían stomped off, handing the tankard to another patron.

A flash of passing neon caught Maebh's attention. A closer look revealed an acid green blouse paired with vibrant purple bell-bottoms worn by a young, brown-haired local woman. But what really stood out was that the blouse was on backwards, with half the buttons clasped in the wrong eyelets.

As the woman made her way to the darkest corner of the lantern-lit tavern, Maebh tilted her head curiously as she observed the local further. The bell-bottoms were several sizes too big, cinched tightly at the waist with a belt but still dragging on the floor. The necklace the woman wore consisted of bottle caps, wine corks and brightly-coloured beads threaded onto string.

Maebh smirked. This woman knew nothing of modern style. Most locals stuck to the style of when they'd arrived or wore simple tunics if they'd been born here. The bright colours and loud patterns clashed horribly, but on this woman, they had an innocent charm. Though clueless, she exuded an earnest willingness to experiment that Maebh couldn't help but find endearing. The backwards blouse somehow suited her, as if she alone could make such a bizarre combination work.

With a wry smile, Maebh shook her head and returned to her own corner, leaving the colourful woman to enjoy her night in blissful ignorance. Some things, it seemed, were best left undiscovered.

"Hi," Ash said, approaching the bar, her slender frame accentuated by her fitted leather jacket and tight leggings. "I came as soon as I could."

Her shoulder-length black hair swished with each step. Though a flush coloured her alabaster cheeks, her green eyes shone as she joined Setanta and Maebh. They hadn't spoken since they'd charmed Newgrange, and Maebh offered her friend an apologetic smile, ready to voice it, but Ash smiled and shook her head, hinting she'd already forgiven Maebh's rudeness.

"Where's your clan?"

"Tom and Ceer started the journey to Newgrange earlier," Ash replied, loosening the lace of a knee-high boot and retying it tightly. Maebh pretended not to notice how her friend's fingers shook as they worked the lace. "They'll be stationed there well before first light to make sure nobody tampers with our protective charms. Let's get moving, too."

"We should tell our clan." Setanta inclined his head toward the tables filled with merry McQuillans.

They each turned to face them, and Maebh rested her elbows on the tall table behind her. Caoimhe was now arm-wrestling Paul, their faces scrunched in strained smiles as neither were willing to be beaten. Malachy poured candle wax down Paul's neck, and it was enough of a distraction for Caoimhe to slam Paul's hand on the sodden table. Raucous laughter erupted from their clan.

Raising an eyebrow, Maebh turned back to Setanta. "Do you really think any of them would understand a word of what you're saying in this state?"

The tavern was stifling, the heat from many patrons and smoke from the firepit causing sweat to bead on Maebh's brow. She had plaited her waist-length hair, but loose tendrils clung to her face. Thankful that she had worn one of her handcrafted t-shirts, she tugged on the hem, looking down at the words 'I'd be jealous of me, too' emblazoned on her chest.

"We should have told them before now," Setanta insisted, frustration lacing his voice.

Maebh stiffened. "And risk Bradan finding out?"

"Ash told . . ."

"Ash can trust her clan and . . ."

"Oi, you two. Shut up and focus," Ash scolded, eyes narrowing. "Set, get your clan out of here and go to Newgrange. They'll listen to you." Ash cast an apologetic glance at Maebh, but she nodded in return, a thin smile finding its way to her lips. "We'll see how sober they are by the time we get there and if they'll be of any use to us, you can decide then. Deal?"

Maebh waited for Setanta to argue, but to her shock, he nodded.

"What will you two do?" Setanta grumbled and Maebh bit down on a smirk.

She had to hand it to her friend; she knew exactly how to handle her brother.

"I'm going to the castle." Ash crossed her arms, already answering his argument. "I have to try to see my brother one last time. I don't care that they keep sending me away."

"I'm going to see if Biróg knows anything," Maebh said. "She's leading prayers at the temples today."

"She seems to know more than we do about anything so it can't hurt," Setanta said, flexing his fists. The revelations about being blood-blessed had shaken him the most. He had spent even more time at the library searching for the term, but so far had found nothing. "Be careful and don't say too much in case Bradan finds out."

"I can handle an old twig lady." Maebh tossed her plait over her shoulder, feigning a confidence she didn't quite feel. What if Biróg's pronouncement was only a ploy set by Ethne? She was a druid, and that's who Ethne had impersonated. She shook off the doubts; Ash had insisted the druid was genuine. "What good is silence now if it'll lead to more death later?"

Setanta exhaled before eyeing her. "Try not to start any fights."

Maebh grinned. "No promises."

A bawdy tune broke out from across the tavern and half the crowd joined in. Rían rang his bell, signalling for the last call to order before he closed The Raven and made the long journey to celebrate Winter Solstice at Newgrange with the others.

"I wish we had more time," Setanta said before brushing a stray hair from Ash's face.

"I know." She took his hand.

Setanta rested his forehead against Ash's and Maebh turned away, pretending to inspect the brewing equipment as she tried to give them a semblance of privacy in the crowded tavern.

"Stay safe." His words were faint but earnest.

There was a tenderness in his voice that Maebh had rarely heard from her brother.

Glancing over, she saw Setanta lean in to kiss her friend's cheek. Ash smiled, giving Setanta an encouraging push towards his waiting clan, but Setanta returned to envelop Maebh in a quick hug. She breathed her brother in, gripping him tightly before he turned and strode out of the tavern, shouting for his warriors to follow. There were grumbles of protest from the McQuillans but eventually they rose from their seats and stumbled after their second in command. Maebh pretended not to notice how nobody looked to see if she'd followed them.

Ash's hand rose to her cheek, and Maebh felt a pang as thoughts of Tiernan filled her mind. He had to be safer where he was than confronting whatever lay ahead for them. They would face the solstice and then figure out a way to free him.

"Ready?" Maebh turned to Ash with forced cheer as she grabbed her leather coat from the stool she'd thrown it on. "The solstice isn't going to wait for us."

Ash nodded and the two matriarchs left the tavern, walking into the balmy spring night of Tír na nÓg. Despite it being Winter Solstice, the air was warm and fragrant with the scent of flowers in bloom. Lanterns glowed along the streets, their golden light casting long shadows. Evergreen boughs and red berries adorned doorways and windows, festive decorations for the longest night of the year.

People spilled out from the temple district, heading in droves toward the highgate, making the journey to Newgrange. At the market square, Maebh pulled Ash into a tight embrace.

"I'll see you there?"

Ash bit her bottom lip, nodding. "We're going to be fine."

Maebh knew her friend was saying it to convince herself, so she smiled, pretending not to feel its falseness. "Of course we will. Go."

She watched Ash hustle toward the castle, knowing her friend was wasting her time. But if Setanta was in a dank cell, she'd do the same. As Maebh's eyes scanned the crowd, she spotted the strange woman in the mismatched clothes heading toward the temple district. She trailed behind her as they weaved through the crowded streets to a quieter section. Maebh wasn't sure what compelled her to follow the odd woman, only that her instincts told her to do so. She turned down a narrow alleyway, emerging between two Tuatha Dé temples.

Maebh crept closer, keeping to the shadows as the woman approached a hooded figure near a wooden door, their silhouettes barely visible in the dark recess of the alley. Maebh's eyes narrowed as the hooded figure became distinct.

Clad in sweeping emerald robes that shimmered like new leaves in the moonlight, her auburn hair flowed freely in intricate braids. Upon her brow sat a simple circlet of birch bark. Maebh would know that twig crown anywhere. It was Biróg.

She crouched low, straining to hear their hushed voices as they entered a temple. Hugging her coat in front of her, Maebh took the wide stone steps to Danu's altar. Biróg and the strange woman continued their conversation as they stood before a reflecting pool, the air heavy with the scent of incense and candle smoke.

Maebh hid behind the maiden statue, one of three aspects depicting Danu, the great mother goddess; the defiant warrior maiden upholding a spear and shield next to the fertile, fruit-bearing mother cradling a baby with a bushel of bounty at her feet. Across from them both stood the third, a stooped crone with her hood obscuring her face, hunched over a staff, twisted with age. Snippets of conversation floated to Maebh over the reflection pool.

"...can't let her succeed..."

"...have to stop the ritual..."

The woman turned, her yellow-flecked eyes honing in on Maebh before enveloping into shadows and disappearing. But before she'd sifted, the corner of her mouth turned up in the hint of a smirk as she'd waved at Maebh—a glimpse of something knowing flashing across the woman's features. Her eyes slitted into a peculiar shape, teeth revealing sharp canines before she dissolved into the darkness.

Maebh strode over, grabbing the druid's arm and dragging her against the crone statue of Danu. Biróg tensed, but her expression remained calm as she met Maebh's eyes.

"Who was that fae?" she demanded, but a searing pain shot through her palms and she released Biróg to find plumes of smoke wafting from her arm. She glared at the druid as she shook out her hand. "Wiccan magic won't help you, druid. What aren't you telling us about Ethne's Winter Solstice plan?"

"I seek only to protect our people. Whatever happens at first light will carve our destinies." Biróg knelt by the flowers and offerings laid at the statues' feet: fish, shells, pebbles and coins glinting in the candlelight. She laid out three coins. "The High King refused to listen. We will share secrets, Maebh McQuillan. But now you must go to Newgrange. Your escort awaits."

Before Maebh could ask what nonsense the woman spoke, her skin prickled, the weight of a steady appraisal on her. She stiffened, placing her hand on the hilt of her sword as she turned toward the entrance.

"Aren't you going to Newgrange?" a cheerful, masculine voice called, before a red-haired highguard appeared across the pond.

Maebh's heart hammered as she spun to find Biróg was gone. Cursing, she strode toward the highguard, a man she'd never spoken to before.

"Were you following me?" Maebh accused, willing her heart to steady.

"I've wanted to talk to you for a while," the man began, and as she strode back to the entrance, his smile widened. "But it's by chance I've stumbled upon you here while on patrol."

"Not interested," she retorted as she pushed past him and down the steps of Danu's temple.

The road leading to the highgate was quiet, and Maebh could no longer hear the merry chatter of those journeying to Newgrange.

Shivering, she turned back to the steps to find the highguard there, and she glared at him as his brown eyes creased in amusement.

"Like I said, highguard, I'm not . . ."

"Micháel."

"What?"

"You meant to say: 'Like I said, Michéal, I'm not interested.'"

"Whatever game you're playing, I don't have time for. I need to get to Newgrange."

Maebh glanced at the sky. Still dark, stars shone brightly overhead. Biróg was a dead end. Full of riddles and more questions. Glancing at the castle, she thought of Ash. Had she been able to see her brother? Was she already on her way to Newgrange?

"You know," Michéal said cheerily, "I've been here one hundred years, Matriarch. With no word from home. Everyone I knew is likely dead."

She looked at Michéal sidelong, his tailored black shirt and pants pristine, an array of wicked knives visible within his reinforced leather vest. She was used to the many highguard that patrolled Tara Court, one guard blending into another, becoming a faceless mass of black fabric and blades. Maebh would not have picked him out from any of the other highguards as being remarkable. His boyish smile widened as he noticed her appraisal. She trudged toward the gate.

"Is Ireland a free state yet?" Michéal asked suddenly, eyes wide and hopeful. "While I joined the Cath, my blood still bled for Ireland. We receive offerings from Fianna over the years—clothes, and books—we haven't had much of a connection to current affairs." He scratched his chin. "Are we free yet?"

"Well, there's the Republic of Ireland, and then there's Northern Ireland . . ." Maebh's heart sank when Michéal insisted she explain. He tried leading her toward the town square, but she refused. "I don't have time to get into political history right now. I have to run my ass off to Newgrange."

"Even if you ran like a Fair One, you wouldn't make it on time," Michéal observed, smiling as he winked. "What if I offered to take you on my horse? You can then tell me all about this border you speak of."

He said it like it was the strangest thing he'd ever heard, and Maebh contemplated taking her chances and running rather than try to explain the last century of Irish history to him. When she glared at him, his ever-present smile grew, as if he knew what she was thinking.

"Gentleman's honour, I will not try to court you while on my horse."

"Oh gods, nobody says that."

"And this is precisely why I want to chat with you more. I'm the youngest highguard here. I'm only one hundred and seventeen years old."

She stumbled, staring at his youthful face. He didn't look seventeen, but he certainly did not fall into the category of being over one hundred, either. Micháel stood about an inch taller than Maebh, with a lean yet muscular physique apparent even under his highguard uniform.

His hair was the most striking thing about him: deep auburn strands framed either side of his sharp cheekbones.

Micháel's eyes twinkled as if he knew a joke nobody else did and would share it if she asked him to. She wouldn't.

"Fine," she said, signalling him to move, and following him toward a stable to the right of the gate. "Let's get to Newgrange."

Before it was too late.

CHAPTER 17
MAEBH

"Never again," Maebh grumbled after stumbling from Mícháel's horse and waving him away.

Thank the gods he didn't follow. That man could talk the head off a Dullahan. Even though she'd tried to use as few words as possible, he left her voice hoarse from answering all his questions.

The early morning sky was lit by lanterns and a thousand stars hanging from the heavens, ready to make way for the rising sun. As Maebh looked at Newgrange, its white stones gleamed in the lantern light. Hundreds of revellers surrounded the monument, decorating the grassy mounds and open fields. Observing Biróg and the Fair One's meeting had left her late, and she had no answers to provide as to what would happen at first light.

Inching forward, the heat of bodies pressed around her, and the sporadic fire pits in the large clearing did little to clear the pounding in her head. She should be focused, but her empty stomach turned at the smell of roasting meats. She would need energy for whatever would come, but she couldn't face eating now.

Noting the charms were still in place as she passed one hidden behind a boulder, she searched for her brother and Ash among the crowd.

Ash found her first. "Are you okay? Was Biróg any help?"

"I'm fine and no joy with the druid, but she was talking to some sort of faerie when I found her," Maebh said. "Did you get to see Conor?"

"No," Ash said flatly, shoulders slumping. "And Bradan refused to see me. We're on our own."

"We're enough." Maebh wished she believed it.

Maebh filled her in on what she'd witnessed as Ash led her to where Tomás and Ciarán stood with Setanta, who assessed his sister as if categorising to see if she was unharmed before saying, "I've warned a few of our warriors to stay alert to trouble, but Malachy suspects something is amiss."

"We don't have time to share everything with him," Maebh said, not adding the fact their mother's former second hadn't bothered to tell them about their Cath plans earlier.

Ciarán gave a grim smile. "We snuck into Newgrange to make sure nobody was inside. It's all clear."

Ash's eyes blazed. "We stay on alert for Ethne. No sign of her yet, but the day is young."

"Unlike her," Maebh noted, but she couldn't stop her sight from roaming the crowd for that silver-haired druid. "I just want this solstice to be over."

"Me too." Ash nodded. "But I'm afraid it's only just begun."

A lump formed in Maebh's throat and she bit into her lip, tasting nothing but her own sorrow. The tattoo inked on her side burned as much as her unshed tears. On unsteady legs, she turned toward Newgrange. She had to get it together.

"As agreed, we'll split up, so we're spread out by the time the chamber fills with first light," Ash said, signalling for her cousins to move to their allocated positions.

The first light of the Winter Solstice held great power at Newgrange. At the moment the rising sun's first rays crept down the narrow passage tomb and illuminated the inner chamber, it signified both endings and new beginnings. If Ethne meant to use that mystical dawn for her dark designs, they had to be in place beforehand. The solstice sunrise was said to possess magic that could tip the scales between life and death, and Maebh feared what darkness it might unleash if left unchecked.

Setanta looked fretful, clearly unhappy with parting from either of them, but he, too, moved away. Ash and Maebh walked deeper into the crowd, closer to the structure. Maebh noted members of Ash's clan standing at strategic positions around the perimeter, keeping watch for any threats. Bonfires blazed, casting dancing shadows as figures whirled and spun to the music of flutes and drums. Laughter and song filled the air, an infectious joy that failed to move her.

Maebh glanced over at Ash's troubled expression and shouldered her playfully. "If the world doesn't end this morning, are we meeting before clan training? Or do you think you'll be too occupied in someone else's bed? An overly tall, broad blonde who needs a good grooming, perhaps?"

Ash's gaze shifted to hers, and she laughed when Maebh wiggled her eyebrows.

"Oh, I'll be there, and I'll be coming from my own tent."

"Setanta will be disappointed," Maebh remarked, but ushered Ash to hurry as Bradan and the other rígfénnid appeared before the base of Newgrange.

This was it. The moments before first light.

Maebh inched closer as highguard formed a line in front of the leaders. Strange. They'd never separated themselves from their subjects before. Perhaps Bradan wasn't as oblivious to the threat of Ethne on this solstice as he let on. If he was anything like his son, he would be no fool.

The sloping hill leading to Newgrange meant that there was already an elevation, so Bradan and the rígfénnid could be seen by most. Maebh was close to the highguard, and although they had stood in front of their leaders, they hadn't stretched as wide as the large monument's base.

"Happy Winter Solstice, Kingdom of Mide," Bradan began, and was greeted with a chorus of cheers.

The inky black sky was moments from lightening as Maebh looked up at him, the High King's deep voice carrying confidently through the cool pre-dawn air.

"As always, only a select few can enter the tomb to witness first light," Bradan said, gesturing behind him. "I'd like to invite my rígfénnid to enter. A gift from me on the solstice."

As the stately men entered the passage, Maebh glared, paying little attention to the rest of Bradan's speech. Why would he put his men in danger? Ciarán and Tomás had ensured the chamber was clear, but surely Bradan wasn't foolish enough to believe the portal was safe on this day?

A tight knot of anxiety formed in her stomach. This moment was monumental. Something so rare, it was sure to contain its own type of power. And Ethne coveted power. So much rested on whatever evil the female had planned to take place before sunrise. The protective charms they had left may not be enough. But they had done all they could for now. All that was left was to wait and see if darkness would be held at bay, or if the longest night would bring only grief and ruin.

Bradan's speech ended to a smattering of applause, and everyone turned their attention to the sky, a hush falling over the gathered crowd as they waited in anticipatory silence. Darkness gave way to the promise of dawn as reds and oranges crept along the horizon, casting long shadows across the stones of Newgrange. The first rays of sunlight had appeared, spilling over the horizon in golden fingers of light. Whatever threat still lurked in the shadows would soon be revealed. Maebh sucked in a breath. They were out of time.

The white stone walls seemed to glow in the dawn's light, welcoming the new day. The grassy mound atop Newgrange was shrouded in shadow, but as the sun continued its ascent, the shadows slowly retreated to reveal its green crown. The air was still and heavy with anticipation as the sunlight crept towards the entrance passage of Newgrange.

All held their breath, waiting. But not Maebh. Fear consumed her as she waited. The fate of the realms rested on the outcome of these next few moments. As the sky lit up in shades of pink and gold, sunlight spilled into the entrance passage, lighting the chamber within.

Nothing happened.

Silence reigned for a few heartbeats, then clapping broke out as those gathered at Newgrange enjoyed the historical moment. Maebh sagged, weak with relief. Darkness had been held at bay. Another day had begun, a fleeting moment of peace amidst the tumult and uncertainty yet to come. But for now, for this precious dawn, light had triumphed over darkness. The solstice had arrived.

A flash of acid green caught Maebh's attention. She stepped closer to the oddly dressed figure who was caressing the white stone wall, shadowed enough that no one else seemed to notice her strange behaviour. As Maebh walked around the base away from the crowd, she noticed that although the odd clothes were the exact match to the woman she had seen with Biróg and earlier in the tavern, the person wearing them now looked completely different. Instead of a young brunette, an old woman with white curled hair and a hunched back sped around the walls. There was no question it was the same outfit, and as the yellow- flecked eyes turned to her before focusing back to the stone, Maebh understood.

The Fair One was now meddling with the tomb. She was fae, but what kind could wear the skin of a human? The female was muttering under her breath, patting the walls as if trying to find the right one. Was she trying to find the charms to undo them?

"Hey! Stop!" Maebh raced closer.

The female ignored her as her hands became more chaotic. An earth-shattering crunch, as though it had emanated from the bowels of the Underworld, interrupted the morning. Maebh's throat closed at the memory of the stone guardians screeching awake. Blinking back the horrible images, her eyes darted to the stones of Newgrange. A low rumble filled the air, shaking the ground beneath her feet. She looked up just in time to see the first cracks form, like black webs along the stones, the massive rocks shifting and then dislodging from Newgrange's walls.

"Maebh!" Ash's scream rang out, but Maebh couldn't turn to her.

For a sickening moment, she just stared as feet away, the stones that had stood for thousands of years crumbled one by one. The old woman came back into view, still pushing the stones and muttering in old Gaeilge. Maebh's vision pulsed as fury simmered through her blood. In one breath she was standing still, watching the woman perform whatever magic that had Newgrange collapsing, and in the next, she was inches from her, gripping her arms. Maebh's lungs contracted as space was no longer a solid thing, but something she'd warped.

In and out of focus, Maebh gripped the woman's shoulders. She needed her to get away before Newgrange fell. The woman tried to push Maebh off, her wails turning to whimpers when her grip tightened. A ringing formed in Maebh's ears as two different locations blinked in and out. What was happening? The pounding in her head was unbearable.

Maebh held on to the Fair One's arm in a vice-like grip as space warped and distorted around them. Her vision flickered rapidly between Newgrange and a peaceful field, the abrupt switches leaving her stomach lurching violently. Maebh blinked hard against the dizzying shifts, struggling to gain her bearings as the landscape changed in a series of jumps too quick for her senses to track or adjust to.

Fianna warriors came into view, rushing toward Newgrange as the stones crumbled and collapsed. Horror filled Maebh as she realised rígfénnid were trapped within. But just as quickly, the scene shifted back to the calm field.

A ringing filled Maebh's ears and nausea churned her stomach as it felt like her body tore apart, only to be hastily stitched back together again. She was in two places at once, shimmering in and out of existence. When her throat was about to implode, she gulped a shaking breath in. Finally, she solidified as they reformed in the field and remained.

The Fair One wailed and struggled, but Maebh tightened her grip, unwilling to let her go until she figured out where they were.

"What the fuck did you do?" Maebh's mind reeled from what she had seen—had it been real? How could a monument thousands of years old have crumbled to dust before her eyes?

"You shouldn't have done that!" the female's shrill voice was rushed as Maebh tried to understand her frantic words.

The nausea and dizziness faded, though a dull ringing persisted in Maebh's ears. She turned to face the Fair One, her fingers itching to unsheathe one of her blades. This creature had destroyed Newgrange, and Maebh had questions that needed answering.

CHAPTER 18
TIERNAN

It was so cold. *Stay*. Just a little more. He grunted against the thousand tonnes weighing in on all sides. *Protect*. He ignored the voices fighting him as he pushed and pushed and pushed. *Maebh*. To the naked eye, he remained stationary like the others. But he'd done it before, and he'd do it again. An imperceptible step so small, not even a Fair One would notice. But he had done it. Before the unnatural gravity holding him here snapped, forcing him back to his position.

It would take years. Far too many for his human life. But he had to believe he'd make it. To Maebh. *Maebh*. That was her name. And he had a name, too.

What was it? He forced himself to try harder. Focus more. Remember. *Protect*. Otherwise, he may as well give in to the stone calling him. Their collective chant in his mind increased, his very thoughts provoking hope. *Stay. Fight*. He wanted to smash every last one of them, including his mother, who remained beside him.

Forever. Tiernan was his name. *Break. Break. Break.*

Shut up, he roared in his mind and for a blissful second the voices stopped. But the numerous beating stone hearts never would, including his.

Darkness was an ever-present companion, but as Tiernan struggled against his enchanted prison, something about the dark captured his attention. The stone guardians were all encased in the same white quartz as Fionn Mac Cumhaill's sarcophagus; the walls speckled with blue-white gems that reflected light from an unknown source. But most of the cave walls were darkened clay of compact earth. Natural shadowed alcoves dotted the cavernous room, but there was something . . . off.

Pushing through the bond, he mapped out the other guardians' positions in their eternal stations. Mind-jumping was a new trick he'd acquired. Thanks to her. The druid often visited. Despite her promise of only one name, she reminded him of who he was, and how he'd wound up here. She'd killed his matriarch and yet she was becoming the only source of his reprieve from the unyielding coldness of the stone guardians.

Her and memories of Maebh. *Maebh*. She had a name. So had he.

Stay. Fionn. Protect. High King. From the constant onslaught of the guardians' internal thoughts assaulting his own mind, he'd pushed back enough to block out most. He'd also started pushing into theirs and found he could see through their locked eyes. It beat the monotony of staring at the one wall and only entryway of the cave. It only served to strengthen his resolve to break free.

Tiernan focused his will, determined to remember more. Fragments of memory stirred. He had fought to save those who left, strangers who had somehow become important to him. He had sacrificed himself so they could escape while he remained trapped here.

Who were they? Friends, companions, loved ones; Tiernan couldn't say for sure. But their absence opened an aching chasm within his heart, fuelling his desire to remember their names, their faces, everything that made them dear to him.

The woman with wild blonde hair and fiery blue eyes. Thanks to the druid, he clung to that one name the most. *Maebh*.

Tiernan would reclaim his memories and his life. And then he would find his way back to those he cared for, to thank them for giving him a reason to fight in the first place.

Weaving through the minds of the other guards, he scanned the surrounding walls and the blackness clinging to them. Midnight pockets pulsed in random places, and he cursed at his entrapment. If he could just walk ten paces, he could see it better. Even from the mind of the closest guard, it was clear there was something wrong. It was not just shadows. The blackness had a presence, rippling back and forth like a snake.

It was inching closer to the guard whose mind he was currently occupying. *Fear. Fear. Fear.* The chant began, echoing through the others. Scared into immobility, Tiernan found he couldn't hop out of the guardian's head as the black presence inched closer. A smoke-like substance, it scorched the exterior of the stone guardian before inching back.

Pain ricocheted through every fibre. Tiernan fled from the guardian's body. He only jumped into the stone body next to him in time for the smoky substance to attack again, this time devouring more of its victim.

The pain was severe, but not as much as before. They were a hive mind, trapped to share each other's thoughts, emotions, and now, pain. The monster retreated and Tiernan saw the guard's arms were no longer white quartz. Was the smoke freeing the guard from his stone prison? As it inched in again, smothering the guardian fully, the man's appearance turned from stone to flesh.

With an intake of a single breath, the man fell to his knees, crying out with his own lungs. It was euphoria and agony combined to be finally freed, but as the shadow crept closer,

Tiernan knew. They all did. The man couldn't utter a word as he was consumed. His face frozen in agony as he disappeared. When the shadow retreated once more, the man was gone. Vanished into the murky depth.

CHAPTER 19
AISLING

The walls of Newgrange crumbled in a deafening cacophony of grinding stone while clouds of dust darkened the sky, shattering the anticipatory silence. Fianna murmured in alarm, peering around for the source. While others had backed away, Maebh had pushed forward, toward danger.

"Maebh!" Ash shouted again, but there was no point. She was gone. A stabbing chill wound its way around her heart, the thought of losing Maebh twisting inside her like a black hole swallowing every ray of hope she had dared to kindle.

Cracks spread through the walls like lightning forks that led to the inevitable cry of thunder as more stones shifted. Grating, grinding noises pierced the air as the stones scraped against each other before crashing in booms that shook the earth with devastating force.

Maebh had been only metres from Newgrange. Too close. Much too close. A hail of stones crashed down right where she had been standing. Ash's heart stopped. No one could have survived that. She tried to push through the crowd, but people rushed past her, jostling and bumping. Great chunks of stone and earth fell, clouds of dust billowing up as the passage tomb collapsed in on itself.

She reached the entrance where screams could be heard from within.

"The rígfénnid are inside!" she shouted, but through the mayhem, nobody heard.

Fire burned her throat as she blinked back tears. She pictured her grandfather amongst the other leaders. A man who was no more than a stranger and would never get a chance to be anything else.

There was no time for that now. Turning in a panic, she searched the many faces that looked on in horror. But none were Set. Her clan needed her. Maebh's face filled her mind, and she bit her lip. Set would need her.

Shouts sounded and her attention snapped to a patrol of highguard escorting Bradan away and ushering Fianna to retreat.

Dust engulfed all within seconds, bringing on an impenetrable fog profound than any night. Two figures darted to her side; she recognised her cousins' midnight curls.

"Ceer! Tom!" she cried. "Fintan Breen . . . I mean, your grandfather . . ."

"Our grandfather," Ciarán corrected, hugging her side. "May his soul continue on."

"And his love remain," Tomás said, before muttering, "not that there was much of it to go around."

Ash and the others stumbled, struggling to keep upright as the earth pulsed and shuddered with groaning quakes.

"What is happening?" She turned to her cousins, knowing whatever Ethne had done, the collapse of Newgrange was not the end.

Ciarán grimaced as he surveyed the ground where fissures yawned wide enough for a man to sink waist-deep, while others snaked off into barely perceptible lines. A bottomless void seemed to yawn from beneath. With each passing tremor more fractures sprouted like some sinister scar tissue upon the land's flesh itself.

"If this was just a natural disaster, the stones would have settled long ago."

Above the chaos, a flock of birds took flight from Newgrange's ruins, black wings beating frantically as they escaped the destruction of the torn land.

Silence fell. An eerie, profound stillness as the dust cloud cleared to reveal what remained. They'd lost their leaders. All but one. Bradan's stallion stamped the rock-strewn ground as his face was a canvas of fury. Surrounding highguard urged him to the safety of the castle and even from this distance Ash saw the war of indecision play out in his expression.

"My place is with my people!" he bellowed, yet highguard urged him forward, an immovable mass against the High King. With a growled curse, Bradan relented.

Spinning his horse back around, Bradan addressed the Fianna. "Everyone, make your way immediately back to Tara Court. My highguard will remain and recover the rígfénnid."

A lump formed in Ash's throat. They all knew there would be no rescue attempt, only a slow and gruelling process to retrieve their bodies.

"I will not let this act go unpunished. We will see the dawn of a new day and with it, fresh resolve to rid ourselves of monsters amongst men."

As the crowd dispersed in distressed groups, chaos erupted around her. People screamed and pushed against each other in wild desperation. Parents held crying children close and searched for escape from the madness. The air turned sour with sweat and panic as wide eyes reflected a contagious hysteria. It was a frenzied mob driven by primal fear and self-preservation that replaced the cheerful festival-goers from moments ago.

Ash called the Breens to join the highguard. Forming a line, they worked in strained silence at first, before laments and prayers to the Tuatha Dé gods rose in the dusty air. She didn't join in. The repetition of hauling stone in the assembled line was gruelling. Every stone painstakingly shifted brought hope and fear in equal measure.

"Look," Ash cried, grabbing Tomás's arm and pointing to where rubble shifted with purposeful motion. A hand thrust out, fingers scrabbling as if to grasp the freedom so near yet agonisingly out of reach.

Without hesitation, the Breens surged into action, shouldering tonnes of jagged stone together, bit by bit until a dust-covered figure emerged.

As the grime cleared, Ash gasped. "Fintan!"

Her grandfather's face was sickly grey. "Others trapped . . . blackness came . . . sucked them in." His breaths grew ragged between words.

The others continued to clear the debris surrounding her grandfather as she sat with Tomás and Ciarán on either side. But all movement stopped when his midsection was uncovered, and his cry rang out.

A serrated piece of rock protruded from his abdomen, a hand clutching uselessly at the wound. But no blood pooled. It moved in currents around the open wound as if looking for a way to escape, but none came. With shaky hands, Ash gingerly moved Fintan's shirt to reveal his chest. His skin looked like cracked canvas, skin darkening in areas as if the blood within were pooling inside rather than seeping outwards naturally.

"Why . . ." Ash began but swallowed the rest of her question as Fintan groaned.

She eyed her cousins as they assessed his chest.

"The protective charms." Ash whipped her head around, searching uselessly for the charms they had placed around Newgrange to prevent blood from spilling. It seemed their charms were working against them.

Despite his age, her grandfather had always looked young, strong. But as his breathing grew shallow and pain wracked his body with wet gasps, he looked his age.

"Hey," she said as his eyes rolled upwards. When she clutched his hand, he blinked, searching, trying to find her once more. "What do you mean about the blackness sucking them in?"

"Opened up . . ." he gasped. "Swallowed so fast. Ran. Almost . . . made it."

His body shuddered a final time before he stilled, mouth agape as he stared at nothing.

Tomás leaned forward, closing his eyelids. Ringing filled Ash's ears as she focused on nothing and everything. She barely knew her mother's father. He had made no effort to seek her out. But to die like that . . .

Ash crumbled, grief consuming her frame while her cousins laid comforting hands upon her quaking shoulders. For the man she didn't know. For Maebh who'd been standing far too close. She searched in vain for Set among the scattered survivors, needing his safety confirmed and his steady presence to ground her. But right now, she was needed here.

Stumbling over the fallen debris, she made it to safety with Tomás and Ciarán behind her. She collapsed to her knees, coughing up dust and earth particles that burned her lungs.

With a quick scan, Ash categorised the destruction surrounding them. Pockets of fire burned through fallen stone. The highguard had moved Fintan's body and were continuing to clear what would have been the narrow entranceway. Most had heeded Bradan's order, leaving the site. Gathering up the tattered remnants of her will, she stood, ready to help again.

"You're safe." Set's voice came from behind her.

Her knees threatening to give way, Ash turned to see him standing unscathed among the rubble. His tall form strode towards her, eyes scanning her from head to toe as his long legs ate up the distance between them. She ran. Her sob filled the air as she launched herself at him. Wrapping her arms around his neck, she latched her legs around his back as he held her close.

Time stood still as they held each other, his broad shoulders shaking as they drew strength from one another.

"You're safe," he repeated, his hand encircling the nape of her neck.

She couldn't answer. But something in her needed his assurance. He was okay, but she was, too. Clinging tighter, she nuzzled into his neck, ensuring he truly was there.

All too soon, Set placed Ash down and took her face in his hands, his fingers stroking her cheeks. His eyes searched hers. "Are you hurt?"

Ash shook her head. "No. You?"

"No." He pressed his forehead to hers with a sigh.

Ash gripped his shirt in her fists. She swallowed past the lump in her throat. How could she tell him about Maebh? She sucked in a rasping breath. Ash sank into him, breathing in the familiar scent as his strong arms encircled her. For a moment, she allowed herself to feel safe and whole again. Let herself forget the horror surrounding them and simply exist within his embrace.

After a long moment, Ash pulled back. "Set, I'm so sorry, but Maebh . . ." The words were lost in her throat, but she couldn't let him find out from another. "Maebh is gone."

Her throat closed as she choked on the last word. He frowned, stroking her lower back.

"What do you mean?"

"She was too close to Newgrange when it happened. Set, I'm so . . ."

"What? No. That . . . that's not possible." He ran unsteady fingers through his hair. "Did you see it? Her fall?"

"I was looking at her right before. She was leaning against the wall."

"But you never saw her go down?"

"Well, no . . ."

"And look, they'd cleared a lot of the debris. Have they found her?"

"No." Ash bit her lip.

His shoulders slumped in relief. "Then she's fine. Completely fine." He hugged her, kissing the top of her head. "I'd know if she wasn't."

Ash looked up at his face, so like his sister's. Now was not the time to argue that point.

"The others will be looking for us. We have work to do."

She nodded. He took her hand, lacing their fingers together. "We face it together."

Ash squeezed his hand. "Together."

The sounds of Fianna returned her to their present, but the thought of the person responsible loomed over them as they marched over the fallen stones.

"Have you seen Ethne?"

"No." Set's jaw pulsed. "I took some of my clan around the perimeter, but there's no sign of her."

Though they could have walked unassisted, the familiar feel of his calloused palm against hers brought comfort. He kissed the back of her hand gently before releasing it, then began lifting and dragging boulders that no normal man could ever hope to shift alone. Biróg's words filtered through. *Blood-blessed*. Set moved the stones with ease, muscles rippling beneath his shirt.

Ash allowed herself a brief, selfish moment to simply drink in the sight of him. Where others faltered, he remained steady. While others crumbled, he endured. Time and again he had proven his strength, in mind and body. He thought what lay beneath was a monster, but it had always been a hero.

No matter what trials lay ahead, Ash knew Set would stand by her side. His hands, so strong as they hoisted stones, were gentle for her. His stormy eyes, now fixed on the ruined landscape, saw the real her. His towering frame, now bent beneath great weight, would fight against enemies that dared approach.

After several hours of moving the wreckage and finding nobody to save, she trudged through the forest with Set, their clans behind them. Trees basked in the afternoon glow, the rays of the sun filtering through the canopy of lush green, painting dappled spots of warmth on the moss-laden ground. The air hummed with the whispers of the wind rustling through leaves and Ash wondered if they spoke of the destruction of an ancient monument.

She'd instructed her cousins to look out for Ethne, but none of them caught sight of her. It was Set who'd convinced her there was no further immediate danger from Winter Solstice. Ethne had played her hand and now they'd all have to wait and see what the outcome was. Why destroy the portal? Was she trapping them all in Tír na nÓg?

Set's weary footsteps were as slow as hers, but she clasped his arm as the clans marched on, needing to touch him, to feel that she was not alone among the rubble, and neither was he. A cawing broke out from a cluster of trees above before a cloaked figure glided towards them. Ash quickened her steps, releasing Set, her hand grasping for her sword as she glared at the lithe feminine figure approaching.

"Hello, little matriarch. We've been waiting for you."

Ash stopped. There was no mistaking that tone, the hint of an echo within. Three voices in one.

"The Morrígan," Ash breathed, fear clutching her throat.

Sallow hands rose, tugging down her hood. The fae's smile was anything but warm. Her features were beautiful yet predatory as she stared down at Ash with a piercing scrutiny. Black hair cut in a blunt angle to her chin fell across high cheekbones and full crimson lips.

"Ash," Set called. "Step back."

Blinking, Ash turned to see Set thirty paces away, axe in hand. Warm breath fanned across her cheek and Ash shivered as her attention snapped back to the Morrígan. How had she got so close to her?

"It's just Macha right now, girl. My sisters slumber."

Ash cried out as the fae grabbed her wrist, squeezing so sharply that her sword fell with a thud to the ground. Before she could fight back, the world warped and distorted. Macha sifted her away from Set and their clans, leaving them behind.

They reformed in a forest clearing. Ash scrambled for the dagger hidden in her boot, but another hooded figure appeared, striking her across the face, sending stars bursting before her eyes. The shadowed male rammed a hood over her head before binding her hands tightly with rope. Pain lanced her cheek, but she bit back her cry.

Through the coarse fabric, she heard another familiar voice. This one, deep and velvety. Another Tuatha Dé Danann. The male fae who'd accompanied Macha to the castle as Bradan announced Aedan's demise. He had seemed too interested in Ash and the others then, hinting he knew something they did not. Had he scented what Biróg had revealed? That they were blood-blessed?

"I told you to wait for me," Tara spat, hauling Ash to her feet.

She stumbled, her head spinning from the brutal blow and disorientation of the sifting journey. Still, she managed to remain standing.

"Do you think my sisters and I incapable of capturing one Fianna?" The Morrígan's voice echoed in her triple tone, both old and young, beautiful and terrifying. It was no longer just Macha. The sisters had awoken.

Beneath the rough hood, Ash's mind raced. Tara, one of the Tuatha Dé; faerie nobility. Her blood turned to ice at the memory of his furious glare pinning her on their first encounter. Ash straightened her stance as much as she could, squaring her shoulders beneath the bristly cloth. She would not show weakness. Lifting her chin, she said, "Take this hood off and release my hands. Then we'll talk."

Tara's reply was a brutal backhand across Ash's still-smarting cheek. Her head snapped to the side, but she did not cry out, biting back the pain once more.

The Morrígan tutted. "Tara, that is no way to treat our guest."

As they marched with her between them, Ash asked, "Where are you taking me?"

Her voice came out steady despite her rocketing pulse. Tara's grip tightened painfully until she whimpered. She dug her nails into her palms, refusing further sounds to escape.

When it was clear she would receive no answer, she catalogued details as they moved; focusing on her other senses to gather clues since the blindfold obscured her vision. Ash stumbled blindly, no choice but to go into the unknown with Fair Ones.

The earthy scents of moss and new growth filled the moist air. Somewhere nearby, an animal growled, but Ash knew there was no predator more dangerous than the captors walking beside her.

CHAPTER 20

MAEBH

Disturbing sounds of stones crashing filtered through the trees as Maebh tied the faerie's wrists with her belt. The female's purple bell-bottoms slouched down to her hips, revealing veined wrinkled skin. The restraint would do little against a cunning creature, but Maebh needed protection, even if it gave her seconds.

With her sword in one hand, she dragged the faerie by her clasped wrists, striding up the highest mound at Knowth. The scattered stones from the tomb dug into her boots, but Maebh paid them no mind. When she reached the summit, she scanned the perimeter furiously, straining her eyes at Newgrange in the distance.

"Fuck." Her heart hammered in her chest.

Through a copse of trees and fields, Newgrange once stood in the distance. Maebh gritted her teeth as she surveyed the destruction. The faint dawn light barely illuminated the distant structure, but it no longer resembled the grassy mound it had once been. Ethne's actions were a violation against Fianna. A mighty passageway between realms was reduced to wreckage because of whatever messed up scheme that woman had concocted. Maebh's hands clenched into fists as fire rose in her throat.

Ethne would not get away with it so easily. The dawn had arrived, leading them into the longest night. Maebh swore she would make the twisted bitch pay dearly.

Leaving the whimpering female on the ground, Meabh patrolled the circular mound.

"Why did you sift us here?" she demanded but the old woman shook her head.

"You did."

Maebh stopped, glaring at the Fair One. "I can't do that."

"You did."

"I. Didn't." But she grimaced. Setanta had sifted with her before, and it had not felt that way as a passenger. This had been different, like the pull to transport her elsewhere had come from within. *She'd* sifted them to Knowth. How was that possible? Setanta was able to travel through realms and locations, but she'd never had the gift. She had thought it had been linked to his ríastrad. Glaring at the faerie to make sure she was still on the ground, a wave of anger burned her insides, but nothing that would lead to her transforming into a monster like her twin.

Willing herself to tap into the pull once more, she tried to sift again, not caring that it had felt like she was moments from death by doing it. Holding her breath, she grasped inward for anything that stirred that strange sensation, but nothing happened.

As the fae rose to her feet, Maebh pointed her long sword toward her. "Stay the fuck down."

The hunched woman stilled, her grey curled hair slick with sweat as her wrinkled, colourless face scrunched in what seemed to be pain.

"I'm just fixing my clothes," the elderly-faced creature said, shimmying her pants upward and sitting cross-legged on the grassy mound once more.

As Maebh glared at the human-masked faerie, she looked for any signs of her glamour. There were usually tells. The female smelled like the off-ness Maebh associated with Fair Ones, but there was no flickering behind her veil to reveal her true form. She cursed before looking toward Newgrange once more. Maebh could make it back on foot, but it would be too late to save anyone. She strode forward, resolve coursing through her veins. She needed to ensure her brother and the others were safe. Ash had screamed out to her, and she had been far too close. Gods, Maebh hoped she made it to safety.

Stopping before the seated creature, her grip tightened on her sword. She could have stopped this. She could have warned the others that it was happening.

"What were you doing to the stones?" Maebh demanded.

"I was trying to stop it," the creature pleaded, standing slowly with her bound hands raised in supplication.

Maebh raised her weapon but stood back warily as her glamour finally wavered, but not enough to see her true form. Yellow eyes glinted through the muddy brown disguise, changing from opal to slitted, reminding Maebh of a goat's.

"You attacked Newgrange. You and Biróg knew that would happen."

She cowered away from Maebh. "I sensed danger and tried to warn Biróg, but she said it was too late."

"Too late? Where's Ethne? Are you all in this together?"

Maebh snatched the front of her blouse, ready to drag her off her feet and shake more answers out of her. But as soon as Maebh's hand closed around the fabric, the creature transformed. Her lined face smoothed, wrinkles fading as glowing youthful skin appeared. Grey hair turned a vibrant blonde and elongated down her back in familiar curls. Her body, previously hunched with age, straightened and stretched, limbs lengthening, torso filling out with curves.

In mere seconds, the frail old lady was gone, replaced by a young woman. Not just any woman. Maebh stared at the faerie as if staring into a mirror reflection. Her own blue eyes shone through, but flecks of gold polluted the otherwise flawless likeness of her own face.

"What the hell kind of trick is this?" Maebh spat, releasing the female's blouse abruptly.

She rose gracefully to her feet, a small smile playing across features that were Maebh's own yet twisted into something alien. "You interest me, so I borrowed your shape for a while."

Maebh recoiled. "Get out of my body!"

With infuriating grace, the faerie mimicked her movements, from the tilt of her head to the tapping of her foot.

"Stop that," Maebh snapped, fists balled.

The faerie smirked, echoing every moment, from combing back loose hair to tapping a restless foot. "So much fire, yet so much left to learn if you'd listen."

But Maebh was through listening. She lunged, but the creature backed away gracefully before donning another face.

The fae shook her head, her swishing blonde hair transforming into auburn locks. Her large golden eyes, the same shade as before, now glimmered with mischief. A long lock of crimson hair fell over one eye, and she flicked it back with a practised gesture.

"I am a púca, and I mean you no harm," the female said, loosening the bindings of Maebh's makeshift cuffs with far too much ease. "My name is Sage."

She had a lilting voice, far different from her quavering elderly tone.

Maebh glared at her, not hiding her suspicion. She had encountered many púca over the years, none that could take the form of humans. "And what do you want?"

Sage tilted her chin up. "To help you, Maebh of Fianna. You are more than your kin."

"Why do people keep saying that?" Maebh grumbled, not lowering her sword as she studied the púca.

"Because it's true," Sage stated, as if it was obvious.

"Blood-blessed?" Maebh asked dubiously before shaking her head. "That doesn't matter. Right now, we need to get back to Newgrange, but I can't sift us there. I don't know how I did it."

Sage nodded, gripping Maebh's wrist before she could jerk away. Light folded to darkness and the suffocating sensation of sifting consumed Maebh once more before they reappeared within the empty streets of Tara Court.

"Why are we here? We need to get back to Newgrange." Maebh stumbled away from the Fair One, who only shook her head.

"You are needed here."

"It didn't work," a sweet, feminine voice said, and Maebh whirled to find Biróg standing in the street of the Tuatha Dé temples, her twig crown framing her bright auburn plaits. When Maebh looked back at the púca, she realised the faerie had combined both her and Biróg's appearances, blending them into one form. Sage smiled serenely at her, Maebh's mouth on Biróg's full face.

Before Maebh could accuse the Fair One of her trick, the druid beckoned them to follow. She retreated up the stone steps of a temple, her disc belt jangling with every step as her robes flowed behind. Sage followed readily, but Maebh hesitated. There was no way she'd make it to Newgrange from this distance. For now, she could get answers from the High King's druid on why she was working with a Fair One.

Sword still in hand, Maebh strode forward, noting Biróg had chosen the temple of Lugh. She followed them cautiously into the stone building. The imposing structure towered before her, etched with carvings of spirals and unknown languages.

Stepping inside, a chill enveloped her. It wasn't the cool day, but the dimly lit domed cavern. Taking an unsteady breath, she coughed out thick air, heavy with incense and the stories of gods and Fianna who'd shared this space. A silent presence seemed to lurk in the depths of surrounding stone, tugging at some wayward piece of her memory, a sense of familiarity in her heart.

Biróg and Sage moved forward confidently, approaching a marble shrine at the centre of the temple. It held a spear that shone with a fiery inner light.

Although wary of Biróg and Sage's intentions, Maebh's curiosity drove her forward. "Why are we here?"

"Lugh represents a master of many gifts, as do you." Biróg turned to Maebh with a small smile. "Don't you feel at home here? Your scent would suggest so."

Sage nodded in agreement. "She smells funny."

Maebh glared between the women as Biróg nodded. "It's her blood."

"You told Aisling Breen we were blood-blessed. Care to finally share what you mean by that?" she asked, biting on her inner cheek to prevent herself from adding anything insulting, and glaring at the púca when she caught her doing the same.

"Lugh can guide you to balance these two natures within yourself," Biróg said, clearly ignoring her question. "Tell me how you feel here."

"Honestly? Pissed off." Maebh clenched the hilt of her sword, angling it before her. "If you don't start answering my questions, I will have to tell our High King that you are harbouring a Fair One in Tara Court."

She smiled when the púca whimpered and Biróg knit her brows as if that thought hadn't occurred to her.

"He doesn't know about any of this, I assume?" Maebh continued.

"He is not of my concern, young one. You are," the druid said, smiling as Maebh glared at her. "I understand your mistrust, but we mean you no harm. Lugh sees the truth within. Let him help you accept what you are."

"No. Fuck this." Maebh turned from the females, but Sage darted forward, blocking her path.

Her large yellow eyes flashed in concern as Maebh swiped her sword in warning. Backing up a few steps, the púca said, "You need to understand . . ."

"I need to get to my family. To see who survived. Don't forget I saw you."

"She tried to stop . . ."

Maebh raised her hand behind her, palm up, signalling for Biróg to shut up.

"If you don't want to tell me anything useful, we're done here."

"You have Tuatha Dé blood within," Sage said, continuing her retreat in quick, jittery backward steps.

Maebh gripped the púca's arm to stop her from falling down the flight of stone steps at the entrance.

"I have what?" Maebh shook her head, releasing Sage. "No. I'm human."

"Do all humans sift?" Sage enquired, cocking her head to the side.

"No, but . . ."

"Can all humans smell emotions?"

Maebh let her silence answer the question even as her mind rebelled against the implication. She couldn't possibly have faerie blood within . . .

She pivoted to Biróg. "Find me when you're ready to share real information."

Chapter 21

Aisling

Ash jerked upright, swaying with the surging rhythm of a horse beneath her, its galloping tempo defying nature. The rough homespun hood shielded her vision, trapping her stale breath. A plea for calmness echoed within her, clashing violently against the need to flee. The blur of unknown landscapes racing past tore mercilessly at her thin grasp at stability. Sifting had been bad, but this was torture.

She had been slumped at a precarious angle, dangerously close to falling forward. How could she have fallen asleep? The hours had bled on in taut silence beneath the thunderous hooves of fae beasts and after she'd struggled uselessly against her captor, her shattered body had won over her harried mind. Ash righted herself, slamming into a hard mass. Tara tutted in clear disgust before moving away on their shared saddle.

She fought the blush crawling up her cheeks. "If you hadn't abducted me, we wouldn't be here."

"If you didn't smell so bad, I could tolerate you."

She gritted her teeth. There was no point in arguing with the fae male. Not when she didn't know where they were taking her.

"Stop fidgeting," Tara said roughly, no better than a growl escaping his lips.

Ash moved again anyway, her bound hands gripping the pommel as she tried to dislodge the hood while rubbing it against her shoulder, but its harsh fabric only irritated her skin.

"Again, if you have a problem, then you shouldn't have—"

"We're here." The Morrígan's voice rose above the rhythmic pounding of horseshoes on dirt.

The horse slowed on a steep incline, and Ash dug her thighs into its sides, but still she slid against Tara's hard frame. He didn't cringe away this time. Her ears popped as they levelled out.

Laughter and the smells of cooked meats and spices filtered through her hood, and she would have thought they'd entered the Fianna's walled town if it weren't for the guttural language being spoken by the unseen people. Fair Ones. She tensed as the horses trotted into a bustling area.

Where had they taken her? Tara halted the horse and dismounted. A rush of unease swooped over Ash by the sudden loss of his body heat against her back. The sun had no warmth against the icy shiver that slipped under her skin. Her senses heightened under the blindfold's merciless darkness, and she picked up the coarse snorting of horses nearby along with the smell of hay.

Blindfolded and bound, it was too dangerous to dismount unaided and she was all too aware of the vulnerability of her situation. With Tara no longer immediately behind her, she was left in a limbo, uncertain of how many unseen adversaries were lurking close. Even her captor seemed preferable to her darkest imaginations of who might be watching her now.

A hand touched her leg and Ash kicked out blindly, but Tara tutted as if dealing with an errant child. There was no way she would out-fight a fae. With a quickness that stole her breath, he grabbed her waist, hoisting her off the saddle. As soon as her feet hit solid ground, he released her. She fell backwards, landing in something that squelched, and there was no mistaking the smell of horse manure. Tara sighed before hauling her up by one arm.

The Morrígan tsked. "That won't help much for the smell you're so offended by."

Ash hated that she jumped at their voices. The sisters were standing much too close. Although they shared one body, their presence filled the space as if there were more than just three entities that made up the infamous female. Slender hands encircled Ash's bound wrists. She struggled uselessly, helpless against immortal strength as the Morrígan and Tara dragged her inside.

A primal dread haemorrhaged within Ash, each beat of her heart echoing in her ears like a foreboding drum as she was guided blindly into unfamiliar surroundings. Darkness under her hood swallowed her vision, enhancing her other senses so every sound echoed within her bones and the damp, cool air licking at her skin sent violent shivers down her spine.

The metallic scent of earth and stone invaded her nostrils, her body attuned to the oppressive claustrophobia of her shrouded world. Even the Morrígan's presence felt far removed, another spectre in this darkness she was pushed into. Her nickname suited her: the Phantom Queen, an elusive presence engulfing darkness with confident strides, leaving Ash grappling for solid footing. Ash stumbled once, then twice, over an unseen obstacle; her breath hitching on each faltering step. Her heart pounded a frantic song, the echo resounding like a haunted dirge throughout the darkness.

The turns they made were like a winding labyrinth, each leading her deeper into an unknown, murkier place. Fear clung to Ash like a second skin, its chilly claws scraping against her resolve, whispering stories of horrors that lurked in the unlit corners of her mind.

Yet, even in her fear, she counted each turn and step. After being dragged down narrow, winding stairs, Tara snatched her hood away before pushing her forward. She fell onto straw-strewn ground. Without another word, Tara and the Morrígan closed a heavy wooden door, the clank of a turning key echoing around the narrow walls.

She didn't need to let her sight fully adjust to know where they'd taken her. In the cold grasp of the dank cell, Ash sat enveloped in a consuming silence, her mind teetering on the precipice of despair. The stone walls around her seemed to pulse with her accelerated heartbeat, their indifferent coldness echoing her growing sense of unease. The door loomed to her right, where iron bands shut tight like teeth in a mocking smile. There was no point trying to open it, even though her hands itched to rattle the handle. She'd heard the lock click into place and wouldn't give them the satisfaction of hearing her attempt.

Instead, she got to work unbinding her hands. Sitting on the uneven stone tiles, Ash hugged her raised knees, finding comfort in the solid mass of her hidden blade still there. With a swift, practised manoeuvre, she rotated it to the worn ropes binding her wrists, the sharp edge biting keenly into the bristly fibres. She stopped only once to ensure nobody was at the door, the rope fraying until falling apart. Sheathing her blade, she wound the rope and stuffed it into her other boot in case she had an opportunity to use it as a weapon. Now all she could do was wait.

Ash's fingers trailed absently over the rough-hewn stone walls, feeling the groove and age of each hidden story locked within their cold exterior as she wrestled with her thoughts. She missed Set. The realisation throbbed painfully, like a wound left open, bleeding rivulets of self-reproach. Why had she walked toward the Morrígan in the forest instead of remaining close to him? The pull had been subtle, the glamour unnoticed until it was far too late. She could still see his face, leeched of colour as she walked stupidly toward a trap set by a cunning female.

The memory of Maebh running toward the crumbling stone invaded her like a shock of icy water. A keening so like the banshee's tore from Ash, from deep within her soul, and she bit on her closed fist for the friend she would never see again. The Fianna blessing played in her mind, but it wasn't enough for Maebh. Her soul would continue on, but more than her love should remain. The matriarch had been disregarded by her clan, even her twin at times, and still Maebh had fought for what was right. The world needed Maebh McQuillan. Ash needed her friend.

With shuddering breaths, Ash willed her mind to think about anything else. With hands still scrunched up, her nails dug into her palms, grounding her against the rising tide ready to consume her.

Bradan should have stopped Newgrange from falling.

The weight of his foolishness battered against her chest; each breath drawn from a fury as strong as dragon fire. He could have warned everyone, should have prepared them, but instead chose to send the rígfénnid into a tomb. All of them, dead. Maebh . . . Set's assurance his sister was still alive replayed in her mind like a balm that wouldn't truly ease, but she willed it to, anyway.

The thought of those deaths and the destroyed Newgrange was a leaden rock in her stomach, sinking deep within her. Their passageway was now rubble because of a mistake that could've been prevented.

A furious tear trickled down her cheek, a lone rebel against her stubborn will. The taste of defeat was bitterly tangible in the cold stagnant air, wrapping its suffocating tendrils around her.

A bone-deep chill coursed through the dank dungeon cell, slithering through the gaps in the stone walls, making the air around her feel glacial and inhospitable. Shivering, she leaned against the rough wall, but jerked away as water dripped onto her head. Looking upward, she followed the water streams until they disappeared into darkness, no ceiling in view. One narrow barred window was positioned low enough to see that it was natural light coming through, but much too high for any hope of escaping through it. Scanning the floor, she grimaced at the pile of musty straw in one corner, the only semblance of a bed. She was unsure how long she'd slept on the journey, but her body screamed at her to crawl over and succumb to the aching fatigue spasming her muscles.

But this was not a home, nor a place of rest. It was a cage, and she was trapped, but she would not yield like a docile animal. The monsters of this world were beyond these stone walls, and she couldn't afford to let her guard down.

She watched the shift in light from the high window, and scuttling sounds in the walls kept her alert despite how bone tired she was. The darkness caressed her consciousness, promising relief. Ash shook it off stubbornly, dragging her exhausted body back toward wakefulness. Each beat of her heart sent waves of resolve through her, every breath confirmation she still lived . . .

. . . Ash prised open her eyes with a start. The cell swam into blurry focus as her cheek kissed the dirty ground—damp stone walls, wooden door shut tight. The barred window let in meagre moonlight. Footsteps sounded outside the cell, getting closer, and she cursed inwardly for having fallen asleep without retrieving her dagger. Ash dropped her head back onto the straw, feigning unconsciousness.

The door swung open with a squeal of rusty hinges, but Ash kept her breathing slow and even. Booted feet approached, stopping beside her. A harsh voice muttered words in a guttural tongue. Then came a discordant shriek of raucous laughter—laughter that pierced Ash to the core, setting her teeth on edge.

The footsteps retreated, the door slamming shut behind them. Ash let out a shuddering breath. She was still alive. Her fingers grazed the hilt of her dagger, and she positioned it so it was within easier reach. For now, Ash let the darkness take her once more. But not for long. For soon the fire in her heart would reignite, and hell itself could not put out those flames.

CHAPTER 22
SETANTA

Storming through the castle, Set moved like a raging tempest, his boots squelching on the marble floor. He had been mere feet away when Macha had sifted Ash out of his reach. Those he passed seemed to sense his weakened tether to humanity, their wary expressions focused on him before scooting out of his rage-driven path. Ash's sword was a heavy weight on his back. Her shocked face as the sword fell when the Morrígan grabbed her replayed on repeat inside his head. His mind was a vat of fury, overflowing and ready to spill, and when it did, he would lay waste to anyone in his path.

He'd ordered both the McQuillan and Breen clans to race back to Tara Court before he sifted. Swinging the doors to Bradan's private wing, he snarled at the two highguard who tried to block him. He jostled through their spear barrier, separating them like stems of long grass.

"Hey, stop!"

Keeping his quick pace, he ignored the heavy footsteps racing in his wake. Set didn't knock as he entered the High King's room.

"Where would the Morrígan take Ash?" Set's voice was not his own, but his monster's.

Guttural and snarling, he held his ríastrad at bay, barely. He had promised the beast within he would unleash him when they stood in front of the Tuatha Dé Danann. Unlike any other time he'd tried to control his transformation, his monster growled in agreement, retreating further, but his claws still clung to Set's will.

Bradan glanced up from his seat beside a roaring fire, Bióg tending to his minor cuts. Her perusal crawled over him like an unwelcome touch, prickling his skin, stirring a tingling discomfort that danced down his spine. He didn't acknowledge her, his focus trained solely on the king.

Bradan's voice cut through the turmoil, iron-hard and unbending. "What are you talking about?" A shake of his head dismissed the highguard who came barging in, poised to restrain Set. "Leave him."

Set glared behind him before striding forward, standing directly in front of the king.

"Macha and that fae male ambushed Aisling Breen on our way back here," Set said, fire burning from within, his hand flexing around his axe handle. "They sifted her away before I could stop them."

"Setanta?" Maebh's voice was breathless as she entered the room, her wild hair half undone from its plait. She stopped short when she saw who was within the room. "What's going on?"

A wave of unspoken ease surged within him at the sound of her voice, his shoulders loosening with every track of her approach confirmation she was in one piece.

"Are you hurt?"

Set had always trusted that instinct would alert him to his twin's distress. Yet, ripples of Ash's worry had found a home in the farthest corners of his mind, introducing him to the uncomfortable whisper of doubt that if something bad had happened to Maebh, he wouldn't know. When his twin shook her head, he reached out for her, drawing her into a hug. Close contact mixed her familiar scent with the unmistakable sharp whiff of ammonia. Maebh, despite her pulled-together exterior, was clearly running on overdrive.

"Are you sure? Because you smell like you're seconds away from a panic attack," he whispered in her ear.

She stiffened, but shot back in a hushed tone, "And you're just a hair's breadth from going full-on Hulk."

"I've got it under control," he assured her, a soft vow that vibrated between them. At her probing glance, seeking answers, he shook his head, shooting down her silent inquiry. He turned and faced Bradan.

"The High King needs rest," the druid began, but Maebh stepped forward.

"The High King needs a lot of things, druid. How did you get here so fast?"

Set glanced between the two women, some unspoken battle warring between them.

"I came as soon as I could to care for our king," Biróg replied in a clipped tone.

"Tell me what happened." Bradan waved the druid off as he stood.

Set ground his jaw, inaction rendering him half-feral. Doing nothing while Ash was gods knew where was unacceptable. He needed to be on the move, on his way to saving her. Not standing in front of Bradan, repeating what had happened. Maebh's dry hand gripped his wrist and she squeezed until he met her gaze. Their eyes were identical in everything but colour, his storm grey to her sky blue.

With a sigh that seeped into his bones, once Bradan had dismissed everyone but the twins from the room, Set recounted what had happened. The king had signalled for them to sit on the plush armchairs, but neither accepted. As he spoke, Set wore a path across the sumptuous carpet in the long room.

"Setanta, I understand your frustration, but you need to understand who you're up against. The three sisters may just be in one form, but they always work together: crow, maiden, and war spirit. They won't welcome you, especially if they took Aisling by force," Bradan said, his brown eyes illuminated by the orange embers of the fire. "As much as I disagreed with Aedan's plámás of the Tuatha Dé, this isn't the first time they have taken Fianna to remind us of their control."

Set stopped before the fireplace, gripping the mantlepiece. With each throb of his coiled muscles, the sandstone surrendered beneath his grip. As the pressure intensified, the mantlepiece protested audibly; a chorus of tiny fractures webbing out, splintering the once flawless surface. "How do you know they've taken her on purpose?"

"I don't for certain." Bradan glanced between the twins; his expression unreadable as he clasped his hands together. "I received a warning. If I didn't change the Cath rules about ridding our kingdom of their kind, the Connacht queen would retaliate. It seems she has done so in many ways today."

"Queen Medb has Ash?" His twin's words, sharp as shattered glass, pierced the air as Maebh collapsed unceremoniously into a chair. When Bradan nodded, she added, "We already warned you Ethne was going to do something. You could have stopped all of this!"

"I will remind you, Matriarch, who you're speaking to," Bradan said, every word laced with caution.

She ignored them.

"And I'll remind you that just because you're wearing a crown doesn't make you less likely to fuck up. Your inaction means this is as much your fault as it is Ethne's."

"Maebh," Set said, moving to stand in front of her as he turned to Bradan. "I'm sorry, High King, we're all on edge."

"Don't make apologies for me as if I'm someone you need to manage!" She glared at Set before turning her fierce expression on the king. "Tell me I'm wrong."

Bradan didn't answer for a long moment, his dark eyes narrowed on her. "The destruction of Newgrange could have been both the Tuatha Dé and Ethne for all we know. Make no mistake, Ethne is an enemy, but so are the Fair Ones."

Set's body quivered with the restraint of leashing his monster, but he was losing. Red pulsed in his vision as his tendons tightened until he was sure they would snap. Maebh stood, racing to stand in front of him, her hand gripping his arm painfully, and he focused on that sensation as he tried to remain in control.

"Where do they take their hostages?" Maebh enquired as she turned to Bradan, her tone still sharp but her glare less likely to find her a cell in the dungeon.

"Rathcroghan, Queen Medb's fortress in Connacht."

Their voices were muffled as Set swam for the surface of his sanity. Fire burned his lungs as Maebh and Bradan continued their conversation, but he didn't hear them. *Let me out*, his monster crooned, and he shivered at the allure to give in. It would be so simple. An intake of breath, a few moments of pain as he transformed, and then his monster would take over. He would not stop until Ash was back. With both of them. As he fought against that pull, something Bradan said snapped him back to reality.

"You're saying we should just leave her there?" Set's voice was garbled. The tendons on his neck strained as his ríastrad pushed to break free.

Bradan nodded solemnly, but raised his hand, palm up when Set stepped closer. "Unless you accept my offer to become my rígfénnid."

Maebh's voice was quiet. "What offer?"

The room was silent for a long moment. Set stared hard at the ground, grappling with the weight of Ash's abduction as he finally sank into a chair.

"Setanta McQuillan, what offer?"

His sister's biting tone cut through his thoughts, and slowly, he looked up at her. "High King Bradan wants new leadership and offered me the job."

Silence greeted him, but his sister's furious glare was louder than anything she could hurl.

"All rígfénnid were within Newgrange," Bradan said, interrupting Maebh as she opened her mouth to no doubt curse at him. "I no longer just want one new leader; I *need* all of them."

"I'm sorry, High King," Maebh spoke softly, her glare indicating she was anything but. "When were either of you going to deign to tell me? As his matriarch, wouldn't it be common fucking courtesy to speak to me about this, too?"

Bradan leaned back in his chair, focusing on Maebh's blotchy face. Guilt punched Set's gut at keeping it from her, but they didn't have time for apologies and explanations. Ash needed them. And his sister's temper was only going to get them both into trouble.

"Maebh, don't, okay?"

"You're just as bad as the rest of them," Maebh hissed, jumping to her feet.

He scrubbed his face as she marched out of the room, ignoring Bradan entirely before exiting.

Set glanced at Bradan, biting the inside of his cheek, but the king only sighed. "We're all heightened after what's happened. Don't worry about your sister. She'll be fine."

The crackling of the fire was the only sound punctuating Set's chaotic thoughts until the weight of his decision became too great a burden in the silence.

"If I accept your offer as rígfénnid—"

"There is no offer, Setanta."

Set bristled. "I thought—"

"You will become rígfénnid," Bradan said, lifting a bell from his side table and ringing it.

Light footsteps sounded before a servant appeared. "Call Bíróg back here. And retrieve a sealed scroll from my desk. It will bear Setanta McQuillan's name." When the servant left, Bradan finally looked at him. "I'm a fair man, Setanta, and I can see you are too. If you want Maebh to remain as matriarch without any reprimand for how she's conducted herself here, and you also want permission to go to Rathcroghan, you need all the help you can get. Your new title as Rígfénnid of Connacht will provide this."

His ríastrád brushed against his internal wall, begging for release. Set's fury simmered, but he tamped it down. "You already had a contract made for me?"

"As my father always said, 'Fail to prepare, prepare to fail.' I may not be a betting man, but I knew you'd see the reason behind this."

Red tinged Set's vision, his emotions warring within. He wanted to charge straight to Rathcroghan and tear it apart until he found Ash, but he didn't trust the man in front of him. The burden was being forced on his shoulders.

"Our former Connacht rígfénnid was never able to appease Medb. May his soul continue on . . ." Bradan paused. Set didn't finish the Fianna blessing, but the High King didn't seem to notice. "You will do a better job."

The sun was low as Set finally exited the castle, a new title and responsibility like a noose around his neck. Bradan had promised a contingent of highguard would be readied for him to leave by first light, advising it was too late to travel in Fair Ones' territory at night. Brisk air greeted him and Set watched the droves of survivors arriving through the highgate. Their wearied bodies pressed close together; hollow-eyed children clung to their guardians with a clear loss of innocence forming their hardened faces. A swell of sympathy washed through him, but the shadow of his concerns for Ash consumed most of his thoughts.

Set passed through the empty stalls in the market square as Fianna trudged forward, weary from their ordeal. Nobody spoke as they entered cottages or walked aimlessly through the narrow, winding streets.

Maebh exited her tent at his approach. The Breens were waiting for Set as he navigated through the tents dotted across the encampment, weaving his way among the scattered firepits.

"When do we leave, Maebh?" Ciarán asked impatiently. As she turned to him, the warrior cracked his knuckles, displaying his arsenal of weapons strapped across his dark leather vest.

She shook her head. "I don't know. Ask Mr Rígfénnid of Connacht."

"Maebh, for fuck's sake." Set glared at his twin, but she wouldn't look at him as she sat with her arms crossed on their low-lying log.

Gasps filled the air, and Lorna stepped forward, clapping her hands. "Is it true, Setanta?"

He ignored his aunt, shifting awkwardly at her gleeful expression. There were more pressing matters on his mind than politics. He'd accepted the role if it meant accessing Rathcroghan to save Ash.

"Where is our matriarch?" Tomás demanded, ignoring the commotion at Maebh's untimely revelation. He stood beside his brother, wearing similar armour and weapons strapped to his body. They looked like warriors Set would love to spar with under normal circumstances and he could certainly use them to fight alongside this battle. Their dark hair and features resembled their cousin's so much that his resolve was cast in iron.

Set looked at the darkening sky and mulled over Bradan's promise of highguard in the morning, and his warnings of the danger at travelling at night. But Ash's sword was a weighted reminder of what needed to be done.

"Rathcroghan," Set said, stepping closer to the men. "And we leave now."

CHAPTER 23
AISLING

Hours, or perhaps days later, the screeching door opened, and Tara stepped into view. If Ash didn't know any better, she'd have thought he was an apparition. His appearance was too clean amidst the dungeon gloom, clad in a pristinely-woven linen tunic and pants. In royal blue, embroidered intricately with shimmering silver threads, it was as if a Tuatha Dé male had stepped out from a courtly painting into the harsh reality of a dungeon cell. His nose wrinkled as he stared down at her, illuminated by the torch lights hanging on the wall behind him. Faint light trickled from the window, hinting at daylight.

"Come."

"Fuck you," Ash said, relieved her voice was strong.

"I've been ordered to bring you before my queen. You are to be made . . . presentable."

Tara sniffed once before wincing, as if such a task were beyond accomplishment. Cursing inwardly at the flush that rose to her cheeks, she backed away, feeling every bit the cornered animal as he entered the cell in one long stride.

"I see you've managed to get out of your bindings."

When he leaned forward, she kicked outward with her boot. He caught it easily and swatted her foot away, but she smirked as he glared down at the mud now on his shirt. With preternatural speed, Tara lifted her, hoisting her over one shoulder. Kicking and beating on his back did little to his swift brutality as he threw her on the ground in the dank hall outside the cell. She glared up at him as he sneered.

"You either walk like a civilised creature, or you're dragged."

Ash spat at his feet.

"Dragged it is," Tara said, gripping her ankles and striding forward.

She cried out when her head fell back against the rough floor, but he did not slow his pace. When they reached a set of deep, narrow stone steps, he released her ankles. Turning, he raised his dark brows in challenge. He would drag her. By some miracle, he hadn't touched the hidden blade and she'd like to keep it that way. On shaking limbs, she stood, raising her chin as she took the first steps. He chuckled as he followed. The spiralling steps did little for her queasy stomach. When they reached an iron door, Tara knocked. Two fae guards let them pass into a muddied road.

As she blinked against the sudden influx of light, a stable loomed into view. Her senses were immediately invaded by the pungent smell of straw and manure intertwined with the vibration from the lively neighing of horses. She was unsure if the churning in her stomach was a result of the smell or her troubling circumstances.

Involuntarily, a gasp ripped through her lips as she dared to steal a swift over-the-shoulder glance. The sight that greeted her overshot her every expectation. What she had perceived as a mere building, where she'd whittled away countless hours in dread, was a fortress. Bradan's map for the Cath had detailed more of Tír na nÓg than she'd ever knew existed. She never thought she'd see any of it beyond the Kingdom of Mide.

But the sight before her defied this notion as an intimidating black monolith, hewn directly from the bosom of a stern mountain towered before them.

"We're in Rathcroghan." She licked her dry lips.

"You're a clever one," Tara sneered.

The formidable stronghold of Queen Medb, wrought from the severe heart of the colossal landform. Ash hadn't thought to ask who Tara worked for. The Morrígan didn't belong to any court, travelling throughout the land on the whims of three sisters, all who sought the allure of power and war. This much she'd known from their scrolls, and it was yet unclear why the sisters had been so heavily interested in her.

The fortress stood defiantly against the backdrop of the sky, erected from jagged black stones that glistened in the brash daylight. Their glossy, sinister sheen was only matched by the magnitude they encompassed, the sprawling breadth and height she couldn't fully grasp from this vantage. It loomed over them, seeming to swallow the air from her lungs. A chill traced down her spine as she took in the sheer scale of Medb's fortress, its ominous presence casting long, dark shadows, seeming to hint at the relentless iron will and unyielding dominance of the queen herself.

Tara gripped Ash's elbow, pulling her toward the stable. From the outside, it seemed to match the fortress in its imposing grandeur; sizeable double doors of seasoned oak greeted them, intricate designs etched into the worn wood. As they drew closer, the overwhelming smell of hay and horses gave way to the subtle nuances of leather and polished metal.

"See that she is hosed down." Tara departed in a whirl of linen and rage, and Ash whipped her head around, taking in the tall stables, neighing heard within.

"There's no point in running." A deep voice drew her attention to where a tall, broad-shouldered man stood in the doorway. "I can't offer a bath, but I can get you a bucket of warm water, soap and privacy."

The human possessed a sturdy build. Brown hair complemented sun-kissed skin and kind blue eyes. Ash blinked in surprise. What was a human doing in a land full of Tuatha Dé Danann? She took a step back as he approached, and he stopped. His smile bowed full lips as he raised his hands in a peaceful gesture, and she bit the inside of her cheek, fighting against tears that wanted to spring forward. Seeing another of her kind broke through exhaustion's barriers and a little of her strength wavered.

Ash didn't know if it was deprivation of sleep, the emptiness of her stomach, or simply the kind face of a stranger amidst fae that had her following him willingly into a stable pen. The man surrounded by such inhumanity seemed so familiar, stirring something within her she was too fragile to handle.

They passed majestic fae horses with gleaming silver and black coats and manes that shimmered with iridescent hues. He led her to a stall at the end, and thankfully no fae beast was housed within.

"Will you take a seat and I'll be right back," he said, signalling to a small wooden stool in the corner. Even though he phrased it like a question, his tone hinted at the unspoken acknowledgement she really didn't have a choice. When the stable-hand returned, he smiled apologetically, holding out folded green satin fabric. "I've been told you must wear this."

Ash stared at the rich material before meeting his eyes. The last thing she wanted was to be dressed up for whatever games the Tuatha Dé had planned.

Placing the bucket and supplies by her feet, he put the dress on another stool by the door before closing it with a faint click. Ash stood, approaching the narrow slit of a window to peer out. Stables stretched as far as she could see, fae beasts snorting and stamping inside their stalls. Reluctantly, Ash forced herself to change out of her filthy clothes, using the sponge and water to clean as best she could. Admittedly her shoulders eased with each cleansing stroke. Staring at her soiled and tattered clothes, she grimaced at the green satin. Lifting it as if it were a fae beast with sharp teeth, the fabric unfolded into a dress with delicate straps.

She hadn't been given clean underwear and she'd be damned if she wore nothing underneath the thin fabric, so she eased back into her knickers and bra before donning the cool, fine material. It felt strange against her skin, but she had no choice if she wanted to maintain the illusion of compliance a while longer. As she dressed, Ash combed her still-damp hair with her fingers, working out the knots and tangles as best she could. Her reflection in the pail of water revealed a woman far wearier than she had ever been.

Though uninjured, hours of lifting heavy stone at Newgrange had left their mark. Ash's arms and back ached, every muscle protesting as she moved. Countless hours of riding a fae horse, of being dragged and manhandled, had drained what little reserves she had left. And now she faced fae politics without food or water for over a day.

She was trapped in a realm of trials and trickery within Medb's court, but she would not face her with anything other than dignity and defiance. Her body may be bruised and tired, but her spirit remained unbowed.

When she opened the stable door, the man was there, a wooden tray in his hands. He handed it to her before leaving once more. A flask of water and a heel of bread with butter were his offerings and she whispered her thanks at his retreating back.

She ate in small bites on her wooden stool, sipping the water until the queasiness in her hollow stomach eased. When she emerged once more, the man smiled kindly at her, his friendly face warming her from the inside out amidst this cold, cruel place.

"I can give you a few minutes more before I have to bring you to them," the man said, concern shining through his blue eyes.

"I'm ready," she said, matching his pace as they walked through the stable. "What is your name?"

"They call me Nik," he answered with a shrug. "I'm not sure what my human name would have been."

"What do you mean?" Unease pooled in her gut.

"I'm a changeling baby," Nik replied. "They collect humans from time to time in order to serve in their kingdoms."

They walked in silence as Ash tried to think of something to say. A fist formed around her gut as she thought of all the babies she'd saved in Mary and Dom's cafe. It would never be enough compared to the humans who were not saved, who had to endure the life of a slave and cruelty of immortal beings.

"I'm sorry," she whispered, taking his hand and squeezing, the gesture oddly intimate between strangers, but feeling natural anyway. Although they'd never met, they were kindred spirits. Humans in a land of monsters.

He smiled at her gesture, but shrugged as they reached the door. "I don't know anything other than my life here."

He opened the door, and Ash's knees weakened at the sight of the fortress once more. She had time to take its sheer size in as she scanned the unending mountain castle.

Medb's palace rose from the folds and hollows of the surrounding hillsides like a slowly awakening beast of stone. Talon-like towers pierced the underbelly of heavy clouds.

Carved from black granite, the castle absorbed what little light managed to penetrate the gloom of the sky above. It seemed to drink in the sparse rays of sunshine, hoarding their gleam jealously within its depths. Ivy and honeysuckle crept over the walls, tracing the lines and contours of the timeless architecture.

The main citadel sat atop a high hill overlooking the surrounding lands. Around it were concentric rings of fortifications: walls, towers and ramparts hewn from the very earth itself.

Ash's attention was diverted as an iron-clad grip latched onto each arm. Two imposing figures clad in red cloaks had assumed the task of escorting her to her fate. She looked back at Nik, who offered a stiff nod before turning toward his stables. She dared a glance at one guard; a pair of deep-set eyes, a mesmerising blend of jade and sapphire, glared back at her. Ash took a step and then another, pretending she had a choice; allowing them to lead her toward the black stone fortress and the unknown whims of an ancient warrior queen.

CHAPTER 24
AISLING

Ash took an unsteady breath, steeling herself as the fae guards allowed her yet another break from the steep climb to the castle fortress. Her thighs burned while every muscle ached as she sucked in air that only hurt her lungs. Sweat soaked through her dress, plastering the thin material to her skin. The breaks the fae guards allowed her were more mockery than mercy. After only a few seconds, a guard nudged her. While she struggled up the steep, winding mountain path, exhaustion weighing heavily on her human body, her fae escorts showed no signs of strain.

"Keep moving, Milesian."

Ash bit back a whimper as she pushed herself to stand on trembling limbs, knees threatening to buckle beneath her. They'd called her many names, and never her real one. Perhaps they didn't know it. More likely, they didn't care. The most common name they used was Milesian, the name associated with humans who'd driven the Tuatha Dé Danann underground, or rather, to this realm. By the sneers and clear hatred shining through these fae, it wasn't just the Fianna who were unhappy with the Peace Treaty that had been struck between their races thousands of years ago.

She refused to look to her right, where the only obstacle between her and a plunge to death was a thin rope. It swung and snapped with every gust of wind so violent, even her hair was a whip against her cold cheeks. She'd given up on trying to keep the skirt below her thighs and she was thankful she'd worn her underwear. The rugged path eventually gave way.

"Where do we go from here?" Ash asked as the guard in front stopped at the edge of a sheer rocky cliff. He smirked, pointing a long finger skyward.

Her mouth dried as she followed his gesture reluctantly. Her eyes rose higher, and higher again, fear coiling in her stomach at the impossibility of what he suggested.

"Here," the guard said, handing her a flimsy rope with glee. "They have these in place for the weak and old of our kind."

His smirk only grew as she grasped it, fate sealed. Foolish defiance was her only ally as she hauled herself up. After a few false starts, she found a rhythm, albeit an awkward, graceless one. Crumbling footholds forced her to scramble upward like a mountain goat, although she was certain she insulted the animal with her clumsy attempts. Her palms were shredded and blood slick, every grasp precarious.

Below stretched only empty air and jagged rocks hundreds of feet down. A gust of wind made the thinning rope undulate like a striking snake, ready to tear free from its moorings. Ash choked back a sob at her options: continue or plunge to her doom.

Pausing granted no respite, the chill seeping into exhausted muscles like icy shards. Wheezing, she willed numb legs to heave her higher yet, nails breaking as she clawed for purchase.

Her escorts glided effortlessly over the treacherous slope, uncaring if she joined them or the crags below. Every graceful movement spurred Ash to climb, irrational defiance prompting her crawl onward even as agony screamed at her to give up.

At last, the vertical rocks veered to a stable edge and she collapsed on it.

"About time," the tall guard muttered, hauling her to her knees before throwing a flask on the ground beside her.

It could have been poison, but Ash unfastened it with shaking fingers, gulping it down. Cool water soothed her insides, but before she could drink the full flask, the guard snatched it away.

"Come on."

Rising on trembling legs, Ash she took in the sheer towering cliff face before them, her vision swimming with the view. There were clear paths more evenly laid out on the mountain side, dotted by alcoves until they reached the mountain peak.

Ash gripped the ropes as the guards led her in a zigzagging climb around jutting rock. Within the rocky outcrops were chambers carved into the sheer stone. Beyond were furnishings finer than any human lord's; sturdy portals opened onto shadowed tunnels delving deep into the stony vastness. The mountain itself was Medb's castle. The fae strode forward, never veering toward the safety of the multiple entryways.

"Why can't we go through one of them?" she asked, her voice barely audible over the wind as she pointed shakily at an alcove.

"Our queen wants you to experience our domain in all its splendour," the taller fae guard said, not slowing his pace in front as he turned to glare in disapproval at her slow progress.

He was striking, with flawless translucent skin and snowy hair that rippled in the blistering winds. His angular features seemed chiselled from alabaster; lips curled in a perpetual sneer to reveal pointed teeth. Powerful muscles shifted beneath a tunic of forest-green silk, trimmed with shimmering golden thread in intricate Celtic knots. His blue eyes watched her with disdain from beneath a cloak the colour of freshly-spilled blood.

The burly guard behind nudged her back painfully, and Ash glared at him before climbing again. The queen was playing games with her. Showing this feeble human just how weak she was compared to the great Tuatha Dé Danann. Her heartbeat pounded in her head as lava flowed through her veins. She may be human, but she was not weak. Not in the sense that mattered. The queen could torture her body, but Ash would not allow her to break her mind. She let that anger fuel her, willing her aching feet to move.

Ash's pulse quickened at every sight of a Fair One. Those who were dressed wore similar satin slips like hers, or low-slung pants that did little to hide what lay underneath, while others wore nothing at all. Their gold and silver-flecked eyes pinned her despite their activities within their chambers. Moans and grunts caught in the wind, and the fae guards paid no heed to the writhing bodies as they delighted in one another's flesh.

Each pair of eyes homed in on her as her laboured breaths and heavy steps faltered past them. A male with wheat-coloured hair and purple-silver eyes reached out, beckoning her to join him as he licked his lips, revealing sharp canines.

"Want to join them, girl?" the second guard whispered in her ear, sending a shiver of revulsion through her.

Bulkier than the fae guard walking ahead, he was no less fair. His locks shone like polished silver floating on the gales. Honey-brown eyes tracked her discomfort with delight. He herded Ash along, as peals of musical laughter rang out when she stumbled past that alcove, even though all instinct screamed at her to run to level ground.

Finally, they reached a plateau, the sight almost beautiful enough to make the hike worth it. They stepped onto a vast expanse that stretched into a courtyard. To her left, a grand fountain cascaded with water, the drops shimmering like diamonds in the dappled sunlight breaking through the clouds. Pressing her hand to her chest, she willed her breaths to even as she let the soothing music of a nearby water fountain do what it could to calm her.

"Move, human," the taller guard said, gripping her arm and hauling her toward a looming arched wooden doorway.

As the guard's hand latched onto her arm, Ash snapped her head upward. Rage bloomed through the haze of fatigue and fear, propelling her steps.

"Get your hands off me!" She wheeled on the guard, ignoring the blur of the world around her as she kicked outward, connecting with his shin. He didn't loosen his grip, but his eyes widened at her barely-leashed wrath. Even though she'd probably caused more damage to her aching feet than his fae skin, it was refreshing, this small taste of humanity in her defiance. "I can walk myself."

He released her as more guards flanked the entrance, their armour gleaming, their delicate features doing little to hide their hungry contemplation as they assessed her passing by. A few smirked. She was a lamb amongst wolves.

The wind lashed at her, as if desperate fingers tried to yank her back. Whether it sought to draw her into the embrace of death or to the safety of the outside world, she couldn't tell.

Her black boots scuffed the pristine marble floors throughout the labyrinthine corridors they traversed as she blinked to adjust her eyes to the torchlight. Ash resisted the urge to fidget with her dress. Distant laughter and muted conversations reached her ears, and with every sound, her heart stuttered and restarted. She had never felt more vulnerable or unprepared for what was to come.

They reached a door unlike any Ash had seen. A living tree stood before them; its trunk and roots merged seamlessly with the stone floor, and its gnarled branches stretched upwards, forming an archway. The tree shivered as she peered at two knots in the wood. A faint rustling could be heard, as if the tree whispered its own tales to those who could understand.

Chatter filtered through the tree as one guard whispered into the rough textured bark, and Ash swore those knots blinked before they separated, forming an opening. An expansive throne room greeted them. The guard's grip was tight as he dragged Ash through the tree. The myriad of fae voices, previously filled with laughter and chatter, went silent. Each pair of ethereal eyes in the opulent chamber turned to her in perfect synchronisation, and she audibly swallowed.

Rough hands shoved her forward, but she righted herself before she could fall to her knees. Refusing to meet any fae's eyes, she took in the cavernous room. Tall arched windows punctuated the walls, allowing daylight to filter through, casting eerie shadows across the intricately carved wooden furniture.

At the substantial distance of the grand chamber, a figure rose gracefully from a mighty throne, its headpiece bearing a pair of colossal bull horns as its crown. Queen Medb stood tall, her unbound blonde hair shimmering against a dress of cobalt blue, a thick waist wrapped in a meticulously-crafted leather bodice, hugging her in a snug embrace whilst playing host to an array of menacingly gleaming daggers hidden in plain sight.

Ethereal, amber-skinned Tara stood beside her in stark contrast in all black. Ash smirked despite herself, noting he'd changed into a clean shirt. Perhaps she would try to kick him again. The Morrígan surveyed Ash with cold eyes on the queen's other side, a crow resting on one shoulder.

Despite the captivating entourage of beauty surrounding her, an undeniable force drew Ash's gaze inexorably towards Medb. She was no stranger to the striking allure of the Fair Ones, nor their sometimes-hideous appearance. For the Fair Ones, extremity was the essence of their existence, extending even to their physical attributes.

But Queen Medb; she was an entirely different phenomenon. Her beauty was not just bewitching, it was piercing; the kind that seared so much Ash's soul wept. It was like staring into the sun; magnificent, radiant, yet overwhelming to the point of pain. Consuming to the eye, yet utterly compelling, demanding the tribute of her undivided attention and admiration. Ash's feet moved forward on their own accord, her very being yearning to be closer to the female. It was beauty that didn't just captivate, it commanded, and it hurt in its stunning intensity.

Ash fought against her trembling limbs, her fingers smoothing out the lush green fabric clinging to her skin.

Medb's voice carried through the hall. "You see, Tara? She changed into the dress we provided. You lost our bet."

Cruel laughter erupted from the crowd, echoing off the high ceilings as Ash's cheeks flushed. How she longed to wipe the smug sneers from the surrounding Fair Ones' faces. As if Medb could hear her thoughts, the queen smiled, beckoning her forward, revelling in her discomfort.

The fae guards gripped Ash's arms painfully and marched her with a speed too much for her human body, the crowd closing in around them. She stumbled before the imposing throne, armrests shaped like wolf heads, ruby eyes gleaming with open maws ready to devour anyone who dared approach.

Tara stepped forward, a vindictive smile on his full lips. "Kneel before our queen."

Another titter of laughter filtered through the gathering. Ash's glare met Medb's knowing smile, fury burning within, overpowering the glamour that would shred her of any dignity or courage.

"No."

A gasp rippled through the assembled courtiers. Medb's eyes flashed, but Ash did not back down. Despite the mountain filled with immortal cruelty, she allowed a small smile to grace her lips.

The air around the queen shimmered with barely restrained power, her eyes flashing black, consuming all surrounding light. A torque of twisted silver hung around her neck, which ended in the heads of two beasts, their beaks open in a silent scream.

No, she would not kneel. Not for Medb, nor any other Fair One.

The queen tilted her head, considering Ash with a scrutiny that held the cold calculation of a goddess who had seen the birth and fall of countless civilisations.

After a moment that stretched into an eternity, Queen Medb's voice rose, breaking the heavy silence with a melodic lilt, like nectar pouring down from the heavens. "Aren't you a fine woman with the audacity of a lioness? Come, sit with me."

Murmurs erupted like a swarm of agitated bees as the assembled Tuatha Dé Danann processed the queen's invitation. Apparently, Ash wasn't the only one who'd expected blood to be spilled.

Tara turned to Medb, a frown creasing his perfect features. "My queen . . ."

"Oh, hush." The queen waved a dismissive hand ringed with jewelled fingers, her numerous rings glittering in the torchlight. "I do not need to reprimand our guest for not bowing. Milesians are savage little things. They must be given concessions for such disrespect."

Medb considered her once more, eyes pinning Ash like a specimen.

"Tell me, little mortal, what troubles you so?" Her voice held no malice, only curiosity.

Ash took a steadying breath before lifting her chin, refusing to take the offered seat by the foot of Medb's throne as the female sat. "Other than the fact you brought me here against my will? I'm grand, not a bother."

Maebh would have been proud of that answer.

The queen let out a small chuckle, sounding remarkably human. "Indeed," she said, a wry smile touching her lips as she leaned against the high-backed throne. "Then we shall get to the point."

With a lazy flick of her fingers again, she beckoned Tara. "She's all yours to question."

An excitement rippled through the assembled courtiers, and the crow perching on the Morrígan's shoulder cawed as the sisters watched, an impassive expression on their face, shushing the creature while petting its head. The courtiers inched closer as Tara stalked forward. Ash had no time to resist, not that she could match this powerful Tuatha Dé Danann. Tara's arms encircled her, binding her arms to her sides. Her exhausted, battered human body was no match for his immortal strength.

Tara lowered his head to breathe in the scent of her hair and she didn't hide her shudder of disgust.

"I haven't stopped thinking about you since I discovered you in Mide," he murmured, his voice lowering to a timbre meant for her ears alone. "About your . . . origin."

There was a contained fury behind his words. A simmering anger that Ash knew she wouldn't live a breath beyond if he unleashed it. Even now, surrounded by the entire court, Tara's wrath would descend upon her with the force of a thunderstorm.

Instinct took over and she kicked between his legs. Ripples of laughter erupted from the room as she spun and ran when Tara released her with a curse.

She made it to the door when a solid force slammed into her, pressing her so hard against the unforgiving bark she felt the sting of it dig into her cheek and neck. She cried out, fighting against Tara as he pulled her close to his body before spinning her and slamming her painfully against the door once more. Tara's fury broke free, his raging emotions flooding the throne room like a fierce wind. Ash cried out, struggling helplessly in his grasp as the court looked on. A play-thing for their amusement.

Ash fought against Tara's iron grip to no avail. The Tuatha Dé Danann was unbreakable, his rage unstoppable. The tree at her back shuddered to life, branches moving like tentacles to wrap around her wrists, restraining them high above her head. The door did not just serve as a barrier to the room beyond; it stood as a sentinel. She cried out in pain as the immortals within the room watched with anticipatory delight.

"Do not mistake me for a man," Tara seethed, inclining his head to her neck and sniffing deeply.

She tried to kick out again, but he trapped her legs with his body, and she had no room to move. "I am a fae male. We take what we want." Tara's face was devoid of any emotion. "And what I want is to taste you."

"Fuck you," she grit out, head-butting him.

She saw stars as a trickle of blood fell from his forehead. As soon as it gushed out, the small cut shrank and the blood congealed. He had healed, but he had also bled.

Tara chuckled as the courtiers inched closer, excitement on their beautiful, cruel faces.

Ash took one breath, and whether it was to scream or beg for release, she'd never know. Tara opened his mouth, displaying elongated canines, as sharp as an abhartach. He pierced the vulnerable skin on her neck. The pain of the wound was instant, and the draw of her blood into his mouth sickening. In the expansive sea of surrounding faces, a chilling void grew, swallowing Ash up from within. Instinctual reactions screamed within her—to run, to fight, to resist—yet she found herself petrified. A chilling flood of fear overrode her senses, leaving her frozen in the unfolding of her fate.

A single tear rolled down her cheek as he pressed her further into the rough tree bark. She hated her useless, weak body. Her vision blurred as he slurped on her life force. Her heart pounded a desperate rhythm against her chest as her mind buzzed with a thousand desperate escape plans. But her body betrayed her, rooted in place by terror. When she finally realised her hands were attached to her will, she attempted to free them, but he withdrew, licking her neck once before releasing her.

She slumped, but the branches held her upright as her blood dripped from his mouth. He studied her, his dark eyes now blackened, as if he wasn't seeing her, or worse, he was seeing into her very soul.

"Human, but not," he mused, licking his lips as if savouring her taste. "Fae but not. Divine."

"Ethniu was playing," Medb's sultry voice echoed through the throne room, the surrounding courtiers parting for their queen and the Morrígan, whose expression was too shadowed to discern.

"What?" Ash tried to ask what they meant, but her tongue was swollen and numb, her vision blurring so there were two of each terrifying being standing over her.

She fell to her knees, the tree releasing her as Tara stepped away. "You will be brought to High King Caicher." Tara's voice was almost gleeful, as if the anticipation of her encounter with their king would bring him joy.

Blackness rimmed her vision, the pull of oblivion too strong for her to resist. She couldn't fight against the darkness that took her, no matter the sweat trailing down her back or the tremble to her hands. She was weak. She was prey. And now, she was going to die.

CHAPTER 25
MAEBH

"Setanta, if you sift," Maebh said for the millionth time, barely constraining the impatient fury creeping into her tone, "you will land blindly in a dangerous kingdom. Don't be such a stubborn arsehole."

Her brother glared at her from across her wide tent, and she matched his expression, refusing to back down.

"I'm not the one being stubborn, Mae. You're not listening to me."

Maebh stood her ground as Setanta paced the expanse of her spacious tent like a caged beast. The lush purple and emerald fabrics adorning the walls cased everything in hushed tones. Her mother's trunk lay sealed in the corner while Maebh's own belongings were strewn atop it, obscuring the temptation to rifle through her late mother's relics.

Maebh's possessions littered the space in varying degrees of use, with ornate daggers and modern creams scattered amongst wrinkled clothes. She loved the lived-in feel to her space, though now her twin was using her clutter as a winding path, deliberately tracing around each item in exasperation at the disorder. He'd been this way when they'd shared a caravan. She ignored him, standing upon lush pelt surrounded by the comfortable chaos as both refused to back down from their argument.

A blend of the familiar scents of crushed lavender and a faint whiff of her mother's presence— an elusive mix of herbs and beeswax from the numerous candles she'd left behind—wafted occasionally from the tent fabric as if in reminder of the formidable woman who once occupied this space.

As Maebh grew older, their relationship only became more contentious as she struggled to meet her mother's impossible expectations for a future leader. "You question me at every step, child; hold your tongue before it trips you up!" she would snap when Maebh pressed too hard. The memories still stung decades later.

Now as matriarch herself, Maebh both resented and longed for her mother's commanding presence. If she were here, would she side with Maebh or Setanta in this debate? The thought made Maebh equal parts bitter and heartsick. She doubted she would ever live up to that crystalline vision in her mother's eyes.

Outside, the sounds of the clan recovering from the Winter Solstice carried through the worn canvas; murmurs of what it could mean, the news of how all the other rígfénnid were dead. Who, other than Setanta, would be called to take on the prestigious role? Lorna's nasal voice was loudest of all. Maebh blocked them out as best she could.

She should be out there, checking in on her clan after what had happened at Newgrange. Instead, she was stuck trying to talk sense into her stubborn twin. Shadows flickered across Setanta's hard expression from her mother's candle lantern hanging overhead.

"If you sift, you could land right in front of Queen Medb's army," Maebh pressed, anxiety gnawing at her insides. She pictured her brother captured or gravely injured, left for dead in hostile enemy land. She swallowed around the tightness in her throat. "What good would that be in helping Ash?"

"Are you willing to risk Ash's life on that point?" Setanta's jaw tightened, the cords of his neck taut. "I don't care if I have to take on the entire Tuatha Dé army by myself. I will bring Ash home."

"Oh, I'm sorry, I didn't realise my brother was suddenly Cú Chulainn."

They glared at one another. But she couldn't fight the shiver of his words as they'd chilled Maebh further. She knew that fervent gleam in his eyes too well, the reckless abandon that arose whenever Setanta had made a decision, no matter how stupid it was.

"You heard what Bradan said. The Tuatha Dé have taken hostages before to ensure compliance from the Fianna. They don't kill them, there would be no point in that."

"And since when did you care about anything our High King has said?" Setanta shot back. "You can't pick and choose when you're a loyal subject."

"You're one to talk," Maebh muttered.

"What's that supposed to mean?"

"You can't just be the hero charging in to save the girl," Maebh shot back, voice laced with a bitterness that tasted like bile on her tongue.

Setanta barely blinked. Instead, he thrust his chest out a bit more, his typically sturdy posture seeming more like a wall than a man. "Yes, I fucking can."

Placing her hands on her hips, she tilted her head to the ceiling, praying for a patience that was non-existent. A headache splintered through her throbbing temples as she narrowed her eyes on her arrogant twin.

"You were supposed to be my second. I'm the matriarch, but you never followed my lead. And now you're rígfénnid." The words spewed out of Maebh's mouth before she could swallow them. "Mam would be so proud of her Golden Boy."

Setanta turned on her, venom in his words. "So, this is about jealousy? Get over yourself, Maebh."

The tent flap ripped open as Setanta stormed into the inky night, the staccato beat of his boots on hard earth echoing his fury. Maebh blinked, gaping at the empty space where he'd stood before hurrying after him, the chill night air raising the hairs on her arms as she left the candlelit warmth behind.

"Setanta, wait," she called out to her brother's rigid back, her breath pluming white in the gloom.

The waning crescent moon cast just enough silver glow for her to track his determined stride toward their clan and the warmth of the largest firepit. Maebh prayed her twin's wrath wouldn't blind him to reason before this night was through. Around them, the silhouettes of her warriors shifted with restless anticipation for the battle ahead. She knew it wasn't the Cath battle they waited for, but the twins' war of words.

Tomás gripped Set's arm, Ash's cousin standing rigid by the fire, moonlight glinting off his bared sword. "Are you ready?"

Before Set could respond, Maebh shouldered forward. "You should wait for the highguard and travel at first light," she insisted, desperation sharpening her tone. "Rushing blindly into Connacht territory under cover of darkness is suicide!"

Ciarán rotated his shoulders as if readying for combat, offering Maebh a pitying look. "I understand your worries, Matriarch. But we're not waiting a second longer to rescue our cousin. Your friend, remember?"

Ciarán's words, dripping with accusation, were like a gut punch to Maebh. As if Maebh didn't care for Ash's safety. Of course she did. But should it be at the fatal expense of her twin? Her chest tightened, the tangible sting piercing through her composure, turning her bloodstream cold in the process. Her eyes slid off Ciarán's face to rest on Lorna, whose smugness was the salt in her fresh wound.

She tried to swallow away the lump in her throat, a bitter sourness that tasted like defeat. It was a moment that challenged her authority, and it happened under the fiercely bright gazes of the people she hoped to lead. No wall of words, she knew, would shield her against this onslaught.

Every muscle in her body seemed to tense as she turned to Setanta, an involuntary reaction as she attempted to assert control over the rapidly spiralling situation. Her fingers felt cold as she tightly gripped his wrist, her desperation tangible in her tight grasp. "Setanta, see sense and listen to me for once in your life."

His hardened expression was a physical barrier he built around himself, a wall even her most desperate pleas failed to penetrate. He shook free from her grasp, stepping around her.

"I gave you my answer, Matriarch," Set bit out. "Stay behind and lead both clans. Bradan has ordered the Cath will proceed as planned."

His countenance brooking no argument, Maebh recoiled as if struck, the sting of his command as rígfénnid hitting their mark: her dwindling dignity. As firepits crackled, her warriors shifted focus from tending to the camp in a bleak silence, drawn to them, waiting for her response. No doubt expecting her to fight. She could scream herself hoarse at Setanta's reckless stupidity and change nothing.

Jaw clenched, she watched her twin walk toward the camp perimeter, his voice carrying as he explained his ability to sift and how he would try to take them with him. Since entering this land, their clear difference between normal Fianna and their gifts had become painfully evident. *Blood-blessed.* They'd never made their gifts widely known, but it seemed her brother had decided Ash's cousins were worthy of being enlightened to his ability to teleport.

Chest aching, she turned her back on their retreat, surveying both McQuillan and Breen clan members to ensure they were uninjured after the events at Newgrange. As soon as decency allowed, Maebh slipped away into the shadowed woods to nurse her bruised ego and racing mind, the confines of camp suddenly suffocating under her irrelevant status. She had to reckon with this diminishment and what it meant for both her pride and their people before Setanta returned.

If he returned.

CHAPTER 26
MAEBH

The echoing tunnels underneath the Hill of Tara greeted Maebh like a wary friend. She strode deeper, her fingertips trailing along cool stone as echoes of her footsteps bounced ahead into the dark. The suffocating press of earth above hung like a shroud, fuelling her urgency to find the chamber's end, and the stone guardians within. Maebh didn't want to be down here, but she needed to see Tiernan; to know he was okay when she was unsure if anyone else she cared about was.

A lifetime seemed to pass with each step as Maebh wound her way through the subterranean maze by torchlight and plummeted without care once she'd offered her bloodied hand to the indent in the wall as payment for entry.

She swallowed hard, imagining where her twin was journeying to, and what he would find there. Maebh gripped her torch tightly, the flames dancing erratically against the damp stone walls, illuminating the embedded blue gems. Ash had to be okay. There was no other option.

Nobody had noticed Maebh had sifted at Newgrange, and Lorna had even remarked on how unscathed she was and how clean her clothes had been, as if that in itself was a crime. She bit down on her cheek. As if living through the destruction had been an insult to her aunt. Another mark against her ability to lead as matriarch.

Glancing above at the seemingly unending abyss, her torch caught the strange substance she'd just waded through after jumping off the cliff edge. It gave off the same smell and look of tarmac after rain in a heatwave. Angling her torch higher, she couldn't make out the ledge she'd jumped from. No wonder this place had been left undiscovered for so long. She'd had to make a blood sacrifice. Her blood. Whatever lay within her veins had the ability to open the entrance to Fionn's resting place. Biróg's and that strange púca's claims that her blood held something more was hard to argue with when it did crazy things like that, but to have some connection to the Tuatha Dé? That was ridiculous. *Of my blood, but more.* Her mother's damned last words surfaced again, taunting her.

She willed herself to step forward, to enter the cavernous room housing the slumbering king. She *needed* to see Tiernan. To know he was real. All the lies above ground were digging their claws into her mind, and it was hard to grasp reality in this impossible world. Once she knew he was safe, she'd tell Ash and Set upon their return. Because they *would* come back.

She'd dressed in her combat clothes: tight-fitting pants and long-sleeved top, but she'd also donned a fur-lined coat. Her breath was visible even in the dim light her torch cast, a violent shiver racing down her spine. Had it grown colder? Or was she the one emanating this icy despair?

A scream sounded before it was muffled and Maebh pivoted, raising her light to find a man suspended in the invisible membrane that stopped death, but could easily cause it if you didn't escape.

"Swim!" she shouted, motioning with her arms frantically as her heart jumped into her throat.

As he twisted, Conor's face came into view, and she stumbled back. Why was he here? How had he escaped the dungeon? As if in answer, auburn hair caught her attention before Biróg emerged beside Conor, tugging him to the ground. Maebh jumped backward, avoiding their falling bodies as they broke through and landed on the uneven ground she'd just been standing on.

"Are you okay?" she asked Conor, helping him to his feet as he gasped for air. What she really wanted to ask was how in the realms did he get here? He nodded as Biróg answered her unspoken question with her musical, lilting voice.

"High King Bradan is a fair man. He has released the boy now that it's clear he is no longer under Ethne's charm."

When Maebh's brows rose, Conor tugged on the neckline of his shirt, revealing a white bandage, a stain indicating a fresh wound lay underneath.

"It had to be done."

Something in his expression told her what she needed to know.

"Conor, you cut yourself?"

"It was the only way I could remove her control."

"That's . . . savage."

Conor released his top, shrugging. "What's a little maiming to free yourself from a curse?"

His expression was so like Ash's, a laugh escaped Maebh. He smiled, but she could see dark bruises under his eyes. A shadow crossed his face, and he diverted his eyes, looking anywhere else. It was as if her mother appeared between them, a reminder of what he'd done at the hands of a wicked monster. He was still a haunted man, and they'd had little time to talk about what had happened.

"I can see you take after your sister for a sense of humour," Maebh said, bumping his shoulder playfully. "We'll get along just fine, Stitch."

His smile returned, but as his attention shifted towards Biróg, a sombre intensity washed over his features. "Are they through there?"

"Yes."

"Wait," Maebh said, stepping in front of the druid. "How did you get through the passage above?"

Maebh's heart quickened as implications swirled in her mind. If Biróg could access the passageway, it meant both Conor and Ethne's claims were false. A thrilling tide surged over her at unlocking part of the mystery they faced.

"We shadowed your steps through one of my cloaking spells. The wind tunnel helped too, so you didn't notice us." Biróg said brightly, no hint of an apology to her confession. "Before your blood dried on the wall, we passed through. And you know why it's your blood alone that works, Maebh. You will accept the truth soon."

The once hopeful tide turned to ice, coating Maebh with the frosted sting of disappointment.

Before she could retaliate, Conor interrupted. "I want to see Tiernan. There must be some way to get him out."

Maebh pressed a hand to her abdomen as if someone punched her. She'd forgotten how close Tiernan and Conor were. She angled her torch higher, Conor's face lit in stark contrast to the surrounding shadows. His brow furrowed as he looked at her, the breeze beating at her back lifting his black curls to show more of his angular jawline. He looked like a tortured angel, with his beautifully symmetrical face. He was so like his sister they could be mistaken for twins if they were the same age.

"I am going to see if it is possible to awaken him without disturbing Fionn Mac Cumhaill," Biróg declared, moving past Maebh toward the cave mouth.

"High King's orders?" Maebh called after her, but the druid didn't respond.

She shook her head at Conor's questioning look and gestured for him to follow as she quickened her pace to walk in front.

They were so close, and yet now that she was here, her legs weakened with every step. Why did she want to see Tiernan like this? She shook off that cowardly thought. She needed to remind herself of how he looked, trapped in stone.

The thumping beats drummed in her ears, and she took a step toward them. When Conor and Biróg followed, she stopped them with an outstretched arm.

"I need to go in by myself first."

Conor frowned, opening his mouth to protest, but Biróg nodded, taking Conor's arm and gently pulling him back.

"I'll call you in. Understand?"

Maebh turned before either could answer. Steeling herself, she took two large breaths before stepping over the threshold and further than she'd dared since Tiernan had saved them. What she didn't tell Biróg or Conor was that this may go horribly wrong. She may become a stone guardian, too. She had attempted to sift since Newgrange, but to no avail. If things went to shit, maybe she could escape by figuring out how to tap into that gift. Turning before she made it to the cave mouth, she added to Conor: "Promise me that no matter what, you won't go beyond here until I say otherwise."

A cloud of displeasure shadowed his features, tugging at the corners of his mouth as it descended into a flat line. His posture stiffened: arms folding over his chest in a shield-like barricade, legs adopting a similar position as if braced for an ongoing siege. He must have seen something in her expression to cause him to relent.

"Okay," he muttered, the single word laced with palpable undertones of his unconcealed discontent.

With that, she picked up her pace, darting around the turn, pausing in awe despite the overwhelming potency of dread the repellent spell caused.

The cathedral-scale cavern was honeycombed with alcoves, rows of slumbering warriors protecting the first High King. Maebh could make out the brilliant white sarcophagus in the distance where Fionn himself rested.

Adjusting to the sickening dread that beat into her, she forced her steps as she scanned the rows of stone guardians. Fianna, encased in stone as they guarded their king until Ireland cried out for his awakening. She sucked in a breath as her eyes landed on Tiernan. Relief softened her limbs like rain, and with a sigh she knew he was safe for now, in this place beyond the surface turmoil's grasp.

Had the thrumming heartbeats quickened as her eyes landed on his? Or had she imagined that as her own heart pumped and spluttered painfully?

"Hey, kitten," she said, standing before him.

Scanning the statues, she spotted her father a few rows behind. The steady thrumming didn't falter that time. When they were about to come alive, their beating hearts had increased before stopping. Her theory was right. She was merely supposed to visit the guardians and abstain from attempting to rouse the slumbering High King. Yet, the fading of her initial fear felt surprisingly vacant, leaving behind a void of hollow emptiness, a deflating resignation that she was invariably distanced from the dangers she had anticipated. Why was such a realisation teetering towards a strange shade of disappointment?

Her eyes tracked up Tiernan's form from his boots to his tense face. He wore a resigned expression that tugged at her heart. What if breaking the curse could be as simple as the fairytales claimed? Before doubt could stay her courage, Maebh rose onto her toes and pressed a kiss to his lips. Nothing happened. Pulling back, she searched Tiernan's face anxiously, hoping against hope that it had worked. A coldness seeped into her.

Lowering herself, she laughed mirthlessly. Of course, that wouldn't work. Only pure of heart or true love's kiss broke spells like that, and she was in neither category.

"Worth a shot, I guess?" she asked her stone friend before sighing.

She turned, reluctant to leave him now that she'd made it here. Jogging halfway down the narrow aisle of guardians, she called out: "You can come in." Conor and Biróg both appeared, and Maebh narrowed her eyes at the druid. "As long as you're not here to disturb the king."

Biróg nodded with an angelic smile, but Maebh would never trust another beautiful, cryptic druid. Their footsteps were barely audible over the thrumming beat, but they both made it through the repellent magic to stand beside her.

"I'm going to investigate," Biróg said before walking away. Sensing Maebh's next words, she added, "And I won't go near Fionn's grave."

Stuffing his hands in his pockets, Conor's shoulders hunched close to his ears. "I'd hoped Biróg had been lying about this and you'd all been playing a sick joke on me."

"I'm afraid not."

"She also told me Ash is currently in Rathcroghan and Set is on his way to collect her."

Maebh observed the druid's ritual, her mind only half-focused on the murmured chanting and gesturing. When she glanced back at Conor, she noted the relaxed set of his broad shoulders and ease of his stance. Gone was the tense, hunched posture from moments before. His brow remained furrowed but without the deep lines of strain she had glimpsed earlier. It seemed the druid's simple explanation for Ash's absence had alleviated Conor's concerns for now, whether truthfully or not. Maebh decided not to contradict the story, seeing little point in worrying him further until they knew more.

She squeezed his arm, offering a small smile as she struggled to find any words that would make any of this okay.

Leaving Conor to stand in front of Tiernan, she wandered over to her father. She opened her mouth to speak, but the words wedged in her throat like a sour lemon. She swallowed hard, but it wouldn't budge. Gearoid McQuillan had been her idol. The one parent who loved her unconditionally. Who'd had the patience of a saint, and a vocabulary that would make a dearg due blush. He'd taught her the best curses and laughed when she'd repeated them. Had howled with delight whenever she'd use them on Gluttons. Her mother would punish her for it, scolding her for turning paying customers away. But if it made her dad laugh, she'd gladly take those punishments.

"I'll get you out, Da," she whispered, laying a shaking hand over his beating cold heart before moving back to stand in front of Tiernan with Conor. With a start, she realised Tiernan was stationed beside his mother. She sneered at the woman from her nightmares. Images replayed in the long nights; Nessa's fist ramming into Tiernan's chest, turning him into the statue he was now. "You make my mother look like a saint."

There was a shift in the darkness and Maebh glowered at it. An eerie presence seeped through the walls and for a horrifying second, she feared whatever had happened to Newgrange was about to bring down the cave. They were thousands of feet underground, and only High King Bradan would know where to find them. She didn't trust her chances of being rescued as she stared up at his son's frozen face. Scanning the dark walls, she spotted a shadow, darker than the natural gloom.

She'd been in the presence of ancient fae before. When they were older than dust and ready for the afterlife, some Fair Ones chose to swap places with human babies to see their last days in the comfort of a nursing mother. Sick bastards. Nobody knew what became of the innocent babes, but Maebh had her suspicions. She didn't think they left them to die, which would have been a mercy. Fae were wicked creatures who played with humans.

Sickened by her own thoughts, she stepped around Tiernan to lean closer to that black spot.

"Conor, do you see that?" she asked, her voice sounding distant in her head.

When he leaned closer, she gripped Conor's arm, angling her head to the growing shadow. It pulsed as if alive, and she wouldn't speak of its presence aloud, in fear of what it might do. She was about to call out to Biróg.

"Run," a low garbling voice hissed, and Maebh's grip on Conor's arm tightened as she whipped her head to Tiernan.

He was still frozen in stone and there was no sign he'd spoken, but one glance at Conor, whose focus was also trained on Tiernan, confirmed she wasn't imagining it. Maebh's vision blurred as all blood rushed to her head. Conor's eyes were wide, his mouth twisted in surprise.

Finally, she recovered enough to whisper, "Tier?"

She stepped closer to him and scanned his lips, hoping he'd speak again.

A piercing cry echoed from the furthest end of the cavern, sending prickling vibrations through the frigid air. The obscure figure of a stone guardian toppled to his knees, his heavy form causing a tremor that rippled through the yawning expanse.

Conor was quicker, but Maebh followed close behind. Biróg reached the guardian at the same time they had. The stone guardian, once a vibrant portrayal of chiselled marble-like stone whiteness, had altered. It was as if an invisible hand was orchestrating a transformation, stroking the stone with an artifact of undeniable power.

The alabaster rigidity of the guardian softened, its ashen complexion acquiring a gradual flush, turning rosy, then olive. The change was systematic yet mesmerising; serpentine veins injecting into existence beneath the sentinel's slowly warming skin, spreading and blooming like cryptic tattoos from a long-forgotten fable. His form, once impenetrable, shivered, sheathing itself in the unmistakable texture of human flesh.

"What's happening?" Conor's voice echoed, bearing a grating edge of urgency.

They only watched in silence, as the guardian, now a man, stared down at his trembling hands. His features, caught in half-shadow, flickered with a potent concoction of pain swirled with an inexplicable wonder.

Conor had almost reached him, his hand outstretched to offer help, when black smoke consumed the man. His face twisted toward them, and Maebh grabbed Conor's collar, pulling him back. They clutched one another as the man's form disappeared in the liquid shadow until there was nothing left.

Something—or someone—was hunting the stone guardians.

CHAPTER 27
AISLING

Ash's eyes refused to open. Her nightmares had been filled with the harrowing face of her grandfather as he died within the rubble of Newgrange. Her muscles screamed in agony, every movement sending fresh jolts of pain through her legs as she rolled onto her back. She was lying on something hard with an incessant scratching along her skin, demanding attention despite her desire for rest.

Tiny needles danced upon her bare flesh in fits and starts, defying any attempt to brush them aside. As consciousness reluctantly asserted itself, the irritation spread; dozens of near-imperceptible pinpricks rousing her. Only as her numb fingers swatted ineffectually at her side did understanding slowly dawn. Hay. She lay amongst the golden grasses, their dried strands retaliating through needling where her form interrupted their drift. With a groan, Ash surrendered to full awareness, the stable's scents confirming her shelter once more.

Another presence caught her attention nearby, and she opened her eyes to find a massive horse studying her intently in the muted grey light. His coat shimmered with impossible colours, brightening the stall they shared and casting shadows. Intelligent gold-flecked eyes regarded her, tracking her every move as she sat up sluggishly and backed away from his muzzle. As if in amusement, the horse lowered himself, so his forehead was inches from hers, blowing out a warm breath in her face before turning toward the stable door.

Heavy footsteps sounded before Nik appeared, a familiar bundle in his hands. "Good. I was about to wake you. Tara's guards brought you here in the dead of night."

She accepted her clothes from him. "I thought they would have brought me to the dungeons."

She cringed at the staleness of her mouth as she spoke, dragging her swollen tongue along her teeth. It was only then she noted a bandage on her neck. She poked it gingerly, remembering Tara's fangs piercing her skin and a violent shiver spasmed down her spine at the violation. Wincing as she shifted on the rough-hewn ground, the movement ignited fire along her battered body. Her palms were thickly bandaged where rope and unforgiving rock had shredded her skin. Even the slightest flex of her fingers sent stinging protests from the inflamed cuts. The agonising climb up Queen Medb's mountain fortress had certainly left its marks.

"They aren't afraid of a human escaping. It doesn't happen. They told me to watch you." Nik looked down at her, sympathy peering through his blue eyes. "I patched up your wounds. They weren't deep and I made sure they won't get infected. I also cleaned your clothes. Thought you'd want them back. They're just about dry."

Ash glanced down at the dark fabric. Although a little worse for wear, they were practically dry-cleaned compared to the dress clinging to her sweat-drenched body.

"I'll leave you to tidy up, but please hurry. We don't have much time. There were no free stalls, but Croí Dubh doesn't mind sharing."

The horse nickered in response, nudging Nik's head before he left, to which the man swatted him away with a chuckle.

Alone once more, they stared at one another, Ash tracking the beast's movement as it took up most of the small space.

"Croí Dubh. Black Heart," she murmured, and the horse looked at her with a deadpan expression.

Ash's legs quaked with exhaustion beneath her as she inched closer to the door where a wooden bucket with warm water, soap and a towel waited for her.

Ash's cheeks warmed before she addressed the horse. "Could you, um, look away?"

Croí Dubh huffed in response, shaking his head before angling toward the open window. They faced the mountainside, a modest paddock in between, but there was nobody around in the pre-dawn morning. Bracing a hand on the wall, she peeled off the dirty dress, rolling her neck in an attempt to release the rigid tension coiled between her shoulders. Gritting her teeth, she washed her skin. After raking her sore fingers through the tangles in her hair, she exited the stall, fully clothed. She'd left the bandages in place, too weak to attempt anything other than to trust Nik knew what he was doing. Her neck didn't hurt, so she'd pretend Tara hadn't bitten her for now. Croí Dubh thankfully didn't nudge her when she departed.

"Through here," Nik called from a narrow door to the front of the stable, and for a brief moment a pang of longing to see her foster parents assaulted her. To be walking down the narrow hallway of their cottage rather than to a miserable stable room in this fae-infested kingdom.

She peered cautiously into the small room, taking in Nik's humble quarters. He sat on a rickety chair by a small table holding a meagre assortment of goods: a worn leather sack, a whittling knife, candles down to nubs and books stacked to such impossible heights she was surprised they didn't topple over at the slightest gust of wind.

"I've made you breakfast," Nik said, gesturing for her to sit on his narrow bed against an uneven wall as he stood over a low fireplace.

"Thank you," she replied quietly as she sat on threadbare blankets.

In the cool morning air, Nik tended the small fire, raking embers to stir life back into the fading flames. He hung a cast iron pot on a hook near the heat. Ash leaned forward, the enticing smell waking her senses.

"This is my infamous stable brew." Taking a clay mug from the mantlepiece, he poured the steaming contents. "Steeped roasted barley, rye and wheat berries that I soak in water overnight."

When he handed the cup to Ash, she breathed deep the beverage's fragrant aroma, scents of roasted bread and cocoa mingling with subtle bitter notes. The first sip brought a burst of flavours unfolding over her tongue, its warmth and complexity soothing her frayed nerves.

"This is better than coffee."

As he poured his own cup, he looked puzzled. "I don't know what that is."

Ash spluttered but recovered quickly. "Take it as a compliment."

"Noted."

He handed her a tin plate of bread and cheese before taking his seat once more to scarf his own food. His eyes never stayed in one place for more than a second, and Ash found herself eating in haste, too. Her stomach was a hollow pit and every bite she swallowed wasn't enough.

As they ate in silence, she peered through a narrow window to a sleepy town, not unlike the Fianna homestead. Though sparse, Nik's little haven spoke volumes in its ordinariness—an anchor against the inhumanity of living amongst self-proclaimed gods.

"I overheard them say you wield the powers of the Tuatha Dé. But that's not possible, is it? You're no fae."

Panic bloomed within her chest, splintering outward like fracturing ice. A lump of cheese wedged in her throat, so she whispered around it. "My parents are human."

Biróg's claims of being blood-blessed screamed in her head, but as she swallowed down the hard lump, so did she push that thought away. If . . . no, *when* she escaped, she would get answers from that druid. She didn't trust Biróg, but she couldn't deny Tara's claims were worryingly similar to what she'd said too. And Ash would rather seek the answers from the druid than a fanged Tuatha Dé.

She was certain of her humanity, but with her ability to sense emotions, Set's ríastrad and sifting gifts, she couldn't deny it any more. *Human, but not. Fae, but not.* They needed to find out exactly what that meant before it caused more trouble. What had Ethne done to them?

"Tara said I will be brought before their High King."

Nik's face leeched of colour, eyes glancing around and out the window. In a flash, he jumped from his seat. "Come on."

She followed him back to the pen holding Croí Dubh. The horse neighed softly, his discerning regard offering strange reassurance.

"Is there any way their claims are true?" Nik probed, gripping the door handle, but not opening the pen. "Can you sift to the human town in Mide?"

Ash frowned, backing away. "No, I told you I'm human. I can't . . ."

"Try."

"But—"

"Your life might depend on it. You must try." Nik's demand was so final.

She cleared her throat, her voice like thin reeds in her in her ears. "This doesn't make any sense."

But she nodded, rubbing her hands together, remembering how Set had explained the sensation of sifting. Taking a steadying breath, Ash closed her eyes and focused inward. Reaching deep within, she searched for that elusive transcendent spark Set had described.

Nothing stirred but fluttering panic. Swallowing it down, she took hold of that fear and willed it into submission, imagining Tara Court. She visualised a taut rope coiling snugly around her core, picturing its fibres drawing tight. A teasing tug pulled at her, a whisper of a connection, but where Set had channelled raw power, she grasped at wisps. The sensation flickered and faded, leaving her grasping at nothing. She opened her eyes with a gasp, finding herself rooted in place while Nik regarded her warily.

"I can't," Ash said, frustration welling as fresh doubts swirled.

Nik offered an encouraging smile. "Over to plan B, so."

He fetched a saddle and bag of provisions, ushering her into Croí Dubh's pen. "This is the best I can offer for escape. If you stay, you're going to die here. He's the fastest horse. Hurry before they come for you."

Ash helped secure the saddle when he instructed her to, but the wrongness of this option weighed on her. "Won't you get into trouble? Why are you helping me?"

He met her eyes calmly. "Humanity is all I have left. They won't miss Croí Dubh." The horse neighed and Nik grasped its muzzle, pressing his forehead against his. "But I will. Go, friend. You know it's only right."

She couldn't have another human life extinguished by her hands. If Nik stayed here, surely it would be as good as killing him herself? A wash of hopelessness threatened to consume her.

She was a Fianna warrior, a matriarch, but she'd never thought she'd have to kill one of her own. If she accepted Nik's help, she could be damning him to death.

She gripped his large hand, squeezing as tears welled. "Come with us."

Nik smiled sadly. "I have my own reasons to stay. Put this on and meet me at the entrance with Croí Dubh."

Handing her a dark cloak, she swung it on, shielding her face in the deep hood. When she met him at the entrance, Nik held a wicker flask and cups, the smell of roasting nuts wafting through. He nodded to follow, so she gripped the reins tightly as they walked toward the quiet town. "Go past the tower. There are no walls. No gates. The mountain is a fortress, and we who live down here are not important enough for protection."

She quickened her pace, her breath piercing her lungs as she kept up.

"Don't look back. If you hear anything, grab the reins tight and press your thighs into Croí Dubh as hard as you possibly can." Nik didn't turn as he patted the horse. "He can take it. He will be the fastest horse you've ever ridden. It's your job to keep your seat, not his. If you're caught and dragged back here, you snuck out while I was tending to other pens. Got it?"

"Yes. Of course." She would not allow him to take the blame for this.

A crack of resolve whipped her spine to straighten. She would not get caught. She stayed close to Croí Dubh's flank, directly behind Nik. Ash tracked the area to a large bell tower near the perimeter of the village. Two guards were stationed there, and Nik stopped in the narrow alleyway between two cottages, shielded from the guards' sight.

"Wait until Croí Dubh tells you to move," Nik spoke softly, quiet enough so she could barely hear.

Ash's heart raced at the toll of the bell.

"It's still early enough that the only people awake are the human workers. Most Tuatha Dé sleep within the mountain, so you just have to get by those guards."

"I don't know how to thank you."

Nik patted Croí Dubh's flank, before nodding in her direction. "Live. Look after my horse. That's the only thanks I need."

With a final grateful nod to the stable hand, she watched him turn the corner of the building, calling out in the Tuatha Dé language. Cheerful voices greeted him, and she risked a glance around the corner to see Nik pouring cups of stable brew for the Tuatha Dé guards. He waved at two figures emerging from a stone building, beckoning them over. More guards. Ash bit her lip, Croí Dubh neighing quietly, stomping his heels as if to warn her to wait. Nik saluted the new guards, angling his flask high to appreciative murmurs.

The bell tolled again, and her breath turned to shallow rasps. This was the changing of the guard. Nik talked animatedly, which led to a chorus of laughter from the surrounding four fae. He pointed to the mountain, and the guards turned at his tale. Croí Dubh nudged Ash and she willed her nerves to take those steps out of the safety of their hiding place. She walked with the horse shielding her as best he could. She barely heard Nik's unknown language or the chuckle of the guards over her erratic heart, but she kept pace with the beast until they made it past the cover of trees to a woodland.

She waited one beat, but she couldn't hear approaching footsteps, nor any sound of alarm to her appearance. It was an effort for her foot to reach the stirrup without a pitiful jump, but once secured, she swung onto the fae horse's back.

"Will they punish him?"

Croí Dubh started into a gallop without acknowledging her question. She'd ridden horses before, but this was no ordinary animal. The horse raced swiftly through the rustling trees, hooves barely touching the ground.

Despite Nik's warning, Ash kept glancing back. Both eager to put distance between herself and Rathcroghan, yet loath to leave Nik behind. He was a stranger, but he was human and had helped her more than he should. She'd no doubt he would be punished for what he'd done, but she couldn't let that guilt in. Not when she needed to escape.

As the woods thinned, a strange prickling rose at the back of her neck. Lightly tugging the reins, she turned in her saddle again, straining eyes and ears for the source of her unease. Croí Dubh seemed to sense it too, slowing to a stop and circling the perimeter.

Through the dappled green shadows, she saw a hint of movement. Ash's breath caught in her throat.

"Who's there?" When only silence greeted her, she shouted. "Show yourself!"

Was it a patrol sent to drag her back? Her hand strayed to the dagger once more in her boot, unsheathing it. Grasping its familiar contours, a dark figure emerged from the forest edge.

CHAPTER 28

AISLING

As Croí Dubh rotated, hooves pounding the soft forest floor, Ash gripped her dagger, eyes trained on the threat lurking amidst the rustling leaves. A single, heart-stopping moment passed before a dark form detached itself from the dense greenery.

"Set!" Ash cried, slipping from Croí Dubh's back in a desperate blur and dropping her blade in the grass.

She threw herself against his imposing frame, clinging to his waist as waves of relief nearly swept her off her feet. Strong arms enveloped her so tightly the breath squeezed out of her lungs. Tremors wracked Set's powerful frame as he planted featherlight kisses against her head. He withdrew just far enough to grip her face between calloused palms, raking wild eyes over every inch. Her body still ached with her injuries, but it was worth it.

"Are you hurt?" he rasped, voice thick.

Ash blinked back tears, relishing the steadiness of his presence. "Just bruises," she managed, clasping his wrists as his fingers brushed lazy circles through her hair. With a heaviness that would break her, she whispered, "Maebh?"

"She's fine. Alive. Still a pain in the ass."

Ash let out a sob-filled laugh, squeezing his wrists as she nodded. Maebh was alive. How? She'd been so close to Newgrange. But it didn't matter. Her friend was alive.

Set's broad shoulders filled his cotton shirt, straining the seams, though the dark fabric was pristine compared to his muddy boots and dishevelled hair. He traced his fingers along her jawline, pausing at the bandage on her neck. His storm grey eyes darkened as they snapped to hers. "Just bruises?"

Her mouth dried at his gravelly timbre, and she stepped back as she squinted at his too-calm face. Sucking in a breath, she opened her mouth to speak, but he cut her off, stalking forward so her feet stumbled, retreating of their own accord until her back was against a solid warm mass. The horse stomped in agitation but didn't move as Set's thick arms encased her, so she had nowhere to look but him.

His voice was lethally quiet. "Show me what's underneath that bandage."

"It's nothing," Ash whispered.

She had no intention of hiding Tara's bite mark, but the words died on her tongue as electricity snapped in the air between them.

Lowering one hand to pull her waist closer, she gasped as the other undid the bandage. His full lips dipped as he eased the adhesive wrap from her skin. She didn't dare breathe as she tracked his expression. He was never as gentle with his fingers until it came to touching her. The bandage came away easily, the cool breeze kissing her tender skin underneath and she winced. His eyes snapped to hers once more.

"What are those?"

She swallowed. "What do they look like?"

He tugged her closer so there was no distance, his hard frame her new prison. "They look like teeth marks."

Ash lowered her eyes, but he lifted her chin until she met his unwavering gaze.

"Yes," she breathed.

"Who?" he growled, shaking his head when she tried to back away. "Are they still breathing?"

Her reply was barely audible. "Yes."

"Not for long." Set released her and whirled toward Rathcroghan, skin flushing an angry crimson. Beneath his shirt, veins and muscles swelled grotesquely large until the fabric tore and fell away.

"Set!" Ash grabbed his arm, his pupils dilated into black pools.

Her heart raced itself into an aching thunder underneath her ribs. He shook off her plea, body rippling larger with each laboured breath. A feral gleam sparked in his eyes, and she gasped when he when blinked. Two eyelids moved within each blackening eye. His ríastrad was breaking through.

"Stop," she pleaded, pressing against his expanding chest as hers fractured. If he turned, he wouldn't forgive himself. "We need to leave. I'm not going back there."

She heard the desperation in her tone, and he must have too. He stopped, shoulders heaving. "Tell me who and we'll take care of it ourselves."

Set's voice no longer spoke through his behemoth build. This voice was a primal thing—a guttural rumble emerging from deep within his throat, syllables strangely formed. This was no longer the caring man who lay with her under the stars or spent hours studying in the library when everyone slept.

In his place stood a nightmare growing into flesh and bone. A beast ready to slay for her. If she didn't stop his transformation, she'd face a titan with enough strength to level this forest or crack mountain stones. And if she let him do just that, they'd all be doomed to the wrath of the Tuatha Dé Danann.

Croí Dubh galloped forward, pushing her aside as he stood in front of Set, who reared back, coiling as if ready to strike the fae horse. Her stomach twisted and dropped as Set released a roar.

"No!" Ash jumped in between them, her arms outstretched.

Within that hellish roar the same protectiveness that kindled Set's care banked embers in his eyes. Even lost to fury's grip, his first instinct remained guarding her from threat—whether real or not.

Set's black eyes didn't waver from the horse's. Blood seeped from his eye sockets which began to move together. Soon one eye would retreat to his throat, and he would no longer be Set. The fabric of his pants tore, clinging in parts to his monstrous form.

"Croí Dubh isn't trying to hurt me!"

Ash shuddered, retreating step by panicked step, Croí Dubh's warm breath a comforting presence at her back. A whine came from deep within Set's throat and she stopped, unable to make herself move. She refused to flee while any hope remained he might yet break free of the ríastrad's thrall. With a sob, she called his name once more, praying reason could resurface amongst the crimson tides now drowning him from within.

"Set, let's just go to Mide," Ash said, daring to stand closer to him despite the horse's nickered warning. "If you leave me here to seek revenge, I'll be alone and at the mercy of whatever else might be in these woods. Look how easily you came upon me. I need you more than you need revenge. Control this. Stay with me. Please."

He stood, heaving, an internal battle she couldn't fathom until finally, his eyes softened when he looked down at her. Slowly, far too slowly, his form shrank. Each ragged gasp drew him farther from his monster's abyss, back to the present. Back to her.

Crimson receded from his flesh as his breaths eased. He reached out to her, and she didn't hesitate. Closing the distance, she threw her arms around him once more. Pressing her ear to

Set's bare chest, Ash closed her eyes, losing herself in the lullaby of his thrumming heart beneath her cheek. Its steady pounding was a chorus singing the song of his restored humanity, like a firm embrace, rumbling down her spine and spreading a warmth in her stomach, drowning out the memory which had done something to her that it shouldn't have.

She felt taut muscle gradually unwind beneath her hands as she rubbed circles over his back. His own arms cocooned her gently, lips pressing a reverent kiss to her hair.

"I'm sorry," he said, and she released a long-held breath at the sanctity of his familiar voice. Like warm honey poured over an aching wound, its purity cut through the haze clouding them both.

Ash lifted her gaze to meet clear grey eyes, finding Set was fighting to conceal the fury that had blazed there so only faint echoes remained. She rested her chin on his chest, drinking in his handsome, haunted face. The ríastrad's traces ran deeper it seemed, but the man beneath had won control once more.

She gripped him tighter. "Don't ever apologise for something you have no control over."

"It's over," he murmured, breath warming her scalp. "You're safe, I promise." And for that moment, clutching each other in the shelter of the looming forest, Ash believed with all her heart that this man would move both earth and heaven itself before letting darkness fall over them.

"Let's go," Set said, stroking her arms. "I need to retrieve my pack and then I can sift us home."

A huff came behind her and she glanced back at Croí Dubh, worriedly. "Can you sift with Croí Dubh?"

Set's brows rose at the name, but he shook his head. "I can only take you."

The horse nudged her back, huffing into her hair. She let go of Set and faced Croí Dubh.

"What is it?" she asked quietly, meeting the fae steed's flickering gold eyes. Croí Dubh tossed his mane, stepping toward her and huffing. "Don't you want to return to Nik?" Croí Dubh nudged her shoulder, the soulful look speaking clearer than any tongue. "Nik asked you to keep me safe, didn't he?" A nod. Ash smiled sadly. "You intend to see that promise through, wherever our path leads?" Another affirmative shake of his mane.

"I see I'm outnumbered once more," Set sighed, running fingers through his wild locks. "I'll be back."

Ash stroked Croí Dubh's ebony mane, refusing to glance at Set's retreating naked form. The horse reached low to the ground, plucking up her dagger and releasing it into her bandaged palm. When Set emerged, he was fully clothed with a pack and a familiar weapon in his hand.

"You brought my sword," she said, smiling softly as Set handed her the trusty hilt.

She glanced at the dull silver blade, one she'd accepted from Ciarán as a replacement after her mother's had been shattered defending Tiernan. Her sigh was as heavy as the blade itself. It was a fine sword, but it would never hold the same bittersweet memories or sing with quite the same voice as the one lost in the cave underneath the Hill of Tara.

"I know it's not the same," Set said tenderly, resting a hand on her shoulder. "But I knew wherever you were, I would find you again to return this, if nothing else."

She slid the sword into its well-worn leather sheath, taking comfort in its weight hanging secure once more at her hip. "Thank you."

Set's smile revealed a dimple that made her stomach drop, but it disappeared too quickly as he studied the fae horse behind her. "I've never sifted with a horse, but I guess we can try."

Croí Dubh stomped backwards, shaking his head.

Ash tracked his retreating form. "I don't think he's willing to risk it."

"Well, I'm not sifting without you. We need to move fast. Can . . . Croí Dubh carry both our weights?"

The horse's lips retreated, baring sharp teeth. Croí Dubh trotted in a circle around them until he stood directly in front of Set. The horse bent his front legs, lowering himself so his rear was pushed close to Set's face.

"I think that means yes," Ash said, biting her lip to contain her chuckle.

"Charming," Set said before vaulting onto the horse's broad back.

Heart pounding, Ash allowed Set to guide her up, nestling into the circle of his sturdy arms. His woodsy scent overwhelmed her senses as she leaned back against the rippling muscle of his chest. His sinewy arms wound securely around her middle, fingers splayed against the fabric over her waist sending heat coursing through her veins. Croí Dubh sprang into motion at some unspoken signal, hooves flying across the forest floor.

She could feel the steady thrum of Set's heartbeat where their bodies met, taking solace in its steady rhythm.

Ash angled her head to take in his square jaw, drinking in reassurance that she was no longer alone. "You came alone into *this* territory. You could have been standing before the Tuatha Dé Danann."

"But I wasn't. Just a cantankerous horse." Amusement laced his words as Croí Dubh made a sound that Ash could have sworn was a curse.

"And Bradan just let you come?"

"You're now riding with the Rígfénnid of Connacht at your back, my lady." When she twisted again in their shared saddle, a rueful smile grew on Set's lips. "Bradan quite literally gave me an offer I couldn't refuse."

"How do you feel about that?"

"The only reason I accepted was because Bradan granted my release to come find you."

There was something in his tone that made her tense. "There's more, isn't there?"

"I was supposed to come as the new emissary for Queen Medb. Bradan had approved my journey, but he told me to wait until the morning and to go with a contingence of highguard. When I returned to camp, Tomás and Ciarán were ready to leave."

"So you left with them? Where —"

"I couldn't wait for them with normal horses. The journey was too slow and that's how I discovered I can't sift with more than one person." Set's grip tightened around her waist for a heartbeat. "All I could think of was getting to you."

"Won't you get into trouble with the High King?"

He brushed a stray lock from Ash's cheek, calloused fingers lingering. "I was never going to wait a full night to find you. I sifted as close to Rathcroghan as I dared and began searching the outskirts on foot. And just as hope was fading, I heard Croí Dubh."

Ash smiled, patting the galloping horse.

"Where on earth did that name come from?"

She chuckled as Croí Dubh neighed.

"I've no idea. But his owner . . ." Another snort from the horse and slight buck had her clinging to the reins. "I mean, *friend*, was a human man." She added quietly, "A changeling."

Set offered another reassuring squeeze. The only sound for miles was Croí Dubh's steady gallop as troubles churned through Ash's mind. Deep in the heart of the Fair Ones' territory, the likelihood of a quiet escape was almost nil. It was only a matter of time before her absence was noticed and someone sounded an alarm, sending the hunters.

CHAPTER 29
AISLING

The countryside slipped by in a blur. Croí Dubh proved himself an expert guide, navigating securely away from all signs of fae habitation. Yet distant howls still split the woodland, haunting the borders where kingdoms collided.

The travellers followed ancient forest paths tracking the River Shannon's serpentine curves as sunset painted the rippling waters in hues of gold and rose. Ash glimpsed movement beneath swaying reeds along the shore, lit from below by the dying sun's light.

"Set, look," Ash called over the rushing river.

He followed her gaze to a secluded cove tucked into the reed-fringed banks of Lough Ree. There, flashes of sleek tails shimmered amber and jade through translucent depths as sinuous forms darted amongst dense growth.

"Mermaids," Set said, as she heard a blade unsheathe. When she looked to the side, he gripped his axe handle as Croí Dubh's steps slowed when they reached a narrow bridge.

Daring to look over the low stone wall, she gulped as long manes floated around ethereal faces pale as foam and scaled tails caused undulating, faint waves.

"Careful, Croí," Ash murmured as the horse's hooves clipped onto the cobbled stone bridge.

Melismatic voices rose faint yet fair upon the waking breeze, their unearthly chorus stirring a longing she knew would only lead to death if she succumbed. She gripped Set's arm, unwilling to allow the slightest chance he'd meet a watery grave. The beautiful females swam under the bridge, mouths gaped to reveal sharp canines. Claw-tipped hands reached upward, beckoning them to jump in.

Each note of their song was a promise of seduction. A pulse between her legs. Set's arm tightened around her, and she bit her lip as she fought the melodic call to shattering bliss. On and on the melody climbed until her body trembled and her chest heaved. Every shift of the man behind her caused more ache and a need so fierce she couldn't bear it.

"Set," she gasped.

His lips grazed her ear as warm breath elicited a delicious shiver. "I know."

She wanted nothing more than to turn around and straddle Set and show him exactly what she needed from him. It wasn't the blade in his hand, but something far more primal. Ash squirmed, biting back a whimper.

"We have to stay strong," Set whispered with a voice dipped in pain and longing as he fought the mermaid's glamoured song.

Ash shuddered, pulling her cloak tight as the haunting singing receded into gathering shadows when finally, they met dry land once more.

"Do you need a break?" Ash asked the powerful steed when they reached the safety of more woodland, though she wasn't sure if it would be for her more than the horse. Croí Dubh shook his mane and sped on, the friction doing little to satiate her desire.

Set's strong chest was an anchor as she leaned against him, although he trembled. His hand splayed on her stomach, but she needed him to move it lower. To let him command her body as she felt his desire pressing into her. She glanced up to see the sweat collecting on his brow. It would be so easy to steal this moment. To wander off the path and let him ravage her, but she forced those thoughts from her mind. Her first time with Set would not be ignited by the song of a siren. It wouldn't be on the edge of enemy territory. She would have all of him organically or not at all.

Finally, familiarity bled into the surrounding woodland.

"We're almost there," Set said, clear surprise in his tone.

They had raced across Tír na nÓg in hours and Croí Dubh showed no sign of tiredness as he galloped on. Warring cries penetrated the dark sky with dripping menace. These sounds weren't from chasing enemies. They were racing toward them, to their haven.

"What's that?" Ash asked, pulling Croí Dubh to an immediate halt. Guttural neighs and mocking laughter rose from ahead, accented by shouts and cries of battle.

Trees thinned and below, Tara Court loomed, the gate closed. Ash's mouth dried at the cause of those cries. A group of highguard defended the gate from a pack of púca. Colossal equine bodies reared and wheeled with odd, lolloping gaits, flanks steaming as they harried a small patrol of highguard who defended the gate. Ash's grip on Croí Dubh's reins was painful, his neighing a clear disgust at the perversion to his kind.

For it was horses the púca had shapeshifted into. But these were neither ordinary nor fae. These creatures had taken on twisted versions of the animal. As Croí Dubh slowed to a stop, Ash squinted at the glowing yellow and red eyes of the attacking beasts. These were not the púca she'd dealt with in cat form in the human world. No number of dairy offerings would satiate their thirst for mischief. They thirsted for blood.

Set dismounted, axe in hand, and she swiftly followed, unsheathing her blade as they inched closer to the thinning woods and the growls and shouts coming from Tara Court. Bodies littered the ground. Men and women in black uniforms of the High King's guard had been herded and separated into weakened groups. The púca swarmed, slashing with sharp hooves, and sinking needle-shaped teeth into flesh and bone.

"Stay here!" Set sprinted ahead without a backwards glance.

Heart in her throat, Ash followed on foot, ignoring his command, hands tightening around the hilt of her sword and Croí Dubh's reins alike.

Beyond the trees' thinning edges, chaos unfolded. Set raced onto the battlefield but dropped his axe as a púca collided into his side. Everything seemed to move in slow motion as crimson flooded Set's skin too swiftly, the fiery tide consuming his form. Bones snapped and reshaped; muscle corded impossibly over rippling skin as wrath incarnate erupted forth with an earth-shaking roar. His form shimmered and swelled, moulting into the rippling ríastrad. With a bellowing cry he gripped the horse-shaped limbs of a púca, pulling it apart until it tore into two.

"Set!" Ash cried, but he launched among the monstrous horses, claws and teeth splitting ebony hides with primordial fury.

By the time Ash and Croí Dubh made it to the highwall, the fight raged in full fervour. She froze, feet rooted to the blood-slick earth. Fianna fought on relentlessly against the tide of aberrations, Croí Dubh launching into the fray to fight off a púca that had turned their way. But her eyes remained pinned on Set. He towered amidst the monsters and men, an incarnation of violence given flesh and bone.

Each strike of thunderous fists or flashes of slavering jaws rent the air with cries that sank talons beneath Ash's ribs. Bile rose in her constricting throat at seeing capability so feral yet borne by the soul who held her own safety gently in calloused palms.

She stood transfixed, even though her pulse raced painfully. Would any trace of gentle Set remain once his ríastrad retreated?

Hand gripping her sword until knuckles whitened, all Ash could do was bear mute witness to the savagery that dwelled within Set and beg any power listening that he survive its fury unfractured.

A púca sent a guard crashing to the dirt, turning its misshapen maw towards Set racing to aid them. Recognition blazed in its gold and crimson eyes: here was a greater prize than any man. It let loose an unearthly howl and lunged.

"Set!" Her scream was drowned out by louder, monstrous roars from the man who held her breath captive.

Without slowing, Set dropped and rolled, plunging his fist beneath its armoured hide. But another abomination was already launching at his exposed back, talons gleaming.

Ash retrieved and rotated her dagger, blade tip between her fingers, and swung with all her strength. It met its target, right in the attacking púca's red eye. It reared back with a roar, giving Set time to finish it off, tearing it apart with his taloned hands.

With Set in ríastrad form, it didn't take long for him to kill the monstrous horses, but many highguard had not survived. Only two remained, injured, but thankfully alive. Ash let out a sigh.

"Come on." Croí Dubh refused to budge, hooves stomping and pulling her back. She glared at him. "What are you doing?"

Shouts sounded, followed by a deafening bellow and Ash's heart stopped.

Another púca charged at Set, but he jumped out of its way in time. Instead of pivoting to charge again, the monster-horse galloped on, retreating into the trees, Set giving chase. Two highguard ran after them.

"Let's go," Ash commanded as she vaulted onto Croí Dubh's back.

It didn't take long to catch up to them, but her head spun at what she saw.

"No!" she cried out, jumping from the horse's back.

Set stood over the fallen púca, his monstrous form heaving as the two highguard approached him, swords drawn.

Ash pulled on the closest guard's arm, but he shook her off, eyes trained on Set.

"He's not a Fair One!" she pleaded.

Her shouts were drowned out by Set's thunderous roar as the highguard closest to him lunged forward, arcing his sword in a deathly swing. Set caught it mid-air, grabbing the blade and breaking it in two.

"Set!" Ash shrieked, but it was too late.

He grabbed the man's head, crushing his skull in one motion.

Silence filled her head, and then a buzzing until her vision swam.

"What did you do?" she choked, and his attention snapped to her. In muted horror she realised his eyes had shifted, one lodged in his throat, the other forming in the centre of his forehead. Blinking, she stumbled forward, and fell to her knees.

"Set . . ." She wasn't sure if his name crossed her lips, but his ríastrad form stepped toward her. Once. Twice.

Croí Dubh pulled on her collar, hauling her away, but Set was quicker. In an intake of breath, he loomed over her. The incessant buzzing filled her head until slowly, his form shifted and shrank. Setanta fell to his knees before her, a silent scream in his mouth.

"Stand up, murderer," a rough voice said from feet away.

Set didn't hear him. His head bent forward until his face was smothered in her lap. Placing her hands on his hair, she tracked black boots that led to an all-black uniform. The highguard she tried to stop sneered at them.

"Setanta McQuillan. There were rumours, but I didn't believe it. Thought it was bullshit." The highguard limped, wincing, but he kicked at Set's side.

"Don't you dare —"

"Shut up, monster whore." The highguard grabbed Set's shoulders, pulling him up. "You will be brought before the High King for murder."

CHAPTER 30
TIERNAN

Tiernan's time was running out. It leeched away with each collective stone heartbeat, a scarce resource slipping between his frozen fingers. Even above the thunderous drumming, he heard the growing power and insatiable hunger of the stalking shadow monsters, scratching at the edges of his perceptions with their raspy, dark voices.

Sluagh, a young, feminine voice said throughout the unified stone mind, but before he could distinguish which guard spoke, the stone clan joined in a chant.

Stay. Fight. Protect.

A couple had talked to him. Strangers with an uncanny familiarity that unsettled his bones. Who were they? Had they known him? They had spoken to him as if they had crossed paths before, as if they belonged to a past he had mislaid. Her lovely face had tilted up at him, cerulean eyes trained on him alone. When her lips had brushed his . . . he'd felt nothing. It was a touch against stone, devoid of warmth. But he'd spoken. One word: run.

Defend. Succumb.

His mind raced, tumbling over itself. The ticking of unseen seconds. A whirlpool of disarray. They had fled when the sluagh attacked another of his stone clan. When had that been? The question echoed, bouncing on the walls of his confused consciousness.

He reached out, mentally grasped for remnants of solid recollections. Straining to map out the faded footprints of time, feeling the edges and the gaps, the before and the after. Yet they slipped, elusive and fleeting. Time, like a trickster, ebbing through his mental grasp.

Focus.

Visitors. A smile, a look. Their imprint vivid, yet their timeline smeared. A red- haired druid's presence, a splash of warmth in cold eternity. But when had they entered his bound reality? Threads of memory tangled, knotted, and frayed. When?

His brain throbbed, clamouring for order amid the echoing chaos. Time spun and whirled in a grotesque dance of infinity, its start and end jumbled, indistinct. Recollection was a mocking haze.

Succumb.

It would be easy to give in to his clan. To stop fighting.

Doubt seeped in, creeping along the fringes. Was he forgetting, or was it that time had ceased to follow any meaningful pattern? Fionn's sentinels unaltered by his jumbled thoughts anchored him to the now. That was what was important. Not the past, nor the future.

A crackling charge, chilling and unsettling, cleaved the heavy air with its sudden appearance. *The shadows are coming*, he shared through the hive mind.

The statue that was once his mother spoke beside him. *We fight, as planned.*

Tiernan could not shut out Nessa Cassidy in this instance. If this were to work, all stone guardians needed to act as one. The sluagh were mere shadow, unseen to the untrained eye, oozing from the gaps in the walls. They slithered like blackened silk.

Stay. Protect. Fight.

Withdrawing from his own stone body, he jumped into the statue closest to the shadow mass, Nessa's stream of discontent following him. But this had been his plan, and he would see it through. The thought quelled his mother's reluctance, but only just. The occupant he shared a statue with now was one of the first to join the underground vigil, a seasoned keeper of the ageless High King. One of the first Fianna warriors. The warrior yielded to Tiernan easily, their shared urgency against the adversary lurking before them.

Jump out on my order, Tiernan commanded. *Like we practised*.

If correctly timed, the shadow would encompass an abandoned sculpture, a hollow camouflage with nothing to devour.

The shadow solidified into a snake-shaped substance, rearing up for its strike.

Wait, he commanded.

Higher and higher it rose until Tiernan couldn't strain his eyes any further.

Now, Tiernan commanded, jumping into the statue beside him. The Fianna was clumsier than him, but as the smoke descended over his stone body, the warrior made it to the statue.

As his thoughts settled alongside Tiernan's, the warrior they'd joined made himself smaller to allow room, but the shared satisfaction of escaping the shadow was quickly replaced by a bizarre sense of discomfort. Being enclosed together in the same stone statue felt like walking in a crowded room, only without the ability to distance himself from others. Their minds swirled within the stone body, thoughts crossing thoughts, emotions spilling into one another, giving rise to a heightened sense of claustrophobia.

Never had Tiernan wished for physical boundaries as he did now, desperate for a curtain or wall to delineate his mental space from that of his stone clan.

Concentrating on the threat before them, he cast a glance at the statue they'd left behind, and Tiernan felt a rush of satisfaction as the shadow entity enveloped it, falling into their trap.

The shadow pulsed around the stone but repelled it as if it were spitting out rotten fruit. Rearing back, it whipped what could have been its head back and forth, as if looking for the Fianna warrior. Slithering closer to Tiernan, it cocked its shadowy head. The Fianna within the stone body convulsed and screamed, his panicked thoughts battering into Tiernan. *Shut up.*

The sluagh was relentless. A tendril of smoke-flesh ghosted across their shared stone cheek, grazing like a lover's caress. The tiny touch birthed an agony so raw, like fire licking through dry parchment. Overwhelmed, Tiernan withdrew abruptly, his consciousness ripping free from the stone guardian and retreating into his original body. His silent scream echoed within the confines of their mindscape.

Retreat.

He collected himself enough to jump back through his companions' bodies, but they had been betrayed by pain, his plan fallen to ruin. It was already too late. The shadow pulsed once before snatching the stone statue that occupied two lives. Tiernan watched, frozen as white stone turned ashen, and no men emerged. Two stone guardian bodies lay in rubble, no momentary reprieve before they were taken like the others. They were nothing. He had done that to them.

Silence filled his head as he returned to his prison.

She had tried to kiss his lips. He'd felt nothing.

CHAPTER 31
AISLING

Ash's thoughts scattered like leaves before an oncoming gale, her ability to focus splintering as Set walked away, blood-soaked and clothes torn.

Croí Dubh nudged her shoulder, and she stared into his gold-flecked eyes. He nudged her again before trotting into the woodland. With an intake of breath, she stumbled over the fallen dead and caught up to Set and the highguard, her aching body a forgotten problem at the numbing horror consuming her. The gates were open, more guards stationed beyond, but thankfully no locals were outside.

"Setanta!" Maebh shouted, pushing through the gathered crowd of black uniforms.

Ash breathed a sigh of relief, drinking in her friend's fiery approach, her wild blonde hair flowing behind her as she stormed forward. She was alive. Set had told her but seeing Maebh unharmed was a balm that soothed her.

"We . . . Tiernan . . ."

Her words were cut short when the limping highguard shoved Set forward. Maebh's glare was a feral and wicked thing that would have any smart person backing away. "Do that again to my twin and I will make you regret it."

The highguard had enough intelligence to eye Maebh warily. "In front of all my guards? Stay out of this, Matriarch."

Maebh's hand went to her blade. "Wrong answer."

"Mae," Set's whisper was barely audible. "Don't. We are going to see the High King."

Ash swallowed a hard lump as Set's twin looked to her and she nodded. Following behind the guard who refused his friends' offers of assistance, the women shared a look that needed no words, whilst Maebh gripped both her and Set's hands. They were both alive, and they were there for Setanta.

Bradan was in the Tuatha Dé temple of Lugh, highguard surrounding him. When he saw their approach, his face lit up with a bright smile.

"I'm so glad you're back, despite leaving unattended." He clasped Set's shoulder, tracking his shredded clothing. He said nothing about Set's bloodied half-naked form before nodding at Ash and smiling at their escort. "Thanks for bringing them here, Donnacha."

"High King," Donnacha began, "You need to know what happened outside. He . . ."

"Leave us," Bradan's booming voice filled the quiet temple, and Ash flinched. The surrounding warriors marched out without hesitation. When it was only them and the lone highguard, Bradan signalled for him to continue.

Donnacha's blood-smeared face blanched as he licked his lips. Before he could launch into his tale, Ash glanced at Set and took in the rips in his clothing, his measured breaths, and bruised, stained eyes. Bile burned the back of her throat as her mind spun, but she stepped forward.

"Can't you see he just protected the entire kingdom from those púca? You should be standing here, grateful for what he's done."

"He also just killed my friend with his bare hands," the guard seethed.

"He attacked Set first!" Ash shouted.

"He should be punished according to Brehon law." Pointing a finger in Set's face, the guard ignored Maebh's warning snarl as he continued. "He took out the púca, but he didn't stop there. He's some sort of monster, High King. He's a Fair One. Full of bloodlust like the rest of their kind."

Blood-blessed. Ash searched the temple as if Biróg would appear at any moment to either confirm the highguard's claims or defend them. But the vast temple was empty, only the stone walls and Lugh's fierce statue a witness to their party.

Silence fell once more, and Ash longed for Set to speak up. But he had the face of a man who'd been through hell. And she'd stood and watched as he'd gone through it. Her heart ached as he refused to defend himself against the harsh words of an ignorant guard.

"Set." Ash stood before him, raising her hand to his cheek. When his grey eyes met hers, she spoke tenderly. "You did nothing wrong."

Set took her hand, rubbing her knuckles. "It'll be okay, Ash."

He tucked her into his side, kissing the top of her head, giving her a reassuring squeeze, as though she was the one that needed comforting. As if his suffering meant nothing. Tatters of an intense battle lay before the gates, blood and bodies the evidence of Set's strength, but also a sign of his lack of control.

Throughout the entire exchange, Bradan remained mute, his brown eyes taking all in. Maebh stood to Set's other side, angling herself between her twin and Donnacha. Finally, the High King asked, "A feral pack of púca defeated my strongest warriors?" With raised brows, he looked at the highguard. "And you're telling me that my rígfénnid single-handedly defeated them all?"

Donnacha's face paled further at the mention of Set's title, but the highguard stepped closer to the High King with a scowl. "What I'm saying is he murdered one of ours."

Ash bristled. "That's not how it happened."

But Set rubbed her arm. "I did kill a highguard."

Bradan nodded thoughtfully, facing Donnacha. He clasped his shoulder as he enquired, "Do you have other witnesses to that event?"

Donnacha jerked a head toward her dismissively. "Just the matriarch."

"Don't you mean monster whore?" Ash returned, glaring at him.

"What did he call you?" Maebh's head jerked toward Donnacha, balling a fist, but Bradan raised a hand, stopping her.

"I trust we have your discretion, Matriarch Breen," the High King said, and a shiver ran down Ash's spine.

"Of course."

The highguard spluttered, "But . . ."

Donnacha gasped. Stooping over, his hands curled around the High King's arm. A sickening sound trickled through the air as in one swift motion, Bradan stepped back, a bloodied dagger in his hand. He glowered at Donnacha as he fell to his knees, clutching his stomach. In another precise motion, Bradan swiped the blade across the fallen man's neck, scarlet blood seeping instantly as his gargled cry filled the space.

They all watched in stunned silence as Donnacha took his last breath. Ash blinked rapidly, eyes trying to process what she'd just witnessed. A heaviness bunched in her stomach as she stared at their High King.

He sighed. "I can't have my highguard turning on my greatest weapon."

Maebh's quiet but lethal voice filled the silence. "My brother is not a weapon to be used."

Bradan's smile was full-lipped, eyes gleaming as he surveyed Set like a grand prize. "Agreed. He is a weapon to be honed."

This was all wrong. Ash's body trembled at the aftershock of what happened. Set looked at her before murmuring, "May we be excused?"

"Not yet," Maebh said, her blue eyes pinned on the king. "We need to talk about Tiernan."

Bradan's shoulders bunched but his face was unreadable. "Now is not the time."

"We don't have any time left!" Maebh stepped face to face with the king, ignoring Donnacha's fallen body by their feet. "I visited the cave. A shadow is destroying the stone guardians. Some kind of fae. If we don't do something, Tiernan could be gone forever."

"I'll get Biróg on it," Bradan said, raising his hand to silence her next retort. "He is my son, Maebh McQuillan, don't think for one moment I want him freed less than you. You have my word."

"Your word is —"

"Thank you, High King," Set cut in, and his sister glared at him.

"I've addressed this with your clans already, but I'd like to remind you all that there are certain situations that can dampen the morale of my people. And as it is our duty to keep spirits high while we defend these parts from Fair Ones, we must keep your little . . . adventure to ourselves, Aisling. For now."

Ash drew back, colliding with Set, who hadn't moved from her back. This new king dealt so heavily in secrets, she wondered how he kept them all straight. "You're asking me to pretend nothing happened? My abduction was a lot more than a little adventure."

"I'm sure you understand. As you're safe now, thanks to our newest rígfénnid, that would be the ideal solution."

"She saved herself," Set said, but Bradan's returning smile was forced, his nod a mere placatory gesture.

Rage built within Ash until her fingers trembled. The ideal solution would have been to refrain from declaring a war with magical beings in a magical realm. But who was she to argue with a king who'd just slaughtered a man sworn to protect him?

"My lips are sealed," Ash managed.

"Good," Bradan said, nodding toward the twins. "You two are excused while Aisling and I confirm an appropriate response to any questions of her absence."

When Set and Maebh hesitated, Ash smiled thinly. "I'll see you later."

Ash crossed her arms, nails biting into her biceps. She wouldn't dare unleash the torrent of furious words battering against her gritted teeth while a dead guard lay by their feet, the murderer smiling at her. The High King clearly prized illusion over truth.

As Maebh and Set reluctantly withdrew, Ash focused on regulating each indrawn breath against her churning disgust. She would need to toe Bradan's line for now. But inwardly she recoiled at it. Raising her eyes to meet his smile, Ash gave one sharp nod to signal her cooperation.

"Before we start, High King," Ash said, angling her head to reveal her punctured neck. "Just know that I'll help with your agenda, but I don't forget, and I'll get revenge."

His sharp grin didn't falter. "I'm counting on it, Aisling."

CHAPTER 32
AISLING

Ash trudged through the empty halls of the castle, the tale Bradan made her recite for over an hour swimming through her brain along with images of Rathcroghan and the otherworldly castle. She'd reported what had happened in Medb's court, and although Bradan had sympathised with her, it was clear that his agenda was not to retaliate against the powerful Tuatha Dé Danann there. She felt little confidence that she would be safe if they chose to abduct her again.

Maebh's revelation echoed in her mind: Tiernan, helpless under the threat of a shadow monster. The High King's promises to help swirled amongst her thoughts. Yet, the icy grip of apprehension coiled tighter around her lungs, plunging her into a cold vortex of worry for Tiernan's fate. A single, stark thought pounded through her mind like a heartbeat: Tiernan had to survive, he just had to. Stepping over the threshold of the castle's imposing entrance, Ash found herself emerging under the vast expanse of the open sky, an evening cloak scattered with twinkling stars.

"Aisling."

She turned slowly, scarcely daring to hope. Conor strode forward with the Breen clan, her cousins on either side of him as they approached from the recesses of a narrow, cobblestoned street that slithered its way through the heart of the castle town. Lanterns flickering in the encroaching twilight cast a ghostly glow on their determined faces, their silhouettes emerging boldly against the backdrop of the ancient stone buildings.

"How?" Ash gasped, pulling him into a hug before holding him at arm's length. "I thought . . . they said you were hurt . . ."

A mere whisper of affirmation escaped her brother's lips, "Yes." The word was accompanied by a smile that struggled to break the chains of his deeply-etched sorrow. His eyes, so like hers in shape, glistened with tears held at bay. His features were newly-angled and haunted from weeks in a dank cell. "But I'm fine now. I want to know how you are?"

A garbled chuckle escaped her lips. Though barely eighteen, her little brother had grown, shedding the last hints of childhood. Now his tall, corded frame was hardened, black curls wind-tossed above eyes too old for his youthful face. Ash drank in the face so like her own, searching for lingering traces of the possession that had warped his mind. Yet gazing into dark eyes, she found only her brother. Ethne's talons had been pulled out. How? She opened her mouth to ask, but her cousins approached.

"Matriarch," Tomás said, pulling her into an embrace that Ciarán joined.

"Your boyfriend left without us," Ciarán said with a glare. "We were coming to get you."

Ash reached backward, searching for Conor's hand. When she found it, she pulled him into their hug, ignoring the sting from her bandaged palms.

"He's not my boyfriend," she mumbled, cocooned by her family.

"Right," Ciarán said with a chuckle. "Whatever you say, Matriarch."

Neither Rathcroghan's dungeons nor Newgrange's collapse had killed her, but her brother's silence just might. With yet another sidewards glance at Conor, Ash bit her lip from asking if he was okay for the millionth time on their journey to the Breen campsite.

Their entire clan trailed behind them, having arrived at the castle steps to greet her return. Not a single one of them looked her in the eyes or asked of her kidnapping. She only hoped Bradan hadn't threatened them to keep that dangerous secret. If she could be plucked right out of Mide, then anyone could. At least she knew her own group, those closest to her, would remain on high alert.

In the distance, highguard were standing watch over their dead comrades so Fair Ones couldn't interfere with them. They would offer them to the sea god, Manannán mac Lir, in the hope he allowed them into the afterlife. She bit her lower lip as Set's defeated face as he kneeled in the carnage he'd created wormed into her mind. Púca had started the battle, but Set had ended it.

Conor caught her eye as she looked toward him again, and they both smiled. Her brother's expression fell crestfallen and he winced, as if he'd remembered he had no right to smile.

"Hey," Ash said, bumping her brother's shoulder. "My tent is over here. It's big enough for the two of us."

"That's because you're matriarch," Conor said and their eyes locked once more, the reason why she was now matriarch a tangible thing lingering in the air. Though only mere feet between them, weeks of silence in that musty cell and years spent apart weighed on them. He scratched the back of his neck, lowering his eyes. "You're supposed to have the tent to yourself."

"I'm allowed to share it with my brother if I want to," Ash said, the false brightness in her tone making her inwardly cringe.

He looked ready to argue again, but she tugged on his stiff sleeve of his homespun tunic, clothes he'd been wearing while in the dungeon castle. They were clean if not threadbare. She swallowed her pain as she made her way to her tent, but not before glancing toward the McQuillan camp. It was a natural reaction at this stage, as frequent and common as blinking, to check to see where Set and Maebh were.

If she was being honest with herself, and she was too tired not to be, it was the tall frame of Set that had her constantly craning her neck in that direction. Spotting him sitting with Malachy, deep in conversation, her shoulders relaxed. She waited for a heartbeat, but he didn't look up, so she retreated inside, limbs screaming from the movement. For now, she needed to ensure Conor was truly all right.

The low ceiling was not an issue for her five foot eight inches, but Conor's taller frame stooped, and his curly midnight hair, the same colour as hers, grazed the fabric, causing friction and making it stand as if he'd rubbed it against a balloon like they used to when they were children. She hid her smile at the memory, signalling for him to take her cot.

"Not happening," he said flatly as he sat on the rug in the centre of the small space, his brows arched in challenge.

They both inspected the area, as if cataloguing what way to argue about who would take the best spot. She had a narrow cot, half-partitioned by a thin curtain, wicker crates stacked high that housed her wooden wash basin, hairbrush and ties, soaps and the one deodorant she'd thought to take from the human world which was painfully depleted. In comparison to Maebh's tent, this one was pathetic. At least Ash's was much cleaner than her friend's, who seemed allergic to picking up her belongings and placing them in any sort of order.

"Conor," Ash began, but a muffled voice called out to request entry. She sighed. "Come in."

Tomás and Ciarán appeared, a cot between them, and on it a rucksack, towels, and an array of weapons.

"Here," Tomás said, signalling for his brother to set the cot down next to the stacked crates. "We'll get you set up in another tent tomorrow, buddy, but we figured Matriarch would want you here for now."

"We kept your belongings safe, Con," Ciarán said, clasping her brother's shoulder.

Conor nodded but didn't meet anyone's eye. "Thanks."

Ash thanked her cousins, and after a beat, they left. She glanced at her brother, who sat on his cot, playing with the straps of his bag. A heaviness weighed on her chest like a lead ball.

"I don't deserve any of this," he said, so low she barely heard him.

"You are the victim, Con," Ash began, moving forward but he shook his head fiercely and when he glared at her, she stopped.

"Mam is the victim. Imogen McQuillan is the victim. I'm the pawn that was too weak to stop her."

She opened her mouth, but no words came out. She wished she were clever enough to say something that would ease his guilt. But what could be said?

"I'm sorry."

For what, she wasn't sure. For it all. For not being there when he'd needed her. For not seeing Ethne for who she truly was. For not getting Conor out of the dungeons sooner than now. She was sorry, but she had a feeling she should be more afraid for what was yet to come.

They stared at each other; the unspoken words charging the air so the tent was unbearably stuffy. He turned away, shoulders stiff and back rigid as he opened his bag and took out clean clothes.

"We should tidy up before we ruin our beds," Conor said delicately, eyeing Ash's travel-worn attire. "And you need fresh bandages."

She glanced down, taking stock. While Nik had worked miracles removing stains from her clothes after Newgrange fell, the hard ride across Tír na nÓg had taken its toll. Dust coated her trousers and shirt, mixed with Croí Dubh's shed hairs. Mud caked her boots and dried sweat ringed her collar. Lifting her hands, she noted dried blood where her palms were and grimaced. She did not want to peel those off, but it was inevitable if she didn't want the area to become infected.

A laugh bubbled up unexpectedly. "I must look a right state."

"I didn't want to say anything," Conor's lips twitched, "but yes, you do."

"Cheeky fecker," Ash laughed and turned to the rustling of her tent once more. "Okay, you two are being extra creepy. Are you just stalking us from outside?"

Ciarán smirked as he and Tomás carried in two more bedrolls, tossing them near her own.

"What are you doing?" she asked warily as they positioned the beds close to the tent opening.

Ciarán rounded on her with theatrically wide eyes. "You're only back from being kidnapped, Ash. Kid. Napped." He sighed, muttering about stupid questions.

Tomás chuckled as he sat cross-legged on his bedroll. "We're on guard duty whether you like it or not, cousin. No arguments."

"Oh, and Con is right," Ciarán said, plonking onto his bed. "We could smell you from across the town, Matriarch."

"I'm too tired."

"Me too," Conor sighed, but before either Ciarán or Tomás said anything, he added with a wrinkled nose, "but you do kind of smell, Ash."

Chucking a wet sponge at her cousins, they scooted out of her room, their rumbling chuckles making it impossible to hold a scowl. Ciarán's hands reappeared moments later with two bowls of steaming water and a howl of laughter before he disappeared once more.

In the small tent there wasn't enough room for privacy so she turned her back to her brother and cleaned up as best she could with visions of having a real bath as much a fantasy as the realm they stood in. She took her time with her bandages, her palms not as bad as she thought they would be. Whatever ointment Nik had used seemed to have healed her hands from her mountain hike.

A pained grunt had her turn as she was drying off.

"Con, what happened?"

Tomás and Ciarán entered the tent, apprehension etched on both their faces as Conor glanced down at his bare chest as if surprised it was covered in thick bandages no longer white but stained with dried blood. When he didn't answer, she stood closer, leaning forward to inspect him, stomach twisting. This was how he'd harmed himself.

"She'd tattooed my chest. I had to get her out."

None of them spoke; each cousin taking stock of what Conor was saying in few words. He'd somehow cut Ethne's possession out of himself. Ash's breath caught as she blinked back tears. What could be said for that?

Eventually, the spell was broken, and they moved into the centre of the tent, embracing in a tight hug once more. Enveloped by her family, she felt safe. For now.

There'd been a part of her that feared what the night might bring when she was alone. She was sure that her kidnapping was not random. They'd targeted her because they were curious about her blood. Perhaps Queen Medb would be content with the answer she'd received, but the Fair Ones would never settle after she'd escaped them. Their pride was far too important. It wasn't a matter of if they would return to punish her. Only when.

CHAPTER 33
SETANTA

Rolling his shoulders, Set coughed out a painful breath. Everything hurt. But he deserved this pain. A Fianna no longer lived because of him. He was a monster against his kind. The thick fabric of his tent did little to keep out the draft that had infiltrated the air. Frost and gusts of frigid air had assaulted them on their return to camp. Or perhaps he was too bone tired to be anything other than cold?

The tent flap rustled but he paid it no heed until a light touch roused him.

"I'm going to clean you up now." Maebh spoke calmly, as if he were a skittish animal.

He drifted in a fog of rage and regret, sights and sensations assaulting him without mercy as she tended him, wiping gore from his flesh with practised care.

There was no hope to find in this sea of red consuming his every thought.

Barely tracking her movements, she knelt before him with a hot cloth and, with a gentleness he didn't deserve, wiped his face. "It's not your fault," she murmured, but didn't continue when he dragged his eyes to meet hers.

Yet Maebh worked on. As bloody waters swirled and staining rags piled, her tending gradually anchored him once more to shore. Piece by piece his humanity was salvaged, brought forth clean yet forever marked by what dwelt within.

At last, her work was done, but still Maebh lingered, meeting his eyes steadily.

He clenched and unclenched his jaw. They'd lost Fianna. Considering the destruction caused, it was a wonder how so many of them had survived, only to be destroyed by púca seeking revenge. And him.

Set knew, as did the High King. Ethne had destroyed Newgrange. But when Ash had been taken, every trail of thought he had focused on nothing more than her survival. Even as they'd travelled home, he would not let his mind wander through his memories, staying alert and focused every second of the trip back. But now, everything from Winter Solstice came crashing back.

"I'll be right back, and we can have that awful nettle tea," Maebh said before disappearing through the canvas door.

He didn't look up, keeping his attention on his clasped hands. Conor had warned them something would happen, and fault lay on them for not figuring it out; and on Bradan who had refused to accept the threat Ethne had posed.

Set had given in to the fear and anger that begged him to ríastrad, but Ash had helped him come back. She'd saved him. Just by being herself.

She was not only soft and caring, but fierce under pressure, a true matriarch. And she somehow wanted him. She deserved more than he could offer, which was only trouble. He wanted to be selfish, to allow himself to get lost in her, but he couldn't put her in that danger. Not when his ríastrad was getting worse. Ash wasn't always going to be there to calm him. He'd almost harmed her before, and he couldn't live with the pain of hurting her with his monster form. His riastrád was silent now. Satiated.

The tent's confines closed in on Set, as if the flimsy fabric walls could suffocate him. The air thickened, his breaths short, an unease gnawing at his insides.

With a sudden swift movement, he swatted the entrance and clambered out, desperate to escape the constriction. Once outside, he sucked in the cold, sharp air like a drowning man gasping for survival. The pristine vastness of the outdoors provided an immediate balm, the phantom squeeze around his lungs easing off.

Set walked in the brisk air in only his boxers to the firepit where a large iron pot of boiling water hung. The clan was used to his body by now, and nobody commented as tired faces merely glanced his way and then back to their own tasks. A job could not be left half done right now, and it was dangerous to be so tired. If Bradan called a challenge, raising his clan's flag, every one of them would have to report to defend their territory or claim another. And Set wouldn't put it past their king to do so, even right after the fall of Newgrange and the battle at the gate. If anything, it might fuel him. With a start, Set realised he no longer had a clear role in the Cath. As rígfénnid, he may be expected to sit it out. Looking across the campsite, he straightened. That wasn't an option.

Nodding at a few of the warriors in greeting, he picked clean clothes from the clothesline they'd erected between two tents. They were stiff and still damp as he put them on, but they were better than nothing.

As he walked on, someone clapped his back as others called out in encouragement. He was proud of his clan for how they'd agreed to keep his rescue of Ash a secret and how they'd followed his orders at Newgrange. If only Maebh had been with them, she could have bonded with them over that awful circumstance. She could have been the one receiving this praise.

Scooping up some water into a breakfast bowl, he ignored Lorna who scolded him about taking their drinking water for preening. He kissed her cheek, but she shooed him away, promising breakfast would be ready soon. His aunt was so like his mother, it hurt to look at her at times. She even treated Maebh differently to Set. His twin didn't help matters by her attitude.

Sitting on a log, he splashed the scalding water on his face and neck; the contrast of heat eliciting shivers in the cold air. Scrunching his toes, he kicked at the hard, white-frosted grass before looking up to the cloudy sky and donning his socks and boots. Spring was no longer the only season in Tír na nÓg.

"Glad you made it back in one piece," Malachy said in greeting, offering a tankard to Set. When Set raised his brows, the former second in command shrugged. "After these days, it's never too early for some ale."

Set nodded his thanks, bringing the cool metal of the tankard to his lips. The ale flowed smooth and reassuring down his throat, the liquid's soothing warmth acting as a serene balm to his frayed nerves.

"You know," Malachy said, taking a long drink of his ale before continuing, "I'll be here for Maebh. If she needs advice."

Set stared at his clansman, but Malachy only continued looking at the fire as it sparked and danced within the iron crate.

"Did High King Bradan speak to you?" Set asked, a heaviness resting on his shoulders.

"You mean aside from keeping Aisling's kidnapping a secret? Yeah. Having a McQuillan as a rígfénnid is the greatest honour. We haven't had that title in hundreds of years."

Set focused on the flames as he took a sip of ale. "I had no choice."

"You're needed where you can make changes," Malachy answered. "The McQuillan clan is strong, but we need more than strength for what is to come."

"What is that?"

"Something greater than any of us are ready for," Malachy said. "Don't you notice the change in weather? Whatever happened in Newgrange triggered this realm into something new."

Lorna moved to join them at the fire, a tankard of her own settled comfortably in her hand as she placed a plate of fried meat and bread onto Set's lap. "I trust you heard what happened with your sister? She was nowhere to be found after Newgrange fell. And when she showed up, not a scratch on her."

"I'm too tired to get into this right now, Lorna," Set groaned as he eyed the plate. His stomach growled as he chewed on a rasher. "We can deal with Maebh tomorrow."

"Maybe the rest of us are tired of picking up her slack."

He looked up to see his sister standing behind the woman, jaw slightly open, still holding the bucket she'd brought to clean him.

"Mae," he began, but she ignored him and marched toward her tent.

"Another reason why you're not fit to lead us, Maebh McQuillan," Lorna called, and everyone stopped what they'd been doing to listen.

Maebh's shoulders bunched, but she didn't turn. Instead, she continued to her tent, disappearing through it and shutting the flap tight.

"Lorna," Set began in reprimand.

A familiar cry sounded and Set jerked his head toward Orla and Eilish's tent. In a flash, he was running, ignoring the fatigue shooting up his feet as he raced over uneven ground. Before he made it, Eilish fell through the canvas door followed by Orla, a carver's knife raised high in the air.

CHAPTER 34
AISLING

Ash tried to see over the numerous bobbing heads but couldn't as she heard Set calling out to Orla. As quickly as they'd ran, the Fianna in front stopped, but she didn't. Gripping Conor's arm and pulling him behind her, she barged through.

"Orla, put it down," Set boomed.

The last people obscuring her view finally moved and she gasped. Orla stood at the entrance to a tent, her sister by her feet. Eilish grasped Orla's legs, pleading, as Orla held a knife against her bound hand. Set stood feet away, his profile a mask of calm as he tried to reason with the distraught woman.

"I can't take it anymore," she said flatly as she sawed at the straps of her harness.

Ash gripped Conor's arm tight in horror as she realised what Orla had planned to do. Set lurched forward, but Orla jerked back, kicking her sister in front of Set as a barrier.

"Wait!" Conor called, pulling away from Ash and stepping beside Set.

Orla hesitated, her face snapping to Conor's. When he took a step closer, she angled the blade toward him, and Ash raced to get in front.

"Stop, Ash," Conor begged without turning, one hand signalling for her to remain beside Set, and the other outstretched toward Orla, placating. "I know how it feels."

Orla's deadened eyes narrowed; the first glimpse of emotion Ash had seen in them since Ethne cursed her hand.

Set's touch was a welcome surprise as he tugged on her fingers, encircling them within his strong grasp. He murmured close to her ear, his warm breath tickling her lobe. "Let him try."

Ash frowned, biting her lip. She remained fixated on Conor's back as he inched closer to Orla and her raised carver's knife.

Orla leaned toward him, eyes glazing as she mumbled. "I can see her aura on you. Did she curse you too?"

"Mine has faded, right?" Conor asked, and when Orla lowered the knife a fraction, he lifted his shirt, showing the bandage. "I got her out of my head. I can help you."

Set sucked in a sharp breath, and Ash's attention whipped to him in question, but his eyes were trained on Conor, his brows furrowed. The entire camp was quiet as Orla stared at Conor, mistrust and fear emanating from her in waves of hot ash.

The air around Orla was thick and suffocating, tinged with the sharp, invasive scent of ammonia. It seeped into Ash's nostrils, overwhelming her senses despite her control over this gift and the numerous surrounding emotions emanating from everyone. Orla's emotions were a violent current, pulling them both into a sea of despair and disorder.

Set's other hand encircled the back of Ash's waist when she attempted to step forward. "Your brother has this," he breathed.

Still, she couldn't help her nervous glances among the crowd, searching for Maebh. She was the matriarch here. If anyone could stop this, it would be her. But Maebh was nowhere to be found. Orla's glances flickered wildly among the crowd, her eyes darting back and forth, searching, too, for something or someone. Perhaps Ethne herself, the cause of this destruction.

Before Ash could pull away again, desperate to keep Conor away from the chaos, the air around Orla shifted, the overwhelming scent of ammonia slowly ebbing. It was a measured change; subtle, like a turning tide.

Ash studied Orla as a vague floral scent floated towards them, not fully bloomed but the unmistakable freshness of buds hoping to burst despite the threatening winter frost.

The carver's knife dropped to the ground. "Okay."

Fianna murmured, voices carrying back to the crowds gathered too far away to overhear. Conor turned but looked at Set as he spoke. "I need an iron blade, seven days hot from a forging anvil."

"Right," Set said, turning, but Conor shook his head.

"It has to be an anvil owned by a blacksmith who is the seventh son of a seventh son."

Ash looked at her brother in askance. "How do you know—"

"I know the forge you need, Orla," Set said, squeezing Ash's waist before letting go and closing the distance to the trembling woman. Ash's jaw ached as she ground her teeth. As if speaking to a skittish doe, he said, "I can take you."

Orla looked down at his hand, scrutinising it as if it were a three-headed ellén trechend. Eilish stood beside her sister, silent, with tear streaks marring her wan face. Orla nodded, accepting Set's hand with her uncursed arm. Ash's stomach dipped as she followed close behind, Set's arm going around Orla's shoulders, the crowds parting for them. Ash, Eilish and Conor followed his lumbering frame toward the centre of Tara Court and beyond to the blacksmith district.

A new set of banners were being hung by the highguard. They stood, Ash holding her breath as she waited for the next Cath contenders to be announced. Should their colours fly free, Orla's hand would have to wait.

They stood as one, held in a vigil as the guard pulled the cover revealing the O'Connors and O'Reillys. Ash's shoulders fell in relief. She was bone tired, and she knew Set must have been too.

She'd managed a few hours of fitful sleep, and she wasn't even sure if he'd slept since Newgrange fell.

The area was quiet, the aftermath of Winter Solstice fresh on everyone's minds. A clashing of steel against iron could be heard in the distance and Set pointed toward one of the forges. Heat greeted them, along with the rhythmic sound of metal casting into something new.

"She's through here," Set said, Orla cradled against his chest as he turned away from the guard.

Orla's eyes were dead once more, as if she'd burrowed deep within herself, not believing Conor's promise of help would come true.

"She?" Conor asked, looking concerned. "I'm not sure if the seventh daughter of—"

"The seventh daughter of a seventh son is more capable of healing than you'd understand, Conor Breen," a feminine voice sounded in the darkened forge. "My iron worked for you, did it not?"

Conor's face flushed, but he seemed resolved as he spoke. "I wasn't aware it was you who'd provided the tools."

"What tools?" Ash demanded, not hiding her impatience. "What did you do?"

"My mind wasn't fully free from Ethne's curse," Conor replied, his eyes glazing over, a shadow crossing his face. "In the tower. I had fought enough to break free from her controlling me fully, but she was still there. Seeing through my eyes. That's why I refused your requests to visit me."

Ash bit the inside of her cheek. She'd never understood why he wouldn't see her, and it had been to protect her from Ethne.

Conor continued. "She'd branded me with a tattoo, one matching the tattoo she'd asked me to mark her with. But mine was made of ink, while hers was made of dark magic. Orla's hand is branded, too, right?"

"Come, let's see." The blacksmith signalled for Set to bring Orla inside.

Guided by Set's imposing figure, they fell into line behind him, winding their way past scattered benches and racks filled with weapons and armour. A wave of intense heat washed over Ash the further they entered. The heat of the stone-encased fire burned bright and hot at the far wall, casting light on the overflowing benches. Ash squinted, shielding her eyes until they became adjusted to the shimmering flames. Set guided Orla onto the bench the blacksmith offered, who then got to work on unclasping the many buckles encasing Orla's hand.

"Be ready," she told Set.

"Grainne, be careful," Set cautioned as he loomed over Orla, who remained impassive to everyone around her.

"How else will we see if it's the same as Conor's?" she tsked before opening the ball- shaped harness.

As soon as Orla's hand was visible, it sprang to life, rising with claw-like nails toward her face. She didn't flinch as they neared but Set slammed her wrist down on the wooden bench. Ash watched, horrified, as Orla's hand twisted at an unnatural angle, scratching the wood as if it were soft cheese, before twisting fully to attack Set's wrist.

He cursed but did not let go.

"Open her hand so we can see her palm," Grainne instructed, raising her goggles higher and leaning close.

After several attempts, he'd managed, and they all leaned forward. A red tattoo marred Orla's palm in the shape of sensuous lips. It was raised, and unlike any tattoo Ash had seen. As if real lips had been sewn to her hand.

"It's the same marking," Conor spoke quietly, as if fearing the hand would conjure the druid.

It quivered at his voice, and he recoiled away from it. The lips smiled widely before opening to reveal sharp canines and a lone ice-grey eye at its centre. Ash's stomach lurched and she was sure if anything other than water and a few bites of hardened loaf had been consumed, she would have vomited. Was a part of Ethne looking up at them now?

"The same treatment should work," Grainne declared, springing to action and moving to her furnace.

The blacksmith's gloved hands roved over the different tools, until she grabbed a poker that looked so hot it glowed more luminously than any other.

"This sword has been heated by the forge for seven days and seven nights," she explained, before gesturing for them to step away. In a wide arc, she rotated the instrument over her head and intoned: "As the sun rises in the east and sets in the west, so this blade will do my bidding. Cast of iron and salt, forged by the seventh daughter to the seventh son, remove this curse from skin and mind, and straighten this warrior's path."

In a swiftness of feminine grace, Grainne pivoted, plunging the red-tipped blade into Orla's hand. The smell of burning flesh filled the room, along with Orla's wails. It wasn't just Orla who cried out, but an animalistic sound filled the space, as if the tattooed mouth had its own voice. Steam rose from her palm, along with a red mist of blood and a sand-like substance. Ash turned to her brother, imagining the same thing happening to him. Her stomach clutched as she sucked in her lower lip.

After several long minutes, Grainne raised the blade. "It is done."

Orla's eyes cleared, and she blinked.

Eilish stepped forward, her hand shaking as she placed it gingerly on her sister's shoulder. Her voice was barely above a whisper, but it was so laden with tentative hope, Ash had to look away. "Are you . . . Orla, are you cured?"

"I think so." Orla's voice was hoarse, as if she hadn't used it in months.

Her eyes filled with tears as she thanked the blacksmith and stood, moving in front of Conor. They looked at one another, as if in silent conversation. He took her uninjured hand and grasped it, nodding at whatever they'd shared. Ash's gaze strayed to Set. She'd expected him to be watching Orla, but instead, his eyes were pinned on her.

Conor asked Grainne for a clean bandage and salve. As they huddled around Orla, Ash smiled up at Set.

"What?" she asked, fixing a wayward strand of hair behind her ear.

"I just love seeing you happy," he said, before thanking Grainne who simply shrugged as if this was just a routine day.

Set motioned for Ash to exit the hot forge, but she hesitated.

"Go, Ash," Conor called, not looking up from his ministrations of bandaging Orla's hand. "I'll see you back at camp later."

Looking at her brother again, Ash nodded and followed Set outside to the cool, crisp air that nipped at her exposed skin like tiny blades. The contrast of heat against the chilly morning caused her to shiver, and she hugged her coat tightly around her as they wandered aimlessly through the busy marketplace.

Stopping at a stall laden with freshly baked scones the size of her fist, Ash breathed in their mouthwatering aroma of warm butter, dotted with raisins. Set withdrew the leather tie binding his unruly locks, extending the cord to the merchant. The vendor's eyes narrowed, scrutinising the offered item.

At last, the merchant's weathered face crinkled kindly. "That'll do nicely for my missus' hair. It's quite like yours, boy."

Ash bit her lip as Set's brows rose, but he thanked the man as he handed over the wax parchment containing one scone. Tearing it in half, he offered the larger piece to Ash. "I don't have anything to barter for jam or cream."

"Thank you," Ash chuckled before biting into its delicate crust. The warm buttery richness burst with citrus sweetness, and she groaned. "It doesn't need it."

Set barked a laugh. "Remind me to always bring you scones in the morning if this is how you sound."

Ash smiled around a mouthful. "If you bring me scones every morning, I may just keep you."

Navigating the lively marketplace, Ash and Set strolled amidst bustling stalls selling everything from fresh flowers and food to intricate handicrafts. The voices of vendors haggling and customers bargaining hummed in the background, giving her a twang of homesickness for when she'd stroll through Dublin city on her way to university. Ash's attention was drawn abruptly when Set nudged her.

"Penny for your thoughts?"

"I was just thinking about the Cath, actually." She met his eyes before straying to the surrounding Fianna world, her voice barely audible above the chorus of the marketplace. "I know we'll be called again soon, and I know that's why we're all here. But I don't know if I want to win or lose. I'm not even sure I care any more."

"I think that's one of the downfalls of being a matriarch, Ash. It doesn't really matter if you personally care or not." His words scathed despite his soft delivery; a cruel truth that she had been denying for some time. "What matters to your clan, matters to you. One team, one goal, whether you chose it or not."

"As matriarch, should I not have a choice? Conor's safe, and when the rest of us are safe, we quit. Don't you want to go home while we still have a home to go to? I have a bad feeling about Ireland. I need to see if Mary and Dom are alive. Truly, I think if Tiernan were free, I'd petition to leave. I don't want to be caught in Bradan's war."

Her words hung heavy in the air, a confession she never thought she'd voice. A gnawing pain spiralled within her, silently echoing the bitterness of her words.

Set reached for Ash's hand. "I'm stuck here now. With my new position, I guess this is home. Forever. So, if it's only Tiernan and his safety keeping you here, then I will take that burden from your shoulders."

Her breath hitched in her throat, icy tendrils curling relentlessly around her spine, sending chilling shivers cascading through her body. The guilt of his statement crept up on her like a shadow in the dying light, quiet and unassuming, yet overwhelmingly present and all-consuming. She hadn't stopped long enough to consider the price Set had paid to follow her to Rathcroghan. He'd given his whole self, his whole future just for permission to save her. Bradan really was the worst of the worst.

Venturing away from the heart of the castle town, they found themselves at the entrance to a quiet alleyway. The lively chatter of the market dwindled into a mere echo, giving way to the rhythmic clatter of a blacksmith's hammer and the distant buzz of artisans engrossed in their crafts. The quieter section was tucked neatly in the labyrinth of narrow lanes.

"Hey," Ash said, waiting for Set to look at her. "I never truly thanked for what you did. I wouldn't want to leave you and Maebh in this place if it meant I'd never see you again. Wanting to go home is only a piece of what I desire."

He flashed a heart-wrenching smile. "I'm listening."

Ash rolled her eyes, swatting his chest. "Cake. Of course. I really want cake. And these little biscuits that Mary used to make for the coffee shop."

"Cake and biscuits, is it? I'll see what I can do." Set smiled as he pulled her deeper into the narrow alley, his calloused hand finding hers.

In stolen moments like these, all uncertainty fell away, leaving only the simple truth: she cared for this man, more than reason dared admit.

Stopping within an alley's sheltered alcove, Set turned to face her, thumb tracing her cheek's curve. His burning eyes flickered between her lips, and her stomach dipped.

His hand found her waist and when he pulled her in, her breath caught. In his arms, all hesitation fled. There was only longing's sweet ache and his silken lips waiting, awakening desires too long suppressed. She was ready at last to surrender fully to the tide pulling her under. His lips grazed her neck first, planting light kisses that made her stomach tighten.

"Are you sure," he breathed, his lips more velvety than she'd ever fantasised about, and as her cheeks flushed, she'd never admit to just how often he featured in her fantasies, "that it's only sweet treats you desire?"

"Hmmm." She bit her lip as her back found the hard rough surface of a wall, arching as he angled her head by tugging on her hair gently.

She felt him smile against her collarbone as his hands inched around her back, lowering to cup her ass before hoisting her up so she could wrap her legs around his waist. They stared at one another, breathing heavily, the delicious anticipatory moment before their lips would meet for their first kiss.

Yet just as he leaned in, Set jerked away with a grimace, skin flushing an angry vermilion as muscles swelled unnaturally beneath tightening flesh.

"Set, it's all right. Stay with me," Ash urged, tugging on his collar, but he staggered back, releasing his hold on her so she fell clumsily, the wall catching her fall.

"Run . . . get away . . . while you . . . can," he gritted out between sharpening teeth, fighting a losing war as his ríastrad took hold.

With one last anguished look, Set let loose an inhuman howl and then sifted. The alley stood deserted, the echo of Set's howl lingering as he fled from his monster. From her.

CHAPTER 35
SETANTA

With impaired vision, Set ran. He'd sifted as far away from Ash as he could, finding himself at the River Boyne before his ríastrad took control. His monster growled in his ear, punching its clawed fists from inside.

We were just getting started.

He'd been so careful around her and something within him thought she was the answer. She was the soft rustling of leaves in a tranquil forest, the hushed whispers of a serene river flowing over smooth stones. She was the stillness of a starlit night. She was his calm. But she was not the answer. She'd just become another problem.

The sense of relief the monster promised at letting go filled him up. But it would do no good. He'd already killed. And the way he'd just felt around Ash. The way she'd looked at him. He should have never trusted himself. With people, but least of all with her. The most precious thing in the world was so fragile compared to a monster salivating for destruction.

He wished with every fibre that he could escape to somewhere safe. A place where he couldn't harm anyone. He clutched his head as a growl emanated from the back of his throat. He closed his eyes, his body turning into a furnace as he folded in on himself. He couldn't breathe as the weight of a thousand oceans pressed in on him. He was fire and ice at the same time; near death and newly born. He felt a million different deaths and even more forms of ecstasy as his monster forced him to open his lungs.

"Hello, Setanta."

Whipping his head toward that sultry voice, the strange lilt he now knew belonged to Ethne. His vision flooded with a pulsating red as he watched the woman who'd murdered his mother materialise in front of him.

"Shall I fetch another fresh-born to stop your ríastrad?"

"No!" Set roared, realising with those words that the last time she placed a newborn in his hands it was not an illusion like he'd hoped. Had she stolen a human child to aid him that night? Had she returned the baby to her parents? Was he the cause of a changeling?

"Breathe, my boy."

An impenetrable darkness shrouded his vision. With a tenderness he hadn't expected from a female that caused so much destruction, she clasped the sides of his face with both hands. He jerked back, but she held firm, proving strength hidden underneath her small frame. Everything about her was a lie.

"Breathe."

As she counted, he had no choice but to follow her guidance, inhaling and exhaling in deep whooshes. The monster within stilled and he opened his eyes.

"I could kill you," he growled as he glared at her.

Alabaster skin was framed by moonlit tresses. She wore a dark robe over her grey dress with multicoloured tattoos covering her from her neck down to all other exposed skin. She smiled. Her grin too wide, displaying pointed canines he'd never noticed before. She glowed as if stealing rays from the sun above. It was only then he noticed they were in the barrenlands where he'd lain under the stars with Ash. The ground was gouged with crevices, its surface a pale powdery substance.

"You could," she purred, as she stepped back. "But you won't."

Silence weighed in the crisp air between them as they surveyed one another.

"Why are you here?" Set had a million questions to ask, and if he didn't start somewhere, she'd disappear with all of them.

"You needed me."

Locking his hands into tight balls, he debated punching her; instead, he forced them behind his back.

"You keep fighting a monster that isn't there, Setanta."

"What do you mean?"

"When are you going to start asking the right questions?"

"Which ones will you answer, witch? Why did you murder my mother? Why did you use Conor? Why are you obsessed with my sister and Ash?"

"None of those are the right ones, but I'll answer you one. Do you want to decide which one?"

His chest was a heaving mass of rage as he tried to control his temper. It wasn't working.

"I have known you, Maebh, Aisling and Tiernan since you were babes in your mothers' bellies."

Ethne sifted out of his reach when he lunged for her.

His control was slipping once more and perhaps he needed his ríastrad to take over and rid the world of this menace. He wasn't strong enough to do it. His monster was.

"Four came into this world, and because of my deeds, four will destroy it." She stepped closer, seemingly oblivious to the breaking tether he had to his humanity. "You are more than your kin."

Set glared at her. "Tiernan is involved in whatever this is too?"

"So much wasted time in the library, Setanta." she tsked. "You need him back. And I can help make that happen."

"How?"

Her answer was in the form of an insufferable smile before she sifted to gods knew where, taking all her damned answers with her.

CHAPTER 36

MAEBH

Maebh strode into the McQuillan camp, kicking loose stones. She glanced over to Ash's tent, but it was shut. Perhaps she'd forgotten about their training session this morning? Maybe she'd slept in? Maybe she was in her brother's tent?

As her clan's voices filtered to her, those gathered around the firepit for breakfast listened to Lorna, who was unfurling the territory map with relish.

"Lorna," Maebh said coldly. Her aunt glanced up with a scowl. "Who is stationed in our territories today?"

"So, you care about the Cath?" Lorna sneered. "Running off to gods knows where instead of training with your clan."

Maebh opened her mouth to retort, but Lorna interrupted. "Where's Setanta?"

Lorna looked behind her as if her twin would magically materialise and she'd no longer have to deal with Maebh.

Clearing her throat, Maebh shrugged. "Off playing at being rígfénnid, no doubt," she said. "Strutting around the castle with the other important people."

Before Lorna could respond, Malachy approached, handing Maebh a dried meat skewer. "Here, Matriarch. You'll need your strength for today's duty."

"She won't be going anywhere," Lorna sniffed.

Maebh smiled at her aunt, keeping her eyes on her as she bit an oversized mouthful and chewed.

A horn blast cut through the town. Paul jogged into camp, brown eyes dancing. "We've been assigned Cath duty today."

He glanced between Maebh, Malachy and Lorna, his eyes never landing fully on anyone.

Maebh decided to put the poor bastard out of his misery. Raising her voice, she stood on a bench. "As matriarch, I will lead us today. Malachy, which territory offers the greatest advantage?"

Malachy considered briefly, taking the map from Lorna's clenched hands. "We have a few acres within the forest, but no clans have ventured to the borders of Mide."

Jumping from the log, Maebh pointed to the map. "The Uisneach is important to the Fianna and would secure a large portion of the kingdom if claimed."

"But it's so far away," Lorna complained. "It would take too long to get there. And then how will we keep it?"

"Don't worry your pretty little head about the big stuff, Auntie. That's the beauty of having a large clan," Maebh said with a savage smile. "We'll barter for horses today. While smaller groups continue to claim territories within the woodland so as not to attract attention to the other clans, a group of us will go to Uisneach. It will mean some of us will have to camp there and then take shifts."

Lorna opened her mouth to speak, but Malachy put his hand on her arm. He nodded, a small smile on his lips. "I like it, Matriarch. We need to take risks when our banner is called. Otherwise, the other clans will gain an advantage."

Maebh bit back her smile. "Then, Uisneach it is. Prepare the clan. Take provisions for three people to camp out. We leave within the hour."

She turned on her heel, eager to be gone from Lorna's sneers. Today, she would prove herself.

"It's strange," Malachy said as they slowed their horses.

Maebh turned to him with raised brows. "What is?"

"That you assigned Lorna to the groups closer to Tara Court."

Sniggering came from the group behind her.

"She has bad hips. Don't you hear them creak with every step?" Maebh grinned before turning to her clan with wide eyes. "I was only thinking of her."

"You were thinking of the headache she'd give," Caoimhe called to which Paul barked a laugh.

"On behalf of the group here, Matriarch," Paul added, "Thank you for thinking about your aunt's poor hip trouble."

A rush of warmth spread through Maebh's chest as they continued through the woodland. The only sound was her clan's chatter.

"We're here," Malachy murmured.

All conversation ceased as her warriors sank into a familiar rhythm, surveying the area. Maebh dismounted and scanned the hilltop of Uisneach, eyes narrowed. The others spread out behind her, watchful.

She led them up the steep hill, hiking through sparse grass and rocks toward Uisneach's summit. As they climbed, she noticed barren patches amid the greenery.

"What do you make of those?" she asked Malachy who kicked at a pocket of infertile soil.

"Bonfire marks?" he suggested but she shook her head.

"Nah. Look around. Too many for that."

Bare circles widened across the hillside in looping patterns too deliberate to be natural.

"They're hooves. Look." She pointed, drawing the others' attention.

They muttered uneasily at the strange tracks circling the hilltop, plants having withered and died within the bounds of each distinct print.

"What creature could leave such a sign?" Caoimhe whispered.

As if in answer, a glacial breeze swept over them as they crested the hill. Before them lay the summit clearing, edges marked by more phantom hoofprints devoid of any growth. But at its centre stood an even stranger circle completely bare, as if nothing had ever taken root there at all.

Paul swallowed thickly. "Something haunts this place."

A mournful howl split the air, raising the hairs on Maebh's neck. She scanned the treeline as multiple answering cries responded in the distance, sounds devoid of any natural animal.

"Weapons out," she ordered, unsheathing her sword and dagger as another ghostly chorus made her flinch. "Stay sharp. Whatever spirit claims this hill, it's not alone."

They fanned out carefully, wary of the woods' encroaching shadows. Maebh approached the central barren ring, kneeling to touch blighted soil. Her fingers came away stained grey as ash. Standing once more, she scanned the land. A chill ran down her spine as her skin prickled with the acute sense that they were not the only ones stalking this land. Turning slowly to survey her clan, a wash of panic flooded her. Something was watching them, too.

A flicker of movement from the crest of a nearby hill drew her attention. The shadows within the impenetrable forest danced menacingly, making the haunting howls seem chillingly closer, infiltrating deeper into the wooden territory.

"Over there," Malachy said, signalling to five hulking figures emerging at the treeline.

Dark spectral hounds as large as ponies, with muscular bodies, riveting and formidable like iron shields, stalked forward. Flames licked where their eyes should be, burning with a malice that sent terror coursing through Maebh's veins.

"What are they?" Paul asked, a sword and axe in each hand.

"They look like . . ." Maebh frowned, "ghoul-hounds."

Malachy snorted despite the monsters stalking toward them. Their coats shed no light, but seemed to drink in what little illumination touched them. Foam flew from jowls filled with too many teeth. Maebh had no time for fear, but hatred settled in her soul for Bradan's dangerous decisions. He'd tasked the clans recklessly and if this were what they would face over and over, plenty would die for his glory, and though she begrudged her clan for their treatment of her, they were still worth more than that.

The largest let out a roar that shook the clearing. It leapt forward with preternatural strength and speed. Maebh swung her blade instinctively, cursing when it sliced through empty air. The hound dissipated into wisps of shadow, reappearing behind her. She kicked off the ground just as its jaws clamped shut where her leg had been.

The others swung at the advancing beasts, but their steel proved equally ineffectual. With chilling howls, the hounds herded them back from the edge of the forest and up the summit once more. Maebh retreated with them, eyes darting for any means to drive off the ghoul-hounds when a dreadful cry pierced the skies. She knew that sound. It was the sound of nightmares.

"The Dullahan," Caoimhe quivered.

Maebh cursed before gripping the woman's arm. "You fucking idiot!"

"What?" Caoimhe bridled, glaring at her.

But it was Malalchy who answered. "You just acknowledged it by name."

Caoimhe's face grew deathly pale as Maebh rolled her eyes and said, "Yeah, so now we can't escape it."

The hounds stopped, sitting on phantom haunches. Their master had arrived.

A towering black steed emerged at the far treeline, headless rider slumped over its back, clothing tattered and eyes aflame. Even from this distance, Maebh saw the neatly- sliced neck above its Adam's apple, before tracking down to the face grinning mockingly as it nestled in the rider's hand.

The Dullahan slowed its approach, skeletal fingers clawing at the reins. Its head swivelled unnaturally, sightless eyes scanning the treeline until locking onto Maebh with an unearthly focus. She couldn't look away. Fear battered against her skull, but her eyes were magnetised to its empty stare.

"Maebh Imogen McQuillan," it rasped, and the arcane power in her full name sent a chill down her spine.

"Shit," Malachy gasped, eyes wide on her. "Don't respond!"

But it was too late. Her name on its lips had summoned her will against her own, and she found herself taking a step forward despite her struggles. When her small clan moved to stop her, the ghoul-hounds attacked with unearthly swiftness. They barrelled into the warriors with the force of infernal storms.

Malachy swung wildly as two hounds descended upon him, steel glancing uselessly off their smoky hides. They bowled him over, slashing with mouths agape as he struggled to wrestle them away. Maebh fought against her mystical binding, forced to listen to her clan's plight helplessly. With an internal roar, she redoubled her efforts, summoning every ounce of will to free herself.

But it was not enough.

The Dullahan tilted its head with a grating chuckle. "Come to me, girl. Your time is nigh."

Its stallion pawed the earth restlessly with every step she took, feet dragging her closer against her resistance. Sweat beaded her brow as she grasped for any means to break its hold.

A flash of neon green filled Maebh's peripheral vision and she watched as the púca appeared out of nowhere. Sage tossed rowan berries before her like throwing stars, and the ghoul-hounds recoiled with anguished howls as blooms exploded across their smoky hides. She chanted and vines writhed, lashing out to ensnare the beasts in thorns brimming with protective light.

As Sage tossed the berries with uncanny precision, their fragrance intensified, spreading through the clearing in aromatic waves. It was no mere perfume, but a fortifying magic. Each burst berry released a fog of scent that seemed almost visible.

Maebh inhaled deeply, drawing comfort and renewal from the rowan magic. Sage reached the others, smearing the berries on each blade before standing in front of Maebh.

She could hear the clash of steel on flesh, the howls of pain from the beasts, but still, Maebh could not move to look anywhere but the Dullahan. His furious stare was death itself, but he did not approach.

The faerie smeared the red juice on Maebh's cheeks, forcing her frozen mouth open to shove some in. Sage closed her small hand over her mouth until she swallowed. Maebh felt the grip on her soul release, and she collapsed to hands and knees with a gasp.

For a moment, everything stilled. Then, with a throaty howl, the Dullahan reared its steed and fled back into the forest, shadows swallowing its retreating form.

As the others stood and collected themselves, Maebh tracked Sage who remained standing in front of her. She had the same red hair, same ridiculous outfit, but there was something different about her. With an olive skin tone, her features were somehow plain when you took them in individually: brown eyes, pink lips; but when you stood back, you could see a perfect canvas.

"You're staring," Sage's voice was the same, a trill.

"You're . . . different," Maebh shrugged before taking the púca's offered hand and standing.

"I heard you were headed here so I thought I'd save you from death."

"Your timing was impeccable," Maebh said with a deep tone of sarcasm. "How did you know?"

"We all know where . . . he roams."

Maebh scrutinised the woman beside her. No, she wasn't a woman. She was a púca.

"How do I explain your appearance to the others?" Maebh spoke in an undertone, feeling the appraisal of her clan as they turned to Sage.

"You can start by introducing me," she answered in a high voice, clearly misunderstanding the question. "Humans are fascinating. Even the ones with Sight."

"Keep your voice down," Maebh shushed her, glancing around.

"You're right, Maebh McQuillan, I apologise. We can never be too careful."

Maebh sighed before spinning to her clan. "Everyone this is Sage. She's a . . ."

"Local?" Malachy asked, then smiled at the púca. "Thanks for saving us."

"It was my pleasure." Sage beamed, glancing at Malachy's outstretched hand. She cocked her head and after a beat Malachy lowered it.

"Scan the perimeter. Make sure it's clear," Maebh ordered, and the others dispersed. She scrutinised Sage. "Did you know your shirt is on backwards?"

The púca looked down at her acid green blouse. "Oh, how silly of me. The buttons are difficult ones in this fashion."

"What are you doing? You can't take your top off right now."

Maebh clasped Sage's arm as the other female hunched over, unbuttoning half of her shirt.

"Come on," Maebh said, holding Sage's opened shirt closed as she directed her toward the horses. "Here, let me help you."

"You are very kind, Maebh McQuillan," Sage whispered, her giant doe-like eyes full of naive sincerity.

Maebh worked through the remaining buttons quickly and Sage turned to face her.

Handing the shirt back, Maebh squinted at the other's chest, her brows furrowed. "What's happening here?"

Sage looked down with a frown. They both stared at her breasts. "I've never seen a female naked form before, so I had to imagine what was underneath."

"And you went for rainbow tits?"

"They are quite appealing, no?"

"You don't have any nipples."

"I'm not nursing a babe."

"Here." Maebh helped her into the blouse as chatter increased. Sage had a lot to learn if she were to blend in and she wondered how she'd got by for so long before Maebh spotted her.

"I'll get you some more subtle clothes to wear when we get back to Tara Court."

"You're not like other humans."

"And you're not like other púca," Maebh said, realising she believed it. "Do you know what happened to Newgrange?"

"I warned the High King's druid, but it was too late by then." Sage flinched before leaning in so close that Maebh felt her breath on her cheek. Her voice was barely audible. "Chaos and destruction are returning."

Maebh searched Sage's face, pulling on the hours she'd spent in the library. That phrase was familiar. "Chaos and destruction," she repeated, and Sage's eyes widened to the point it was clear she wasn't human.

Whipping her head back and forth, she cocked her ear which had turned pointed. "The wind speaks."

"Woah, what the hell, Sage?" Maebh grabbed the púca's arms, whispering. "You're going to give yourself away. Calm the fuck down."

Sage's hair receded, displaying full animal ears as the woman shrunk in size. Her glamour was faltering.

Chaos and destruction are returning.

At first, Maebh's mind struggled to catch up, the significance of those words eluding her in the soft rustle of their surroundings.

Then, it struck her; the pieces falling into place like a puzzle snapping together. The Fomorians, whispered of in legends passed down through generations. Maebh replayed the countless nights she had spent nestled under blankets, captivated by the tale-spinning of her clan seanchaí. Diarmuid's voice, enriched with a deep, resounding tone spun tales of the Fomorians as an ever-looming spectre.

They were the black ink staining the rich canvas of their heritage, beings of relentless chaos and unabating destruction.

Bits of history, folklore, and cautionary tales about these monstrous entities crept back into her mind, causing her pulse to quicken. With each recollection, the gravity of Sage's revelation weighed heavier, triggering a sense of primal dread. The momentary peace after a battle won suddenly felt like a thin veneer, a fragile illusion masking an impending storm.

"The Fomorians are returning?" Maebh faltered, jumping at the unnatural hiss that came from Sage before she transformed into her true form. "But they were banished to the human realm."

The fae spoke, in a whisper so hushed, Maebh had to lean closer to hear. "The Fomorians are like the Tuatha Dé. Two kinds. The lessers were sent to the human realm, yes. But the royals were banished to the Underworld. They will return."

CHAPTER 37
AISLING

"We have so much to catch up on, it's not even funny," Maebh stated before dragging Ash by the arm through a narrow dirt road.

Morning light bathed Tara Court as its people stirred. Streets bustled with activity, merchants rolling wares from wagons or arranging displays in the market square. Though sombre notes remained from Newgrange and the púca attack, overall, a spirit of resilience spread in the stone village. But when Ash tracked where Maebh's target was, she dragged her feet.

"No." Ash pulled away but couldn't break free from Maebh's strong grasp. "We are not going to The Raven. It's morning."

"Day drinking is the best kind of drinking," Maebh said, raising her brows as if Ash were the one being unreasonable. "You were kidnapped by the Morrígan, for fuck's sake, and the only version I have of that is Set's, which is pretty thin on details."

"Can we please leave it at that?" Ash spoke wearily, just thinking about her nightmarish time in Rathcroghan made her feel sick. At Set's name, Ash swallowed, a lump forming in her throat, spreading to her chest in burning waves. She dragged her feet, until Maebh stopped. "I'm not going anywhere until you tell me if Set is okay."

Waiting to hear of Set's state was like prodding at an open wound, both painful and impossible to resist.

Ash had gone back to her tent after he'd sifted away, and waiting to hear from him had been a torture she had never thought she would have to endure. As hours drifted by and the tent's canvas walls began to close in on her, she'd gone to the McQuillan camp, only to be told by Lorna that Set had returned and was 'resting'.

Even though Ash was a matriarch, and Lorna only an elder to another clan, she'd felt like a wayward child in front of the formidable woman who had literally shooed her away. Ash had retreated to her tent, convincing herself to let it drop until Set was ready to see her. That would last about five minutes before an anxious yearning to see him took hold. But every time she dared to move the tent flap aside, a wave of humiliation swept through her, pinning her back. It felt as if Setanta had yanked his hand away, leaving her to wobble and fall.

The burning urge to confront Setanta wrestled with her dread of what he might say. He had warned her about his ríastrad, but he'd always made his attraction to her very clear. It hadn't mattered before but now his ability to warp spasm seemed to be the towering shadow of uncertainty that draped them both.

Maebh stood silent for a moment, observing her. Ash had known enough of Set's struggle with ríastrad to understand the toll it took on everyone around him, especially those closest to him.

"Ash," Maebh started with a softer, more compassionate tone than she'd ever used before which made Ash's eyes pool with unshed tears. She did not want sympathy. But Maebh continued, "Setanta's ríastrad isn't just a change in his physical form. It takes a mental toll on him as well. He has to deal with the aftermath, the guilt of potentially hurting those around him. And this time, he almost hurt *you*."

"But . . ." The denial of her statement died on her tongue. He'd almost hurt her before. In the underground cave when Tiernan had turned to stone. Over the past few weeks, she'd convinced herself of the impossibility Set would harm her, but what would have happened if he'd stayed in that alleyway with her?

Maebh turned to face her fully. "When he emerges from an episode, he needs time. Time to recompose himself and come to terms with his actions. Sometimes, he's not so much avoiding you, as he is trying to protect you. It's his way of keeping distance until he's certain he won't pose a threat."

"I just want him to know that . . ." Ash hesitated, tucking loose hair behind her ears. What did she want him to know?

But Maebh only smiled, squeezing her arm reassuringly. "Setanta cares about you. But he may take time to process what happened, to let it sink in. It doesn't mean he's rejecting you or pushing you away. That would make him an idiot."

A surprised burst of laughter tumbled from Ash's lips, filling the air between them.

Maebh let go of her arm and gave her an encouraging smile. "Let's give him some time, okay? Today, let it just be the two of us. You need it, trust me. Neither of our banners are up today. What else do you have planned?"

Ash sighed, letting Maebh direct her through the crowds. To be honest, hanging out with Maebh sounded like a much-needed distraction after everything that had happened.

Warriors gathered in clusters. Those whose banners were called to take part in the Cath were deep in conversation, swapping stories and strategies for the day ahead. The Raven stood at the edge of the square. Maebh jumped in front of it, twisting before raising her arms as if she were showcasing a grand prize to a TV show contestant.

Grinning, Ash rolled her eyes before pushing Maebh through the open doorway. As much as Ash had dragged her feet, they both needed this. Everything else could wait. Friend time came first this morning.

The Raven was dim and quiet in the early morning light. Dust motes floated lazily through beams of sunlight filtering in through the grimy windows. The air was still and musty, carrying aromas of spilled ale, pipe smoke and roasted meats lingering from the previous night.

Tankards and plates sat abandoned on tables, and Rían could be heard in the back room cursing about early risers.

"I feel like I haven't seen you in ages. I stopped by the camp yesterday, but Lorna scowled and said you weren't back from your Cath run yet."

"Rule number one, bestie, when it comes to me, you can trust Lorna about as far as you can throw her. We got back around supper time, but I was *dealing* with some stuff." Maebh led Ash to a secluded corner booth, expression darkening as she slid onto the worn bench by the large stone hearth, its fire long gone out, leaving nothing but cold ashes.

"What kind of stuff?" Ash unsheathed her worn sword, angling it against the red brick wall by the hearth. After her abduction, she didn't want to be too far away from her blades. It was the only way her cousins agreed to back off a little from babysitting her.

Maebh pressed her palms into her eyes. "I don't even know where to start. I guess with Tiernan?"

"Yeah. Conor filled me in." A knot of worry tangled tight within her as a shiver travelled down her spine. Her fingers twitched involuntarily, reaching for her worn blade to find solace in its presence, but it didn't give the same comfort her mother's blade once had.

"About the shadow things? On the walls? And Biróg? Gods, I need a drink."

Maebh gestured to Rían, who dutifully ignored them. Ash didn't miss the way Maebh's attention flitted around the room, her eyes darting from corner to corner of the empty tavern. To some it may seem like her friend was merely taking in the rustic wooden beams and décor of the tavern she loved so much. But Ash knew better.

Beneath the playful edge to Maebh's voice and demeanour lay a subtle undercurrent of tension. Gradually, Ash let her mind's barrier relax, her gift of sensing emotions flowing to the front. As she focused on Maebh, a peculiar fragrance began to curl around her senses. Anxiety. She recognised it, a scent as distinct as it was unsettling. It had the biting tang of cold, metallic fear mixed with the sharp bitterness of uncertainties. The smell was like burning tyres, dark and acrid, coating her senses with an uneasy alarm that was hard to ignore.

It was overpowering and a little nauseating, and Ash stared at her friend's wide smile, wondering how she performed so well when beyond Maebh's calm exterior was a turbulent ocean of anxiety's chaotic presence.

Ash reached over, squeezing Maebh's hand. "Biróg said she could help. She knows more than we do about whatever that shadow is."

Maebh's sigh was deep but she nodded. "I tried to kiss him."

Ash angled her head and Maebh's cheeks flushed. "Tiernan. I thought it couldn't hurt. All of those bullshit stories about a first kiss breaking spells. Turns out they really are bull."

"Okay, you really weren't lying when you said you were dealing with stuff."

Ash watched her friend carefully, sensing that something else sat heavily on Maebh's mind.

"I met a púca in a bar," Maebh eventually blurted.

Ash pulled a face, looking at her before cocking her head. "Why does that sound like the start of a bad joke?"

"I told you I have a lot to fill you in on," Maebh exhaled before squinting at the bar. "A whole shit-heap."

Ash nodded seriously. "We share the shit-heap of many. Hit me with it."

With a deep breath, Maebh recalled the last Cath and what Sage had told her about the Fomorians.

"Where is the púca? Maybe it was involved with Ethne's plan?"

Maebh shook her head. "No, she wasn't."

Ash stared at Maebh, the resolution clear on her expression. She wondered if Maebh knew she also emitted a wave of protectiveness when she spoke about the Fair One.

"Look at what attacked the wall. Púca can't be trusted. You can't know for sure . . ."

"You'll understand when you meet her. She's different from other fae."

"We've only dealt with lesser fae since we got here, except for the bastards that kidnapped me," Ash said, her brow furrowed as she tried to catch up with Maebh's revelations. "And The Dulla—"

"Don't say his name!" Maebh clapped a hand across Ash's mouth, panicked eyes darting back and forth as if the malicious faerie would appear out of thin air.

Ash pinned Maebh with a look until finally, her friend released her. "Sorry."

Wiping away Maebh's sweaty handprint, Ash continued. "Tuatha Dé Danann and Fomorians have had their own feud since before humans existed. How are we supposed to deal with this?"

"No fucking clue," Maebh announced, leaning back in her chair.

Both women called out for Rían when he passed them with a stack of dirty dishes, but again, he ignored them.

"Can we talk about Set? Is that weird for you?" Ash asked.

"I think we need to. Maybe your problems will take my mind off the other ones."

Ash tried balancing her dagger on the table for distraction. "Is he really all right after what happened?"

"He's fine," Maebh sighed, scraping at a stain on the table with her fingernail. "Dealing with it the only way he knows how. Avoidance."

"I just wish he could trust me with it. I understand he needs time, but he needs to know I'm not afraid of him."

"Maybe you should be afraid. And besides," Maebh said dismissively before rising and walking backwards toward the bar where Rían reappeared. "He's a dick. I'm a dick. It's part of being a McQuillan twin. It's our thing."

Maebh's silky voice and Rían's short gruff responses filtered back to Ash as she stared glumly at the marked table.

Ash's mind filled with images of Set as his skin morphed into the monster. She should heed Maebh's warnings, but there was clearly something wrong with her. Ash wasn't afraid of Set's ríastrad. If anything, she believed he would protect her against harm in both forms.

"Rían says as payment for the drinks, we have to clear the dishes from the tables."

When Ash studied the discarded plates and tankards, she raised her brows.

Maebh chuckled. "So, I told him to fuck off, we're matriarchs."

"Then why are you clearing dishes?" Ash asked dubiously as Maebh piled plates from the nearby table.

"He offered breakfast, too. So, get up, buttercup, we've got work to do."

Ash smiled. "Mam used to say that."

"I'm sorry," Maebh said softly, setting her plates on a table and turning to face her fully. "I didn't know."

"Don't be sorry, Mae," Ash picked up the dishes and meandered to the next table, piling more on. "I think remembering things like that helps."

"I . . . " Maebh swallowed thickly, following behind with her own stack. "I find that hard. If I talk about Imogen. About happier times. Stupid tears always come."

"Crying is good," Ash said, bumping Maebh's side as they continued around the room. "I cry all the time."

"My mother always expected me to hold my tears in." Maebh rolled her eyes and put on a cold voice. "Show no weakness."

"My mother taught me crying is as natural as breathing. There is strength and cleansing in tears."

Maebh smiled, scrunching her nose. "They probably hated each other. Imogen would have called your mother a new age hippy."

"And Cara would have called your mother a bitch."

"Your mother would have been right."

It took the women nearly thirty minutes to clear away the remnants of the previous night and tidy up the empty tables and benches. By then, a few more early risers had wandered in, seeking breakfast to start their day. A stairwell in the back led to the inn's lodgings. Creaking floorboards and muffled voices could be heard as the other residents stirred.

Steaming tankards of Rían's special mead and two hearty breakfasts were waiting at their table when they returned from the last off-load to the kitchen where the tavern owner's son stood sullenly over a basin.

"Totally worth it," Maebh said around a mouthful of eggs, devouring half her plate within minutes.

Ash grunted in agreement, dipping soda farl into her fried egg. She ate more slowly, savouring the honey-glazed sausage, the burst of hot flavour enveloping her tongue from the grilled tomatoes. Each bite was savoured slowly as she relished the luxury of a hearty meal after surviving on mere dry bread and cheese. The taste of the scone had been divine, yet this was another level to remembering she had tastebuds. As she parted her lips for another bite, a pang of longing struck her. An image of Mary working her magic in the kitchen surfaced in her mind. Gods, she missed her foster mother's cooking; an indulgence she wasn't sure she'd ever sample again.

After their bellies were full and half their drinks consumed, a warmth had spread over their table from the rising noises of the tavern filling up. Other patrons' conversations blended into a low, comfortable din.

"Did you hear about what the Collins' did?" Maebh asked as she scraped her soda bread around her plate to soak up the egg yolk.

"They were on duty, right?" Ash asked, her cousins having filled her in on the Cath since her 'little adventure'. She gritted her teeth at the secrets piling higher than the dishes they'd stacked.

"They found a faerie troupe that were hiding in the forest. They came back from their shift with necklaces of wings and teeth."

Ash halted her fork mid-air. "Are you serious?"

"I'm afraid so," Maebh said, her mouth twisting in disgust. "They passed me in the square, congratulating one another on their haul. Apparently, other clans are not only competing in the Cath, but they are also taking souvenirs to show off the fae they 'redistribute'.

"And the High King isn't forbidding this from happening?" Ash set her fork down, pushing the remnants of her food away when Maebh nodded.

"Oh, I forgot to tell you about something else that happened on Winter Solstice."

"There's more?"

But of course there was. Maebh had vanished and no matter her front, there was no way she would have abandoned everyone. She had been the most vocal at trying to stop Ethne. But they hadn't stopped her, and now they were left in wreckage.

"I sifted," Maebh said quietly as her brows creased. "I saw the púca—Sage is her name—doing some weird magic spell beside the stone. Then I heard the first cracks. I thought she was the one causing them, so I somehow triggered my sifting ability to move myself and her away into the woods. Not before I saw Newgrange fall."

Ash's mind whirled as she took in Maebh's revelation. A pang hit her stomach, hardening it, as she longed for such a gift. To know that she could escape if she was ever taken again. That a dungeon in Rathcroghan and the whims of Tuatha Dé like Medb, Tara or the Morrígan wouldn't hold such power over her. Perhaps it was a twin thing that Maebh and Set now possessed this gift, linking them in ways she could never share?

"What happened then?" Ash forced away her petty thoughts.

"I met that twig-wearing druid, Biróg, who told me we have . . ."

"Tuatha Dé blood?" Ash finished and her friend's face confirmed it.

"How did you know?"

Ash gestured to the raised bumps on her neck, the skin had turned purple. "When Tara tasted my blood, he said the same thing."

"What the fuck happened to us?" Maebh downed the rest of her drink, slamming it on the table.

Ash mimicked her, relishing the now lukewarm sweet drink as it trailed down her throat. What *had* happened to them? Why did all these strangers know more about them then they did? It was becoming harder to deny their accusations. They each had a set of gifts that no other Fianna had.

"Okay, it's your turn to get our next round."

Ash glared at her. "I literally worked just as hard as you to get that first one."

Maebh only winked before leaning back on her chair, arms raised behind her head.

"Fine," Ash sighed. "But when I come back, you're filling me in more on Tiernan."

Maebh's smile froze as her blue eyes darkened. Ash sat back down, squeezing Maebh's leg. "Hey."

Her friend leaned forward, face inches from Ash's. "He would have freed us by now. We are failing him, Ash."

"There was no shadow creatures this morning when you went down there, right? And no other guardians were taken?"

Maebh shook her head, but Ash could tell she wasn't fully listening. "Biróg said it's a form of sluagh. She's placed iron and herblore charms around the cave that she claims will keep them safe."

Ash tilted her head. "I thought sluagh were hosts of the dead that stalked above ground. I've never heard of them lurking in caves."

"Things have changed since Newgrange. Can't you sense it?"

As if in answer, Ash shivered as the tavern door swung open to admit more Fianna. Eternal spring had disappeared from this realm, and with it came weather more in line with the human realm.

"I need to ring Mary and Dom," Ash said, a lump forming in her throat. "I'm afraid of what I'll find out. If time has shifted. Or if they're still . . ."

"They are alive, Ash." Maebh stood. "I'll get the drinks."

CHAPTER 38

AISLING

By the time Ash and Maebh exited The Raven, the morning hours had long since slipped into afternoon. Stepping into the bustling lane, Maebh shielded watering eyes with one tanned arm, linking the other through the crook of Ash's elbow as they ambled along. "Gods, why is it so bloody bright out?"

Ash chuckled but squinted to the daylight. "That's what will happen when you spend your morning tucked away within The Raven's dingy light."

"If Rían heard you now," Maebh rebuked her, tutting.

Together they wove between passersby going briskly about their business, dodging the foot traffic clogging the narrow streets. Merchants called out their wares from boisterous stalls while children weaved giggling games around adults' ankles. After the sombre events of recent days, it lifted Ash's heart to see the village thriving in a resilient routine once more.

"We need food," Maebh declared.

"Again," Ash agreed as her stomach rumbled.

They made it to the square where wooden tables were laid out. Boars roasted on spits while other vendors sold dried fruit and candied apples.

"What do you fancy?"

"I'd kill for a bag of chips smothered in salt and vinegar."

Ash's many nights out in Dublin swarmed through her mind. High heels and sore feet and greasy food after dancing with friends. What would they make of her if they saw her now? Matriarch to a clan of warriors, wearing the same clothes for far too many days in a row.

"Come with me," Maebh said, winking, even though their arms were still linked, and Ash had little choice as her friend darted to a vendor at the far side of the square.

A large frying pan sizzled as they approached, and Ash's tastebuds perked up. Peering inside, steam greeted her, as did chunks of frying potato and onion.

"It's not a bag of chipper chips, but it's the closest thing we've got."

"I love you." Ash exclaimed, squeezing Maebh's arm. "This is exactly what I want."

They sweet-talked the cook stirring the savoury food into giving them a generous portion; in exchange, his daughter would dance with Ciarán Breen at the next ceili. Ash promised it would be done, and smirked at the young woman who blushed but couldn't hide her own smile at the exchange. She lumped the paper bag to overflowing.

"Whoring your kin," Maebh scolded in between piping hot chunks of potato. "What sort of matriarch are you at all?"

"A hungry one," Ash said, stuffing her own mouth and groaning at the greasy goodness. "This is better than chipper chips."

Maebh sucked on a soft onion with a popping sound and smiled before nodding to a bench. They gobbled up the contents, fighting over the last potato chunk. A pale hand slipped between them, scooping up the remaining piece.

"Hey!" they shouted in unison, squinting up at Conor, who only shrugged.

"You may re-think stealing our food when I kick your ass on the training grounds, Stitch," Maebh threatened.

"When do you want to go?" Conor said, a smile in his tone.

Ash loved seeing that. His brown eyes were clear, amusement dancing on them. "Stitch?"

"Yes, because he's a tattoo artist and he also maimed himself," Maebh said, shrugging like the nickname was obvious.

Conor threw his head back and laughed. "I wondered why you called me that. Now I definitely want to fight you."

"Come on then. Let's get your two cousins and make it fair. I wouldn't want to break you when Ash has only got you back."

"Oh, and tell Ciarán about his date to the next ceili," Ash said with a grin.

"Do I even want to know?" Conor chuckled, shaking his head before turning to Ash. "You coming?"

A familiar figure strode toward the centre of the district, and she stood abruptly. "No, you go on. I'll catch up later."

Her feet carried her away before she truly registered what she was doing. Discarding her empty paper bag into the next fire pit, she followed Set into the blacksmith quarter.

They'd got so close. She'd thought they'd actually kiss, but then he ran. Maybe he enjoyed their banter up to a point, but he was unwilling to get into anything serious? He'd told her once that he'd decided not to get into any relationships after Orla. Why did she think she would be the exception? She was a fool.

The area was less crowded than the food district, but plenty of warriors milled around the different forges. It would be impossible to miss Set's looming form, at least a head above everyone else. With every step, her nerves screamed at her to turn and go back to the safety of her brother and clan. Not because she was afraid of him hurting her physically, but her heart was far more tender.

Set ducked into the largest forge. Grainne's. Ash waited outside, unsure whether to follow him or not. Hesitation turned to fear, and her legs wouldn't have moved her further even if she'd wanted. Loitering outside, she waited until it was officially clear she was stalking him. Just as she turned to leave, he reappeared. His golden hair shone in the afternoon sun, a wide smile on his face as he called a farewell to Grainne. When his eyes met hers, his smile faltered.

And then vanished.

"Hey," she said, a blush rising to her cheeks.

"Hey." He tucked his hands behind his back where he held a large box, looking anywhere but her. "What are you doing here?"

Shit. This had been a terrible idea.

"Just . . . wandering around," she said lamely before adding, "Maebh dragged me to The Raven. I was heading home until I saw you and thought I'd say hi."

He smiled, but it was strained, and she wished the ground would swallow her into the Underworld.

"I was just returning manacles to Grainne," Set's voice cut through the rhythmic clang of metal against metal, his eyes transfixed on the blacksmith engrossed in her craft.

A gnawing sensation scraped at Ash's insides. As he said it, a slight falter hinted he was trying to hide something from her. Absurd thoughts swirled in her mind, poisoning the awkward riddled air. Gods, had he come to Grainne to flirt with her? Ask her out? Was he interested in her?

He was always finding excuses to touch Ash, or so she'd thought. Perhaps he was tactile like that with everyone. Maybe he saw her as someone else to flirt with, along with a lengthy list of others. To quell her spiral, she carefully unbarred her gift. Pulling in a slow, deep breath, she was assaulted by the scent of Set's feelings. His emotions weren't the spicy fragrance of attraction or the sweet smell of infatuation.

Instead wafting towards her was an entirely different aroma. Set's scent was edged with the unmistakable hint of discomfort. The decaying odour of dampened wood and overripe fruit combined into a distinct smell, one that cast a light onto the unease that was quietly brewing beneath his strained smile.

"Okay. I said hi. Bye."

Dashing around the crowds, she muttered to herself until a firm hand grasped her shoulder. "Ash, wait."

She didn't want to turn to face Set, but he angled her around. Staring at his chest, she remained silent. He sighed, bringing his hand from behind his back. A long, narrow wooden box wrapped in a green silk bow hung between them. Ash regarded it, puzzled, before finally peering up at his face. His beard had grown over these past days, but she thought she could detect a blush on his cheeks for once. Releasing her shoulder, he scratched his chin.

"I wanted to surprise you, so you caught me off guard. Will you please take the box?"

He shook it, but nothing rattled. Ash cocked her head to the side, trying to recover from her spiral of embarrassment to this new knowledge.

"You weren't returning manacles?" She asked it slowly, hesitantly, as if she was learning a new language.

"Well, yes, I was. But Grainne has been working on this for me for a while now and she'd promised it would be ready as a Winter Solstice gift. Since that day went to shit . . ." Set paused, and Ash couldn't help but note the nervous energy radiating from him.

Passersby chatted around them. Despite the flurry of the market, everything was muted as Set stood before her. Inspecting the long box, the size of his arm at least, she toyed with the green ribbon, smooth and slippery to touch. He took her elbow, leading her to a walk.

"Are you going to open it?" Set ventured, placing it into her hands.

It was heavy. As if breaking a spell, she smiled before nodding, a flutter of excitement dancing with the relief in her chest. The seat she'd just vacated at the market square was still empty, so she plonked down on it. He sat silently beside her as he watched her hands. His gaze was a caress as her fingers clumsily worked the knot. When it finally loosened, it fluttered to the ground, but before it did, Set caught it between his large fingers.

"Here," he said before tugging on her hand.

With gentle slowness, he pushed back her jacket sleeve, bunching it to expose her wrist to the cool air. The contact of silk on her skin was nothing compared to each time his fingers grazed her. Mesmerised by the way his fingers wrapped the fabric with such care around her wrist, she watched them dance in an elegance that did not marry to how deadly they looked when holding his axe. As always, he was a beautiful, lethal contradiction.

Ash stared at the neat bow on her wrist, angling it in every direction.

"Now open your present before I take it back," Set said in a very Maebh-like tone.

She chuckled before lifting the stiff lid. Her heart stopped and then restarted in a thunderous beat as she looked at the sword lying in crushed velvet.

"I know it's not the same as your mother's," Set said quietly, peering over her shoulder at the weapon. "And I know it won't mean as much, but I wanted you to have a blade worthy of sitting on your hip. Beautiful and sharp. Forged from something real and magical."

She traced the pattern on its hilt. The guard and pommel were intricately adorned in symbols and a language, elegantly shaped. The blade was etched along the fuller with a pattern of swirls.

Finally, she found her voice, although it was thick. "It means so much more."

Set leaned closer, his thighs pressed close to hers as he traced a scrawl on the handle. "Every sword needs a name. It's up to you what you call her, but I had this engraved as a reminder. Le croí gran."

"Pure of heart."

"Like you."

As the dawning realisation of her feelings threatened to overwhelm her, she kept a firm handle on the only response she could muster. Words were not enough, but they would have to be for now.

"Thank you."

"And about what happened . . ." he began.

But Ash grabbed his hand, shifting the box to the side so she could look in his eyes. "I'm not afraid of your ríastrad. I'm never going to be. And I'm not foolish enough to think I can help you control it. I'll be more careful in the future if that's what you need from me. I'm sadder that I haven't seen you since. I'm embarrassed to admit that I'd been questioning whatever this is between us."

Set wrapped a steady hand around Ash's shoulder, pulling her close. "Of all the things in the world we have to wonder about, how I feel about you is never going to be one."

"Promise?" she asked, holding a breath.

He leaned his head to hers and closed his eyes, sighing. "With everything I ever hope to be for you, Aisling Breen. I promise."

Each word filled the space between them with an invisible bond, tying them closer than ever before as they sat together, allowing the world to drift by them as Ash rested her head on his shoulder.

"Will you come with me to the tree?" Ash asked after a few minutes of companiable silence, sheathing and tying her new sword to her belt, realising she'd left her borrowed sword at The Raven. She'd get it later. "I want to check in on my foster parents."

They walked in hurried steps toward Tiernan's tree, the exact moment his magic ward kicked in apparent with Ash's irrational urge to turn in the other direction. Pushing through, she grabbed Set's hand until the haze cleared and the giant oak tree appeared before them. Set stroked her palm with his thumb before releasing her and she couldn't hide her smile as she knelt before the waterproofed box housing Tiernan's equipment. He'd genuinely thought of everything, it seemed, right down to the drastic change in weather this realm had suffered.

The now familiar pinging rang out as they waited for Mary or Dom to connect their call. On and on the ringing went, and with every shrill sound, her stomach tightened further. It cancelled out.

"Maybe they're not home," Set offered.

She shook her head. "They never let it ring out."

With a shaking finger, she pressed the button to connect the call again.

After the fifth attempt, her panic was a living mass beside her.

"Ash," Set said calmly, "breathe."

Her vision swam as she tried to figure out what to do. A ping sounded, but it wasn't the connection she'd hoped for. Studying the screen, she read the blue box that had appeared.

"It's a prompt to connect to your parents' webcam," Set said, craning over her shoulder. "Tiernan must have encrypted the laptop in case something like this happened."

Without hesitation, Ash hit confirm. The screen went dark, and she thought she'd hit the wrong button until shadows darted in and out of focus. Set reached over her and increased the volume. Shrill shrieks and hisses exploded from the microphone and Ash's heart stopped.

Flashes of light illuminated the cottage kitchen. The laptop was on the dining table, the same spot Mary and Dom spoke to her whenever she called. But she couldn't see either of them in the destroyed room. All she could make out were overturned chairs and puddles on the ground, too dark to determine.

"Oh, gods."

More cries came through.

"Those don't sound human," Set said, as if that would reassure her.

"I have to go to them," Ash choked, gripping Set's arm and trying to stand but her legs wouldn't obey. "But how can we get there? The underground tunnels will take too long, and Bradan won't let us go anyway. Set, I have to help them!"

"*We* have to," Set corrected, taking her in his arms and helping her stand. She stared at the screen, willing and dreading a glimpse of her family. He didn't let go of her waist as he kissed her forehead. "I'll get us there."

CHAPTER 39

SETANTA

It was a fool's plan that had Set standing on the white-powdered crevices of the barrenland. But he couldn't see another way to help Ash.

"Are you here?" he called out to the dusk-ridden sky.

It was still bright enough that he could see his warm breath hitting the crisp air, and he clasped his hands close to his face, puffing into them as the unforgiving signs of winter settled into his bones. A snap to his left had him facing toward it, axe unbuckled and in his hand a moment later. A troupe of faeries leapt from a nearby trunk, but they didn't come nearer to him. He stared at them as they danced around one another, their translucent wings shimmering.

"You called for me?" Ethne's sultry voice was too close, and he whipped around as her warm breath tickled his ear. Rubbing his shoulder against the side of his head, he eyed the female across the expanse of earth, nowhere close enough to have breathed on him.

"Did you mean what you said the last time?" Set called loudly, even though she could probably hear him from this distance.

In a blink of an eye, Ethne stood metres from his face, a gleam in her grey eyes. "You'll have to be more specific. I say a great many things."

His hand shot out, but she'd already sifted out of reach, but not as far as her last trick. Gritting his teeth, he bit back his retort. He didn't have time for this. None of them had, especially Ash's foster parents.

"Help me help her." Set's shoulders dipped as he realised this was a reckless and stupid idea. He really was a fool when it came to Aisling Breen. He'd lowered himself to ask the help of a murderous creature.

"You've witnessed what is happening, haven't you?" Ethne was before him once more, but all malice was gone from her face. "You've seen the human realm."

"Ash's family . . ." he said but teetered off, not wanting to give Ethne too much ammunition to use against him.

"Bradan and his merry men will not help the human lands. He has an agenda, and it does not include saving humankind."

"And what's your agenda?" Set seethed. "You're the cause of the humans being attacked."

"I have no desire to kill humans. I want you to see who you truly are."

In the time it took for Set to turn toward Ethne, she clicked her fingers and his blood burned to excruciating degrees.

"Don't fight it. Embrace your ríastrad."

Breathing became impossible as a red film coated his vision. A rage consumed his thoughts before he could do anything other than roar. Piece by piece, his body transformed into the monster he hated.

Finally, we're free.

Taller than his human form, he towered over Ethne. Her angelic face tilted up at him with adoration, and he cocked his head as his monster swarmed around his mind, looking for a way to merge with him. This was different. In a heaving breath, Set realised he was still present of mind. The urge to snap Ethne's neck was there, but his will to fight against it was strong.

"You're still here," Ethne crooned, stepping closer, no fear in her eyes.

He could feel it then. The joining of two halves. His human self, still seeing through the eyes of a monster.

No, the other half crooned. *Not a monster. We are a wolf amongst lambs.*

"You can do anything you want in this body, Setanta." Ethne stepped even closer, placing a hand as high as she could and only reaching his navel. With a bright smile, she even turned her back on him.

His other self strained to close the distance. It would just be a matter of reaching out with one arm and clutching her throat. One simple flex of his fingers and her neck would break. *Kill her.*

His hand was no more than an inch from her white-blonde hair when she angled her head toward him, a wicked smile on her lips. Gripping his hand, she led him to one of the deadened trees.

"Snap this tree in half."

"What?" Set's voice was garbled, as if he were speaking through a mouthful of acid.

"You want to break something. Go on."

Angling his enclosed fist backward, he barely needed any momentum as he pummelled the tree until there was only a stump sticking out of the ground. As he turned to Ethne once more, she pointed to a boulder.

"Pick that up."

With less hesitation this time, he hoisted the boulder above his head, rotating before throwing it across the land. It cleared to the other side and rolled down a steep hill. He raced to peer over the edge, seeing steam rise from scattered hot springs near the edge of a healthy forest. So the barrenland hadn't reached much further than his last visit.

"See your strength. Take control."

"How?" he asked, feeling his body temperature cooling, his voice turning back to his own. He shrunk down to normal size and grimaced before looking at his shredded clothing. Freezing, he scowled at his human flesh. It knit back together, the stinging watering his eyes, but he hissed and blinked the tears away. It was just like after he turned with Ash, but he had put his accelerated healing down to the magic in potions given to him by the High King's druids.

"How?" he asked again, looking for any signs of the torn flesh and broken body he was accustomed to after turning. He was whole.

"It's you. It always has been. Two halves in one vessel. You have the power over your body."

"I never have before."

"You have. Once you realise the truth, you can control your warp spasm. More than Cú Chulainn ever could. He wouldn't listen, but perhaps you will."

"You knew Cú Chulainn?"

"He was a vain sort of character. Always preening himself. I must admit he was a good lover, even if he sought praise for every pleasure he gave. More work than worth."

Set growled, not hiding his frustration, which seemed to only delight the wicked female before him. "What do you mean he wouldn't listen? What is the truth I need to realise?"

"You fear turning, don't you?" Her question suspended in the air. At his confirming nod, she ventured further. "When you ríastrad, that fear is no more. You're already a monster. Submit to him and he will submit to you. Are you afraid now? Or do you feel the power you harness?"

Set chewed over her questions. Images of his unleashed beast flashed across his mind, raw and terrifyingly powerful. There was truth to her words. He wasn't the same man in ríastrad; the beast roared while the man watched, the fear held at bay by the tangible, electric thrill of untamed power enveloping him. He was caught at the crossroads of dread and exhilaration. Fear didn't vanish but mutated, losing its foreboding edge to accommodate an intoxicating, primal strength. It was an internal tug of war, fear versus power, and he was the rope stretched taut in the fray.

"I'm not . . . broken." He said this more to himself, but she chuckled.

"No."

"Back in the other realm, I'd wake up broken, My mother always had to . . . tend to me." He hated speaking about Imogen to her murderer.

When he glared at her, Ethne smiled sadly.

"Your mother's intention was to leash you. She understood your immense potential, yet instead of teaching you this simple truth, she played the apothecary, drugging you with a druid's potion that resulted in those injuries. That, combined with a hefty dose of sedatives, ensured she could puppeteer you. It prevented her worst nightmare from manifesting."

"And what was that?"

"For you to pull the strings instead."

Set found himself adrift in a sea of unsettling revelations. His relationship with Imogen had been complicated, but he'd honestly believed she'd had his best interests at heart. And unlike Maebh, he'd had comforting images of his mother, but they were contorting before him into twisted silhouettes. Her apprehension, wrapped in layers of love and watchfulness, acted as bars of his cage, deforming his perception of himself before he encountered his true might. His perspective on the chains of her love hardened, morphing it from a blanket of security to restrictions to overcome.

The power his mother feared from him was the one pulsating in his veins, as much a part of him as his heart or mind.

"Can you help, or not?" Set's sigh hung in the air, countered by Ethne's stare until a set of clothing materialised before him.

His eyes narrowed as he examined the pieces, an all-black ensemble of top and pants.

"Would you rather stand here in rags?"

He didn't answer as he donned the new fit, each piece snuggling against his physique like a tailored glove. Even the boots, sturdy and secure, melted into his feet as if they were custom-made just for him. The thick, formidable fabric of his top and pants was woven to endure, a specially reinforced design poised to accommodate weapons, serving as an agile battle-suit. Scooping up his discarded axe, he slotted it into the reinforced loops, its weight settling familiarly against his side.

"You need me to help you get in and out of the human realm," Ethne stated, and he nodded reluctantly as she continued, somehow knowing his worries exactly. "And you don't want to sift because the realms are dislodged."

"Because of you," he shot back but she ignored him.

"What will you give me in return?" Ethne's voice swirled around him on the breeze. Set turned, and she cocked her head to the side before sifting in front of him once more. "What is it worth to you? To help your . . . friend?"

Set bit back the retort to say something stupid like 'everything' even though he realised it to be true. As if she heard his thoughts, and he was beginning to realise it was a possibility, she smiled.

"Would you give up your ríastrad?"

He blinked. And then blinked again. "What did you say?"

Ethne circled him, but he did not allow his back to be exposed to her this time. Following her rotation, his hands rested on both hilts of his axe and sword.

"You have no idea of the power you possess, my boy. And it seems you do not appreciate it."

As if his monster heard her, it brushed against their inner bridge, not so much trying to break free as it usually did but acknowledging her words. Set ignored them both.

"I can't get rid of it. I've tried."

Recounting his childhood attempts, he'd naively sought out different Fianna within Ireland who claimed to have cures for curses and Fair One trickery. None of it had worked. When his mother had found out, she'd beaten him. That in itself had been a shock, as she'd always saved the worst of her brutality for Maebh. The same cords of guilt wrapped around his gut at that. It hadn't mattered how strong he'd become; he'd never been able to save his twin from the wrath of their mother. It was a shame he'd live with forever.

"I have lived many lifetimes," Ethne said. "If I told you I could help you with your plans to save the human realm with Aisling, and in exchange, I asked for your ríastrad, would you accept?"

Set weighed the words in his mind as the monster within stirred and raged against that bridge. It did not want him to agree, and hope grew from that realisation.

"You can take out my monster?"

He could be freed as the price for what he wanted.

Ethne smiled as she nodded her head. "Heed my warning, boy. You and your ríastrad have bonded. Whether you acknowledge that side to you or not."

Again, his monster banged against the bridge, its claws scraping and clinging to his mind, begging him not to listen.

"I don't care," Set said, stamping down on his howling mind as his blood pumped too quickly. If he stood like this for much longer, he would turn again. "Get it out."

Allowing Ethne to come close enough to touch him was a battle of wills. He ignored his screaming heart and his pounding head as she placed a pale hand over his heart.

"You must also carry a secret," she whispered in his ear. "A simple geas. You have studied countless scrolls and have debated what I am. I will tell you, but it is your secret to keep."

"What . . ."

"Do we have an agreement?"

He tried to consider everything she'd said, but none of it mattered. Ash wanted to get to the human realm, and he'd promised to take her. If the price was a monster he never wanted, then he would gladly pay that over and over. "Yes."

"I am a Fomorian royal, Setanta McQuillan. Born from the realm of chaos and crowns. A land stolen from my people by the Tuatha Dé Danann. I have no battle with Milesians. With you."

Solid ground pressed on his back as the world shifted and the stars blinked down at him. Ethne smiled, her hand still on his chest as she leaned over him. Jerking his head around, he took in their surroundings. They were still in the barrenland, but time had passed. It was no longer the muted colours of dusk, but full-blown night.

"How long?" his voice was groggy, and he desperately needed water.

"Almost done," Ethne said, signs of strain in her voice.

Set tried but failed to move, but even the smallest jerk had him biting back a cry.

"Don't move," Ethne warned before lifting her hand.

At first it looked as if she clutched at nothing. Some invisible force was pulling away from her, but then he saw it. A writhing shadowy thing blacker than the night stretched toward his chest, as if trying to go back in. He watched, equal parts fascination and revulsion as she gripped the shadow substance higher. With her free hand, she lifted a long shaft, forcing the substance into the pointed tip. Blinking, Set only had enough strength to lift his head. It was a spear.

"You have the power to sift, but Aisling does not. She can sift while holding this spear if you ever separate. But I warn you, Setanta. The spear will taint her or anyone else with the slightest touch. You are its master and should never part with it."

Set's head was under siege as a wave of agony lashed at his core, blindsiding every nerve in his body down to his feet. Shaking, he attempted to steady himself, his hands clutching around his midsection like a vice, yet the violent tremors defied his control, his body spiralling into a cold shudder. Set allowed Ethne to help him sit upright. He gripped his arms tightly around his waist, unable to control the violent gnashing of his teeth. He was a cold, hollow shell. Empty.

"Your ríastrad is contained within this spear. Here." Ethne offered the weapon to him, but when he couldn't lift his arm, she helped him.

The spear was warm to the touch, a salve against his icy skin. Through trembling fingers, it pulsed with an inviting heat, a soothing welcome to the frost coating his bones. Strength radiated from it, as if by its very touch it had the power to heal the wasting sickness plaguing him.

"You are now but a mere man," Ethne whispered, but he had no strength to lift his eyes from the spear.

Intricate swirls and patterns formed the hilt, an ancient language long forgotten. It was old; he could feel its presence. Older than dust. Older than the Fomorian before him. He marvelled at its beauty as he examined it from bottom to its lethal, sharp point. It hummed a melody under his grasp, a hot blue light radiating from the symbols as he stroked the hilt. With every breath, strength returned to his bones. Not as strong as before, he realised, but strong enough for any man.

Ethne's usually glowing skin was dull, a faint sheen on her brow. "How does it feel?"

Set looked down at the beautiful spear. His monster was within. It brushed against the hilt once more, and he almost recoiled. But it was not malicious, he realised. It was the gesture of an old friend. He gripped the spear, angling it so he could lean on its unbendable force, and stood.

"It feels like it should always have been mine."

She smiled as she stood slowly. "You must name it."

Set didn't think twice. "Lámfada."

"Of the long hand," Ethne's voice was full of glee, but Set did not turn toward her as he listened to the humming of his spear. "You will be able to sift between realms without missing time."

Knowing all he needed to do was think of his exact location and he would sift there, he thought of Ash. A warmth that started in Lámfada seeped to his hand and enveloped him. Breathing out, he stepped forward and into Ash's tent.

She'd been pacing and stopped mid-stride as she spun to face him. At the sight of her, he knew what he'd done was worth it. Ignoring the flu-like ache to his bones, he met her halfway to the centre of her small room.

"Where have you been? You promised we would find my foster parents."

"I can bring you the human realm." Set angled the spear in front so she could see it, but when she reached up, he jerked it away. "Don't touch it!"

There was a mutual flicker of surprise flitting across their faces at his sharp reaction. Collecting himself, Set licked his parched lips.

"Ash," he started, his tone softened but every bit as earnest. "I'm sorry. The spear is . . . mine. It's only safe to use in my hands. Will you trust me enough that you'll never touch it?"

Ash studied him, her eyes dancing with a myriad of emotions before they landed on a resigned acceptance.

"Fine," she agreed, her voice tinged with an unease she didn't attempt to disguise. "I tried to find Maebh, but she's guarding a McQuillan territory all the way out at Uisneach."

"We can sift to her now and bring her if you want," Set offered.

Ash looked at him, a battle clear in her emerald eyes, but she shook her head. "We've wasted enough time."

He swallowed hard, biting back the revelation of what he'd been doing during that wasted time. It didn't matter. She didn't need to know about the sacrifice he'd given willingly to a Fomorian royal. With a jolt, he realised his tongue swelled at the thought of revealing that secret. He'd agreed to a geas without an ounce of his consideration to the magical binding.

Instead of burdening Ash with anything further, he simply nodded. "Let's go."

CHAPTER 40
AISLING

Darkness coated the cottage. As gravel crunched under her feet, Ash willed her heart to steady as her other senses warred for attention at the danger lurking within her old home. She was not unacquainted with danger, not after her kidnapping, but this was a new kind of fear. One wrapped around two people with kind hearts.

Glancing behind, her eyes narrowed toward the space they'd entered the realm on the deserted country road. Bright spots danced around her vision, a light-headed sensation tugging on her stomach as she willed herself to fully adjust before they encountered anyone. Or anything.

With a shaky breath, Ash crept forward, gravel betraying each careful footfall. She found herself holding her breath with each step, inwardly cringing at the minuscule betrayals beneath her feet.

Set, however, was a different story. Merging with the shadows in a dance only he seemed to know, he moved with a haunting grace that left no trace behind, not even a rustle. His presence was like a wisp of smoke, there but not. And she was damned if he didn't look exquisite doing it.

Her eyes slithered over his figure and the new attire covering his muscular frame. Even as a throb dipped in her lower stomach at the mere sight of him walking, a pang of resentment snaked its way up her chest. The boundless hours of his absence, each tick-tock a sting to her patience, and he'd returned with a new spear and sexy battle-suit while she'd been pacing her tent, ready to tear her hair out. He had made her promise to wait for him, and she had no other choice but to do just that.

Amidst her internal storm, she bit down on her lower lip, but a grunt of dissatisfaction slipped past her defences, breaking the silence. He looked her way, but she ignored him. Set's late, fashionable return had brought relief, but had also added a touch more vinegar into her already sour mood, a bitter aftertaste that she would need to swallow down.

Usually, the farm buzzed with animal noises, but an ominous hush fell like a veil. Light never failed to spill from the cottage's open door and windows, yet restless shadows prowled where warmth and comfort once shone. Glancing left, her heart froze. Gone was the comforting bulk of Newgrange's brooding watchful guard over their home.

"Look," Set breathed, stepping toward the hedge separating them from the passageway. "It's gone here, too."

Heart hammering, her gaze fixed on the shadow across the field. Set's torch flared to life and a moment later, it trained on Newgrange. Or what was left of it.

Scattered piles of loose stone replaced orderly concentric rings with no sign of a grassy mound; only rubble and fractured ruins remained. The sight of it here was worse. Mary and Dom had refused to leave despite her warning. Her breaths were laboured with some nameless grief. For losses too profound for tears alone.

"Do you think they could be over there?" Ash's voice was not her own.

Set inched up beside her, every tensing line of his form alert for any threat. "Let's check the cottage first."

His new spear gleamed dully in the starlight, poised yet unraised. Dread wound itself around Ash as darkness swallowed her cherished home. The gravel drive crunched beneath each careful step, her senses straining for clues of what they would find.

She glanced at her watch but cursed at her bare wrist. She'd taken it off soon after arriving in Tír na nÓg, the constant circular motion of the clock hands jarring, a reminder that she was no longer linked to this world.

"I hear something," Set murmured, signalling for her to stop, and wrapping both hands around the long spear.

As the cottage came into view, Ash froze. The front doorway yawned unnaturally wide. It was hanging off its hinges, an indent in the middle as if a powerful force had opened it, the wood splintered with webs of destruction.

"Is there a back door?"

Ash nodded, her throat too tight to speak. She tugged his arm, and they walked as quietly as they could past Dom's shed positioned between the house and surrounding fields and barn. The door to the shed was also open, something Dom would never have done. It was his pride and joy. A place to house all his tools and paint. The man was constantly on the go, tinkering with old machines and engines, or daubing fences or any surface he felt needed 'a lick of paint'.

She stopped, daring to glimpse inside, but only darkness greeted her. Her boots crunched on something, but when she flipped the switch, the light didn't work. Peering down, she lifted her boot. Shards of glass.

"The lightbulb burst," she whispered to Set who stood outside the overcrowded shed, illuminating the space for her.

Dom had always needed to duck his head upon entering, and she couldn't imagine Set trying to squeeze through. Gods, where were her foster parents?

As they approached the cottage, Set switched off the torch once more. Ash stepped deliberately across the threshold of her foster home, listening . . . nothing but their muted breaths disturbed the silence. They searched each room, finding them devoid of life. Bare, hollow chambers greeted them where love and laughter once resounded, now echoing with a stillborn emptiness no steps could breach. No answers greeted their investigations, only deepening questions beneath this home's haunted veil.

"Where are they?" Ash asked as they returned to the chilly night air.

A cry echoed from the adjacent cafe, spurring Ash into motion. Racing through the splintered door frame, her eyes locked onto a squirming bundle at the room's centre, a wailing infant the sole sign of life amid this vacant shell.

Set barrelled in behind her, coming to an abrupt halt at the sight before them. He gripped her shoulder, but she shook him off, running to scoop the tiny baby protectively into her arms. Its wails faded into whimpers, but then turned into cruel laughter.

"Ash, put it down."

She stared into her arms, breath catching in her throat. Where a baby should be swaddled in cloth, shadows writhed and swelled, growing as if it consumed the very darkness of the night.

Lowering the creature, she retreated step by careful step as the jet-black mass morphed and writhed until a shadowy form grew into a hunched, cloaked figure. The dense folds floated on a phantom wind, veiling lean limbs that ended in shrivelled feet, their jagged broken nails sharper than daggers.

A pale face speckled with age spots leered from beneath its tatty hood and fixed on Ash with limpid blue eyes that had seen many lifetimes.

"I knew you'd be back, girl." The figure's voice dragged like talons down granite, a groan laden with vengeance. "Did you fancy yourself rid of me after our last encounter? Your life is mine, girl."

"You!" Ash gasped as she realised it was the dying fae she had saved a newborn from in this very cafe.

"Me," it snarled, lunging towards her. Ash shoved a table into its path, tripping the faerie. Set rushed forward, jabbing with his spear but meeting only air.

With a thunderous roar, the creature wrenched the weapon, laughing wickedly before throwing it aside and pouncing. Gnarled hands closed around Set's throat, hoisting his kicking form aloft with an unnatural strength at odds with its emaciated physique. Tattered robes slipped from bony shoulders as it reared to its full towering height. Sinew and tendon stretched taut over jutting bones, corpse-like flesh hanging like pockets.

Ash's blade sang in the dim light and made a sickening noise as it pierced the creature's back. Black ichor oozed from the wound, but the faerie didn't release Set, who gagged as he scrabbled at unyielding wrists. The creature smiled at her. With methodical cruelty, it tightened merciless fingers, crushing Set's windpipe further. Trembling, horror coiled her gut as she willed, for the first time, for Set to give in to his ríastrad. There was no sign of a crimson flush to his skin, or an enlargement to his frame.

"It's me you want," Ash said, charging forward. "Let him go."

Set's gasp sounded painful, but the fae had dropped him. That's all she needed. Ash drew her sword, swinging at the faerie's throat. The blade sliced leathery skin and the creature hissed. Gripping the dagger in its side, the fury in its eyes turned into malicious glee.

"Killing you with your own blade would be fun."

It swiped at Ash, but she jumped back, falling onto a table and toppling over its side. Set was on his feet, but the faerie backhanded him, sending him crashing into another table.

Wheezing in pain, Ash clutched at the discarded cutlery strewn on the floor before spying a saltshaker. Hoisting herself up by the edge of a low couch, she smiled against the pain. She'd started this battle months ago when she'd saved a baby from becoming a changeling. She'd use the same tricks she always did when dealing with these immortal bastards. She hurled the saltshaker at the fae's face. It howled as the glass broke, white granules exploding on impact.

Ash scrambled to her feet, unsheathing another dagger, and climbed onto the faerie's back. Wrapping her arms around its throat, she tightened her hold with one arm as she stabbed her blade into its eye. Its thrashing stopped as it fell to the ground, lifeless.

Ash rushed to Set's side, helping him up. "Are you all right?"

"Other than my pride being wounded from how that thing kicked my ass?" Set chuckled but winced as he rubbed his throat. "You're amazing."

He leaned on her for support before they retrieved their weapons and made their way outside.

As they left the cafe, Ash looked back at the destruction wrought by the faerie's attack.

"We have to go to my clan's camp. Niamh promised she would stay close. She may know where Mary and Dom are."

Set nodded. "Lead the way."

Hand in hand, they left the ruined cafe, leaving her foster family home behind, abandoned in this new world where monsters no longer seemed to lurk but thrived. The human realm had not gone unscathed by Newgrange's implosion.

CHAPTER 41
AISLING

Under the watchful gaze of an ink-black sky littered by stars, the River Boyne surged forward with a fervour not unlike the urgency coursing through Ash. For miles, she and Set had walked guided only by the moon in the ghostly twilight, weaving a silver path through the darkness for them to follow. In this human realm, it had felt unnatural. There were stretches of land unscathed by streetlights in Ireland, but the road they'd found themselves trudging wasn't typically one of them.

With her hand painfully clenched around her sword hilt, she flinched at yet another chorus of growls, too sophisticated, and much too like a conversation, to be mere animals. As with every other time, Set's new spear pulsed with a faint light. He'd been cagey about his new weapon, but she would do as he asked and trust him.

Nothing disturbed their journey, but Ash couldn't shake off the unsettling feeling seeping into her bones. It was as though the night itself was alive, and countless unseen eyes were studying them. Finally, scattered lights of what Ash hoped to be the Breen clan caravans were like a beacon. She hurried her steps.

"They have electricity," Set said, taking her hand in his and squeezing. "You told Niamh to look out for them. We saw no signs of Mary or Dom at the cottage. I'm sure they'll be here."

Ash only nodded, her pace quickening as her throat closed tightly around the sorrow she refused to acknowledge before she had any proof her foster parents had been harmed. She'd hoped Niamh had taken heed of her request to stay close to the cottage on Winter Solstice. Her cousin had wanted to take Ash's place as matriarch. Niamh hadn't made a move against her to remove her title, but Ash still wondered if the other woman would obey.

Tiernan had put restrictions on their clans' funds as a threat to the elders while they were in Tír na nÓg. Since the clan had split, the elders and a few others staying behind while others had followed Ash to participate in the Cath, she wondered what reception she'd receive from them now.

Damn them anyway if they chose to refuse her birthright. All she cared about was ensuring her foster parents were safe, and to see what state this world was in after Newgrange collapsed in Tír na nÓg. If what they'd just faced at the cottage was any indication, this world was doomed to the hands of the Fair Ones.

"Who's there?" a gruff voice shouted out as they approached. She heard the unmistakable sound of a shotgun clicking.

"It's Ash. Aisling Breen," she called out. "And Set McQuillan."

Set squeezed her hand, but remained face forward, his form tense, the spear once more in his grip. Murmurs floated towards them until the voice called for them to approach.

"Ash!" Niamh cried before breaking through the pair of Fianna standing watch at the perimeter of the caravans. Her familiar athletic frame was a stark relief to the shadowed silhouettes behind her. "How? I'm so glad you're safe."

"Matriarch." Emer appeared behind her wife, and the title was not lost on Ash. Emer added quickly, "Mary and Dom are here. Niamh saved them as you asked."

Ash's legs gave way but Set held her upright. Her foster parents were alive. They were safe. She repeated this in her mind until she believed it.

"Where are they?" she managed to croak out at last.

"Come, we'll take you to them."

As they hurried behind the couple, Ash felt all eyes of the remaining Breen clan on her. Peeking through caravan windows, and the few bunched around a low burning fire, she nodded at them, and they nodded back. The clan was silent. No chatter, and even though it was night, it was still early enough that there should have been children playing.

"In here," Niamh said, signalling to the largest caravan at the centre. Her mother's caravan. Hers.

Hesitating at the door, she raised her shaking fist to knock, but she didn't have to. The narrow door swung open, followed by both Mary and Dom peering down at her. Wordlessly, they descended the steps and embraced Ash in equal bone-crushing hugs.

"You're okay," Dom said gruffly.

Ash didn't fight her tears, but thankfully they weren't filled with anguish. "So are you."

After several minutes of relishing their warm embraces, Dom extracted himself. Mary kept her arms wrapped around Ash's shoulders as they both watched him stand in front of Set who'd been quietly watching their reunion along with Niamh and Emer.

"I told you to watch out for Aisling," Dom said as Set accepted her foster father's outstretched hand. Dom pulled him into a hug. "Thank you for bringing her back to us."

"Actually, Dom," Set said, clapping the older man's back before grinning at Ash. "She saved me."

"That's my girl." Dom hugged her again.

"Come in," Mary said, gesturing for them to enter the caravan. "I'll put the kettle on."

When Ash moved to step inside, she turned when Mary added tightly, "You both are welcome for a cuppa too."

Niamh smiled. "Thanks, Mary."

Ash smirked when Set entered last, the entire caravan tilting as he bent over to squeeze through. Mary busied herself in the kitchenette as everyone else sat in the various seating spaces. It was a large caravan compared to most, with a circular table at its centre and a narrow hallway that led to her mother's old bedrooms. Ash jolted, having to remind herself that it was now all hers. And Mary and Dom's, as it seemed.

She made to help Mary, but her foster mother shooed her away. Ash couldn't help smiling at the familiarity of it.

"What's been happening here?" she asked as she sat on the empty seat beside Set, across from Dom.

"As you predicted, the first light of Winter Solstice was the start of all this," Niamh said, gesturing with her arms like it explained what she'd meant. "Newgrange fell."

"Was anyone hurt when it collapsed here too?" Set probed, leaning forward so his elbows rested on his thighs.

Ash frowned, piecing together the significance.

"No, thankfully not," Mary said as she placed a tray in the centre of the table. "But that didn't last long."

Everyone helped themselves to a cup and Mary poured steaming tea from Ash's late mother's pot into each one. "We were able to convince the authorities that it wasn't wise to reopen so soon after Cara's murder. Thank you, Aisling, for warning us. Who knows how many more lives would have been lost?"

"What about your side? How many were killed?" Niamh asked, taking her wife's hand.

Before she could answer, Emer asked, "And what about Tiernan? Is he okay?"

Ash and Set shared a look before she answered. "Tiernan is alive . . ."

"But?" Emer probed, her tone flat as she leaned away as if putting distance between them would make what Ash had to say less damaging. She was tall, like Tiernan, her sharp cheekbones and elegantly long neck so like her cousin's.

"We found the caillte," Ash said softly, her eyes meeting Niamh's and then Emer's as they gasped. "They are in an underground cave, protecting Fionn Mac Cumhaill's grave . . ."

She trailed off, throat closing around the words as she met Emer's frightened eyes. How could she tell Tiernan's cousin what had happened?

Set's hand found hers, squeezing gently as he took the burden from her. "The caillte and other Fianna are in a magical enchantment, standing guard over Fionn. I'm sorry, Emer, but Tiernan is now among them."

Emer reeled back with a broken cry, face crumbling as she seemed to fold in on herself. "No! What do you mean? How? Not our Tiernan . . ."

Niamh gathered Emer close, tears pooling in her own eyes as she stroked her wife's hair. She raised her devastated stare to Ash and Set. "Can he be saved?"

Ash disentangled her fingers from Set's to lean forward earnestly. "I swear on my life, we will find a way to free him and the others." She blinked back the burn of her own grief. "I won't leave him down there."

Emer's weeping pierced Ash's heart. But she meant every word. Tiernan would walk in the sunlight again. She had to believe it with unbreakable conviction; the alternative was too terrible to face. Emer remained quiet for some minutes, face pressed into her wife's shoulder. The rest sat in mournful silence, the weight of sorrow and uncertainty pressing down on them all.

Emer sat up with a shuddering exhale, eyes rimmed red but resolve steeling her expression. She reached a trembling hand across the table. After a heartbeat, Ash took it gently.

"Thank you for telling me the truth," Emer rasped, a lone tear slipping free, sliding down her golden-brown cheek. "I know you'll bring him home."

Ash clutched her hand, wishing she could erase the pain etching such deep lines. Despite their differences they were united in this, no matter the outcome. She gave Emer's fingers one last comforting squeeze before leaning back, Set's arm resting around her shoulders before tucking her into his side in a warm embrace.

"Aedan O'Dwyer is also among Fionn's guard," Set said softly, his head inclining to Emer as her eyes widened.

"And that's why my uncle is now High King?"

Ash's head spun as the truths that were hidden in the other realm were laid out on her mother's small table. Her breathing grew less ragged. Even though there was pain in their revelations, there were no secrets to hide under Bradan's watchful eye.

"And what of Newgrange?" Niamh asked again, "Did anyone get hurt in Tír na nÓg?"

"The rígfénnid were the only ones in the chamber when it happened. There were a few Fianna killed in the fallout. Fintan Breen was amongst the dead."

Everyone remained quiet, sipping tea as they let that news settle. Niamh's lip trembled as she raised her cup to her lips in a shaky grip. When she set it back down, she said, "I didn't know him, but it's hard to hear our grandfather was a casualty. Did you get to spend any time with him?"

"Not really," Ash said hesitantly, not wanting to reveal her dislike for the man and how cold he had been.

Emer blew on her tea before sipping and then added, "As soon as the walls to the ancient stone crumbled, all chaos loosed."

"Fair Ones came out of hiding," Niamh shuddered. "We've been camped here, but we were outside your cottage that morning, just in case."

"And a good thing, too," Dom said, slurping from his mug. Ash's heart warmed at the sound. It had annoyed her countless times, but thinking how she might not have heard his habit of drinking tea as if he wanted to consume the entire contents in one go, she would never scold him about it again. "A collection of those beasts came for us."

"In retaliation for all the changeling attempts we've stopped over the years in the cafe," Mary chipped in. "It seems those monsters had been waiting to act out their revenge for saving babies."

"So how did you kill them?"

"We had a stash of salt and iron bombs," Dom explained as if it was standard policy to carry such things.

"And then we came in with our weapons and finished the job," Emer said with a smirk.

Before Ash could challenge Dom on his choice of weaponry, Set asked, "And what about the rest of the world?"

"That's the thing." Nimah's brows puckered. "It's only Ireland."

A buzzing rang in Ash's ears. "What . . .?"

Silence smothered them as they grasped for reason.

"It's like the Fair Ones are isolating us from everyone else. Nobody to help us escape." Mary's grip around her mug was bone white. "We've been cut off from the rest of the world. They've imprisoned us here for slaughter."

Those words hung suspended over the group like a leaden shroud. One terrible truth closed the maw of hell upon them: if escape was impossible, then so was rescue. Their forsaken homeland was a trap, and its captives numbered in the millions.

CHAPTER 42
AISLING

Ash gripped her mug, hoping the warmth of its contents would anchor her to this news as her mind fought to keep up. "You can't leave or communicate with other countries?"

"We're the new Bermuda Triangle," Dom said gruffly. "Lost behind a veil. We still have access to television and the internet. But it's confined to this country, and only those with generators to link into to the electricity grids."

"Seriously?" Set stood, the caravan swaying as he wore a path in the narrow space. "Apocalyptic type stuff?"

"Exactly that," Niamh confirmed and shivered. "All those zombie movies have nothing on what has been going on here."

Ash took a shaky breath, her heartbeat racing as quickly as her thoughts. "And we have no idea what the rest of the world makes of our disappearance? Or if they are experiencing this in their countries?"

A humming filled the room, Set's new weapon glowing once before going quiet. He reached back to grip its shaft as all eyes trained on him.

"Where did you get your spear?" Dom asked, his eyes narrowing.

Set released it before frowning. "It was a gift. It doesn't matter right now."

Ash's face snapped to him, unwilling to back down when he merely shook his head. Sighing, he nodded. He would tell her later when they were alone.

"Are you hungry?" Mary asked before standing and going back to the kitchen area.

Ash's stomach gurgled in answer and Set chuckled. "I'd take that as a yes."

As the others talked about what was happening, Ash watched quietly, basking in her new scenery. Mary was in her natural habitat, preparing a meal from odd ingredients that she could find. Tears rimmed Ash's eyes as a wave of relief washed over her at the sight she feared she'd never witness again. Dom and Set talked strategy, and what they could do to fight back. Emer and Niamh sat on the narrow-embedded couch, holding hands, and talking quietly with one another. Their heads were pressed together so Niamh's red hair tangled with Emer's black plaits. It was oddly comforting, surrounded by this unlikely group.

Sooner than Ash thought possible, Mary presented a meal of fresh tomato soup, sourdough bread and a cold platter of fruit, cheese, cold meats, and crackers. After they ate in comfortable silence, Emer and Niamh excused themselves, advising they would come again early in the morning with the elders. The thought of facing Mrs O'Malley was as welcome as inviting a dearg due to breakfast but Ash reluctantly agreed.

"You two take the room at the back," Mary said, washing the dishes while Dom dried, the pair synchronising into a familiar routine that Ash had seen countless times over the years. "We're sleeping in the small room at the front. We didn't want to take your room, even though Niamh tried to insist."

Ash's cheeks heated as she stared down the corridor. Set's voice was low but strong as he said, "I'll sleep on the couch."

Dom and Mary looked at one another and Mary snorted before saying, "You can hardly think we're old fools, Aisling

Breen. You're a grown woman and since we're facing world-altering events, there's no need for pretences, now is there?"

It wasn't a question. Dom winked at Ash as she got to her feet, but she didn't miss the cold appraisal he gave Set as he rose, also.

"Goodnight," Dom called, and Ash's cheeks were a furnace as the couple chuckled after them.

Cara's old room was to the right, but she couldn't bear the thought of entering that sacred space. Not yet. A hollow ache blossomed in her chest at the mere idea, memories of her mother sneaking their bittersweet rays into the cracks of her heart. Ash had left through stubbornness and naivety. Knowing that Cara had been trying to protect her from Ethne, she felt . . . no. She couldn't go down that road of regret. She wouldn't have met the couple murmuring in low voices to one another at the other end of the caravan. No decision that led to her becoming family with Mary and Dom should be considered a mistake.

As she inspected the familiar narrow door of her mother's room, she remembered the nights as a girl when she crawled into the bed beyond, seeking refuge in Cara's soothing arms.

Tears stung Ash's eyes, but she stubbornly blinked them away. That room demanded tears in private, and now was not the time to open that door and with it, the aching wound that would never truly heal.

"Are you feeling all right?" Set asked quietly behind her, his presence a warm comfort at her back.

Nodding, she didn't trust her voice to answer. With a shaky breath, she entered the small room to the left. It had a pull-down single bed and not much else.

"I can sleep on the floor," Set offered, taking off his boots.

When she turned to him, she noted the dark circles under his eyes.

"When was the last time you slept?" she asked, taking his hand, and tugging him onto the bed.

It was a little musty, but it was clean enough.

He sighed. "I can't remember."

"We'll share, even though it's a little snug."

When his light brown eyebrows rose, she smirked.

"Okay, fine. It'll be more than a little snug. I can't face taking her room. Not yet."

"Hey," he said, tucking her in close to his side and kissing her forehead. "I understand."

She could have stayed like that in his arms forever, but they were both too tired.

"We should get ready for bed," she said, extracting herself and leaving the room to use the small bathroom down the hall. The lights were off elsewhere, Mary and Dom having retreated to their end of the long caravan. With a spark of surprise, Ash noticed a familiar bag filled with her belongings and her heart fluttered. They'd taken her clothes with them.

Pulling out sleep shorts and tank top, she used the bathroom and freshened up, thanking the heavens for the spare toothbrushes and paste she'd found in the overhead cabinet. Looking down at the cotton sleepwear, she marvelled at how something so simple could feel like a luxury. And gods how she'd missed the floral smell of Mary's fabric softener.

She padded back to the room, noting the firepits at the perimeter of the campsite and the rustling of footsteps from the clanspeople on patrol. She'd have offered to take a shift, but exhaustion weighed on her bones. Dragging herself through the door, she told Set there were toiletries he could use, not missing the appraisal he gave her bare legs and curves no longer encumbered by a bra. Goosebumps raked her body, and she was acutely aware of her breasts underneath the thin material.

When he left, she took a shaky breath. Ash settled onto the narrow mattress, drawing blankets to her chin as shadows closed in. A war of fleeting pulses raced through her as she thought of the man in the room beyond. Not that they could do anything under the same roof as her foster parents. They hadn't even had a proper kiss. Was it inappropriate? Mary's words replayed in her mind. With everything going on, why was she second-guessing this? Why should she care about what others thought?

The door closed, so she lifted her eyes to find Set. And gulped. He'd tossed aside his clothes, now standing with dark boxers around thick hips, leaving taut muscles exposed. Water streamed down ridges chiselled from hours spent perfecting lethal skill, tapering from broad shoulders down to a firm waist.

His chest, arms and those sinful thighs rippled with potent strength, chiselled into a pattern too intimate to name. Ash traced higher past sculpted pecs and an eight-pack worthy of legends until meeting his smouldering gaze.

"I hope you don't mind." A rumbling chuckle rolled from Set's chest. "I wanted to freshen up. Should I be concerned that Mary left some of Dom's clothes for me again? These were the only things that fit. Kind of."

He snapped the waistband of his briefs with an audible smack, drawing Ash's stare helplessly downward.

"Eyes up here, Breen," he said, clicking his fingers.

"I'm not even sorry," she found herself saying before lifting her gaze slowly to his.

Electricity sparked between them as heat raced through her from head to toe. She rose from the bed, drinking him in. Nothing else existed. Not when this man stood before her.

"Why are you looking at me like that?" His voice was husky, enticing her further.

"Like what?" she murmured.

"You know." He dipped his chin, grey eyes ensnaring her. "Like you want to do something more than just eye-fuck me."

"Hmm?" was her only response as she took the last step to stand in front of him.

"Do your worst, Breen."

Rising to the tips of her toes, she captured Set's lower lip, sucking it slowly between her teeth. He groaned, hands encircling her waist, hauling her against him. She wrapped her legs around his hips, their bodies flush, and this time there was no sign of his ríastrad to ruin it this time.

There was nothing tame in what blazed between them, and she didn't see any reason for their first kiss to be any different. She opened her mouth eagerly as his tongue met hers, their mouths syncing in a dance of fire that burned through her body. With each stroke and nibble she sank deeper until only the press of their bodies against each other existed and how he worshipped her mouth with his.

A toilet flushed, followed by Dom's rattling cough. Ash froze before Set chuckled, gently breaking their kiss. He rearranged them comfortably on the narrow bed, still entwined.

"To be continued?" His eyes shone with amusement, with a hint of that molten steel that stole her breath.

She smiled into his chest, breathing in his familiar scent before flicking his nose.

"Hey!"

She rose onto her elbow, staring down at his shadowed face as he rubbed his face. "It's time to tell me about your new spear, Setanta McQuillan."

They glanced at where it rested by the wall. Set shifted awkwardly, rotating so he lay facing her, fist holding his head up so their eyes were level.

"Okay . . ." Set bit his bottom lip, a sheepish look shining through his grey eyes. "It's just that I . . . can't."

"What do you mean?"

"It's complicated."

An outraged squeak escaped her when he spun suddenly, pinning her wrists, his weight deliciously immobilising.

"Stop trying to distract me!" She fought half-heartedly, knowing with his strength she hadn't a chance.

"Just know that you can trust me."

Huffing, she caught his bottom lip between her teeth once more, nipping until he released her.

"Vixen," he accused, a glint in his eye.

"Fine, Setanta McQuillan," she murmured as she nestled into his warmth, relishing his solid frame. "I'll trust you, but you would tell me if you were in some kind of trouble?"

"I'm fine, Ash. Don't worry about me," he said sleepily, kissing her forehead. Reassured, she rested her head over his heart once more, its strong cadence soothing away the torrent of nagging fears that could wait.

CHAPTER 43
SETANTA

Soft tendrils of golden light peeked through the curtains, rousing Set gradually. Ash's warm, soft body was a delicious addition to his morning. Her legs were tangled with his beneath the bedcovers. A content smile curved his lips as he traced lazy patterns up her back, delighting when she moaned sleepily under his touch.

"Good morning, beautiful," he murmured, his voice rough from sleep.

She rolled towards him, emerald gaze meeting his. As her fingers wandered through the scruff of his beard, one leg encasing his thigh, a familiar frisson shot through him, desire sparking deep and immediate.

"Did you sleep well?" she asked, arms reaching out towards the ceiling in a gratifying stretch, her back arching off the bed, offering him an enticing view of her perfect body in the thin cotton sleepwear he'd insist she take back to the other realm.

"Nope." He flicked her nose. "Somebody snores worse than a clurichaun."

Before she could protest, his lips sealed over hers, a slow taunting tug of lips and teeth.

"I have morning breath," she whispered into their shared space, receiving his grin in return.

"I know."

"Cheeky fecker."

Chuckling, he hauled her on top of him, and her beautiful eyes widened. The dawning realisation of his need reflected in her eyes before she straddled him, rotating on his hard length in a slow, taunting movement as she lowered her mouth to his.

"Breakfast is ready!" Dom's rumbling voice called to them from the far end of the caravan.

"That man," Set grumbled.

Ash laughed before detangling herself from his embrace. "To be continued."

After washing up and dressing, the scents of breakfast cooking led them to the kitchen where Mary shot them a shrewd look. "The lovebirds arise! Sit yourselves down. You must be hungry."

Set offered Ash a wolfish grin as her cheeks reddened, but it quickly disappeared when Dom coughed pointedly, crossing his arms as he stared at Set until he sat opposite him.

While Ash set the table, Dom slid piping mugs of tea their way.

A brisk knock at the door burst the comfortable bubble enfolding them. Ash stiffened beside Set as Mary opened the door.

Set kept his face impassive, shoulders squared as Mary ushered the visitors inside.

"Good morning, all." Niamh breezed in, plonking on the small settee with Emer, followed by a wide-shouldered woman with white hair.

"Good morning, Mrs O'Malley," Ash said tightly, her eyes floating past the woman to the empty doorway. "Where are the rest of the elders?"

"We thought it best if I met with you while they tend to the rest of our clan. We share the same . . . views about you, Matriarch."

Set's jaw locked at the veiled insult, the desire to leap to Ash's defence burning in his veins. From the charged silence of the surrounding table, he wasn't the only one. But he restrained himself, for this was her clan and her battle to fight. Against this thickening silence, the rhythm of Mary's movement between the kitchen domain and the dining table created a muted soundtrack. The soft, intermittent clatter of plates somehow pierced the strained atmosphere, offering fleeting respite from the unsettling standoff as Ash and Mrs O'Malley regarded one another.

A faint glow seeping from the back of the caravan caught Set's peripheral vision. He blinked in surprise as the familiar glow of his spear emanated from where he and Ash had shared a bed. For the first time in far too long, he didn't fear the transformation that used to follow every wave of anger. His limbs felt no strain, his muscles remained pliant and his vision steady.

Ash took a long drink from her mug. Setting it down, she smiled sweetly. "And I have my views on you, Mrs O'Malley. Elders are much easier to replace than matriarchs."

The older woman glared at Ash while Dom chuckled. "That's my girl."

Set fought back a grin, biting the inside of his cheek to steer away the rising amusement. However, as Ash raised her mug in false salute to Mrs O'Malley, it was too hard to leash, and it stretched across his face in a wide smile.

His attention swerved towards the generously laden plate Mary passed his way. Although Ireland was under fae siege, she'd managed to produce a feast. A tantalising array of food was spread before him; blackberry and apple tart infused with a tangy-sweet aroma, French toast drizzled with rich, amber honey, perfectly poached eggs on sourdough toast to satisfy any lingering hunger.

"It's a mishmash of everything, I'm afraid." Mary shrugged before joining Dom.

"It's delicious, Mary, thank you," Set said around a mouthful of tart, noting her blush as she fussed over pouring Dom another mug of tea along with her own.

At last, everyone had found a cordial, if not tense, rhythm.

"Have Niamh and Emer filled you in?" Ash asked after Mrs O'Malley's face turned from puce to a blotched white once more.

"Yes," she sniffed, gripping the handle of her mug. "The elders and I consider it is time the clan returns to the human realm. You only tasted what was out there last night. We need full numbers for protection."

"I won't leave Tír na nÓg until Tiernan is freed."

All clatter halted as Mrs O'Malley stood. But before she could respond, Emer and Niamh rose from their settee, coming to the table edge.

"Thanks for looking out for my cousin, Matriarch," Emer said solemnly. "It is only right that the clan remains in Tír na nÓg, Mrs O'Malley."

"You don't get a say, Emer Cassidy."

"But I do," Niamh interrupted. "I agree with our matriarch's decision. Tiernan wouldn't let any of us remain trapped. He is a part of our clan and we'll do everything to get him back."

"Whatever is happening in this realm is linked to Tír na nÓg," Set added, scratching his beard. "As rígfénnid, I'll petition to our High King to send Fianna warriors here to protect the humans and our remaining people here."

"Bagged yourself a rígfénnid, cousin," Niamh said with a whistle, shooting Ash an approving glance "Nice."

"I see the elder opinion is not appreciated here, then." Mrs O'Malley reached the door, swinging it open to emit the frigid morning air. "I'll report this back to your elders, Aisling."

With a resonating click, the door closed behind Mrs O'Malley.

"That went well," Mary said brightly.

After a heartbeat everyone dissolved into laughter.

"I guess that's par for the course with Mrs O'Malley," Emer chimed in, her wide lips wearing a smirk so like her cousin's, Set realised.

Watching Ash's interaction with those surrounding them, he knew that the longer Ash lingered, the more challenging her eventual departure would become.

"Are you ready?" Set interlaced his fingers with Ash's.

Dom's towering frame rose from the table as the laughter died down.

"Take care of yourselves," Dom rumbled as everyone stood from the table. "Don't do anything I wouldn't do."

Ash gave him a tight hug. "That's a wide scope to operate under."

Dom smiled, kissing her forehead before Ash moved to Mary. "I love you both so much. Thanks for everything."

"This isn't goodbye, my girl," Mary murmured into Ash's ear. "You'll come back to us."

Set shook Dom's hand, the other man's tight grip lingering as he pulled him close. "Look after her, won't you?"

"We'll look after each other, I promise," Set replied solemnly, giving Mary a hug as Niamh and Emer embraced Ash.

"You bring Tiernan back safe," Emer said to them both.

Ash held her gaze, nodding, swallowing hard as she glanced to and from her and Niamh. "Look after my family and the clan," she choked, turning swiftly and disappearing to her room.

Once inside, a small duffel bag on Ash's back, Set gripped his spear. "Let's go back."

CHAPTER 44
SETANTA

"Are you sure about this?" Set asked Ash, tugging her back to his side as they walked the cobbled streets of Tara Court.

She chuckled but allowed him to guide her into his arms. He nuzzled her hair, breathing in her scent of lavender and the citrus wash she'd used in her morning shower.

"I'm not sure of anything," Ash sighed, squeezing his midriff, and leading them into a stroll. "But we agreed. Telling Bradan about Ireland is the best option. The country is overrun by Tuatha Dé, but we can help."

Set nodded and let her move away from his side, only to grab her hand as they walked through the unusually quiet streets. They had sifted back only moments ago, and when both their clan campsites were empty, they angled towards the centre of the town.

The solid weight of his new spear bore on his back, and it eased the building tension of the revelations of the previous night. When it had pulsed in the caravan, he'd feared Dom would ask to inspect it, or that someone would touch it. Ethne's warning rang clear in his mind; he'd never let anyone be corrupted by the spear. A hum pulsed from behind, but Ash didn't seem to notice it. He reached backward to stroke the warm steel and it quietened. His monster lay within that blade, and it was as though it was reminding him of their so-called bond. Set couldn't be corrupted by a monster that was already part of him even if they'd been separated by the magic of a cunning Fair One.

"Up ahead," he murmured as they made it to the centre square, forcing his attention away from his ríastrad and how his body felt weaker since they'd been parted. A large assembly had gathered feet away, all muttering to one another.

"What's happened?" Set asked a local woman who looked at him as if he'd grown two heads.

"Were you not here for High King Bradan's announcement?"

Ash stepped forward. "What did he say?"

"Fair Ones," the woman whispered, looking around as if to ensure none were standing beside her. "They caused Newgrange to fall. High King says the Peace Treaty is all but broken. You really didn't hear?"

Set was a loss for words before he scrambled for understanding as the woman regurgitated Bradan's explanation. The High King had lied about Tiernan, and he was continuing his tangled web. Set's stomach hardened as he ran a hand through his unruly hair. They knew the truth; the destruction sprang from Ethne's scheming alone, not some orchestrated Tuatha Dé plot. She was a Fomorian royal, and his lips tingled with the reminder he could not tell anyone that truth.

The local woman eyed them sceptically and as Ash frowned at him, he looked at their intertwined hands as she winced.

"Sorry," he whispered, releasing his painful grip.

Ash only shook her head before saying hastily, "We were distracted."

The woman's brows lifted as she tracked their closeness, and he felt her eyes roam his black battle-suit with clear appreciation. "I'm sure you were."

"Come on," Set said, ignoring the woman's snigger as Ash spluttered. Spotting Malachy and Maebh to the side, he tugged her over.

"What do you make of that?" Malachy asked, not bothering with greetings. The gruffness that made up the former second would seem rude to most, but Set could see the worry etched on his sun-weathered face.

"It's bullshit," Set said, trying but failing to rein in his anger.

His sister didn't seem to share the sentiment. Looking between the two, Maebh asked, "And where were you two all night?" Her tone was playful, at odds with everyone else. Ash gave her a look that would have anyone else shutting up, but not his twin. She winked. "Are you finally a thing?"

"Now is not the time," Ash said, which only made Maebh snicker. Set couldn't ignore the twinge of disappointment, but he wouldn't push for more than she was willing to offer. Ash nodded toward the castle. "What exactly did Bradan say?"

Maebh sighed. "The Cath rules have changed. Our banners will be called more frequently, but we will take shifts with the highguard as well as training and . . . redistributing any fae still in Mide."

A knowing silence settled on their small group. Glancing around the assembled gathering, anticipation and excitement were ripe amongst the warriors and Tara Court residents alike. The Cath was no longer about gaining acceptance into this land. It was solely a fight against the Fair Ones. And while Set appreciated how frustrating Fianna life had been, being forced to aid and abet fae, he knew this wasn't the right approach either.

Squeezing Ash's arm, he kissed her cheek. "I'll be right back."

She nodded, her porcelain face strained. Maebh only smirked wider as he headed toward the castle. Set heard Ash murmuring to his sister, no doubt filling her in on what they'd discovered in

Ireland and how Set would request aid from Bradan. Whether the High King would listen was the issue.

Set was swiftly allowed entry and led to where Bradan and others were enjoying a feast. As he stepped into the great dining room, savoury fragrances of rich stew and roasted meats were present, but his sharpened senses quickly analysed the different smells. The deceptively thin layer of rich foods were the emotionally seasoned aromas of the assembly's energetic, yet somehow apprehensive ambience. It was as if each enticing culinary aroma picked up an undertone of emotion; the citrusy excitement, the metallic fear, and the acerbic contempt forcefully tagging along with every whiff of food, making it unmistakably more than just a feast.

Set glowered. Since all of this happened, his gift of empathy was easier to decipher. It had always been his sister's ability; or curse, if you asked her. He'd been happy to not share the same affinity to it, but now, he couldn't deny his senses had heightened.

A chill ran down his spine and he stiffened, but nothing stirred within. Reaching behind to the spear, he gripped it, the smooth metal a growing comfort as time passed. It pulsed in response. This was usually the time he'd feel his monster fight to come out, but only silence greeted his mind.

He'd tested himself countless times while lying in bed with Ash, and nothing had happened. There was no danger in being with her now. The spear was a solid rod at his back, the presence of his monster illuminating it even now. But there was nothing menacing. It seemed as if the ríastrad was no longer a threat once encased outside his body.

Ethne did that for him. She was a heinous Fomorian, but she'd saved him from himself, and he couldn't deny that one truth.

"Come, join us, Setanta." Bradan gestured to a seat beside a warrior from the Collins clan. "Meet your fellow rígfénnid."

The black-haired clan leader nodded at Set, quiet compared to the others who chatted incessantly over mouthfuls of food and hearty swigs from ornate goblets. A servant emerged behind him, drawing out the heavy high-backed chair for him to sit. When he motioned for Set to remove his spear, Set shook his head, subtly adjusting the position of his weapon to sit comfortably.

Bradan pointed at the man beside Set. "This is Deaglán Collins, Rígfénnid of Leinster."

Set nodded at each introduction through the different provinces, who each acknowledged him but promptly returned to their conversation and gorging.

A great feast lay at the middle of the table as more servants lined the walls, jugs of different beverages to hand. Bradan's eyes were a weight on Set's profile, so he leaned to the closest dishes, piling his plate. A bronze-roasted turkey and boar took up the centre of the long banquet table, while seared racks of different meats were interrupted by golden pockets of crispy potatoes, glazed carrots and green beans swimming in a buttery dish further down. Set's stomach rumbled in appreciation, despite the hearty breakfast Mary had provided.

"So, this is the infamous McQuillan boy," Deaglán said, lifting his glass in salute. "Rígfénnid of Connacht."

Set looked at the man with a smug smile, leaning against his chair, flexing his muscles under the tight-fitting black fabric. "I'm no boy."

Another servant was by his side, before he had time to do anything else but accept a goblet thrust into his hand. Smirking above the rim, Set raised it before sipping the too-sweet drink. A mask was needed in front of these people. One Maebh donned often. He could borrow it from his sister for this. As a McQuillan twin, they were used to this type of reception.

"And what do you make of our decision, Setanta?" Bradan's voice was quiet, but everyone stopped talking.

Set tensed, placing his goblet on the table, speaking carefully. "I understand where it's coming from."

What he'd come to speak to Bradan about seemed like a dangerous conversation to have after the High King's speech. Bradan had said 'our decision' and he wondered if the other rígfénnid had had any say. And if so, Set's position as one of these leaders was already under jeopardy to have missed the chance to vote. He'd never wish away a moment spent with Ash, but he did regret not having asked more questions of Malachy and Maebh about what exactly had been declared.

Sure enough, Bradan said, "You heard the new rules have changed. Fianna are called upon to fight against our oppressors. The Cath is still important, but we need a full capacity of leaders to guide our warriors and people in the trials to come."

A murmur of agreement rippled around the table. Scrapes of cutlery against plates filled the room and Set stared at the barely eaten food on his plate before him as his stomach squirmed.

"I want to go to the human world and check in to see if they need our aid." When Bradan only looked at him with a stony expression, Set pressed. "You said that the Peace Treaty is broken. There are Fianna in the human world. They are abandoned to the whims of the fae."

"Our fellow humans have their government. We have ours."

"But . . ."

"I am dealing with the Taoiseach, and he is aware of what has happened. Newgrange collapsed in their world too."

"They know about us?" Set said before hastily adding, "Was anyone hurt?" His neck heated with his almost slip. He'd begun spinning his own lies, but he wasn't as good at it as Bradan.

"No." Bradan lifted his glass, taking a long sip before continuing. "They've always known who we are. Our people put up with the scorn of humans in that realm, travelling around in performing shows, but government officials have always known. It is why we are never truly questioned. When throngs of us go missing to enter this realm, they cover it up."

Set let that sink in, absent-mindedly stroking the rim of his wine glass.

"Come," Bradan said before standing. When the other rígfénnid stood, he shook his head. "Only Setanta."

Set winked at Deaglán as he rose and followed the High King even though his heart hammered in his chest.

Following Bradan to the lower levels of the castle, he willed his heart to slow. The spear at his back whispered as they descended stone steps that turned to clay. He couldn't make out any words but there was a cautious urgency to its tone. Torches lit the gloomy damp path and Set had no doubt where Bradan was leading him.

"I want to show you what we no longer tolerate." Bradan's voice echoed through the tunnel.

Accepting the torch from the High King, Set held it aloft, hoping to see beyond the mere feet he could. Lámfada responded to his thought, a blue hue emanating from his back. The High King stared at the spear for a moment but didn't comment. The familiarity of the rough walls reminded Set of the Hill of Tara tunnels. He glanced to the side, wondering if Bradan knew how close his son may be to this spot.

A putrid smell hit his nostrils. Shit and blood and gods knew what else filled the dank space as the walls narrowed until Bradan had to walk in front so as not to touch the dripping walls. An iron door stood before them, cries echoing from beyond.

A rustle sounded and Set's skin jumped as a highguard in black armour came out of the corner of obsidian darkness. A heavy iron key in hand, Set couldn't make out his face as he nodded wordlessly to the king. The clank of iron and a turning of a key, and then the repulsive smell intensified as stale air hit them. The cries quietened upon hearing that sound, as if they didn't want to draw attention to themselves.

Set swallowed the bile forming in his mouth as he took in the many forms within the dark cells. Was this where Conor had been? The spaces were crammed with small bodies, and if Set didn't know any better, he would have thought Bradan had imprisoned children, but the withered faces and animal features told him enough.

Swarms of fae backed away from the cell doors, the ones at the front shaking violently. Some of the creatures were as thin as twigs, hair the colour of autumn leaves and eyes as large as duck eggs. Others were covered in coarse dark hair, long yellow teeth poking out of wide mouths, jagged nails raised before them in pleading gestures so human it made Set's throat close over. Others were as dark and corporeal as shadows, iron manacles hanging from the walls anchoring them from taking on their true forms. But Set could not fear these creatures. Not when they were trapped like wild animals, most bearing deep gashes from the blades of man.

"I thought we were escorting the fae *out* of Mide?"

"We are . . . for most of them," Bradan said. "These are criminals who refused to leave. Who had the audacity to fight back when we'd tried for the peaceful approach. Something their kin do not bestow upon us if we venture to their lands."

Bradan led them further into the dungeon and Set resisted the urge to cover his nose and mouth with the crook of his elbow. Another pitiful cry filled the air and Set saw its owner as they neared a set of chains housing a small man. Not a man.

A wizened face surrounded by matted hair that was probably auburn, covered with so much dirt and blood that it was hard to tell in the darkness. He wore tattered trousers and a ripped shirt that showcased the many cuts and bruises scarring his body.

Angling his light higher, Set tracked the iron chains suspended from the unseen ceiling, jangling with every wince and movement the creature made. His small wrists had large welts where the metal had burned his flesh, so much that bone peeked through. But no matter how much it burned, the fae couldn't seem to stay still.

Set gripped his torch tightly, subtly stroking his axe at his belt to ensure it was still there. Not for the clurichaun before him, but for the monster beside him.

"This one killed a highguard."

The clurichaun whimpered before rasping out, "He killed my family. All of them, dead."

"They were attacking my man."

"They were babes," the fae wailed. His head fell back before pinning Set. His sea-glass eyes bloodshot. "Please."

Set knew then that one word would haunt him from this day on. Because it was not a plea for freedom; it was a cry to help end his misery. Set had killed a highguard. But he was not chained, nor was he condemned to torture and death.

"Set, I will give you more time with your clan while the Cath is on. But as rígfénnid, I want you by my side. I see strength in you beyond your physique. You are strong of mind, and you know there are sacrifices and unsavoury things that we must do in order to win the war against the Tuatha Dé."

Set stilled, as did all the many ears before him. Bradan had openly declared war in front of these fae. Set hadn't heard his speech above ground, but surely the High King hadn't been as foolish then? There was no way any of these fae would survive beyond these walls.

"Show me you understand," Bradan said quietly.

Set looked at the High King for a long moment before frowning at the clurichaun at their feet. Handing his torch to Bradan's outstretched hand, he unclasped the button securing his dagger. It felt heavier in his sweaty hand, the smooth wood unyielding in his grip. The clurichaun stilled at the sight of the blade before straightening as tall as he could. He reached Set's thigh, his neck bent far back to look up at him with clear eyes.

"Thank you."

Set nodded once before raising the dagger. In a swift and powerful motion, he slit the fae's throat. A thundering silence filled his head as his soul blackened further.

CHAPTER 45

MAEBH

Ash circled Maebh, her steps on the dew-covered grass tracing a careful path, but Maebh tracked her with patience, her blade gleaming despite the dark morning.

"Ready?" Ash challenged, her breath rising between them.

"Always."

The chill morning air was saturated with hues of grey and purple, the sun reluctant to break the horizon as they trained. As quick as a viper, Ash darted forward, only for Maebh to effortlessly dodge to the side.

"You're getting better at that."

Ash rolled her eyes. "If you were a man, I'd accuse you of man-gloating right now."

"How dare you; that's worse than mansplanations."

Ash preened. "I say it like it is, sister."

With a swift kick, Maebh sent Ash stumbling backward, all humour draining from her face as she clutched her mid-section.

"Was that necessary?"

"Absolutely."

"Again." Ash swiped at her dark brow, bringing her ornate sword in front, fierce determination on her face. Setanta's gift to Maebh's best friend gleamed as the sun finally peeked over the treeline in the distance, the steel not yet scarred from battle. The sky melted into a warm palette, streaks of buttery yellow unfurling across its canvas, warding off the purples and indigo hues that clung stubbornly to the heavens. With how things were going, the smooth blade would be riddled soon.

Maebh mirrored Ash's stance, feet planted firmly in the wet grass. Though exhausted, her body buzzed with restless energy that only combat could satisfy. The highguard training nearby were a mere background noise that held no relevance to the women's spar.

A playful smile played on Maebh's lips. "Are you sure?"

The only response was Ash's familiar huff of laughter before launching another practised strike. Maebh deflected the blow.

High King Bradan's decree, demanding the warrior clans integrated training with the royal guard as part of the ongoing Cath, altered the landscape in more ways than terrain alone. Now highguard and warrior clans mingled where once they were separate, alliances tense and fledgling despite the shared purpose of defending their kingdom in a battle all but declared.

The two women ignored the training fighters as some stopped to watch and shout encouragement. Combat was another dance Maebh had fallen in love with at an early age and she refused to allow men to ruin it by offering their opinions on how she performed. The symphony of steel clashing and precise footwork, the to and fro of the deadly tango, was an intoxication best served without unsolicited judgement.

"Croissants," Ash shouted over their dance, continuing their other torturous game.

Maebh sidestepped her advance, deflecting her blade and pivoting. Their first encounter at the Dublin café played in her head and her heart warmed. Neither had realised the friendship they'd form.

"Apple tart," Maebh countered, and the two women laughed, no doubt both remembering how Maebh had charmed that same dessert from the café server.

Ash was one of few people Maebh had ever truly let in, and there was no doubt they'd bonded over their collective losses. With a catch in her breath, Imogen's death intruded once again as she continued her swordplay. But her mother's searching eyes in that dim tunnel filled her vision, Maebh's knees dampening on her mother's blood, all while Imogen had looked beyond her to seek out her son. Watching her mother die would plague every good thing, Maebh was certain of it.

"Fluffy pillows," Maebh grunted, her advance catching Ash off guard, listing off another item she missed from the human realm.

Ash stumbled back but regained her footing, glaring at Maebh before puffing a breath out and raising her sword once more. Maebh drowned out the sound of appreciative shouts from their spectators.

"Have you spoken to Set since last night?" Ash asked quietly. She advanced again, and a few highguard moved closer within hearing distance. It was a half-hearted move and Maebh easily deflected.

"Yes," Maebh sighed, angling their footwork to move away from eavesdroppers, not before noticing a familiar face amongst the king's guards. Michéal smiled brightly when he noticed her attention, but she pivoted her back to the red-haired man. "Bradan is hellbent on getting rid of the fae from this land. He's selected rígfénnid from warrior clans. No locals."

"Did he tell you about the dungeons?"

Maebh nodded briskly as her stomach bunched. Bradan had gone too far. The other clans were on his side, taking sick trophies during the Cath. The High King was bloodying their hands, including her brother's.

"Hey," Maebh said, arcing her sword lazily. "You know what else I miss?"

"Coffee," they said in unison, and when Ash laughed, Maebh took the opportunity to kick her friend's legs, causing her to fall on her back, much to the delight of Michéal, who called out for Maebh and clapped. She gave him a scathing look before turning her attention back to Ash.

Standing over her raven-haired friend, she laughed. "You still leave yourself open on your left side."

"And you, my friend, continuously mollify any notions I have that I'm a fit warrior."

"You are fit," Maebh said with a wink. "I'm just fitter."

They meandered over to their belongings, as Ash politely acknowledged their onlookers, who shouted out pointers to her for their next sparring session before dutifully leaving them to get back to their posts.

Before Michéal could open his mouth as she passed, Maebh said, "You're stalking me."

"Not at all," Michéal chuckled, stuffing his hands in his pockets as the highguard around him sniggered. "I heard of two matriarchs sparring and had to see it for myself. We get so little entertainment here."

"So, you don't find hunting innocent faeries as good sport?"

"Careful, Maebh," Michéal said, scowling before casting a pointed look at their surroundings. "Enjoy your day."

He gestured for his highguard to follow, leaving Maebh to watch his back.

"What was that about? *Who* was that?" Ash asked.

The formidable wall of Tara Court loomed in the distance as they wandered toward their usual spot skirting the woodland. The court's stones, weathered by centuries of relentless elements and heavy history, stretched toward the cloud-littered sky as if reaching for the heavens to touch the gods who'd left this world and its inhabitants to fend for themselves.

"Potential trouble." Maebh's sigh was deep as she took the wicker basket Ash carried, waving her toward their favourite area.

An orchestra of birdsong, sweet and innocent, wove melodic tendrils through the chilly morning air. But the sound wasn't as beautiful as previous mornings, and it took a few beats before Maebh realised it missed the interwoven soprano strains of pixies that had always alleviated the natural song with an ethereal lightness, making its absence even more impactful.

Ash shook out their tartan blanket before laying it on the dew-laden grass as Maebh discarded her sword and hunkered to rummage through the basket she'd borrowed from Rían. Barters and loans were the main currency in Tír na nÓg and Maebh had soon learned that she didn't have a lot of either to go on. It was lucky for her that the rest of the McQuillan clan were resourceful and although they begrudgingly recognised her as matriarch and she barely hid her contempt for them, she took advantage of their supplies. One couldn't be too picky after weeks of living in this realm when she'd stolen the last of Setanta's coins.

"We're on duty tonight," Ash murmured, handing her a cloth-covered bread roll.

"So are the McQuillans. Not that my clan particularly cares that I'm their matriarch. They'll go ahead with whatever plans my aunt concocts." Maebh uncovered the still warm bread, inhaling it deeply before biting into it. Groaning loudly, she grabbed a handful of grapes from the basket.

"I'm calling you on your bullshit," Ash said, taking smaller bites of her own roll. She shook her head when she opened her mouth to retort. "Set is rígfénnid, and you have that clan without his interference. You know how much I like your brother, but he was a hindrance to your leadership. Remember when we first met, and you stuck up to Professor Mathews for me? You give zero fucks. I believe your t-shirt even said something like that at the time."

Maebh chuckled. "I miss my clothes."

"My point is, stop letting others tell you what to do. Do you want to be matriarch?"

"Well . . ." Maebh hesitated. Her mother had trained her to be their leader whilst dismissing every attempt she made at performing as one. "It's my birthright. I shouldn't have to fight for it, but I've never been given the chance. They want me to prove myself. Fuck them. I've done as much as anyone else who is born into this role."

"You sound like someone who has given up to me." Ash nudged her shoulder. "You're just going to lie down and let them take it from you?"

"I'm not lying down, Ash. I'm just . . . dealing. Okay?"

They ate the rest of their breakfast in silence. When she finished, Maebh hugged her knees, one hand absent-mindedly doodling in the moist soil. Wearing the Breen combat fatigues, she had stubbornly bated her aunt at every chance. She wasn't fooling anyone, let alone herself.

Ash's voice broke through her thoughts. "I've seen your leadership skills, Maebh. The way you look out for others, the way you can instantly command attention when you arrive. If you could see what I see, you'll realise you were always meant to lead."

They shared a look, her friend's green eyes sparkling with a warmth Maebh could feel spreading into her chest. Ash was right. She had one foot in the game. She couldn't continue pretending she didn't care what her aunt said or wearing clothes to clearly piss her off. But would anyone listen? Years of wearing her mask of indifference was not an easy thing to cast aside.

"All right, clan," Maebh said as she rose from her weathered log. "We have a long night ahead. Let's get to guard duty."

They were gathered around a crackling fire after sharing an evening meal, one Maebh had secured by successful bartering some of her mother's jewellery with a local fish merchant. She hadn't hesitated. Imogen had had terrible taste; gaudy necklaces, real gold, but completely not Maebh's style. The clan had relished the fresh catches. Even Maura had been pleasant to Maebh while she'd cooked the large pieces of meaty haddock along with seasoned potatoes and vegetables, though Lorna had given sceptical glances, insinuating her trade had been distasteful. It hadn't stopped the woman from gorging on two helpings.

The winter night held a bone-chilling cold, more extreme than any they had yet to experience in this realm. Maebh secured her fur-lined coat, tugging on leather gloves she'd also found within Imogen's belongings. There were untouched troves within the ostentatiously-sized tent, but Maebh had avoided most of them. Despite her feelings towards her late mother, she would be a fool not to enjoy the extravagance of the luxurious bed and the comforts Imogen had lugged into this land.

"I want to patrol tonight, Maebh," Orla said quietly from the log she shared with her sister.

Eilish shook her head, gripping her sister's arm. "You're not ready."

"We need people to stay here," Lorna said, stepping in front of Orla, blocking Maebh's view as if she didn't exist. But her voice was soft as she spoke to the other woman. "There's no shame in waiting to heal after what you've been through."

"I'm done being cooped up in this encampment," Orla bit out, jumping to push past Lorna. Her dark eyes beseeched Maebh as she asked, "What do you say, Matriarch?"

As Orla's words echoed in the frosty air, Maebh caught a whiff of the powerful, earthy aroma of a forest after rain and the unyielding resilience of aged wood all rolled into one. Orla's resolve hung around her like an invisible shield.

"Matriarch," Lorna sighed, turning to face her. "Your mother would have done what's right for the clan, and you should too."

As Maebh glanced between Lorna and Orla, an internal tussle erupted, and she chewed on the inside of her cheek. From the murmurs of agreement with her aunt, siding with Lorna was the safer vote to earn some respect from her clan. Yet as she looked upon the brunette's raised chin, her eyes daring her to be more than just a puppet, she couldn't help but see her own flaring determination to prove herself. Hadn't Maebh herself fought for validation of her strength and free will?

Maebh smiled brightly at Orla. "Let's go. Show them what you're made of, Corrigan twin."

CHAPTER 46
TIERNAN

A biting chill coursed through his veins as the shadows infiltrated the cave walls, their presence a palpable threat to his king's very existence. What started as spider-thread fissures were now unmistakable gouges to a black void; ever-expanding, ever-consuming.

Each crevice, once as insignificant as the veins of a leaf, had twisted and snaked its way through the cold cave, swallowing darkness and stone as only living nightmares could do. Within these voids rippled the sluagh; undulating, alive, and hungry.

Half of the stone guardians had already been consumed, reduced to nothing more than rubble scattered along the cave. His memories continued to slip away, fading into the void, and like a spool unravelling, he uselessly grabbed for any thread to his identity.

Ethne had christened him with various names, but it had been the voice of the elusive stone guardian that had named the shadow monsters stalking their cave. She had maintained a peculiar distance from the rest of the stone clan, one that he had fought to gain when he was first trapped, but that battle was lost. Despite half the guard crumbling under the host of sluagh festering around them, she had managed to conceal herself. How could she isolate herself amidst their shared existence?

Protect.

He remembered Ethne's name, but the woman with golden hair was no longer an anchor tethering him. Her name was lost to the crashing waves of a storm even Manannán mac Lir could not calm. His own name was lost too.

Tiernan.

A wash of familiarity cloaked him as he wrapped that name around his mind. The stone guard had spoken, her voice cutting through the incessant chant of the others. Fionn Mac Cumhaill was in danger. Their duty was to protect him. But the sluagh remained attached to the walls, perhaps by the enchanted charms the red-haired druid had scattered around the cave. He jumped from body to body, searching for the female's voice who remained hidden within his stone clan.

Tiernan leapt from one stone form to the next, phasing into their thoughts as they continued their relentless chant to stay, protect, fight. He dived deeper, wading past the repetitive prayer, a plume of fragmented memories offering glimpses into who each guard had been. There was a man, once a poet and one of Fionn's oldest friends. Beside him was an older woman, one of the fiercest Fianna highguard who'd set out to find the ancient king.

On and on, Tiernan threaded until he stopped before a young woman. The clothes of this statue were too modern for any of the original Fianna or highguard ensnared by Fionn's enchantment. As Tiernan contemplated the stone sculpture, she held an air of nostalgia encapsulated forever in stone. Clad in a pair of low-rise jeans, her feet were encased in oversized flat boots. An array of wicked-looking daggers peeked under a puffer jacket that lay open to show a graphic tee that brought a faded memory of the golden-haired woman who'd kissed him.

As Tiernan jumped into her statue, he was not met with a cascade of memories, but an unrelenting fortress of rage. A surge in his gut that felt oddly like a swift kick propelled him through the remaining statues and a force of memories barrelled into him, a sudden rush of images consumed him. Among these fleeting remnants, one figure persisted: a formidable man.

His stature was substantial, built like the ancient oaks of lore, black curled hair tied against a thick sun-weathered neck as he battled a host of ferocious Fair Ones that could only be Fomorian. The man's movements were too graceful for his mountainous form.

The warrior manoeuvred over the battlefield filled with monsters and ethereal fae; his dance so fluid and instinctual that it was as if he was merely a part of nature, a force of the universe expressing itself. His weapon shone, a radiant club that commanded art and destruction, striking true with crippling decisiveness. The luminous club consumed darkness, and Tiernan felt a kinship he couldn't put into words, a sense of unity shared between the souls of warriors. This wasn't another guardian, but an entity out of legendary tales, a figure cloaked in the mystic folklore of his homeland. An earlier incarnation, a being, who in centuries past, fought against the monsters of this realm and stood victorious.

Fight. Fight. Fight.

Gasping, Tiernan found himself hurtled back into his own stone form. A biting coldness seeped into his skin as a sluagh hissed into his ear, close enough to feel its icy breath without touching him. The shadow host had moved away from their black pockets and were swarming once more around the stone guard. Those charms had not worked for long.

Fight.

Tiernan recoiled, and it took a thunderous heartbeat to realise he'd moved. Looking down at his brown skin, no longer stained by white granite, relief jolted him into another step before dread poisoned his newfound freedom when shouts bounced across the room, and he stared at the other guards racing toward the sarcophagus nestled deep within the grotto.

"Come on, Tiernan!" the young woman called, dark hair flying behind her as she raised a sharp dagger in the air, her Ugg boots slapping against the damp ground.

Tiernan reached for his sword, wishing it were a club from the vision he'd seen. Launching into step beside the woman, a chilling familiarity of his entrapment triggered a grim realisation: Fionn Mac Cumhaill's resting place had been threatened.

They joined the row of guards, their ranks considerably depleted.

Form a protective wall, Nessa Cassidy ordered, and he grit his teeth against his mother's instructions but followed suit, the stone clan compulsion compelling him.

As they pressed their backs against the raised sarcophagus, a desperate last stand against the predatory shadows slithering ever closer, Tiernan turned to the woman.

"What's your—"

"Sinéad," she said, staring straight ahead at the sluagh swarming so tightly there was nothing but darkness pressing around them.

From the curtain of shadows emerged two figures in perverse humanoid forms. A shudder of dread snaked down Tiernan's spine as he took in their grotesque features. They stood upright, mimicking human posture, yet their entities blurred and distorted at the edges, their boundaries impossible to fix. They seemed to exist as beings with substance and formless apparitions alike that continued to merge and reform with the lurking shadows.

One cocked its shapeless head, the gesture a mockery, the cruel perversion of humanity sending the taste of bile creeping into the back of Tiernan's throat.

Stand your ground, Lorcan Breen commanded, and with a jolt Tiernan realised he'd had some connection to his daughter before his last life ended and this one had begun.

"Focus, Tiernan," Sinéad commanded, and he straightened when the monstrous forms stalked forward.

Their sauntering gait was a deliberate, slow, almost dignified stride, but beneath it Tiernan tracked the predators savouring their impending victory. Each step drew them closer to the stone guards and to their slumbering king in an agonising taunt, a promise of impending doom.

Weapons ready.

The stone guard raised their collective blades in unison. The figures paused, their heads turning toward one another, an insidious rumbling laughter resonating within them. The sound, like scraping glass and rattling bones, ricocheted off the cave walls.

The perforating dread within Tiernan peaked as the shadow beings continued until they were feet away from the stone guard line, drifting in and out of their personal spaces. It felt like a hunter circling its prey, toying with its food before going in for the kill.

Tiernan knew that someone was about to die. It could not be their king. But they could not fight against these monsters, only stand before Fionn's resting place until one by one, they were consumed and destroyed. Was this his turn? Would he die without remembering who the woman with golden hair was?

Before he could manage another thought, one menacing silhouette of the shadows veered into his space, and a surge of revulsion thundered through Tiernan's veins. The reek of decay filled his nostrils, and the sheer proximity of the darkness sent icicle jabs of fear stabbing into his senses.

He struck out with his long blade, his insides churning with a dread-induced fascination as his sword jolted forward, groaning as frost crept along the steel from the shadows until it broke into two, leaving a mere stump in his grip. The sluagh lunged forward and Tiernan stiffened, but the monster stopped a breath away before snatching the guard next to him.

An ear-splitting scream filled the air as the man dropped to his knees, and the stone clan knew the terrible inevitability before their clansman; none could look away. A cold hand found his, and Tiernan gripped Sinéad's palm as the kneeling man's pained eyes swung upwards, locking with his. The light in his eyes eclipsed by growing fear, his pupils dilating into dark chasms as his mouth twisted in a grimace.

"Your name is Ultán, and you served your king well," Sinéad whispered.

Ultán's expression slackened, his eyes moving to hers. He nodded, his shoulders slumped even as the sluagh hovered over him, growing thicker and larger before snatching him headfirst into its large, shadowed maw, the sickening sounds of a quiet, squelching crunch filling the cave. The process was painstakingly slow, the sounds repetitive yet eerily rhythmic until the shadow consumed him entirely. No rubble lay by Tiernan's feet. No sign Ultán ever existed.

The humanoid shapes seamlessly melted back into their dark wall, their distinct forms swallowed up by the monstrous shadowy expanse. It was as if they had never been separated, their brief independence a mere puppet display conjured by the cavernous shadows, who retreated towards the cold crevices of the cave, a promise of their imminent return.

A compulsion to stay in their formation overtook Tiernan's body and he did not fight it. Sinéad's hand retracted from his own. Defeated and exhausted, Tiernan discarded his broken sword and it clanked against another familiar one he remembered belonged to someone he used to know. It didn't matter, his missing past was not important. A crushing weight pressed against his spirit as his limbs cemented once more in a frozen vigil.

It matters, Sinéad said into his mind, and he knew the others couldn't hear.

He didn't bother responding.

The black voids eating the stone clan were not only destructive but also generative. The walls were birthing grounds for a growing army of sluagh, pouring out shadow soldiers like an unending tide of inky devastation. With every passing moment, they swallowed more light, more hope, creeping ever closer to their king. With a heavy heart and a resignation to his inevitable fate, Tiernan braced himself for the sluagh's next attack.

One he feared they would not survive.

CHAPTER 47
MAEBH

"Go away," Maebh groaned into her pillow as an unrelenting finger poked her cheek.

Without opening her eyes, she already knew it was too damned early to be awake.

"Maebh McQuillan," a delicate voice whispered close to her ear, hot breath tickling her cheek.

She tensed. She knew that voice, and it wasn't from any of her clan.

Peeking one eye open, she looked up at . . . herself. Not-Maebh smiled brightly before blinking once, cocking her head to the side. "Did I wake you?"

Wrenching back her blanket, Maebh sat upright, pulling Sage closer. Squinting at *her* unruly blonde curls to her blue eyes and pouty lips, she pushed the púca to sit on her bed.

"What are you doing here? If my brother sees you . . ." Maebh shuddered, remembering Setanta's haunted face after slaughtering both púca and Fianna who'd attacked him. He still hadn't spoken about it, and she'd only gleaned the story from Ash.

"I don't look like that," Maebh finally said, looking at the dishevelled clothes she'd loaned the púca, plucking strands of hay from Sage's top, who only frowned down at herself. "Where have you been sleeping?"

"The stables, mostly." Lifting her hands close for inspection, Sage said, "I thought I copied your appearance perfectly."

"You didn't. My boobs are bigger."

Sage placed her open palms to her breasts as if measuring before reaching out with both hands towards Maebh's chest, who slapped her away. Sage pouted. "How can I make it better if you won't let me?"

"I don't want you to look like me." Maebh jerked her covers up, crossing her arms against the cold morning. She would have to wear a jumper to bed in future. Damned eternal spring her ass. "Why do you want to look like me anyway?"

"It was the only way I could get inside your tent unnoticed. You told me to not look so conspicuous. So, wearing the skin of a known Fianna is a good solution, yes?"

Maebh's face scrunched as she eyed the tent entrance. It must have been later than she thought. They'd patrolled until the early hours, Orla keeping up and seeming more upbeat than she'd been since cursed. Knowing how much it had meant to Orla made her aunt's scowls worth it. Clattering of pots and conversations filtered through the thin canvas.

"Did anyone from my clan see you come in here?"

"Yes, all of them," Sage said brightly. "The blonde woman who looks like you but older and crosser bid me good morning, but she didn't smile when she said it."

Maebh cursed. "You walked by Lorna looking like me? At this time?"

"It was the only way I could —"

"Yes, you said that." Maebh cursed again and Sage shrank back. She sighed. "Don't be scared of me. I say mean things, but I'm not going to hurt you."

Sage's large blue eyes, *her* eyes, were doleful, and Maebh flinched. She never would make that expression and she didn't like her doppelganger doing it either.

"You need to shift into someone else so we can both leave."

"Right," Sage said. "Any suggestions on who?"

This would be the longest day of her life.

"You also need to change into fresh clothes. Honestly, why you can't just transform into a cat? Life would be easier."

"I like being human," Sage shrugged, twirling in a circle until she spotted Maebh's mother's trunk in the corner. "I'll change now."

Maebh rose from her bed, her empty stomach churning. "Wait . . ."

But it was too late. Sage peered into the open trunk. "Those are pretty." She turned with wide-eyed wonder. "Why don't you ever wear them?"

"They were my mother's," Maebh said dismissively, trying to calm her racing heart and fight off the disappointment. She hadn't known what she'd expected to be in the trunk.

"They have your name on them."

Maebh stilled, staring over at Sage who arched a brow that made her look more like herself, and to her dismay, her mother.

"Please shift into someone else," Maebh said quietly, and Sage must have heard the desperation in her tone as she did so instantly, and the brunette merchant woman who was promised a dance with Ash's cousin stood before her.

Maebh stood, her head swarming with an incessant buzzing. On trembling legs, she cautiously approached the knee-high trunk, Sage stepping aside to reveal a treasure trove of remarkable clothing and weapons. Each piece was intricately crafted from rich, opulent fabrics: sumptuous silks and fine leathers, glistening velvets, and thick furs. Tracing her fingers over her embroidered name, she marvelled at the blend of feminine elegance designed for combat.

Her attention snapped to the array of weapons nestled amidst the folds of fabric: swords with unique hilts, gleaming daggers, throwing knives, and a collection of belts and pouches presumably harbouring druid potions.

A whirlpool of scattered thoughts stirred within Maebh as she surveyed the overflowing contents. Imogen McQuillan had been cruel and demanding, a formidable force that had shaped her upbringing. Yet, here lay evidence of her mother's legacy, a heritage that was now entrusted to Maebh's hands. Had Imogen known of the looming danger? Had she considered Maebh's potential matriarchal inheritance sooner than she had let on?

Drawing a shaky breath, she reached out, her fingers carefully selecting a garment—a closely-fitted vibrant tunic, richly hued and emblazoned with golden Celtic motifs. As she held it against her, she turned to the long mirror by the dressing frame, gazing at her reflection.

"That suits you," Sage said. "You should wear that."

Maebh gave a slight smile at the remark before tearing her gaze away.

"Here," Maebh said, rifling through her own stash of clothing and pulling out a simple tunic and pants that would not look amiss on a merchant. "Put these on behind there."

Sage disappeared behind the dressing frame, giving Maebh a much-needed moment to breathe and think about why her mother had a trunk full of clothes set aside for her. She slipped into the new tunic and pants, both hugging her figure perfectly. The emerald hue of her top seemed to enrich her sun-kissed tan, while the dark fitted trousers showed off her curves. Her blonde curls fell wild and free, and for once, it didn't bother her. In the full-length mirror, she wasn't just Maebh anymore. She looked at a matriarch. Standing straighter, she realised she looked like her mother. The golden motifs woven into the fabric made her deep blue eyes shine even more vividly.

Turning once more to the trunk, she burrowed down until she found a short blade and matching sword. The weapons felt familiar in her hands, as if they had been waiting for her touch all along.

As Maebh closed the trunk, the weight of Imogen McQuillan's legacy settled upon her shoulders. No matter how awful she had been as a mother, there was no denying how strong a matriarch she had been. Could Maebh ever prove herself, not only to her clan, but to her mother's memory? These clothes seemed to suggest Imogen had thought Maebh may forge her own path; and she wanted to.

Maebh would do what her brother had been begging for since their mother's death. It was time to embrace the challenges that awaited her and carve her own destiny as a warrior matriarch worthy of the formidable Fianna clan.

Half an hour later, Maebh and Sage exited the tent.

Of course, the entire McQuillan clan were sitting around the scattered logs having a late breakfast after their patrol duty. All scrapes of spoons against bowls and conversations stopped upon seeing them.

"Matriarch," Lorna said, making it sound like a joke. "I just saw you come home at an ungodly hour. And you left a stranger unaccompanied in your mother's tent."

The púca grabbed Maebh's hand, fear radiating from her in a sharp intrusive scent of ammonia. To everyone else it would appear like two lovers holding hands after a night together. Maebh did not care if that's what they thought. They'd seen her with many lovers over the years. She would not allow her aunt to make little of her in front of Sage.

"Just because nobody would touch you with a druid's pole, don't begrudge the rest of us some fun."

A ripple of laughter filtered through her clan, and Maebh's smile widened. Perhaps Lorna did not have as many supporters as she'd once thought. Lorna's oldest friend stepped forward, thin lips twisted, but Maebh lifted her hand to the elder. "Don't join in, Maura, you'll only hurt yourself."

"The devil lives on your wicked tongue, girl," the woman spat.

"Call me girl one more time and see how wicked I can be." She tugged Sage by the hand. "Come on . . ." Shit, she couldn't remember the local woman's name. ". . . hon. Let's get breakfast."

A few of her clanspeople chuckled and nodded their heads towards her as she passed. She winked at them. It was a stupid battle, but she'd won it.

"What if the woman you're impersonating is here?" Maebh asked Sage doubtfully as they weaved around the already bustling market stalls. Slowing her pace, she eyed the tables. The baskets and tables usually teeming with fresh produce were only half full. Had she been asleep for the entire morning? The announcements for the Cath and highguard training usually happened before noon and as she looked to where the flags usually billowed, none had been raised yet.

"I'll shift if I see her." Sage pulled on Maebh's hand. "Come. I want to show you something."

Her soft voice was uncharacteristically dire, so Maebh followed sceptically. The púca never seemed concerned by the danger of being caught by another Fianna, content on remaining in Tara Court despite her kind being slaughtered for trophies. Maebh opened her mouth to ask if she was aware but closed it. How could she say it without hurting or scaring the creature? Perhaps that's what Sage needed to realise she shouldn't remain. Maebh was about to start the awkward conversation when they reached the farmlands.

"Look," Sage said, pointing to the farmers in their vegetable patches.

"They aren't milling." Maebh climbed onto the wooden fence dividing the fields that were constantly worked on to get a better look. White dusting covered the normally green and gold grounds. "There's frost."

"When Newgrange was destroyed, the lands of our peoples collided. So did the wind and unforgiving seasons. We have never had to worry about things such as harvesting for winter."

"So, the markets don't have enough food to barter?"

"The people don't have enough food to eat."

The castle loomed in the distance as it did in every area of Tara Court. The fields were on higher ground, like the Hill of Tara, to catch sunlight despite the high walls protecting them. None of that would matter if they had no crops.

Maebh shielded her gaze against the overhead sun. "Bradan will figure out a way."

"The human High King concerns himself with many things. I fear this is not one of them," Sage said. "I have more to show you."

The púca strode on, but not before shifting behind an abandoned work shed. Now, she was a Fianna warrior from another clan. One that Maebh knew of but had never spoken to.

"What's the name of the woman you're wearing?" Maebh asked, and Sage shrugged. "How come you don't ever change into a man?"

The púca turned, her unfamiliar freckled face scrunching. "I did before. I didn't like the feel of it. Too many parts."

Maebh nodded with a shrug; she couldn't argue with that logic. They reached the quiet market, its merchants huddled in groups. Worry radiated from them, and Maebh cut off her gift as best she could as they passed. It reeked of dank and must. She'd started rationing her favourite perfume soon after arriving for fear of it running out, so her normal defences were depleted, and the familiar shielding fragrance of myrrh and tonka bean was not as potent.

The streets narrowed and became dirtier, and she realised they'd reached a part of the market that she hadn't ventured into despite being here for weeks. It had always seemed off, as though her ability to read emotions and people was telling her that the people who came here were not ones she wanted to know.

Her nose wrinkled as rusted iron and old pennies assaulted her. Sage's face was equally unsettled as she walked closer to Maebh.

"You smell it too."

"What is that?" Maebh asked, eyeing the Fianna who loitered here. The stalls were more barren than the main square and sold random selections of broken dishes and dirty blankets. "Who would want to barter for any of this?"

Sage nodded toward the crumbling walls behind the tables, where crudely painted symbols were scattered. It was almost like graffiti; a sight Maebh hadn't seen since leaving the human realm.

"They sell other things to the right people," Sage whispered as they passed the hooded men and women who watched them with unfriendly gazes.

"Like what?"

"Not here." Sage quickened her steps as a merchant stood past his stall, crossing his arms and glaring at them.

Maebh opened her mouth to ask him what his problem was when a flash of auburn hair and black clothes caught her attention. She tracked Micháel as he spoke softly with a few of the merchants, who were on much friendlier terms with the highguard than either of the women walking through their turf. For once the man didn't see Maebh as he darted behind a stall and disappeared through to the building behind it. Sage tugged on Maebh's arm again and they retreated to the main section of the court.

"Did you sense it?" Sage asked as Maebh puckered her brow. She added, "The magic?"

Maebh stopped in her tracks, turning to face the inconspicuous backstreet marketplace. "What does that feel like?"

"This particular kind of magic smells like iron. Feels like dread."

"How would I sense magic?"

"All Fair Ones can," Sage said as if that explained anything.

"Sage," Maebh began, tucking a loose curl behind her ear. Why was her hand shaking? "We've been through this. I'm not fae."

"You have Tuatha Dé Danann blood within."

"So you say, but . . ."

"If it looks like a sow, smells like a sow, then it's a sow."

Maebh sighed. "That's not the saying."

Sage's brows raised as if that didn't matter. And really, it didn't. Maebh's breathing slowed as her heart rate pumped furiously. There was no way she was a Fair One.

Right?

"What is being blood-blessed? If I have fae blood, how did that happen?"

Sage nodded, well . . . sagely, which severely riled Maebh. She kicked at loose stones, scuffing her new black boots.

"It is time to seek the answers."

Placing her hands on her hips, she glared at the púca. "And just how do I?"

"Biróg."

"The twig crown lady who only answers questions with questions?" Maebh rolled her eyes. "That's just great, thanks."

Sage's smile was wide. "You are welcome."

The now familiar trumpet sounded in the distance and Maebh groaned.

"Change into someone else."

By the time Maebh reached the castle main entrance, another brunette by her side, most clans were approaching from the encampment area.

Another trumpet signalled and they collectively turned to the parapet in the distance. Highguard stationed by the flagpoles unravelled banners showcasing which clans were next to take part in the Cath. The first was a red hand, palm open against a yellow background. She searched for Ash in the crowd to see her reaction to the Breens' call. Three more clans were called, and Maebh settled herself for another day sparring with highguard when the last banner was unfurled and her breath caught at the sight of the white wolf on hind legs, front paws outstretched against a red background.

It was finally the McQuillan clan's turn to fight. Watching her banner placed alongside the Breens', her resolve snapped into place like the wind catching the fabric. She would ally with Ash, and she would not take no for an answer this time.

CHAPTER 48

MAEBH

The market square was a flurry of movement as warriors marched to their designated assignments, while the locals looked on. Their arrival had been entertainment from their normal routines at first, but as the days had ebbed into weeks, Maebh had seen a dip in the courtesy they'd once shown. Nobody had thought the Cath would take this long. But now, with all the strange events taking place, including the bad, it seemed she and the other warriors were now welcome once more.

A symphony of chirping birds filled the air and Maebh looked toward the stone walls where countless nests had been constructed. It was as if an army of birds had made Tara Court their home. The weather had chilled in this realm, so perhaps this was their form of migration? Her curly hair bounced with each step as she made her way toward the McQuillan camp. Anticipation surged through her veins, but the increase of her heart gave away the nervous flurry forming.

She rehearsed her speech. Lorna and Maura would not interrupt her. She wouldn't allow it. She'd sent Sage away, begging her to keep out of the Fianna warriors' way. The púca promised she'd be fine. Now was not the time to take a Fair One under her wing, but she couldn't ignore the niggling feeling worming in her gut when she watched Sage walk away. Somehow, she felt responsible for the creature's safety.

"All right," she called to her warriors, who were in the process of strapping on different blades and weapons.

They didn't stop, but at least they'd turned to look at her. She smoothed out her new coat, her embroidered name like a beacon on her chest.

"We are going to clear the River Boyne from merrow and we are going to ally with the Breen clan," Maebh said, her words rushing from her. She took a breath, eyeing her aunt who only smiled at her. Taking that as a terrible sign, she forged on anyway. "I think it's the best plan. The . . . headless horseman was a sign that things can get too dangerous in smaller groups. The merrow are just as deadly. They will put up a fight. When we are successful, we will receive more points. I've looked over the rules, alliances are allowed."

Lorna sighed dramatically. "Maebh . . ."

"No, Lorna. It's about time you realised I'm in charge. I've decided this is our best plan, so we're doing it."

"Setanta already decided that this was our best plan, so we're ready to go." Lorna sneered as someone coughed. The others wouldn't meet her eyes and Maebh had to take that as confirmation. Lorna waved a hand, lowering into a mocking bow. "You're too late to order us, but by all means, keep talking."

A parade of onlookers had seen them out of the castle gate, shouts of well wishes following them as the warrior clans marched out of Tara Court. Other clans scattered in different directions, maps in hand as they planned to target different areas of Mide. Maebh followed behind Ash and Setanta as the Breen and McQuillan clans marched toward the river.

It had been Maebh's bloody idea, but the clan behaved as if Setanta was the hero of the hour. Had they forgotten she'd suggested this alliance and it had been her twin who'd shot it down? As if signalling Setanta through snarling thought alone, he turned from the front line, beckoning her to join them. Her scowl only deepened as she fought the urge to stick out her tongue.

After several miles in her foul mood, she ignored everyone, even Ash who had tried to get her to take part in their brainstorming over where they should tackle first.

Truly, this was a waste of her time. She should be concentrating on how to free Tiernan, or finding Biróg and getting answers on why Sage thought she was a Fair One. Her clan obviously didn't need her as matriarch with Golden Boy Rigfénnid Arse Face taking the lead. There were too many indicators that led dangerously toward the púca's accusation for Maebh to totally shut down the possibility. But how could she be a Fair One and be completely oblivious to that fact? If she was, then so was Setanta. He had the ability to ríastrad. A trait best known for Cú Chulainn, who was a Tuatha Dé Danann . . . No, she couldn't spiral down this road. Not yet.

"Mae," Setanta said from beside her and she blinked back her surprise. When had he sidled up to her? She searched, but Ash was nowhere in sight, and they were walking further behind the others. "What's your problem?"

She debated punching him in the gut, but that wouldn't have been the mature, matriarch-like approach.

"You are," Maebh said, elbowing him in the stomach. She felt satisfied at his flinch. Although it was hard muscle she'd hit, at least it had hurt. "Why did you go behind my back about allying with Ash? Why are you even here? Aren't you supposed to be too important doing rígfennid stuff in the castle with all the other big, strong men?"

Setanta's brows rose as he rubbed his stomach. "Honestly .. . I've been taking care of things since Mam died. You've barely been around and when I arrived at camp and you weren't there, I thought it best to take charge like normal."

"So, you're going to give me shit over being ten minutes later than you were after the banners fell?"

"No, that's not what I'm saying," Setanta said slowly, as if talking to an irrational child. Her arm twitched, the impulse to elbow him again almost too strong to deny. "If you want to take over and actually *be* matriarch, I'm all too happy to step back, Mae."

She pursed her lips as he looked down at her. He was too calm. There was no sign of his temper flaring, and it oddly made her feel less sure.

"What's with the new spear?"

"What?" Setanta visibly tensed as his hand raised behind his head to tip the new weapon, facing her as if to further shield it on his back.

"Can I see it? she asked, reaching around him.

"No," Set answered, far too loudly and quickly, the stench of his possessiveness rolling off him. It was a complex aroma that filled Maebh's nostrils and she cringed. Dark and elusive, it was tinged with the proprietary mustiness of old books jealously hoarded away. He backed away before shrugging. "This is something I picked up from Grainne's forge. I wanted to thank her for all the help she gave us with Orla and Conor, so I bought it from her."

"With what?" Maebh asked, tasting rotten fruit signalling a lie between them.

"None of your business." Setanta looked at her, his face a mask of stone. "Who was in your tent this morning? Malachy mentioned a local leaving with you."

"None of your business, brother."

They stared at one another as the secrets grew between them like a spider's web. Neither answered the other's question and they walked through the woodland in tense silence. Setanta, once a ticking time bomb, walked in stoic resolve, eyes scanning the surrounding trees and bushes with a calm that did little to settle her. What had changed in her brother? Was it Ash?

She mumbled something about scanning ahead to make sure they were taking the most direct route, and walked swiftly until she caught a glimpse of a pair walking with identical raven black hair.

"Hey," Maebh called, and both Ash and Conor slowed to allow her to catch up. "My clan is boring. I'm walking with you guys."

The sun was high in the afternoon sky by the time they made it to the River Boyne. The devastation of Newgrange was still strong in the air. Highguard and a group of Fianna clans could be seen in the distance, clearing the rubble that once was the ancient stone passageway.

"Where do we start?" Maebh asked but immediately wished she hadn't bothered.

Setanta spoke over her. "We have two merrow hats. The water around the nest is poisoned so only the hat wearers can enter until we can retrieve more protection."

Ash offered Maebh her hat when she saw her studying it. It was crudely sewn from what Maebh dreaded to think was a red hide, turquoise feathers jutting out, all possibly from the same unknown creature. Maebh lifted it closer, and the feathers tickled her cheeks, as soft as silk with a scent of brine.

"Why is the water poisoned?" Malachy asked.

Ash peered into the river, her pale pink lips downturned. "Because male merrow scales emit a toxin and when they nest, it pollutes the water until the perimeter around their nest is contaminated for humans. Fish and other creatures aren't affected by it as much. But it's an effective way for them to protect their merrowspawn while hunting for dinner, too."

When all eyes were drawn to Ash, she shrugged. "After they attacked, I researched them. My . . . the couple I lived with had a library full of Irish lore at their house. Mary had a thing for collecting old classics, and I knew she had a section on the merrow and mermaids of Ireland. You wouldn't believe how much real information is in there. Humans truly do know about the legends; they just don't realise they're real."

Maebh handed the hat back to her friend. "We'll station around both sides of the river. Both clans will work together to take on anything that comes out. Just because we're hunting merrow, doesn't mean that's all that's down there."

Set stepped closer to Ash. Stooping a little to meet her eyes, he spoke softly. "I think it's best if Malachy and I go first. We can take on the first group of merrow, lure them up here for you and Maebh and the others to grab their hats."

"Wait. What? I planned to go," Ash said and Maebh realised if her brother didn't hear the hurt in Ash's voice, then he was an idiot.

"We are working together, and everyone has their strengths . . ." Set trailed off.

Yes. Her brother was most definitely an idiot.

"When you and Ash fought the merrow the last time, were you the only one to kill them?" Maebh asked, stepping beside Ash.

"No. Ash killed one. But she was incapacitated soon after."

"Because they had caught her off guard, right?" Maebh retorted. "You were more prepared because you weren't ambushed. We're the ones ambushing today, and Ash is more than capable of handling herself. I know. I've trained with her."

Set's nostrils flared as he glared at her. "Mae—"

"Matriarch's decisions are final over *her* clan, or have you forgotten who's in charge, brother?" Her tone was light, but there was no mistaking the fire behind her words.

"Only when it suits her," Lorna's scornful words were loud enough to be heard by all, but Maebh chose to ignore her.

"I will go first," Ash said, breaking the loaded tension between Maebh and Setanta.

"And the other hat, Matriarch?" Set asked, jaw set so tightly that she was sure he'd break a molar.

"You can use it. I'm quite happy to stay dry for now." Maebh moved to the back of their group, noting Conor was located there too.

Paul, Caoimhe and a group of Breen warriors retrieved one of the retractable bridges along the winding riverbed, using the set of wooden wheels and steel bands connected to the bridge via a labyrinth of ropes and pulleys. Malachy shouted orders as the warriors turned the wheels in unison until the reinforced planks slid smoothly across the river.

"You stand up for Ash, but not yourself." Conor had come closer, and Maebh didn't turn to look at him, watching as the pair discarded their outer clothing, leaving just their tank tops and pants on before putting those ridiculous hats on. They began convulsing and Maebh watched, mesmerised as gills formed along their necks. Before they dived into the dark water, she saw webbed hands and feet. Gross.

"I don't see the point," she began, finally turning to Conor who was still studying the space their siblings disappeared into. "Why try to change their minds of something so deeply ingrained? They all believe I'm a failure."

"But you're not."

Maebh blinked. Before she could respond though, he stepped toward the water where everyone waited. What would Tiernan do if he were here? Surely, he'd be by his matriarch's side. Would he have noticed her true feelings like it seemed only he had? He didn't share the same gift she, Ash and her brother did, yet he saw her and understood her. She wished more than anything that he were standing beside her, lecturing her on being an ass and just to take part already.

Was he still himself? Or had the stone prison turned him like the others?

CHAPTER 49
SETANTA

The dark, cold embrace of the rushing river weighed heavier on him with each stroke of his arms. The current tugged him down as if Manannan Mac Lir, god of the sea, were embracing him into his watery kingdom. But this section of the river was no better than a tomb. His eyes were already adjusted to the darkness, a thin film having snapped into place as soon as he put the cohuleen druith on.

Glancing backwards to Ash, he noticed her eyes were filmed with the same protection barrier; her normally emerald eyes glistened like gems under the dappled sunlight filtering through the river's surface high above. She wouldn't look at him, her pale skin a blue hue in the depth of the river, reflecting the muted light that permeated the depths.

He was a fool for suggesting Malachy go with him instead of her. Maebh had made things worse, like she naturally did, and he hadn't been able to explain his reasons to Ash in front of both sets of clans.

If anything happened to her . . .

It wasn't because he thought she was incapable of fighting for herself. Glancing her way now, only in a black tank top and pants, her bare legs long and strong as she kicked through the heavy current, Set marvelled at her vitality. She was a leader to a fierce clan, and she had proved her strength when taking charge at Newgrange. Her midnight hair flowed behind her with each strong stroke, exposing her long, elegant neck. His blood heated at the thought of planting soft kisses until he reached her collarbone, a whimper from her beautiful lips. He couldn't trust that he wouldn't put his clan in danger, that he wouldn't destroy the world if any harm came upon her.

She was a distraction. She was his downfall. And he couldn't bring himself to care about the danger in that. His spear hummed at his back, as if the monster within agreed with his thoughts. An empty pit had formed within his stomach every time he searched for his monster, a mix of relief and something he couldn't place when he'd realise that he no longer had to fear his ríastrad. A peace had cocooned around his heart, one he'd never felt before. One that had partly to do with the spear, and more to do with the woman swimming at his side.

He opened his mouth to speak, but remembered too late that they were underwater. Instead of swallowing suffocating water into his lungs, however, it flowed in and filtered out of the gills that had formed on his neck. Weird.

"I'm sorry," he said, the words bubbling between them, but clear as if speaking on land.

Her gaze snapped to his, but her unhappiness only seemed to deepen as she continued to pump her arms and legs, expanding the distance between them. When Set reached her, he tugged on her hand, rotating them until they were face to face. With one hand around her waist, her arms threaded the water to keep them both from rising. At least she hadn't pushed him off.

"I was an asshole up there, and I'm sorry for suggesting that you wouldn't be suitable to come in first."

"You can't undermine me in front of my clan. In front of yours. I'm matriarch, Setanta. Something you need to accept. For both me and Maebh."

Set winced. Only his family called him that, and he felt the sting of his full name on her lips like the reprimand it was.

Ash's words jabbed him like a dig into his side, something his twin often enjoyed doing. He berated Maebh for not leading, and knew he'd been challenging her choices when she did try. Set had always thought he'd be Maebh's second in command. Although Imogen had been the one to lead, she'd listened to Malachy's council. Now he was forced into being rígfénnid, and soon he wouldn't have any say in the McQuillan clan.

"I promise I won't do that again." He stroked up her bare arm and smiled as she shivered. "Are you ready?"

Ash tugged his arms, drawing him closer, her supple lips parting. When he angled his head to close the gap, she shoved him away with a teasing smile. "Let's go find some monsters."

"Vixen."

Her chuckle sent a wave of bubbles to tickle his face.

They swam deeper until they reached the rocky bed. His vision swept across the riverbed, tracing the discarded fishbones that lay strewn amidst the silty landscape. These remnants whispered of the dangers that lurked in the shadows, and of the merrows' predatory nature. Ash picked up what looked alarmingly like a human femur before dropping it where it made its slow descent. A putrid smell filled Set's nostrils and he pointed ahead to where tall grass undulated in the current. An oily substance marred the dark water the closer they swam to it and his heartbeat kicked up a gear as even more discarded bones trailed along the riverbed.

Intricate patterns adorned the surface of the nest, woven with meticulous care. Swirling designs and gentle curves, reminiscent of the flowing currents, danced across its exterior, imbuing the structure with an otherworldly charm. Vibrant hues of green, borrowed from the river's depths, enlivened the walls, creating an enchanting spectacle of colour. The beauty of the world was tainted by the knowledge that danger awaited them.

As they drew closer, he noticed the openings strategically placed in the nest's construction. Narrow slits, resembling windows to an underwater realm, adorned the domed ceiling. These openings no doubt served as the merrow's hunting grounds, allowing them to peer outside while keeping their precious merrowspawn safe within.

Ash unsheathed the dagger strapped to her thigh, and he copied her by unstrapping his spear. It was almost weightless in the dense water, but its now familiar smooth handle was a reassuring presence to his over-heightened mind. Set fought the urge to pull her back as Ash parted the long grass and then disappeared through its thick foliage. Before her lower legs disappeared, he was parting his own sections of the thick grass. Stopping every few seconds to listen, they continued in until an echo of grunts filtered through.

Heavy silence bore down on them as they slowly crept forward, using the grass as an anchor and shield. On and on they went until finally muffled sounds could be heard up ahead. Set gripped Ash's ankle, but she'd already stopped. He reached her and they waited behind the thinning grass. Shoulder to shoulder, they parted the grass just enough to see through.

From what he could make out, they'd reached the epicentre of the nest. Merrow clustered in groups in the large clearing, swimming back and forth around high pillars of gel-like balls that reached to the top of a woven grass ceiling. Tracking the narrow holes that formed long open slits on the roof to peer from, Set counted how many merrow were patrolling and how many were tending to the balls. A flurry of movement caught his eye to the tower closest to him. Within the gel, something black and small moved. A tiny claw pressed against the soft membrane. His throat dried. They weren't balls; they were merrow eggs.

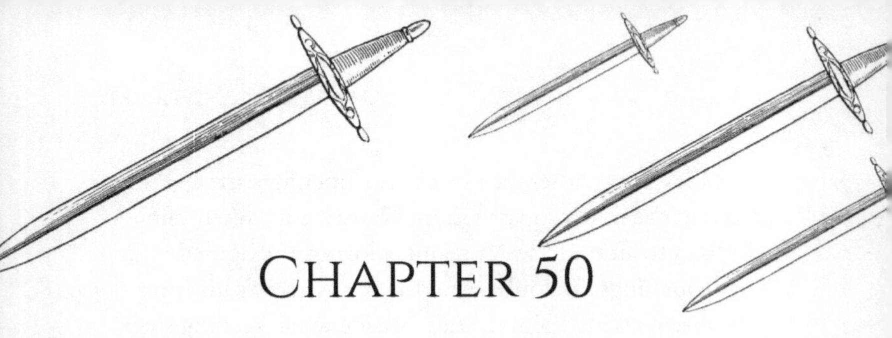

CHAPTER 50

AISLING

The nest loomed around them, its imposing presence closing in as Ash listened to the grunts of merrow barely visible through the grass wall she dared to part.

Structures, rising like stalagmites, housed the merrowspawn. Each cluster of the fish-like eggs formed a vertical tower, reaching toward the ceiling of the nest, their translucence shimmering under the gentle light that filtered through the river's surface, even this far below. The sight was undeniably breathtaking, but tremors of unease coursed through Ash at the monsters within reach.

Swimming above their domain would only alert them, and that was probably how they caught their prey. She imagined herself standing above the surface, looking at the star- speckled reflection, not realising these monsters were watching her underneath, ready to drag her below.

She ignored the boulder that landed in her stomach, churning as memories of that night came back to her. The helplessness she'd felt as they dragged her deep underwater. She had been sure she was about to die. Her heart raced with the echoes of that fateful day, only to be saved by Set.

His shoulder grazed hers in a solid comfort, his eyes scanning the nest before them. She couldn't help the memory of their piggish faces inches from hers as their clawed hands tore her clothes and flesh. Their grunts and squeals as they communicated with one another, no doubt of the plans they'd had for her.

She gripped her dagger tightly as she floated, scanning them now. It was only when Set tugged her shoulder she'd realised she'd been festering in that memory, inching within sight of a group of merrow tending to the nearby pillars. Swimming back before they could notice her, she nodded that she was okay. She would not be the one ambushed today. Set's gaze lingered a moment longer, but she turned to survey the little monsters in their home. His choice to take Malachy over her still stung like a wound, but now was not the time to dwell on it. He'd said sorry and had seemed genuine, so she'd let it go.

The merrow gruffly communicated with one another as they circled the pillar, their scaled green bodies shining from the luminous eggs. They were easy to kill one on one. But they never were alone. Merrow nested together, and had learned that their strength was in numbers, clearly seen in the clusters within this one nest while the females of their species lived in open seas. Mermaids. They were far more civilised, but no less deadly. Riding on Croi Dubh's back with Set at her back, they'd almost lured them to a watery death with their siren song.

Ash had learned a lot since that day she'd been attacked. Her scars, both visible and unseen, had forged her into something new. Something that would not yield to the darkness and fear of monsters.

It was now she who hunted them.

The merrowspawn themselves were a sight to behold. Their spherical forms, reminiscent of delicate fish scales, glowed with an ethereal light. Hues of blues, purples, and pinks painted their translucent iridescent surfaces, movements hinting at the growing creatures within. It was as if each egg contained a fragment of river magic, waiting to hatch and join the merrow domain. A place where life began, no matter how monstrous, and continued its mysterious dance beneath the surface. Clustered together in threes like otherworldly columns, they reached towards the ceiling of the merrow nest.

They needed to act before they were discovered, but Ash watched the merrow tend to their precious towers with careful devotion. Each merrow moved with a grace that belied their rugged appearance. Their dedication to nurturing their offspring was evident in every fluid motion, every touch of their webbed fingers against the delicate orbs.

Ash signalled for Set to retreat while angling toward another spot, where the towers were spread farther apart than the other clusters and only two merrow tended. As they swam out of sight and weaved through the grass walls, Ash steeled her nerves. It did not matter how beautiful the merrows' movements were as they cared for their offspring, or how they hovered in a choreographed ballet of care and protection. Reaching the spot she'd chosen, she parted a layer of grass to view the new position. The two merrow were within arm's reach, their webbed hands delicately brushing against the eggs. One hummed a haunting melody as it worked, a lullaby of the deep.

Heartbeat steady as she adjusted her grip on her dagger, the weight of Ash's role settled upon her shoulders. She tensed as phantom pain lit up her stomach, icy fire tracing parallel tracks where vicious claws had shredded flesh. Jaw clenched, she embraced the fury rekindling beneath her breast. Set's longer weapon would be easier to target enemies at a distance, especially ones with deadly claws, but Ash preferred closer range for this. She was ready to confront her fears, to protect her clan, and to prove to herself and to the world that she was no longer the vulnerable soul they had encountered before.

Positioning her blade before her, she motioned for Set to follow her lead, waiting on him to disagree. To her surprise, he nodded, not insisting on taking point.

Propelling forward, a surge of strength coursed through her veins as she swam into the clearing. Grabbing the nearest merrow, she tore its hat off while simultaneously slitting its throat, silencing him forever. The shock of her presence still held the remaining merrow in place, its beady eyes widening, giving Ash the chance to strike again. She swung her blade, injuring but not killing it.

Set was a blur beside her, two hats already in his hand. She hadn't even seen the two merrow he'd attacked and killed, but now they were floating above them, oily blood pooling from their punctured chests. He gestured for her to retreat as the creatures screeched, swarming toward them from their merrowspawn towers in the distance. But that would not do.

Her eyes landed on the one she'd injured, its blackish blood polluting the water. It snarled in her direction, needle-sharp teeth exposed, one claw extending to her. With a swift arc, she sliced through its arm, and even underwater she heard the crunch of bone as her blade carved straight through. The merrow watched its clawed hand float between them as Ash took that distraction and stole its hat. The result was instantaneous, its face turning purple as the magical effects of its hat ceased, causing its lungs to fill with the putrid water.

This time when Set barked that they should leave, with the remaining creatures screeching as they swarmed toward them, Ash kicked off from the riverbed, propelling herself upward. Clutching her hats in one hand, she hacked through the grass ceiling, widening the narrow window slit so she could squeeze through.

The echo of pursuit reached her ears as she broke free before a violent burst of grass and seaweed punctured through the ceiling and Set appeared through his own hasty opening. Her legs scissored through the water with unyielding force as they escaped to dry land and their awaiting clans.

Breaking through the surface simultaneously, Ash gasped, tearing the hat from her head, allowing her lungs to draw in the sweet air once again. Their group, positioned downriver, ran toward them.

"It's not a race," Set called as he jumped from the water, extending his hand and lifting her easily as claws snatched at the surface where she'd just been.

A smile tugged at her lips. "Says who?"

"It's not over yet." There was a glint in Set's eyes, a sparkle that only came to life when he was thoroughly amused. Coupled with the way water droplets clung to his rugged beard then raced down his sharply chiselled jawline, the scene before Ash was nothing short of mesmerising.

Running footsteps of their warriors increased but Ash stepped closer to Set, her heart taking an involuntary leap as light bounced off his wet skin, his chest heaving as water trailed down the rivulets of his abs and he sheathed his spear.

"Eyes up here, Breen."

"Not yet."

Her gaze roamed over him with undeniable thirst, drinking the sight of his beautiful body. He chuckled, and as his deep sound rippled through the intimate space between them, her eyes travelled to his mouth. Those lips, the slight parting as he caught his breath—she wanted to capture this moment as much as she wished to ensnare those sinful lips with her own. To bask in his laughter and his warmth that would only leave her craving more.

"I love the way you look at me, Breen," Set murmured.

There was an inescapable gravity to his presence, an implicit captivation that forced a soft sigh from her lips as he smiled at her. And despite herself, despite the whirlwind of their surroundings, she found that she wouldn't want him any other way.

"That was close," Ciarán whistled as the others gathered around them.

Ash tore her eyes from Set as her cousin snatched the two cohuleen druith from her and handed the other hat to Tomás. Snarls sounded from the water, and they stepped away from the river's edge as the numerous beady eyes of the merrow appeared, but they did not advance. Instead, one by one, the merrow retreated underwater, unseen once more.

"Here." Set threw his hats to Malachy and Maebh who both caught them.

Maebh grimaced at the wet fabric. "I wish it was in a different colour."

The river surface rippled before four merrow broke the surface, grabbing Paul, who had been standing too close to the river edge. The McQuillan warrior cursed as two of them clawed and gripped his legs, causing him to fall with a thud to the mucky ground. Before his full body could submerge, Set reached him, pulling him back single-handedly while unsheathing his axe and hacking the water demons. One slice. Two. Paul crawled back a few paces before jumping to his feet, dagger in hand. "The next hat is mine."

"Deal." Set said, clapping his clansman on the back before strutting toward Ash.

She couldn't help her smirk before scanning the now calm water. "They're expecting us now. Could be just below the surface, waiting."

Set nodded, gesturing to the four other hat bearers. "Put your hat on when I give the order. The initial sensation is a shock, but you'll adjust quickly. Jump in together, weapons drawn."

Ash tugged his arm before he could signal anyone to place their hats on. "Wait. Watch."

She pointed toward the river water. The current was as strong as it always was, but as they watched, small bubbles appeared sporadically. "There are quite a few of them waiting for us now. There will only be a few guarding their merrowspawn so that will be easier to target if we can get past them."

"Wait," Set said, his brow furrowing. "You want to kill the offspring?"

Ash licked her lips, saltwater lingering on her tongue. She'd spent years protecting newborn babies from being snatched by such monsters. Guilt, thick and invasive, unfolded within her. As dominant as a shroud, it blocked out rational thought, making each word she'd spoken feel like a betrayal to her own conscience.

Ducking her head to avoid meeting Set's eyes, Ash let the truth spill out of her. It felt like slicing her own flesh, the pain echoing in the hollow cavern of her heart. "They didn't think twice about trying to kill me, Set. They are monsters from their birth."

Set looked to the depths, as if being able to see the towers of unborn merrow below them. "We'd never see the stars if darkness didn't cloak the night." His grey eyes pinned her a moment after as he took her hand. "Life is about balance. Maybe they see us as the monsters?"

Ash stopped. The world fell away as the surrounding clanspeople became nothing more than the trees and river. His tone hinted at the words unsaid, the ones he wanted her to hear. She placed their joined fingers over his beating heart. "You're not a monster, Set. Even on your worst day. You are not."

Set gripped her face, leaning down to brush his lips against hers in a featherlight caress. "Not any more."

As they watched, the bubbles spread out, wider than the six hat bearers.

"We need bait." Maebh stood beside Ash, leaning forward as she scanned the river. "Spread out. Each ridiculous hat wearer goes with three or four clanspeople."

"We're not risking anyone's safety," Set said, his tone flat. "That's your plan?"

What was with these two? Ash looked at her own brother, her brow furrowed. Conor stood near the back, his face scrunched as he watched the river sweep by.

Maebh clicked her tongue and moved around Ash to stand in front of Set. The McQuillan clan backed up a few paces and Ash copied, realising they had far more experience when the twins got into an argument.

"No, Setanta," Maebh said, too quietly. "This is my dodgy as fuck plan, but I'm open to hearing yours. Oh, you don't have one. Great."

"We go in together. Once they don't have their hats, they are practically defenceless. We grab and come up. Someone be ready to retrieve the hats and divvy them out." Set's words were final. When he glanced at Ash, eyebrow raised, she turned to Maebh.

"I told you before," she said to Maebh but looked back at Set. "So now I'll tell you again. Don't place me in the middle of your twin drama. Now is not the time to argue. Set, Maebh's plan is sound. Any plan we form is dangerous. Look at what we just accomplished."

"That's settled, then," Maebh said, turning her back to her brother who only glowered at her. "Paul, you take my hat. I'll go in without one as bait."

CHAPTER 51

MAEBH

Maebh tightened the strap of her leather gauntlet, her heart pounding in her chest. The plan had been set in motion, and now she found herself standing at the water's edge in her underwear, her sight fixed on the turbulent currents. Beside her stood Orla, ready to be bait despite the urging of her sister to stop this dodgy as fuck plan.

"Matriarch," Paul said again, the hat clenched in his strong hands. "I don't like this. You should have the hat and I can be bait with Orla."

"Nope," Maebh said before smiling. "You need to get your revenge on that little water hound."

"I'm looking forward to being bait," Orla said, shoving Maebh's shoulder. "Sure, it'll be a bit of craic, Matriarch."

Maebh chuckled, but she couldn't help but feel a pang of guilt for putting her in such a dangerous position. Orla needed this as much as she did. Setanta loomed beside them, silent, but ready to go with her plan. All but Eilish had readily agreed, despite Setanta's argument against it. Even Lorna hadn't bothered to give her any grief. She and Maura were at the back of their group, ready to retrieve the cohuleen druith they stole to redistribute to the waiting warriors.

There was no time for hesitation, and no time to second guess herself. She was finally acting like a matriarch, and her clan were actually listening. Taking a deep breath, she glanced up at Setanta, who only nodded gravely, ready to dive in once more.

"On your count," Ash called from her position downstream with the Breen clan.

Two of Ash's warriors would also act as bait, surrounded by the hat wearers to protect. They'd distanced themselves from where Ash and Set had resurfaced, but there was no doubt the merrow underwater were tracking their movements.

"You ready?" Maebh asked Orla, her voice steady despite the turmoil within.

The other woman nodded, her grip on her weapon firm.

With a swift motion, they jumped in. The water erupted with a flurry of movement. Merrow swarmed around them, clawed hands and sharp teeth gleaming in the dim light. Slashing her blade through the water with deadly precision, Maebh met scaled flesh of the monster's abdomen, barely avoiding the swipe of his claws. Other bodies had plunged into the water, but the water was too dark, the beasts too fast, to follow how anyone else was faring. She needed to get a cohuleen druith.

The merrow lunged for her once more, screeching as Maebh delivered a powerful blow to its neck as his nails dug into her side. Gritting her teeth at the sting, she pressed a hand to her side. It was shallow, but her head pounded with the lack of oxygen. Keeping the merrow in sight, she tracked Orla's fight with another merrow where she easily killed and claimed its hat. With a swift manoeuvre, Maebh disarmed the merrow, snatching its hat from its head.

She wasted no time in placing it on her own, feeling a surge of power course through her veins. The hat melded with her, body seizing at the surge of magic coursing from her head, a fiery transition taking effect. Gills slashed across her neck like blades slicing skin and she cried out, realising she could breathe.

Blinking a second lid into place, her eyes adjusted to the dimness of being below the surface. Swirling in the water, Maebh tracked Orla's retreat to the surface, a hat gripped in one hand. Maebh wanted to shout at the other woman to place the hat on her head and follow their plan, but there were too many merrow between them.

The merrow, with their sinewy bodies and iridescent scales, darted and weaved around her. They lunged with ferocity, their claws slashing through the water, leaving trails of shimmering droplets in their wake. Maebh met their onslaught head-on, her blade an extension of her will. As a merrow closed in, jaws gaping wide, she twisted her body and delivered a swift strike, the blade finding its mark with a resounding impact. The merrow recoiled, a trail of blood clouding the water as it retreated.

The battle raged on, a flurry of flashing blades and thrashing bodies. Maebh weaved through the chaos; her senses heightened underwater. She could hear the muffled clash of weapons, the grunts and cries of her clanspeople, and the haunting echo of her own heartbeat.

Water resistance proved both friend and foe. It slowed her movements, creating a sense of weightiness, but it also afforded her a measure of control and precision. She took advantage of the fluid environment, relying on her instincts and training to anticipate her adversaries' actions.

A merrow lunged at her from the side, teeth bared in a primal snarl. Maebh spun in a graceful pirouette, her blade slicing through the water in a swift arc. It howled in agony as its arm was severed, the dismembered limb floating away in a black haze.

Her breath came in short bursts as the battle wore on, her muscles protesting the strain. Yet, she fought on, fuelled by a mix of adrenaline and determination. The water around her grew murkier with each passing clash, swirling with a whirlpool of dislodged sand and silt.

Another merrow lunged at her, fangs bared. She parried its attack, her muscles straining under the water's resistance. It swiped its deadly claws but only tore at her gauntlet and she plunged her blade into its neck before stealing its hat. Maebh dove further into the depths of the water, the weight of the world lifting off her shoulders as the liquid embraced her body.

The battle beneath the surface was a symphony of mayhem and motion, illuminated by the muted light filtering through the ripples above. She could finally see the others, fighting their own battles with the water demons, and with relief, she noted more had joined, now wearing the cohuleen druith. Pivoting, she spotted Orla a short distance away kicking up to the surface once more. Her eyes narrowed in on her hatless head. Why hadn't she placed a hat on her head yet?

As Orla reached the surface, Maebh cried out a warning that she could not hear as a scaled body shot for hers. The merrow plunged two claws into Orla's sides, dragging her underwater. Maebh surged forward, dodging merrow who tried to reach for her, but her warriors had surrounded her, fighting any creature who dared to attack.

Orla's movements were swift and calculated, her strikes hitting the merrow's back. Yet, the merrow, born of the water and therefore bred for its every movement, twisted and turned with uncanny grace. The monster did not release its grip on Orla, dragging her further downward, a mix of black and red blood concealing them from Maebh's sight. She signalled to Setanta, pointing frantically at Orla's predicament. Even under water she heard his curse, as his powerful legs pumped toward their clanswoman.

Her stupid plan would get Orla killed. She swam faster, watching Orla's axe hack at the merrow's hands. Set reached them first, his spear gripped in one hand; he thrust it toward them, bubbles violently swirling as his blade struck true with a satisfying thud. The creature let out an anguished cry, its blood mingling with the swirling currents.

Maebh yanked the cohuleen druith from the dying creature, placing it on Orla's head. The clash of steel resonated through the depths, a desperate battle for survival raging on around them. She didn't dare look to see who was winning as Orla's eyes rolled to the back of her head.

"Orla! Can you hear me?" Maebh slapped her cheeks, willing her eyes to open as panic slid down her throat, gripping tightly.

"She's lost too much blood." Set's clipped tone reverberated through her.

Maebh only nodded, not making eye contact with him as terror clung to her like a weight that threatened to drag her to the riverbed.

"Bring her above water," Set said, securing Orla's arm around Maebh's shoulder, her head lolling to the side. "The clan is too preoccupied trying to protect you. They're not looking out for each other."

Maebh's gaze snapped to him, but he was already diving further down to join the others. She allowed herself one glance, relief flooding her at the sight of the Fianna warriors advancing further toward the grassy domed nest. They were winning.

Gripping Orla's midriff, she kicked her legs furiously towards the surface, breaking through the veil of water. Gasping upon impact of fresh air, she dunked underneath to pull her hat off and then Orla's before treading to the embankment. Conor was the first to make it to them, helping her hoist Orla out of the river as the warrior evaded consciousness. His eyes locked on Maebh's as blood oozed from their clanswoman's sides.

"You're safe now," Maebh whispered, as she pressed into one of Orla's wounds as Conor did so with the other, with panic-filled eyes. Maebh all but sobbed, "Stay with me, Orla."

But her eyelids did not flutter as her skin turned ashen.

"What happened?" Lorna demanded, knees dropping beside Maebh with a first aid kit in her hand. She shoved Maebh with an elbow, taking over with pressure on her wound.

Maura appeared beside Conor, a tad gentler than Lorna, but urging Conor to move so she could tend to the injury.

"She needs this," Lorna instructed, angling a vial to Orla's lips. "Don't just sit there, Maebh. Open her mouth."

Jerking from her aunt's harsh tone, she squeezed Orla's mouth, cringing at the bloodied stains she left on her pale skin. Finally, Orla spluttered as the distinct putrid smell of a druid's healing tonic filled the air.

A hand grasped Maebh's and she looked down to the bloodied grip as Orla rasped, "Thanks for saving my life down there."

"It was Setanta," Maebh said numbly.

But Orla shook her head, eliciting a fit of coughing before she managed a weak smile, her voice just above a whisper. "It was both of you. The golden twins."

Maebh's heart twisted as she squeezed her hand. She didn't have it in her to correct the injured woman. Not now, when Lorna was eyeing her with suspicion. She knew that wasn't the full story. And they all knew it was her who had put Orla in danger in the first place.

Guilt twisted inside her, and she could barely smile at the emerging warriors, cheering as the final merrow had been killed.

The battle had been won, but at what cost? She looked around, searching for those who were injured. None as serious as Orla, but it was her decision that caused those wounds. She'd created scars, and she'd nearly ended a life.

CHAPTER 52
AISLING

"You look . . ."

". . . like shit," Set finished, a broad hand diving into his mass of wet curls as water trailed along his neck, slowly descending to his abdomen.

Ash held her breath, following the movement, appreciating how often she got to witness the artistic perfection of this man when wet. He wore his leather strap across his chest, the now familiar sight of his spear peeking up behind his head, and only a towel hung low on his hips. Her breath hitched before she smiled at the memory it elicited.

It seemed a lifetime ago Set had carried her all the way from the merrow-infested river to the safety of her family cottage. Only to wind up in nothing but a towel in her small car, driving the pot-holed country roads of Ireland. He had been breathtaking then, and he was even more so now, despite his wild hair.

Ash suppressed a chuckle, clutching her washcloth and vanity supplies to her chest, acutely aware she was only wearing a sports bra and shorts underneath an open white shirt which did nothing to shield her from the cool breeze. Awareness prickled along her skin.

"I wasn't going to say that." Ash moved forward onto the next stepping stone, avoiding the damp earth in her flip-flops, as the queue shortened to the bathing tents. Primroses and forget-me-nots had pushed up between the cracks in the stone, perfuming the air.

Set mirrored her step, matching her stride as they inched forward. "But that's what you're thinking."

It was busier than normal, which probably had to do with it being warmer than usual since Newgrange crumbled. Soon after the arrival of the warrior clans, the High King had erected a series of bell tents, each containing large wooden bathtubs, situated by a well overlooking the farmlands and their campsites. Steam rose lazily from the largest communal tub, where a handful of warriors and villagers soaked tired muscles.

"We all had the same idea, it seems," Ash mused, spotting the familiar faces of their clans across the communal baths, many already lounging in the warm water.

"A treat for how much territory we claimed yesterday," Set said, a smile playing on his full lips before lapsing into a frown. "I had to spend ages convincing Maebh it was a triumph."

"She took Orla's injury to heart," Ash nodded. "I told her it wasn't her fault. How's Orla holding up?"

"Recovering much faster with the druid tonics I have access to at the castle."

She couldn't resist smirking. "Being rígfénnid has many perks."

Two matriarchs marched down the adjacent line, pushing in front of a warrior about to enter a private tent. Although murmurs of irritation echoed down the queue, nobody confronted the leaders.

"As does being matriarch." Set pointed at the woman in front of her, next to enter a tent. "You could do that same trick."

"I could," Ash agreed solemnly. "But I'm not an arsehole."

Set threw his head back and barked a laugh. "Fair enough, Breen."

The setting sun cast a warm glow over the surrounding fields, where farmers could still be seen tending to the last of their evening chores. In the distance, children's laughter and the smell of cooking fires drifted from the town square. The bell tents cast shadows as hanging lanterns were brought to life as the sun took its final bow for the day.

"Bradan has offered me a room within the castle," Set said softly, and Ash tensed at the acrid smell emanating from him.

"You're unsure if you want it?" Ash asked, and when he nodded, she added, "Because of what happened in the dungeon?"

Set only dipped his chin stiffly, his lips pressed tightly as his throat bobbed. A familiar flush of anger rose within Ash at what Bradan had made Set do. How could their king demand a task as cruel and heart-wrenching as ending another's life? Fae or not. Set, who saw goodness in all things, did not deserve having his gentle spirit scarred in such a way.

Ash's palms itched to shake some sense into their High King who should protect his people, not inflict wounds upon their souls. Set had put the poor clurichaun out of his misery in as humane a way as he could but like Maebh, Set was hard to convince that the guilt did not lay on his hands.

She offered a gentle smile, hoping the reassurance in her expression might soothe in some small way. His worth and goodness were as steady as sunrise, too bright to be dimmed by hateful orders commanded in darkness.

Shaking himself, as if to fend off the memories of that horrific event, he nodded toward the castle. "If I take a room there, I won't have an excuse to escort you to your bathing chambers, my lady."

When he bowed low, Ash giggled before moving to the next step as the woman in front entered the now vacant tent. "I hardly need an escort."

"You have one all the same. And one that insists on taking your burden."

Before she could object, Set plucked her bundle from her, his eyes lingering on her exposed midriff. Goosebumps erupted along her skin, a blush working its way to her cheeks as the heat of his gaze trailed along her taut stomach, rising to her black bra and back down to her matching shorts.

"Eyes up here, McQuillan."

"I'm not even sorry."

Resisting the urge to fidget, she stood before him as he took her in. They were feet apart, but his perusal—the way he licked his lower lip when he slowly appraised her body—felt like there wasn't enough space to breathe in his presence. A chorus of laughter erupted from a nearby outdoor tub, and as if a spell had been broken, his attention snapped to its occupants before he invaded her space. Tugging her shirt together, he frowned, and a weight landed in her stomach.

When he caught the confusion in her gaze, Set leaned close, his breath tickling her earlobe. "I want to be the only one who gets to eye fuck you."

Swallowing, Ash didn't trust her voice and she found her own lip between her teeth. Loud voices carried across the breeze and they both turned in the direction of a group of warriors regaling a tale from their recent fae clearing. Despite Set's heated glances and words that made her question her feminism, she scrunched her nose at their glee at tormenting the smaller fae.

More wooden tubs were scattered around the bathing area, and many chose to group together. They'd all grown up in large clans with little space. They trained to perform in travelling shows across Ireland, so there was little time for modesty.

Ogling Set's half-naked form as discreetly as she could, modest wasn't a word Ash would ever have used to describe him. Biting the inside of her cheek, she only wished she'd made it to the bathing area sooner so she could have been a shameless pervert and watched him bathe. The smell of soap and Set filled her nostrils, a combination of cleanliness, oakmoss and leather, adding a refreshing touch to the spring water boiling in the iron cauldrons up ahead.

"Aren't you finished washing up, Set?" Paul called as some of the McQuillan clan trailed away from a nearby tub.

Caoimhe added, "Or do you suddenly want to go wash up again now that a certain matriarch is heading that way?"

"And he still hasn't parted with that spear," Malachy commented, adding quietly, "I wonder if our Setanta is trying to overcompensate?"

An eruption of laughter exploded, and Ash couldn't help joining in. Set's face flushed but he shouted across to Malachy, "My sister has had a bad influence on you."

More laughter filtered by as Set shoved into Malachy and Paul as they passed.

When he turned to Ash again, he smirked and winked. "Now, that's not a bad idea."

"What's not?" she asked, hating how breathless she sounded.

"Don't worry, I'm only keeping you company until your tent is free, Matriarch, warrior's honour." He inclined his head, stray locks falling into his face before chuckling. "My mother wouldn't have allowed this, you know."

When Ash looked at him in question, he pointed to his hair. Some of his plaits had come undone, overgrown hair sticking out at odd angles. "For me to look so unruly. 'Savage warrior, but styled' was her instruction."

"What way do you want to look?" Ash probed.

"I haven't really thought about it," Set said, looking up to the darkening sky. "It's not important considering everything going on. It just reminds me of her and how much hell she would have given me over it."

When the woman exited the tent, Ash took a deep breath. "Come with me."

Set's eyes found hers and she took his hand. He ducked under the heavy opening as she tugged him inside with her, ignoring the bemused looks from the other Fianna as she closed their curtain, concealing them behind it.

CHAPTER 53

AISLING

Lit candles and flowerpots were scattered around the rough stone tiles laid out to avoid the muddied ground within the bell tent. A lone wooden table housed small jars of sweet green herbs to add to the bath, from camomile, lemon balm and mallow to brown fennel. Grabbing her supplies from Set and dumping them on a free space, Ash turned to him once more.

The tent was large enough to fit a small clan, but it had suddenly shrunk in size. Set took up so much of the already hot air, she found her breath laboured and her heart erratic. The tub had finished draining, so Ash busied herself with the taps linked to pipes attached to the heated cauldrons outside. Her breath shaky, she peered up at Set, who hadn't moved from where she'd left him, his eyes pinned on her every movement.

"I'll help take out your plaits," Ash said, pointing clumsily at his head as if he didn't know what she was talking about. "And then you can decide what you want to do with it. *You*, Set. It's your hair, and your choice."

Set blinked at her, as if she'd said something profound. His ear-splitting grin made her stomach flip and she found herself smiling broadly at him in return.

"And here I was thinking you were trying to seduce me into taking a bath with you," Set said, chuckling.

"Well . . ." Ash said, waiting for him to look at her. Shrugging out of her shirt, she unclasped her bra, discarding both on the table. Her face flushed in satisfaction at his wide eyes, homing in on her breasts. "I also need to take a bath."

She waited until his eyes reached hers. He opened his mouth to say something, but before he could, she hooked her thumbs into her pants, lowering them inch by inch, never wavering her gaze, until they, too, fell to her feet. She didn't miss the way his eyes turned from grey to molten steel as he took in her naked form.

He swallowed before huffing out a low breath. "Beautiful."

She trailed her hand along his chest as she passed him, stepping into the bath as it continued to fill. Unsure what to do next, she tucked her knees up, hugging them. He seemed to notice her sudden nerves and stepped forward, unclasping his spear, and discarding his own belongings beside hers. Picking up a jar one by one, he dumped a healthy dose of each herb into the water, the wooden bath filling with an intoxicating scent.

"May I join you, Matriarch?"

The way he said her title had her toes curling. Ash nodded, her throat bobbing as he discarded his towel, and she greedily roamed every muscle, his perfect form as he stepped into the bath, lowering before facing her.

"Are you sure?" he whispered, eyes full of gentle understanding. He would only go as far as she led him.

With that comfort, she smiled, inching forward so they shared breath, the steaming water pumping into the bath now reaching her lower stomach. Kneeling before him, she stroked her fingers along his arms, tracing the perfect curve of his lips until they landed in his hair. His eyes roamed her body, but his hands remained on the tub edge, his fingers gripping it forcefully as if he were afraid to touch her.

"You have beautiful hair."

His laugh was a full belly one. "I'm sitting here, naked as the day I was born, and you tell me my hair is beautiful?"

"Well, it is, Setanta McQuillan," Ash said, slapping him on the shoulder, but grinning. "I'm sure you don't need me to tell you how perfect you are."

His hands finally left the sides of the tub, finding their way to her waist. The calloused pads of his palms traced along her lower back and, when he didn't stop, she gasped as he cupped her ass, tugging her closer.

"I want to hear you say a lot of things, Breen," he purred in her ear, sending a violent shiver down her spine. He squeezed her cheeks. "But most of all, I want to hear the sounds you make, because I think they'll break me."

He kissed her, and it was as though a veil had pulled back, revealing a world only they could touch, the symphony of their hearts beating along with the steam and water cocooning them. His fingers roamed, tracing upwards to cup the curve of her face delicately, as though holding something rare and precious, so at odds with how he'd groped her only moments ago.

The fervour of his touch burned a glow onto her skin while his thumb traced the contour of her face, seeming to memorise each dip and arch. His eyes held a deep reverence for her as he softly traced his thumb down her chin, then her neck, to stroke between her breasts before grazing her along her ribcage. Heat pooled low in her stomach, and then lower still as he pressed his tongue between her lips, ushering her into a different realm; where the world was nothing but them.

The heat of his tongue against hers ignited her senses, sparking an uncontrollable flame within her. She melted into him, her hands gripping his arms, her body inching closer in response to his touch. The distance which had once separated them collapsed as she straddled him, ignoring the overflow of water splashing over the bathtub as his hard length pressed against her stomach. Her breath hitched and she gasped slightly, opening her mouth further to deepen their kiss.

Too soon, Set pulled back, turning his head and groaning between heavy pants. "Noises like those will ruin me."

She leaned forward, ready to continue, but he nodded toward the closed tent. "I want you, but not with so many people around, and if you keep kissing me like that and making those beautiful, tortuous sounds, I won't be able to stop."

She was about to protest, but chatter filtered by as a group of warriors passed. She sighed again, but this time it was not in satisfaction. Reaching upwards, she turned off the water and signalled for Set to turn, getting to work on loosening his plaits. Lifting a bar of conditioning soap, she lathered it in her hands before massaging it into his scalp. Noise permeated through the thin walls, but otherwise, it was just the two of them as she worked. He tilted back as she worked her fingers through his damp locks.

After rinsing, she picked up the comb he'd given her, knowing she had her work cut out for her to rid his hair of all the tangles.

"Do you miss anything from the human realm?" she asked, her voice sounding loud in their quiet bubble.

He hummed as if he wasn't really absorbing her words, so she gently tugged.

"Hey," he said, cocking one eye open before smiling. "My life was pretty full on with our shows and travelling, so I didn't see much of the human realm."

"But Maebh seems to have."

Ash recounted the long, long list Maebh had of all the things she missed. Set's smile was thin-lipped as he nodded.

"My sister had a way of pissing our mother off. It was like another gift. Imogen didn't want us mixing with locals or going out without other clanspeople. So naturally, that's what Maebh did. Our clan is more sheltered than you realise. It was like my mother knew a Cath was coming, so she made sure our clan did nothing but perform shows and train for it."

Ash listened in silence as she combed out his hair.

"Since coming here, I've found peace," Set spoke softly. "I don't have to hide who I am here. There's nobody to judge me."

"You can always be yourself around me. I know the darkest parts of you, Set." She rotated fully, kneeling between his legs, touching his chest, feeling the steady beat of his heart. "Your darkness is a part of you and that's okay."

He closed his eyes as he crooked his head to the roof. When he looked at her again, he was guarded. "Aren't you scared of what you saw me become?"

She studied his wary expression, visions of his ríastrad slicing through men and monsters. But she also saw the broken man he became after.

"I'm not scared of your monster, Set. I'm scared of my own." She smiled when he looked at her in confusion, so she continued. "Yours is a physical entity but everyone else's monsters are hidden. If I let you in, I'm not sure you'll like what you find in my shadows."

"We're all dangerous if we choose to be."

His arms encircled her, and they stared at each other. Like before, they were sharing secrets, but this time, there were none left unsaid. Nudging her closer in invitation, she let him pull her in, straddling his lap once more.

"Now it's my turn."

"For what?"

"To wash you." Set lifted a soap from the table. "So I can have fun making you dirty again."

Her thighs squeezed around his and his eyes darkened. She spoke in an undertone. "I thought you said you wouldn't do anything here?"

"I'm going to sift you somewhere where no one will hear how I make you scream."

Set lathered his hands, beckoning her to lean back. Mesmerised by his command, she obeyed, inching away, her head resting on the tub edge as she watched him prepare. He started on her raised knees, his broad hands disappearing into the warm water, as he rubbed all the way down her outer thighs. She resisted the urge to squirm, but just barely.

He worked slowly, the heat of his fingers trailing along her stomach before skimming the underside of her breasts. He used lazy strokes, a trail of soap bubbles marking her skin as he roamed her body like he had all the time in the realm. When one hand moved between her breasts, she arched her back, silently begging for him to touch her more. Touch her in the places she burned for him. But he only smiled, his eyes never leaving where his hands explored.

"Rinse yourself off and then I'll wash your hair," Set instructed, and she glared at him.

"I can wash my own hair." She heard how petulant she sounded, but built-up frustration outweighed her ability to care.

"I'm doing it," was his only reply.

They stared each other down until she cursed softly, dunking into the water. She heard his laughter from under the surface.

Pouring the shampoo from the glass jar, the tent filled with the aromatic smell of lemongrass as he lathered it onto her scalp. She moaned as he massaged her head and his hands stilled.

She twisted enough to look at his face and he lowered his hands to her shoulders, his long fingers stroking her throat lightly.

His eyes were that delicious liquid steel again as he loomed over her. "I can't take my time like I'd hoped. I need to get you out of here . . ."

She heard the promise in his unfinished sentence, and she dunked under water again, taking charge of rinsing out her hair. She hastily applied her conditioner and rinsed as Set stepped out of the bath, gathering their belongings. But he didn't put his towel on, and Ash stared at his hardened frame. When she tore her eyes away, she found herself looking into his eyes, where there was no amusement, only heat.

"Let's go," he said huskily, one hand extended to help her out of the bath, while his other held their belongings, including their towels and his spear, a glow emanating from the tip.

"You're sifting us out of here naked?"

"I'm not wasting another moment before I can finish what we've started, Breen." Set pulled her close and they were folded into darkness.

CHAPTER 54
AISLING

When Ash's eyes adjusted to the muted light, it took her a moment to realise where they were. "The barrenland?"

She contemplated the clearing as cool air raked a shiver through her. Desolate but beautiful.

They studied one another and she couldn't help but remember the last time they'd been here, laying under a thousand blazing stars confessing their deepest secrets.

He turned to smile at her before nodding in the direction he'd started walking. "I saw a hot spring."

She followed, steam breaking through the ground as the surrounding crevices widened, and the path became trickier to follow.

"Over there." Set pointed to a steaming pool at the bottom of a hill and she quickened her pace in the hope of warming her chilled naked form once more.

Until now the land had been level, as if flattened by a giant, and as they walked down the hill, Ash couldn't help but think they'd unlocked another mystery to this magical land as she took in several shallow pools, steam rising to the clear dark sky.

"Get in." Set's voice was a command and a promise of what was to come, filling her with warmth and heady anticipation. Ash could do nothing but obey as it slowly burned away any insecurities she had by standing naked before a man she considered more beautiful than any Fair One she'd seen.

His gaze was a physical caress as she took his offered hand and lowered into the bubbling spring. When he followed her in, only rising steam and the gurgling of the hot spring filled the space between them, the warm kiss of the water soothing her naked body.

"I've thought about this moment for so long." His lips slid along her jaw, lowering to her neck and her back arched. His hands gripped her hips before tugging her to him.

"It's a pity it took you so long to act on it."

"Aisling Breen, you'll be the end of me." He nipped her lower lip, a teasing sting before a sensuous kiss. "I've never had sex in a hot spring," Set murmured against her skin, and she gasped as one hand drifted to cup her backside and the other rose to stroke a hardened bud.

"Neither have I." Her own hands roamed his chest, fingers trailing along the ridges of his torso before dipping below the water. She gripped him and he groaned. Despite how much she ached for him, she glanced around. "What if someone sees?"

"If someone sees," he nipped her throat, causing her hand to tighten around his length, "we'll give them a good fucking show."

He smirked when she laughed, his eyes dancing as he watched her. "I want to make sure you laugh like that every damn day."

Stroking him once, she released him before stepping out of his hold, inching away until her back hit the wall of the pool.

Ash watched him as she slid her hands along her bare skin, around her breasts, her stomach. Set's eyes darkened as he tracked every place she touched. When her hand slid beneath the water his mouth parted, an expression so ravenous she could feel it on her skin.

His body already showed her what she needed to know, but she asked anyway. "Are you enjoying the show?"

His breath was shallow as he answered, "I need to touch you."

"Come here."

He pivoted her as he sat, and she straddled him, her head falling back as his mouth found her breast, his hand lowering once more to her ass.

Ash's hips moved of their own accord, and she bit her lip as she moved against him, working her hips to find the friction she desperately needed. He squeezed her ass, lapping his tongue against her hardened peak.

"Set," Ash gasped, unsure how she planned to finish that sentence but needing him to relieve the dull ache between her thighs.

As if reading her thoughts, he hoisted her up off his lap, and turned, placing her on the edge of the pool. His hand gently pressed her back against the slick rock before slowly pushing her thighs apart. The cool night air kissed her skin as she braced herself on her elbows, tracking his hungry eyes as he murmured in approval.

Set lowered himself and she arched into him, her head falling back as she whimpered. He circled his thick arms around her thighs, pulling her closer to the pool edge.

"You're so beautiful." His mouth closed around her with a possessive growl, and everything fell away. All reason to life, to the challenges that faced them. She was his, and he was hers and this moment changed everything.

There was no warning as he inserted two broad fingers and she cried out, and her chin dipped to watch what he was doing to her. There was something so carnal in seeing him between her legs. When it got too much, her elbows gave way and she fell to her back.

"Set, I can't," she panted, her eyes watering as she tried to keep her head raised.

His eyes scorched into hers as he continued with his sinful mouth, only pausing enough to command, "Come."

Her vision blurred as her head hit the rocky ground. He wrung out every wave of her pleasure and only through a blissful haze did she notice he'd begun stroking himself as he now stood in the water looking down on her.

"Seeing you this way . . ." he grunted, squeezing his shaft.

Rising on wobbling legs, she pulled him to sit on the edge of the pool, straddling his muscled thighs. Lowering herself, slowly, she held her breath as his thick length stretched her; her eyes rolled back as a delicious sensation filled her. Set's hips bucked as he nudged further in, and she moaned his name on his lips.

"Aisling," her name was a plea, and she sank down with a moan.

With hips undulating, she claimed his mouth, feeling him everywhere as their movements grew more fevered, his thrusts slamming into her.

"Fuck, Ash." He groaned against her heated skin, and she sank her teeth into his shoulder as all reason abandoned her.

She whimpered as she crested once more, and Set cried out her name as her body clung to him in all ways. Still riding the wave of pleasure, Ash turned, digging her nails into his broad shoulders as she arched back, head falling back as he thrust so deep she forgot where he ended and she began. Set held her hips with a bruising grip as he found his own pleasure, the air filled with the sound of their laboured breathing.

When the euphoric waves finally subsided, they stilled. Chest heaving, Set positioned her so she was sitting across his lap, strong arms enveloping her as she curled into him. He stroked her hair, kissing her forehead.

"Can I say something, and you don't have to say anything back?" His words broke through Ash's haze, pulling her from promised dreams, and she realised she'd fallen asleep.

The sky was a muted purple. How long had they been there? The water was still hot, Set's steady heartbeat under her cheek, their breathing perfectly in time. She never wanted to leave.

Realising he was waiting for an answer, she whispered. "Sure."

With a soft laugh, he kissed her before saying, "My mother used to chain me after I turned."

Ash lifted her head, a frown playing on her lips as she looked at him. "Set, I'm so sorry."

"I'm not finished," he said, tucking her back into his side. She watched the empty land surrounding them as he continued. "Her chains weren't only physical. I've been in chains my whole life. Imogen expected perfection, and so did my clan. Orla was never there for me. She used me for what she wanted, and I thought that's all I was good for. I have a darkness I've fought so hard to contain because who could love someone as monstrous as me?"

Ash laid her palm flat against his chest. "You can't think you're unlovable because of a darkness you can't control. It doesn't define you."

"So, you think I'm loveable?"

She heard the smile in his tone and she bit her lip.

"I think you're all kinds of things." She kissed his chest where his heart lay. "Loveable is one of them."

"I could never protect Maebh from my mother, and the burden I carried was always just below the tipping point."

Ash imagined the world Set had lived in, realising it was a hell she couldn't fathom. Lifting up once more, she raised a hand to run her fingers down his cheek, tracing his jaw and neck until finally resting over his heart.

He closed his eyes at her touch but opened them again. "Then I met you. When I'm with you, my chains are loosened. You're the key that unbinds me."

Ash nuzzled against his neck, kissing him tenderly. It wasn't a conventional love story. But it was theirs.

CHAPTER 55
MAEBH

In the warm afternoon light, Maebh's eyes swept across the open field that served as the training ground. The high walls of Tara Court loomed in the distance, a constant reminder of the protection needed against the Tuatha Dé Danann and—a chill snaked down her spine—the Fomorians.

A dense canopy of ancient trees sighed secrets at her back, the woodlands harbouring notably less fae than before. She hoped it remained that way. Fianna were no longer the ones to cower and fear. Perhaps the Cath was serving the purpose High King Bradan had planned? They were finally fighting back against the Fair Ones. And winning. The Kingdom of Mide was almost clear, and although there had been instances of retaliation, most of the territories were held by the warriors who'd cleared them. Set's display against the púca had been enough for the fae to stay away.

No clan had encountered any of the higher breeds of Tuatha Dé. The Morrígan and Tara had not returned since they'd taken Ash. Considering the destruction of Newgrange, perhaps the Tuatha Dé had other things to concern themselves with? Or they did not care. The whimsy of immortals was a dangerous thing.

The training ground reverberated with a symphony of steel and grunts as Fianna honed their skills, both warrior clans and highguard alike. Scattered strategically across the field, sturdy wooden posts loomed, looking as though they were sprinkled across a vast chessboard. Atop each sat the targets, circular straw bundles, their centres marked with a hardy bullseye painted in contrasting black and white. They were distanced at varying lengths, challenging the archer to adjust for both distance and wind variation with each arrow let.

A now familiar voice rang out as Micháel shouted. "Ready! Strike!"

The air thrummed with the unmistakable chorus of bowstrings snapping, followed by the swift surge of arrows piercing the sky. There was a gratifying rhythm of thuds as each arrow found its mark, sinking into the straw targets with formidable precision.

A quiver filled with arrows lay by Maebh's feet, and although she'd improved since training with the highguard, she'd still have to train harder to match Micháel's quickness and accuracy. She hadn't forgotten his presence at that half-hidden market. What had a prominent member of the High King's guard been doing there?

If what Sage had said was true, the merchants were selling contraband items that went against Brehon law. If caught, Micháel would be in serious trouble, never mind the sellers involved.

As if summoning his attention by thought alone, Micháel glanced her way, so she immediately turned her attention to her clanspeople. Straightening her back, her focus fixed on the assembled members of the McQuillan clan.

"Listen up, everyone!" Maebh's voice rang out, cutting through the sounds of clashing steel. "We have a lot of ground to cover today. Let's focus on swordsmanship and combat drills."

A few clan members nodded, while others searched the crowd and she gritted her teeth. Setanta's absence was still a constant battle, even though his position as rígfennid was a sense of pride within her clanspeople. Repeatedly grasping and releasing her sword handle, she gnawed her bottom lip as she marched her clan to another station.

Setanta had agreed to the promotion without consulting her, and she knew he'd done it to save Ash, but her friend was a big girl who hadn't needed Set's help. Maebh brooded on how her brother was now tied to this land and this realm. It was clear he'd reacted without thinking about the consequences of that.

Maebh took a deep breath, and a few satisfying pops sounded as she rotated her neck, releasing built-up tension. That was another day's worry, and she would use his absence from training to beat down anyone who first sought his approval for her commands. Maebh's eyes scanned the group, ensuring they were attentive before she singled out individual instruction. Ones that just so happened to be searching for the former second in command.

"Sean, your footwork needs improvement. Keep your stance steady and maintain your balance," she directed, her voice firm. "And Patricia, remember to follow through with your strikes. Don't let up until your opponent is disarmed."

The two young warriors stared at her for a long moment and when she arched a brow, they quietly murmured their agreements, pairing up to go over her direction.

As Maebh stood overseeing her warriors spar, her heart heavy with the responsibility of leadership, a subtle movement in her periphery caught her attention. It was Orla. She was alone, in the corner, repeating the warrior forms they all knew by heart with a steely determination that was new to her.

Maebh's focus was drawn to her, like a moth to a flame, her heart twisting painfully in her chest. Orla's movements, though more fluid than before, still bore the signs of her recent encounter with the merrow—a slight hesitation here, a small wince there. The curse's after-effects clung to her like an invisible shroud, but she broke through it valiantly each time.

It was Maebh's decision that had put Orla in that situation, her tactical use of warriors as bait. Orla had volunteered, and she had let her. She had given her the chance to prove herself as a warrior again after the curse, but it had almost cost Orla's life. Guilt gnawed at Maebh. It didn't matter that no one else seemed to blame her, not even Lorna, insisting it was a necessary decision in the heat of battle.

But now, watching Orla, Maebh swallowed hard, a knot in her throat. She would not allow her clan to see her crumble here, but a sickening tide warred within, her stomach spasming as she watched the other woman.

A sting that drove home her reality— every decision, every command, had weight. It was felt by those she led, altering their lives in irrevocable ways. With a bracing breath, she accepted that guilt, wore it like armour, because it too was now a part of her leadership—a part of her.

Orla cast a look her way, catching Maebh's attention. There was something unusual about the glint in Orla's eyes that drew Maebh to make her way towards her fellow warrior.

Orla met her halfway, sheathing her sword. "I want to thank you, Maebh," she began, her voice steady.

Maebh cocked her head, puckering her lips, the bitterness in her voice evident. "For almost getting you killed?"

Orla shook her head with a soft laugh, notes of a tangy citrus a stark contrast to what she'd once been; gone were the smells of despair that had once cloaked the cursed woman. "For being the only one who doesn't treat me like a helpless child. Eilish hovers over me, the clan constantly questions me on how I'm feeling, but you're the only one who doesn't wrap me in cotton wool." A small smile tugged at the corners of Orla's mouth as she continued. "You're letting me move on with my life. As short as it may be with your grand plans."

Maebh couldn't help the laugh that escaped her lips as she bowed theatrically. "You are very welcome to be the first to follow my bad ideas."

Maebh gestured for Caoimhe and pushed Orla toward the other woman to pair off. As the training session progressed, Maebh's attention was unavoidably drawn to Micháel, who stood at the fringes of her clan's combat drills.

When he spotted her attention, his mouth twisted in a grin before he stood beside her. "You're looking lovely, as always, Matriarch."

She avoided reaching up to move a stray strand of hair from her face, her scowl deepening. She'd worn her hair in warrior braids, intricately woven and adorned with strips of leather and small silver beads. It had taken longer than her normal half-assed attempts, but it finally held her normally unruly hair firm. Well, most of it.

"We're here to train, not to talk shite," Maebh spoke sharply.

She smoothed down the sleeveless tailored leather vest, fitted trousers hugging her curves, tucked into knee-high leather boots. Her mother had sized her up from head to toe, and she didn't know how to feel about it. It had been the same battle she'd had over the dancer uniforms. Imogen had designed and ordered them to wear ridiculous costumes while performing. She couldn't help the niggling feeling this was another costume, and another act. But that was her aunt's judgmental voice in her head, so she chose to ignore it.

Micháel beamed mischievously, his eyes lingering on her. "And there's that McQuillan charm. I see your clan are finally listening to your instructions. The ones that showed up, anyway."

Maebh looked discontentedly toward her group. She'd already noted who was absent. Her aunt and a few of the older clanspeople weren't in attendance alongside Setanta, and she sighed. She had hoped more would turn up than this.

"You belong with people who respect you." Micháel placed his hands behind his back as his brown eyes squinted toward the sky.

"What are you talking about?" Maebh demanded, her full attention on him now.

He glanced her way before watching her clan. "You're not being used to your full potential here. There could be a place for you where you don't even know yet."

Maebh didn't follow his gaze, staring at his profile as she tried to decipher Micháel's cryptic words. "And would that place be in the dodgy backside of Tara Court?"

When Micháel turned to her, she added, "I saw you disappear into an old warehouse in a back lane covered in graffiti."

"And here I was thinking it was me doing all the chasing." Micháel sniggered when she rolled her eyes and turned back to her clan. He waited a beat before he leaned in closer, his voice dropping to a near whisper. "There are things at play here that you're not ready to hear. I promise, though. When you are, I'll tell you. But for now, can you do me the favour of keeping that little titbit to yourself?"

Micháel's dimpled grin was wide, but she could smell the tension surrounding him if his pinched expression didn't give it away. A flare of curiosity sparked in her, but she had enough to worry about. Whatever this highguard was entangled in she was sure she didn't want to be involved. Maebh nodded, refocusing on pushing herself and her clan—the ones who bothered showing up—to excel.

After the gruelling session, Maebh grabbed her cloak, inviting her clan to The Raven for a tankard on her. As the frigid air kissed her sweaty skin, she hugged the dark cloak closely to her, its rich blue hue shining in the still present sun. She secured the silver clasp, adorned with a family crest, around her neck. Slowly, day by day, that symbol no longer held her in the grip of fear it once had. As they made their way to her favourite tavern, she debated ways to punish the rest of the clan.

The Raven was a place where secrets were uttered amidst the clinking of glasses, and as Maebh entered through the nondescript wooden doors, its familiar atmosphere washed over her—the warm glow of candlelight, the hearty laughter of patrons, and the mingling scents of ale and roasted meats.

"Grab that table and I'll fetch our drinks," Maebh told her people.

The McQuillans took up a lot of space within the already full tavern, but they'd make it work for one drink and then Maebh would take her time in one of the bathing huts. Tiernan's frozen face filtered through her mind, a punch of guilt targeting her lungs. She was no closer to freeing him and the taunt of her failures echoed around her in the merriment of the low-lit room.

Standing at the long bar where Rían was dutifully ignoring her, a flash of silver chains on a slender neck caught Maebh's attention and she groaned as she tracked a short woman with curled brown hair and ample curves join a group of highguard. The woman smiled sweetly, accepting a full tankard and plate of the tavern platter at the centre of their table. She narrowed in on the woman's familiar tunic and pants, now dirtied, too long for her short frame, and a little worse for wear.

The púca hadn't heeded her warning. Sage was still within enemy territory and was about to eat supper with the most dangerous predator for her kind.

Highguard.

CHAPTER 56
MAEBH

Deciding Rían was taking too long, Maebh manoeuvred around the narrow opening, helping herself to two full pitchers on the low shelf. When Rían turned and glared at her, she winked.

"I'll be back to collect a tray of empty and hopefully clean horns, Rían," Maebh called as she darted away.

Passing by Sage and her new friends, she inwardly cringed as the púca tried to join in on the highguard's conversations. Sage's eye contact lingered just a touch too long on the man beside her, her eyes alight with a peculiar yellow glow that mortals wouldn't possess. Maebh had come to recognise that telltale shimmer, a flicker of otherworldliness that Sage struggled to conceal.

Setting her pitchers down with her group, Maebh promised she'd be back with the drinking horns.

"Take your time, Matriarch." Caoimhe lifted a pitcher to drink straight from it, as the others grabbed for it, cursing and laughing.

Maebh studied the púca who'd clearly joined a table of humans to eat their food. As Sage bit into a piece of roasted meat, her teeth elongated into sharp, pointed fangs before returning to their human guise. Maebh's eyes widened as a jolt of panic shot through her. She eyed the highguard at the table. It was a small slip, and hopefully nobody else would notice, but it was becoming clearer to her that the púca needed someone to teach her how to behave more like a human before she was caught and punished for remaining in Mide.

Why had Sage insisted on staying amongst enemies of her kind? Because that's what they were, Maebh noted, as a clan bearing necklaces made of faerie teeth glinted in the candlelit room as she collected the horns and returned to her clan.

A filled horn was passed to her by Caoimhe, and she took it graciously, trying to interject herself into their light-hearted chatter. However, watching Sage's awkward attempts to mingle with the highguard was so embarrassingly unbearable that she found herself downing the contents of her horn in just two swift gulps.

"Why can't you borrow money from a leprechaun?"

"Because they're always a little short."

Sage's laughter came a beat too late, a forced sound that lacked genuine mirth. Her eyes flickered with confusion before she quickly adjusted her reaction to match those around her.

"A Fianna went for a job interview in a human stable. The interviewer asked, 'Have you ever shoed horses?' to which the Fianna said, 'No, but I told a Dullahan to fuck off.'"

Maebh flinched. Again, her laughter was too late, and this time one of the men noticed.

"I've got a good one for you, Sage," the highguard sitting closest to her said as he nudged her elbow. "Have you heard about the one-eyed púca?"

Maebh felt Sage's tension as the cracks of her disguise frayed, her eyes narrowing into yellowing slits for a heartbeat.

"No," Maebh said, jumping from her seat to plonk down at an empty one at their table. "I've got one for you. What does a highguard call his wife?"

"What?" the highguard asked, his face still stretched in his last laugh.

"Cousin."

Silence filled the space as the table full of highguard stared at her. Maebh took a large slug of Sage's tankard before saluting them and tugging the púca to stand. "Come on, they clearly don't know how to take a good joke."

A trickle of laughter bubbled from Sage's lips as she let Maebh pull her away. The McQuillans were deep into another round, so Maebh took her to the long bar where Rían was busy pouring several tankards at once before disappearing out back and reappearing bearing food platters. Maebh nodded at him, but he only grumbled in return before shouting at a group at the far end of the tavern to collect their order.

"Thanks for getting me away. I thought I was doing a good job at deceiving them."

Maebh's eyes narrowed on Sage. "Why did you join them?"

The púca shrugged. "I was hungry."

"Where have you been sleeping?" Maebh asked, but by the straw strands and dirty smudges, she could guess.

"In a barn in the farmland district," the púca admitted. "It's warm and you get used to the smell."

"But no one else does when you walk by." Maebh wrinkled her nose and sighed, eyeing Rían as he slammed more drinks down on the ever-increasing number of patrons approaching the bar. "Are you impersonating a local again?"

Sage looked down at her small, curvy frame, the splattering of light brown freckles on her nose and forehead creasing at her puzzled appraisal. "No. This is my own conjuring of how I would like to look if I were human. As you warned, I narrowly avoided detection by a merchant who almost caught me this morning."

"If you insist on staying in Tara Court, and gods know why," Maebh said, straightening as an idea formed, "then you need somewhere better to stay and to be able to eat without having to trick Fianna into letting you sit with them. You're no beggar."

Sage cocked her head to the side in a clearly animalistic gesture. "Then what am I?"

Maebh smiled brightly at Rían, whose eyes narrowed in response when he finally stood before them. She didn't waver as she answered. "A tavern wench."

"I don't have time for this, girl," Rían said gruffly as he carried another pile of dirty plates that had been abandoned at the side of the bar, discarded by patrons who'd given up on table service.

"My point exactly," Maebh said, signalling for Sage to take the remaining plates, and shoving her around the tall counter to follow behind the burly tavern keeper. When he saw them behind him, he growled but allowed them to pass into the back kitchen where one cook banged pots and plates and a young man hunched over a large basin, scrubbing the plates that were dangerously towered high beside him.

"Da, I can't do this any longer," the young man complained, raising his pruned hands, his sour demeanour equally as impressive as Rían's but less so with the frilled apron hanging dirtied and wet from his neck.

Rían ignored him as he barked more food orders at the cook.

"All she needs is board and food as payment and you have yourself a live-in helper."

Rían paused, halfway through the doorway to the loud tavern. He glanced back, studying Sage. Maebh glanced at the púca, cringing when yellow flecks sparkled in her eyes, the shadow of another form glimmering underneath for a fraction before her face steadied once more. Maebh dared to glance at Rían. He didn't react to the oddness, but only said, "She starts in an hour."

Rían's son groaned. "Can't she start now?"

He ignored him. "Gather your belongings and come back here before closing time or you'll be locked out for the night. It's not easy work and I'll make no allowances for your weak arms. You pull your weight or you're out."

Maebh stopped Sage's hand before she managed to grip the other one, no doubt to literally pull herself forward. "She'll be here."

"Can she speak?"

Maebh elbowed her.

"Yes," Sage replied quietly, wincing from the jab.

By the time they made it out to the front, the McQuillan clan had left. Dragging Sage outside, Maebh sighed at the darkening sky as the sun dipped below the highwall, casting a faint glow over the cobbled and dirt streets as the torch-lighters made their way through the scattered posts, lighting each one with practised swiftness.

Sage's hand gripped Maebh's arm tightly.

"Hey!" Maebh grimaced, but Sage dragged her further into a dank alleyway, its narrow walls wedged between the tavern and the adjoining inn.

"You've done me a great favour tonight, Maebh McQuillan. It is time I repay you in kindness."

With a swift movement, Sage sifted them away from the tavern and into darkness. After several blinks, Maebh's eyes grappled to adjust to the faint blue hue reflecting off the uneven stone walls, her heart pounding a staccato rhythm against her ribcage.

"Why did you bring me here?" Maebh asked, her voice echoing in the hollow corridor, swallowing her words with a greedy, haunting echo.

"You need to see him," Sage said, tugging her forward by the hand.

A lump formed in Maebh's throat, fear coiling inside, attempting to escape like a caged animal clawing her insides. She wasn't sure if Sage meant Tiernan or her father, and both men fought for dominance in her mind. "Has something happened? Biróg promised the sluagh would be taken care of." Her voice came out more strained than she'd intended.

"Come." Sage infuriatingly quickened her pace, ignoring the plea layered in Maebh's words. Sage, despite her shorter frame, was hard to keep up with as she charged ahead.

As Maebh and Sage plunged deeper through the passageway, the stone walls inched closer, almost shifting with their every movement. The once familiar smell of damp earth and stale air was now tainted, stinging Maebh's nostrils and she recoiled. It carried a hint of something colder, an eerie perfume from the belly of the earth, so ancient it shivered down her spine.

The passage opened at last into the vast cavern. As usual, Maebh found herself pausing before the threshold, her pulse syncing to the once deafening, now distant rhythm of the stone guardians' collective heartbeat. The pulsating energy seemed quieter; the all-encompassing dread that usually accompanied her visits minimised as if held at bay.

"Is there something wrong with the magic of this place?" Maebh pondered, stepping through the opening without any trouble. "The repellent spell?"

Sage nodded, her pale fingers extending into the yawning abyss before them. Maebh squinted, peering into the inky darkness. The dim light struggled to reveal its secrets but soon the scattered mess came into focus.

A curse flew from Maebh's lips before she clasped two palms over her mouth, a strangled gasp on the brink of escaping. Rubble was strewn across the floor; boulders and smaller fragments speckled the extensive space as if the cave had coughed up its heart. But Maebh knew better. Those fragments of stone had once been men and women. Fianna trapped within stone to guard Fionn's tomb.

Her gaze flew in frantic zigzags until landing on a dozen or so stone guardians. All that remained surrounded the sarcophagus at the far end of the cave. Tiernan, her father, the others. They had to be amongst them.

"Please." Her whispered prayer ricocheted off the ragged walls as she clung to the desperate hope of her stubborn will. She raced forward, ignoring the carnage of stone she tripped on in her path.

The guard faced outwards, and as she felt tears stinging the back of her throat, she didn't fight the sob that purged from her heart as she stared up at Tiernan's frozen face first. Circling the small number, it didn't take her long to see her father; then Ash's father and Tiernan's mother amongst the remaining sentinels. Unfamiliar faces looked back at her too, and she wondered at who they were and where they came from before finding her way in front of Tiernan once more.

Even frozen in stone, Tiernan's face showed echoes of the man she knew; the kindness in his smile, the worry lines on his brow. But etched deeper now was the terror of his final moments, the cold grip of helplessness as the magic took hold.

Maebh swallowed past the rising lump in her throat.

"Just seeing Tiernan this way . . ." she halted, lacking the words to explain the endless wound his state inflicted.

"You want to save him, right?"

Maebh turned her glare on Sage who inclined her head, waiting for an answer.

"Of course."

"Is blaming yourself helping?"

"No amount of apologies will make up for what I've done," Maebh said quietly. "For what I've failed to do."

Biróg had no answers despite her promises. The druid had stormed into their lives with claims about their blood, only to disappear with all of her secrets. Maebh's inability to save

Tiernan or her father from this fate weighed on her with each step, like a physical burden dragging her down. It wasn't just heavy; it cleaved into her, the sharp edges carving into the fabric of her spirit, threatening to plunge her into a darkness she would never escape from.

"Have faith that your efforts will yield fruit in time."

As she stood before Tiernan's stone form, Maebh reached out a hand to lightly touch his arm. Though made of lifeless rock, she could almost feel his spirit trapped within, screaming to be set free. A single tear rolled down her cheek.

The cave's dim light emanated from the gem-infused walls, bathing everything within reach in a spectrum of blues. Shades of indigo, azure and turquoise played across Tiernan's features; somehow the dancing light soothed her.

As Maebh stared at Tiernan, movement caught her eye. A shadow emerging from a cave crevice, gliding silently towards one of the stone guardians. And Sage.

"Look out!" Maebh raced toward the púca who turned wide-eyed as the shadow reared back. Like an open jaw, the monster contorted as Maebh barrelled into Sage, the two of them falling to the damp ground.

Panting, she twisted to see the shadow engulfing a guardian's head and shoulders before it crumbled into dust.

A familiar sensation curled in the pit of her gut, and she glowered at Sage as the world surrounding them twisted and condensed as the darkness folded into them. A biting coolness slapped her cheeks as they lay near the temple of Lugh, its stone pillars looming over them.

Detangling from Sage, she jumped to her feet, her pulse pounding loudly in her ears. "Why did you sift us out? I have to go back to Tiernan. To my dad!"

"But . . ." Sage looked confused, inclining her head, yellow eyes glowing in the flickering torchlight, "*you* sifted us."

Her words slammed into Maebh like a wrecking ball. Her mind spun as her legs threatened to give way.

"How do I control it?" Maebh begged in a shallow breath, heat flushing her face and neck as she stared toward the Hill of Tara. She'd never learned how to control this gift, and Tiernan and her father may now lay scattered in rubble because of it. "I need to sift back!"

"The sluagh will kill you."

"Then I'll kill it first." Maebh grabbed her sword from her belt, determination hardening her features.

Sage's eyes widened. "It appears your self-preservation is a glamour. Because the Maebh in front of me is a fool." Maebh glared at the púca and to her surprise, Sage glared right back. "That thing will eat you alive."

"Tiernan would risk his life for me. My father . . . I have to try."

"I know you want to save your loved ones," Sage said. "But you'll be no help to them dead. You need a plan, a back-up."

Maebh bunched her fists in frustration. "I could have taken that thing."

"That thing eats rock," Sage countered. "You wouldn't have stood a chance."

"I can't do this alone." Maebh grasped her sword, hating to admit Sage was right. The thought of abandoning them again made her blood boil. Maebh took a deep breath, forcing herself to think logically. As much as she wanted to rush back in, swords blazing, she needed a plan. A smarter approach. She met Sage's countenance. "No more hiding behind a High King's commands."

"What are you planning?"

"One thing I never thought I'd do," Maebh said, homing in on the warrior campsite fires glowing in the distance. "To ask for help."

CHAPTER 57
AISLING

Relishing Tara Court's peaceful night, Ash strolled through the quiet streets toward her campsite. Half her clan were on patrol while the others staked out their claimed territories. As she rounded the corner, one silhouette stood out amongst the shadowed marketplace stalls, and she smiled. "You're out late."

Set's hardened features softened as he lifted his hand in greeting.

He shrugged as he reached her, the taut fabric of his fitted jacket flexing against his broad build. "Another rígfennid meeting about everything and nothing."

Ash glanced up at the full moon shining down on the castle town. With stalls locked up for the night, the square was deserted. Few lights shone in the surrounding homes that lined the winding streets. A calm fell over the fortress, a momentary reprieve; Ash breathed in deeply, clinging to it. Set snaked an arm around her waist, standing behind her.

"I'm sorry I haven't been around," he murmured into the shell of her ear, and she shivered.

Turning, she stroked her fingers up his arms, his tendons tightening underneath her touch. "You can't say no to the High King."

"The only person I can't say no to is you, Breen."

"Is that so?" she breathed as he tugged her closer.

"It is." Set backed them into a deserted alleyway and she released a surprised laugh. When he'd pinned her against the rough wall, his grey eyes captivated her as he whispered, "Tell me what you want and it's yours."

So much had changed recently but being with Set still felt right. Looking up at him now, Ash took in the lines and planes of Set's face as he towered over her. His eyes, a symphony of grey hues, bordered by a starburst of long dark lashes, held an ocean's depths. They were captivating, and when Ash dared to meet them, she felt like she could drown, lost and found at the same time.

Setanta McQuillan was an intoxicating blend of gentleness and hardness that allowed her to be both strong and vulnerable in equal measures. The familiar flutter in her stomach spread to her chest, a bittersweet cocktail of anticipation and anxiety that only he could stir.

"Anything?" she asked, her voice barely audible, yet her tone carried a weight that hung in the short distance between them. When he nodded, she smiled. "Then I want you."

Set leaned in slowly, kissing her forehead, her cheek, before tipping her chin up to claim her lips. Ash's hands instinctively found their way to his chest, pulling him closer by the leather band of his spear harness. Her world narrowed down to the sensation of Set's lips, the touch of his hands. His mouth was soft yet urgent against hers, speaking in a language only their hearts could understand and for some unknown reason, tears prickled against her closed lids.

Set's fingers brushed strands of hair away from her face before gripping the back of her neck, angling her head to deepen their kiss. She rose to the tips of her toes before he grabbed her waist, hoisting her high so she could wrap her legs around his midriff, her back slamming against the rough wall.

Squeezing him tight between her thighs while linking her feet behind him, he moaned into her mouth, his hands cupping her backside before one hand roamed to the front of her pants, tugging on the button before it sprang free. Ash pressed herself closer to Set, desire building between them. His hand roamed, slipping underneath the band of her pants. Ash gasped and arched into his touch.

A pointed cough sounded from the alley entrance, and they stilled.

"Go away," Set ordered, and Ash buried her face into his shoulder, chuckling despite her erratic breath. Peering over Set, she found Biróg standing at the alley's entrance with her arms crossed, an amused smile on her heart-shaped face.

Ash's cheeks flushed red. "Biróg." Set gripped her waist, pivoting his head to stare at the druid, but not relinquishing his hold on Ash. She tapped his shoulder and finally he released her. "We . . . um . . ."

"Young love," Biróg said with a knowing laugh. "But there are matters we must discuss."

Ash frowned, looking up at Set.

When they hesitated, the druid added, "About Tiernan and your fathers."

Ash's mouth dried, her fingers closing the button of her pants shaking. "Let's go."

Set grabbed her hand, his expression guarded against the druid as his spear shone in the moonlight. Ash's mind buzzed as they left the narrow alley and followed Biróg beyond the highgate and into the dense woodland.

"Who is that?" Set's voice echoed through a silent grove, and Ash followed his line of sight, her eyes landing on two figures bathed in the muted moonlight flooding the secluded spot. But the druid didn't answer as she continued without turning.

Dread pooled cold and heavy in Ash's stomach as her feet carried her forward until two familiar faces greeted them.

Maebh and Conor wore similar grim expressions, mirroring her apprehension, pulling forth a sigh from her. "Do you know what this is about?"

"I was at the cave." Maebh's face leeched of colour. "Things have gotten worse. We need to save them."

Before anyone else could speak, as if drawn by some powerful magic, they congregated by Biróg who knelt on the ground, drawing symbols in red sand from various jars and clay pots scattered in a semi-circle around her. Ash watched, her eyes fixed on Biróg as the druid worked with a captivating sense of calm and focus, oblivious to the shadowed figures that had quietly gathered around her.

Dressed in a flowing gown of emerald, her red hair piled high on her head, Biróg looked every bit the druid of lore. She moved with an ethereal grace, her hands intrinsically aware of their task. Reaching for a jar filled with vivid, crimson sand, its grains sparkled under the moonlight that managed to seep through the dense canopy.

Humming softly, the druid's fingers dug into the jar, gathering a handful of the precious grains before moving over the ground with delicate precision, and slowly a familiar pattern began to form. The symbol of triskele, a complex triple spiral that held significant meaning for druids' rituals. As Ash traced a similar tattoo on her wrist, she couldn't help but think of her mother whose tattoo she'd copied.

"What are you doing?" Maebh asked impatiently. "I've told you, we are out of time. No more cryptic bullshit."

Biróg looked up calmly. "There are some truths you must know. Sit and I will show you."

A series of glances passed between them before Ash's focus alighted and remained on her brother. He'd improved since being released from the bleak dungeon. The colour had returned to Conor's face, and his eyes no longer held the ghostly shadows of his ordeal. However, his current expression was strained, a mirror to her fears. Battling the dryness in her throat, she reached for him. "Con, are you okay?"

His dark features twisted as he took a shuddering breath. "I'm trying to make sense of it all," he paused, running a hand through his black hair with a heavy sigh. His eyes wandered off towards the grove, squinting as if the answer he sought would reveal itself there. "Tiernan . . . being trapped as he is," Conor's voice strayed into a whisper. "We are brothers in everything but blood. He was always there for me, and I wish I could do the same for him."

In the ghostly silence that followed, Ash felt the unspoken agony hanging thickly in the air.

"You will," Ash said, a firm conviction lacing her words. Brushing aside her own whirlwind of emotions, she tugged him into a hug, an attempt to quell the storm brewing inside him.

Her eyes strayed to Set, who stood a few steps away, spear glinting from his back. His face was guarded as he watched Biróg hover over her pots, but as he met Ash's stare, warmth filled his eyes. He mouthed 'Okay?' and she nodded with a small smile.

"We all will," Maebh chimed in from beside them. She gestured grandly at Biróg with her chin, a small smirk tugging at her lips. "Even if it means having to listen to an old crone."

Her words were followed by Set's low chuckle, and they all glanced at the druid who continued her work as if she hadn't heard Maebh's comment.

Conor drew in a shaky breath. "I barely remember Dad; my memories are so faded. But they don't deserve this. None of them do." His voice was barely audible, carrying the weight of their shared worries.

With a collective sigh, they agreed silently to Biróg's invitation and sank to the ground, forming a circle around the druid. Biróg resumed drawing in the sand, chanting unfamiliar words under her breath. The moonlight took on an eerie glow, bathing them in silvery light.

"Palms out." Biróg's command rang clear in the otherwise silent forest. The red sand warmed in Ash's palm, and she watched as the druid scattered the crimson grains on the others' outstretched hands. "Close your eyes."

After a heartbeat of hesitation, Ash obeyed, her eyelids shutting like curtains over the reality of the grove. A tingling wrapped around her arms, and she gasped, opening her eyes to see a red light writhe around her wrists in a chain that glowed hot to the point of pain. It rose, joining the three others' so they were all linked with the fiery magic. She couldn't move; her wrists were bound, her lips frozen so she couldn't call to the others who each remained motionless with outstretched hands, the red sand also burning into their flesh.

A heaviness pressed on Ash's head, forcing her eyes shut once more. The pain subsided when she finally gave in, and Biróg's chanting washed over her. Colours swirled behind closed lids, and through whatever magic the druid conjured, she knew the others experienced the same sensation. They were tethered to this moment as their surroundings transformed to another dark wood draped in moonlight. A figure knelt, long black hair rippling in a chill breeze, a bare swollen belly upturned to the moon.

"Mam?" Ash's voice was barely above a whisper, and her mother didn't hear. Even if she'd shouted her name, she wouldn't. Ash stared down at herself, semi-corporeal. She was in a vision. Ethne had done this to her before when she'd seen Fionn Mac Cumhaill and the first Cath. Ash stared at the twisted scene before her, and her heart stopped. This was different. This was worse.

Cara was not the only person here. Two other pregnant women sat cross-legged. Imogen McQuillan and Tiernan's mother, Nessa Cassidy, with Ethne standing in the centre.

"Watch," Biróg's voice echoed, unseen.

Ethne held a vial over Cara's stomach. Red liquid dripped onto her, but it didn't slide off, but sizzled as it formed patterns into her skin. Cara screamed yet no sound carried, only anguished trembling contorting her youthful features. Ethne didn't wait until she lifted another vial and turned to Imogen and then again to Nessa, repeating the motions so each woman contorted in agony.

Unable to peel her eyes away, Ash watched the scene unfold with a strangled breath as Ethne chanted and the women writhed and spasmed, trapped in an invisible torment.

A wave of emotions jolted through Ash, some hers, but more from those surrounding her through the tether on her wrists. She felt the hot flare of Maebh's disbelief followed by Conor's distress, an icy mixture of concern and alarm seeping into the shared glowing chain of their bond. And, echoing in the far corner of her consciousness, resided Set's reaction—a feral blend of apprehension and silent dread.

Their mothers jerked in unnatural angles, blood-smeared bellies heaving and undulating with each movement. Shadows swirled, and Cara and the others vanished into utter black.

With a start, Ash woke, mind reeling, her hands clenched where her beating heart struggled against the shackles of her ribcage. When she peered down, she winced at her wrist, her tattoo criss-crossed by a thin red band, but the link was broken. Only her erratic thoughts warred for attention, her mind no longer connected to the others. Biróg studied her grimly and then the others as they, too, gasped awake.

"So now you know," the druid said, clasping her red, stained fingers.

Maebh glared at the woman. "Now we know what, exactly?"

"Ethniu infused your mothers' wombs with Tuatha Dé blood, granting you with abilities no human has ever possessed."

Conor interjected. "I don't have any special gifts."

Biróg smiled. "No, child. Cara Breen agreed to the ritual while pregnant with Aisling. But she knew better than to taint you with the same fate."

Maebh leapt up. "What does this have to do with saving Tiernan?"

Biróg remained calm. Despite Maebh's comments at her being an old crone, the red-haired beauty was flawless, bathed in moonlight. "Understand first, act later. Your mothers consented but did not fully understand what Ethniu's ritual would do."

"Ethniu." Ash mused, the name stirring something from her nightmarish ordeal in Rathcroghan. "You called her that before. Do you mean the daughter of Balor?"

"The Fomorian ki . . . ki . . ." Set stuttered, his face paling as he choked on his words.

"The Fomorian king," Ash finished, and he nodded gratefully, wiping his brow.

Focusing on Set, Ash cocked her head as he gripped his throat and coughed. "I'm fine."

"She is known by many names," Biróg nodded, a sad smile on her lips. "But Ethniu was her first. And because of her deeds, you are blood-blessed, gifted with abilities from the Tuatha Dé blood, but it comes at a cost. They see you as a threat."

Maebh began pacing. "Thanks for the history lesson, but I don't care about any of this! Tiernan is in danger. The Tuatha Dé can get in line. We need to save him."

Biróg spoke gently. "Your abilities may offer help in saving him. But you must know them first."

Caught in the throbbing silence, Ash watched, her eyes widening as Maebh stormed forward, hands reaching out to grab the druid's robes, hoisting Biróg effortlessly into the air.

"Mae!" Set stepped forward, but Maebh glared at him, eyes darkening from cobalt blue to black.

Power seemed to ripple beneath her skin, almost tangible in the still night. She glared back at the druid struggling in her vice-like grip. "You've been holding this secret from us since we got here," Maebh accused, her voice deepening to a guttural wrath igniting her words into flaming arrows. "And you have done nothing useful to save our family."

Ash's hand clasped around her open mouth as she glimpsed something else, a flicker of change so incredibly subtle she almost missed it. Maebh, who was always firm and steadfast, stood a bit taller, her athletic figure casting a longer shadow under the silver glow of the moon. Her grip on the druid seemed steadier, her strength more pronounced. It was a sight that would've been inspiring if not for the underlying sense of dread it brought.

Remembering Set's transformation into the formidable, crimson warrior, Ash felt a shiver of recognition creep up her spine. The same scarlet hue that painted Set's skin during his episodes seemed to echo as a barely-there glow, casting an otherwise sun-tanned Maebh in a warm, blood-touched light. Dizziness tugged at Ash. Was her mind playing tricks on her due to worry, or was this the first hint of Maebh awakening to her gift, or curse, as many would consider it?

Maebh's changes were nowhere near as drastic or terrifying as Setanta's, but the potential implication was hard to ignore.

"Blood-blessed," Ash spoke so softly she wasn't sure the words left her lips, but everyone turned to her, even Maebh.

Ash's chest tightened with a mixture of fear and denial as she approached her friend, placing an arm on hers. "Put her down, Mae."

"Not until she tells us why she's only sharing this with us now." Maebh's voice echoed, her fierce tone punching holes in the silent mantle of the grove. Biróg's legs dangled uselessly, her gargled pleas for Maebh to release her punctuated with her pale hands slapping at Maebh's raised arm. But even as the confrontation raged on, Ash's mind raced to process the hint of an unsettling truth that the night had eerily begun to unravel.

"If you don't calm down," Ash said, licking her lips before pressing forward, "you're going to ríastrad."

The surrounding night appeared to hold its breath, silently waiting for Maebh to accept her words.

"Mae, she's right," Set came to her side, a quiver in his voice unlike anything Ash had heard before.

Fear radiated from his eyes as he stood beside his twin.

A strange heat radiated from Maebh, perceptible only as an elusive shimmer in the moonlight as her features sharpened.

Maebh lowered the druid slowly, taking several steps back as she studied her hands, and when she finally looked at Ash, horror painted her face.

"You have a choice," Biróg said, between coughs as she tried to compose herself. "Your gifts can be used to save your kin or destroy the world."

CHAPTER 58
SETANTA

The days had been long, but not in the magical way they once were. Twenty-four-hour days, sixty-minute hours; and their clocks and phones had started to work. They were all indicators the realms were irreparably changed. Set had forgotten how much longer everything seemed to take when time was a physical factor. The air itself smelled different, as if it also knew time was no longer a secondary thought, but a living, breathing entity. He hadn't realised he'd miss the whimsical nature of Tír na nÓg. Something had shifted in this realm, and in the human realm.

Set feared it was not for the better of humankind.

He tossed on his bedroll, exhausted from Biróg's revelations and Maebh's insistence on guarding Tiernan until they freed him. Maebh hadn't given into the ríastrad, but Set could see it. She had her own demon living within her, not fully awakened, and he hoped for his twin's sake it never did.

She'd revealed the truth to some of their clan . . . her clan. He was still a McQuillan, but he no longer served under her rule, and he no longer trained or fought with them in the Cath. But Maebh had grown into her rule. Half of the clan readily served her. She'd decided on top of the Cath and highguard training that those she trusted would rotate patrolling the underground cave.

It was his duty to report this to the High King, but he wouldn't.

The Tuatha Dé Danann were not happy with the Fianna. And Bradan reciprocated that sentiment, as did most clans. They had Tuatha Dé blood. Maebh, Ash, Tiernan and Set shared blood with fae. What would the High King do to them if he knew that piece of information?

Sighing so deeply he felt it in his bones, he wished he'd asked Ash back to his tent. He had barely had time with her the last few days, just stolen moments in between meetings.

Shifting again, Set wondered why he bothered trying to sleep. With a heavy sigh, he closed his eyes.

"Hello, my dear boy." Imogen stood in a grey silk gown, her skin glowing underneath a full moon.

"Mam?" Set asked shakily, taking in the barrenland they stood on. The vision of her smeared in blood while Maebh and he were unborn pierced his mind and he ground his jaw, drinking in this version of her.

She was too beautiful, deathly pale, a caricature of his memory of her.

"This is wrong." He glared at her. "You're not my mother."

Imogen smiled, her lips growing wider and wider, as if invisible strings were pulling them apart. She stepped closer, her hair lengthening and lightening into silver-blonde, her body broadening with curves, colourful tattoos appearing to ink themselves along her bare arms. A sweet scent filled the air, like burning incense at a funeral pyre.

"Ethne."

She inclined her head before turning to face the same direction as him. "It's interesting what you've done to the place."

Steam rose through the crevices and shadows danced along the broken earth. An acrid taste pooled in his mouth. The barren expanse of land, though lifeless and desolate, wore an uncanny aura that made his skin prickle uncomfortably.

Through the rising steam and dancing shadows, Set scanned the fractured landscape, looking for the source of his unease. There was something off about this place.

Everything seemed slightly distorted, like a warped reflection in a fun-house mirror. The area was too quiet, its stillness unnerving. Even the quality of the moonlight felt odd, too cold and white, devoid of its usual soft, silvery glow.

Set shook himself. "I'm dreaming."

"You're half right."

He opened his mouth to ask, but she answered in his mind. *We both are.*

"So, we're sharing this dream?" Set stepped away from her, arms crossed. "Who is in control of what happens?"

"You, of course. Think of me as a guest."

An unwanted one.

"We both know that's not true."

"What do you want, Ethne?" Set grimaced, reminded of what Biróg had told them. "Or should I call you Ethniu, Fomorian *princess*?"

He'd almost swallowed his tongue when he'd tried to name the Fomorian king thanks to this female's geas. Ethne had said she was a royal, but he hadn't realised she was the daughter of Balor of the Evil Eye, a legend whose eye could poison and weaken anyone he looked at. After countless hours studying the castle scrolls, Set berated himself for not uncovering this.

She lifted her chin. "I have no shame in my origin, boy. You know who I am, so you know my story."

"Your father locked you in a tower and you fell in love with a Tuatha Dé Danann," he said dismissively. "The very kind that you seem hate."

She sneered. "Said like a man who hasn't lived a life where females are seen to serve and obey. You know part of my tale. Know this, Setanta McQuillan. You cast Fomorians as the villains, but it depends on what side of the story you're on. What role you've been handed."

When he didn't answer, Ethne raised her pallid hand, twirling it above. The broken ground disappeared below them and a stone floor rose so rapidly, Set wasn't sure if he was falling or if it was rising to greet him. Either way, the impact was strong enough that he stumbled to his knees.

Cursing, he stood, taking in the unfamiliar circular room. "A tower."

"My home as a babe," Ethne intoned, her figure gracefully moving towards a slender strip of an unadorned window. It was no more than a set of narrow openings, allowing thin fingers of sea-breeze to filter in. Not turning back toward him, she added, "My prison."

As Ethne rested an elbow on the sill with a heavy sigh, Set took in the elegant bed nestled opposite the window, offering a glimpse into the rumbling heart of the sea's freedom to the outside world. From the high-reaching ceiling hung a large wooden chandelier, holding beeswax candles, its flickering light breathing some warmth into the cathedral-like chill of the tower room. Against one wall, an oversized armchair snugged under a narrow shelf crammed with aged parchment rolls and leather-bound books.

"Why are you showing me this?"

"Because you wondered whether this was just a dream. It is, but we are sharing it through our minds. We are linked, Setanta McQuillan. Far more than you realise."

A headache was forming as he tried to keep up with her.

"I didn't enter your dream uninvited." Ethne arced her arm and once again they were standing in the dust-choked soul of the deadened forest. "You brought me here."

He was about to deny her claim but a shift in the air hinted at a foreboding truth. It wrapped around him, penetrating his thoughts with an unsettling clarity that nearly stole his breath away. He felt his mental walls crumble, leaving him raw and vulnerable under the weight of the revelation. His head buzzed with conflicting thoughts.

Swallowing down his unease, Set moistened his lips, the sharp taste of uncertainty giving a bitter hint of what was about to unfold. Now that he had unintentionally summoned her into his dream, he might as well seize the opportunity. "I wanted to ask you something."

"Ask."

"Is there a way to save Tiernan?"

Ethne stepped backwards, toward the steep hill. "Prove to me it's worth sharing that information with you."

"How?" Set asked before adding with a sigh, "What do you want from me?"

"A simple geas," Ethne said, shrugging as she continued her departure. "I came to you when you summoned me. All I ask in return is that when I call upon you next, you join me."

Set stared at the female warily, his throat dry. The geas she'd already placed on him had nearly choked him. "If I agree to come to you when you ask, will you remove the other geas? Allow me to speak about who you are."

Ethne's voice was a velvet whisper as she paused in her retreating steps. "Once you join me, the other geas will lift, but not a moment before, and you cannot utter my name or this encounter until I call on you. How about that?"

"This is some sort of trick."

She waited, face impassive as he warred with his mind, fully aware she could hear every thought. If she could hear his thoughts, could he somehow hear hers if he knew how?

Yes. Ethne's smile was wicked.

A cunning creature, too smart and too long in this world for Set to outwit.

She chuckled. "I agree."

"Enough," Set bit out. "The geas is that I come to you when you call upon me next? Once?"

Ethne inclined her head.

"And I can leave after?"

"If you want." Ethne tilted her head, silver-blonde hair cascading over her shoulder. "But maybe you won't."

"Doubtful," Set murmured, but nodded. "Fine."

As the words left his mouth, Set felt something shift within him. It was subtle at first, just the faintest tugging sensation in his core. But once the agreement was made, the tugging violently twisted into a wrenching ache that radiated through his entire being.

He gasped and doubled over, clutching at his chest as unseen bonds lashed around his soul. It felt as though an unbreakable chain was being wrapped around his essence, binding him irrevocably to Ethne's will. He fought against the geas with every fibre of his being, but it was no use. The magical bindings were already taking hold.

Through the haze of agony, Set smelled something burning; it took him a moment to realise it was coming from within. His veins lit up as though liquid fire now coursed through them, searing his internal flesh. A scream tore from his throat but was cut brutally short as the fire reached his vocal cords.

Finally, the pain faded, though it left him wracked and shaking on the ground. He felt hollowed out and stretched impossibly thin. A piece of his soul now belonged to Ethne.

He'd blacked out that last time she'd placed a geas on him; he hadn't known it could feel this way.

Groaning, he pushed himself up on trembling arms and met her stare. For the first time, fear took root in his heart at what he had recklessly agreed to. The geas was sealed; all that remained was when she'd enact her claim.

With only a wicked smile in farewell, Ethne retreated further downhill. Rising on unsteady limbs, he tried to follow her but couldn't. Looking down, his feet were cemented in the scorched earth.

Her words floated toward him before she sifted out of sight. "You have a special place with Aisling. Take her there. Follow the shadows to find the key. Release Tiernan and all trapped within."

"Wait," Set called, struggling but failing to break free. "You wanted to awaken Fionn Mac Cumhaill. Why haven't you?"

Silence answered him as shadows detached from every tree and rock, waiting for Ethne's departure. They came for him as if swimming underwater until they latched onto his skin. He fought, but they were immaterial, nothing solid to grip onto, even if they could hold him. Set reminded himself he was in a dream. That she also had control and these must be a parting gift. But higher and higher they rose until he was blinded by them. He opened his mouth to scream and swallowed them.

CHAPTER 59
AISLING

Ash exited her tent to find Tomás and Ciarán in a stand-off with some Collins clansmen. Again. She muttered a slew of curses Maebh would be proud of.

"Just because you claimed more territory, you think your shite doesn't stink," the Collins warrior sneered before spitting on the ground by Tomás's boots. Her cousin tracked the movement with a calm Ash knew led to violence. The warrior wasn't smart enough to stop from adding, "High King Bradan won't select a clan like yours, tainted by the Breen butcher boy. You'll not win the Cath, no matter how many Fair Ones you cast out of this land."

Tomás and Ciarán stole a glance at each other, identical grins stretching across their faces. Watching them, Ash contemplated letting them have their fun. The warrior had dragged her brother's name into his taunt, and the resulting laughter from the Collins warriors only ignited the smouldering anger within her cousins. As fire skirted along her veins, her face and neck warmed as she fought against the urge to join in.

The atmosphere grew taut with an unspoken electrifying tension, snapping and crackling in the air like a live wire, mounting with each passing second the warriors stared at each other. She knew her cousins could handle themselves, yet the numbers were uneven, and the situation was quickly disintegrating into a potential brawl. They didn't need the High

King's attention on them when they were using some of their resources to guard the cave without his knowledge.

Her cousins stepped closer to the two men in front of them until their foreheads pressed against theirs. As they gained the attention of surrounding Breen members, more joined behind them, numbers swelling. As scornful laughter and jeering rose from both sides, she heard the unmistakable sound of steel sliding from sheaths.

"Tom, Keer," Ash said, stepping between the clans. "Enough."

The brothers eased their tension enough to slide their blades back into their sheaths, though neither gave away an inch of the ground they stood on. Casting a swift glance over her shoulder, Ash realised not one member of her clan had withdrawn either. The Collins warrior instigator tore his focus away from them to grin at her. Breathing deeply, she willed herself to remain calm.

This was the same man who'd claimed she'd murdered her mother on the first night of the Cath festival. Back then, she had relied on the protective shield of her cousins. But her journey since that day had refined her. The slurs from a baseless man no longer held the power to unsettle her as they used to. He opened his mouth, but she cut him off.

"I'm assuming you have something clever to say, but not today. Go back to your matriarch like a good little boy."

His face turned puce, features contorting as laughter filled the air behind her. Before he could recover to retort, a commanding woman's voice rang out from behind him.

"Aisling Breen."

The warrior's smile was feral as he stepped aside with a wink. A woman with dark hair pulled into a severe bun strode forward, straight-backed, hand resting casually on her sword hilt. Her jacket held the Collins coat of arms with 'Matriarch' emblazoned underneath.

"Fiadh Collins," Ash acknowledged, nodding her head.

She remembered her mother speaking of the other matriarch. She'd been the same age as Cara, and they'd never liked one another. By the rude conduct of her clan member, Ash had little hope they would become allies any time soon.

"Well, if it isn't the lost kitten who's come crawling back. Rumour had it you fled like a frightened child after Newgrange," Fiadh sneered, her tone soft and playful. Raking her assessing eyes over Ash, her voice turned cold as she uttered, "Colour me unsurprised."

Ash bristled, Bradan's order to remain quiet about her abduction a barrier between this woman's accusation and the truth. She kept her tone even. "I went seeking answers beyond these walls. And I haven't fled this Cath. I believe we are above yours for territory."

Fiadh huffed a derisive laugh. "Pretty words, but we'll see if you can keep your territories." Her eyes flicked proudly to her clan and Ash caught sight of the hideous trophy necklaces bearing parts of fae victims they'd tortured from their claimed territories. The woman added, "Not that I envy your prospects."

As Fiadh turned to leave with her sniggering clan, Ash caught a pulsing darkness, like a shadow expanding with the moving sun, as Set appeared behind a nearby tent. He wore his all-black battle-suit with weapons attached to a myriad of pockets. As his spear caught the sun's rays, it shimmered, the sharp point glinting menacingly.

He scanned the campsite, each swift movement of his gaze matching the rise and fall of his broad chest, tension lining the set of his jaw. The moment his attention locked onto her, the frantic motion stilled. It was as if invisible threads pulled them together, his intense look anchoring on her in the sea of his chaos.

Ignoring the others, she barely breathed until she was face to face with Set.

"What's wrong?" Ash lifted a hand to his face, stroking away wayward curls. "Were you in the cave? Has something happened?"

"No." He didn't smile, his eyes flashing with something she couldn't read. "I didn't get much sleep last night. And my dreams . . ." he shuddered, his face blanching. "They didn't end well."

"Let's go for a walk," Ash said, taking his arm.

He nodded, sweat gleaming from his brow, but his hand was warm and strong when he clasped her fingers around his, leading them toward the woodland. "We need to talk."

A cold sheen of sweat broke out across Ash's forehead and back. Her palms grew clammy, but Set didn't seem to notice, his grip steadfast on hers.

"Have you discovered something?" Ash said in a faint voice. After Biróg's ritual and Maebh's insistence they were running out of time, they'd agreed to concentrate solely on freeing Tiernan, Cath be damned. If Tiernan's father would not see to it, then they would.

Set looked down at her with pursed lips before changing direction, angling deeper through the dense trees.

"Do you trust me?" Set's deep baritone made her shiver as she glanced up at him.

She didn't have to ask where they were going as the familiar pathway to their barrenland greeted her. Not many people took this path through the woods and the only sounds she could hear were those of the wild animals and birds.

"Of course," Ash said, lengthening her strides to keep up with him before she repeated herself. "Set, did you find something?"

"I know how to save Tiernan."

"What?" Ash's heart jumped before she gripped his arm until he finally stopped. "Then why are we going in the wrong direction? We need to get the others. Does Maebh know?"

Her throat restricted as unwanted hope swelled dangerously, heavy enough to crush her lungs if she let it grow.

Set's face was unreadable as he glanced to the trees and then back at her, his shoulders stiffened. "I need you to trust me."

Ash searched his face, wariness seeping from his cool grey contemplation and she couldn't help but remember how he'd looked when they'd found him in the tunnel after Imogen's gruesome death. She released a heavy breath as her dry lips parted.

"Okay."

He provided no further explanation as they trekked through the woods. The overhead assembly of tree branches interlaced to form a thick, leaf-laden canopy, filtering out most of the sunlight. Deciding whether it was still daytime, or if the encroaching dusk was arriving prematurely, became increasingly challenging.

Shadows pulsed around them, and all greenery seemed to dull the further they walked. When High King Aedan had first brought her here, Ash had thought the deadened white wood and scorched dirt earth had been an ominous sign. She'd believed the High King's claims that it had somehow been the human realm polluting this land.

But the times she spent here with Set had made her see the beauty of this place; the small purple flowers that grew from the jagged crevices near the hot springs and the trees that held a silver light through the crevices of white bark, shimmering during daylight. The air was dry when they first entered, but the further they went and the closer they grew to the rising steam, it transformed into soothing wafts.

Set reached behind, unsheathing his long spear as he stepped onto the powdered earth. Everything was cast in unnatural shadows. The once bone-white trees that surrounded the large meadow seemed to shiver in anticipation as Ash stood beside him. Kicking up loose debris, she tracked Set's tight grip on his weapon, studying his tense face.

"You need to tell me what's going on."

Set looked troubled as he looked around them, stepping further into the wide space. "She told me to come here."

"Who?" Ash urged. His expression strained, mouth contorting as he tried to form words, but no sound came out. She'd seen enough to guess. "Ethne? When did you see her again?"

When he remained silent, a boulder dropped into her stomach, its weight grounding her in an uncertain reality. His eyes briefly met hers, their pained expression communicating a silent plea that tugged at her core. But before she could decipher his silence, his focus sharply reverted to the treeline.

"Setanta, what's happening here? What did she say?"

As if in answer to her mounting fear, the treeline came alive with unsettling noises. They rose in harsh whispers initially, baying winds carrying the faint, garbled sounds of unseen mouths. As the seconds stretched on, the noises grew louder, disembodied voices gnawing at the silence.

Each shriek crawled under her skin, their elusive origin beyond the dense wood a question left unanswered like the entire conversation with the man at her side. Ash unsheathed her sword, fingers curling around the hilt. The chill of the metal, worn slightly through practise but untested in true battle, seeped into her skin. It offered a meagre comfort, the sensation as hollow as her lungs that refused to fill her with certain breaths.

"I want to tell you, Ash, but I can't," Set said, placing his back to hers as they circled their perimeter. The noises stilled as if listening to his voice. Waiting for his confession.

As Set drew in a lengthy breath, there was a noticeable shift in his voice. It emerged softer, almost intimate, as if he could hardly believe the words he was uttering. "Have you noticed I haven't had to ríastrad? This spear holds my monster. I . . . she . . . I'm finally free."

"What?" Ash whispered, turning to face him as his revelation hit her with the force of a gale, leaving her momentarily speechless. She wanted to ask how but her voice was lost to a surging tide of surprise.

She searched his face, looking for any sign this was a joke, but only raw vulnerability pierced through his eyes.

A soft laugh slipped past her lips as she let herself believe him. He broke into a grin, and then a laugh, eyes brimming with tears as he nodded.

"I'm finally free, Ash. She . . . I . . ."

When he grimaced, clutching his throat, Ash stepped closer, but he shook his head, swallowing hard.

As Set's words hung in the air, the spear in his hand responded. Its surface came alive, emitting a glow of blazing white, a hint of blue pulsing rhythmically, like a living, breathing entity. Each pulse cast a vivid light, which ebbed and flowed in captivating waves, creating a hypnotic dance of shadows across the woodland floor. She reached one hand out to touch it, but Set snatched it away, shaking his head frantically. "Don't touch it, remember?"

Ash took an involuntary step backwards, lowering her hand as she tracked his fierce expression. A tightness formed around her ribcage, the surprised joy at finding out he was no longer caged by his ríastrad replaced by the confusion of his overreaction. "Set . . ."

The shadows writhed around them, encircling just beyond their feet.

"Follow the shadows," Set murmured and Ash's eyes darted to him.

She turned, trying to keep the shadows in sight, but they slipped in and out of her vision, elusive as smoke. Despite her efforts, the darkness possessed a will of its own, darting around the shifting treeline and playing a perplexing game of hide and seek. "Are these sluagh?"

The haunting chorus emanating from the treeline abruptly amplified, making the woods ring with sounds that ranged from guttural whispers to high-pitched wails, fraying Ash's nerves as her grip tightened on the only weapon she had. Normally with Set by her side, she wouldn't doubt their chances, but he was hiding something.

She stole a glance at him, his rugged face adorned with an inscrutable mask. His usually vibrant eyes, now glazed and bloodshot, were shadowed underneath with strains of blue. His unrelenting hold on his spear gave away the tension he was trying to conceal. He had asked her to trust him. He'd always had her back. This was the man who followed her across the dangerous lands of Tír na nÓg, not knowing what he'd find. He'd agreed to a title that he'd never wanted to save her. Of course, Ash would trust Set.

"Let's follow the shadows," she said, voice steady despite the beating turmoil within.

At her words, the strain etched on Set's face eased, a glimmer of relief sparkling within those bloodshot eyes. It was as if she had unknowingly answered a silent plea he'd been wrestling within. With a nod, he released a breath, his shoulders lowering. Straight backed, he took a step toward them, and she joined his side.

The shadows, mere pitch-black silhouettes before, now took on a deeper character. They quivered; their inky, intangible forms shifting and morphing under the blue luminescence of his spear. As Set and Ash ventured forward, the shadows wove a path ahead, flickering occasionally under the spear's light before continuing their withdrawn dance deeper into the unknown.

CHAPTER 60
AISLING

"Why didn't you tell me about your ríastrad?" Ash cast a sidelong glance at Set, her eyes narrowing as they trailed the retreating shadows leading them beyond the barrenland treeline. She didn't bother hiding the tinge of hurt in her voice. "You've had that spear since . . ."

She trailed off until realisation widened her gaze and she glared at him. She'd been beside herself, waiting anxiously for Set's return when they'd believed Mary and Dom were in danger. He'd reassured her, asked her to remain patient, promising a swift return when he'd arrived with a new battle-suit and spear.

Set's lips tugged down awkwardly as he grimaced.

"I should have told you sooner. Everything I've done." Set's voice fell for a moment before he turned to look at her, an earnest resolve shaping his handsome features. "You must know by now, Ash. Every choice I make, it's always with you in mind. I love you."

The words struck her like a well-aimed arrow, robbing Ash of her breath. Tethered to the spot under his earnest appraisal, her world whittled down to those four, pivotal letters. Love. Such a simple word, yet it bore heavy implications, filled with untold promises.

She could taste the underlying sweetness of his declaration, laced with a melancholic undertone that caused her lip to tremble. As she peered up at him, tears threatening to spill, the encroaching darkness of the woodland deepened the lines of his face in ways that made him seem even more genuine, more real.

The shadows wavered and swayed, jumping from one brittle tree onto the next. One jumped too close to her face, and Ash recoiled with a shiver.

"You don't have to say it back." Set spun away before she could fully process the depth of his revelation. "We must find a key. It will save Tiernan. Our fathers."

Ash hesitated. She ignored the niggling guilt at not saying those words back, but they were too precious to utter in a time like this. "We'll find another way to save them, Set. Biróg . . ."

". . . is as in the dark as we have been for months." Set shook his head. "We must free them now. Maebh will never forgive me if we don't try everything."

Despite her instinct to run in the opposite direction, Ash followed. With each step, the sky darkened. Leaves rustled faintly, brushing against each other like spectral whispers in the encroaching darkness while the gentle hum of woodland life dwindled to nothingness. The forest hushed, as though donning an eerie, muted mask.

The softening heartbeat of the forest felt unfamiliar, laden with an unnatural stillness before a storm, sending a shiver cascading down Ash's spine. The tiny hairs at the nape of her neck prickled her skin as she silently plucked a dagger from one of Set's sheaths. He slowed his pace but didn't question her as the charged tranquillity punctuated the forest.

A monstrous roar ruptured the weighted silence, echoing through the woods. They halted. It wasn't just a sound, but a force that pushed against them, throbbing with raw power and primordial terror. Low and guttural, chilling in its intensity, as if the voice of the forest itself had turned bestial.

"What was that?" Ash's breath was an erratic drum, calling on any creature to seek her as prey.

It wasn't Set who answered but the shadows, as they encircled them before conjoining as one only feet away. Set was at her side, spear in front as those inhuman wails emanated from the shadows, which vibrated and writhed as they cried out and growled in multiple voices.

The shadows elongated and thinned until a jagged line rose from the ground, higher than the trees.

"Do you see that?" Ash asked, not trusting herself, as the sounds intensified only to become muffled as though behind a closed door.

"It's like a seam from a shirt," Set said, raising his spear toward it and tracing upwards.

She could see it then, the shadowy edges as if it were stitches holding something in place.

A noise like tearing fabric filled her eardrums and she resisted the urge to cover them, instead gripping her sword and dagger, angling them toward the shadowy seam. They both took several steps back as a taloned white hand, larger than any she'd seen, broke through the shadowed lines parting before them.

"Run," Set's voice broke through her terror as another hand appeared and whatever was behind the shadows pulled and clawed its way through.

All sound muted as more of the monster's bleached body became visible.

"Ash," Set said, pulling on her arm as he shoved her behind him. "Run."

"I'm not leaving you," she gritted out before stepping in front of him.

Set only nodded before striding closer to the creature, thrusting his spear outward, stabbing one hand. A guttural roar rang out, but before Set could pull his spear out, he lurched forward.

"No!" Set cried as the monster gripped the blade with its other hand. "Ash, help!"

"Let it go!" Ash shouted, but she sprang into action as Set's face turned ashen and he clung to the spear as if his life depended on it.

With a wide arch, she brought her sword down on the beast's arm. It was not a clean cut, but the blade sank in deep enough for its hand to spasm, releasing Set's spear. She pulled her blade out as the arm disappeared into the shadows.

"Thanks," Set breathed as he gripped his weapon before securing it on his back and unsheathing his axe instead.

He turned to Ash, but she cried out in warning as more hands appeared, the monsters ripping through the shadows too quickly.

"We need to get help," she said, tugging him away from the scrabbling hands. "We can't fight this on our own."

The only thing Ash could hear was the pounding of her blood as she willed her legs to move faster. Set was just ahead of her, and by his continuous turning, she knew he was running much slower than he liked to stay with her. She dared a look behind and wished she hadn't. The bleached monsters were gaining.

The things chasing them collectively went quiet as if they knew they were homing in on their prey. They had been heading towards Tara Court to alert the highguard, but once the creatures could be heard chasing them, they veered deeper into the woods and away from the innocent lives. Ash had hoped they'd have come across other warriors or highguard out patrolling the reclaimed lands by now, but so far all they'd managed was to get further away from the barrenland and Tara Court.

A whoosh of air hit her face before a large mass collided into her side, causing her to fall.

"Ash!" Set was on the creature before she could roll. Before she could even get a good look at it, he flung it through the thick bush. "Let's go."

Ash was on her feet and running once more, this time allowing Set to hold her arm and drag her to a faster pace. Her feet almost didn't connect with the uneven ground, but she could hear them. With every step, the otherworldly monsters drew dangerously closer.

Her lungs protested as they plunged through the forest, and she knew it was no use. She opened her mouth to tell Set they needed to stop and fight, but a keening wail pierced her ears, and she cried out as her arm was jerked and Set stumbled to the ground, a creature on his back.

She could see it now.

Moonstone-white, it was humanoid-shaped in most ways, with skin hung loosely from thin bones. Its muscles undulated under its slick skin as its friend reared from Set's back, pinning him to the ground with hoofed feet. Hairless, red-pupiled eyes took up most of its face. Where a nose and ears would have been, only diagonal slits appeared. Ash ran towards it as it opened its jaw wider than any snake's and was about to latch onto Set's shoulder with its fangs.

She raised her sword and slammed into the monster, shoving her blade into its midsection. It slid in easily, missing bones but getting stuck in muscle. The monster screamed, knocking Ash back with its arm. She hit the ground by Set's feet with a groan.

Set shouted at her as the monster writhed above him, its hulking form twisting to face her. The beast snarled, a deep, guttural noise that echoed through the night. Saliva hit her, and the smell of decay invaded her nose, the foul spray coating her face. The creature's spittle was thick and stringy, stinging her skin with its acidic touch.

Screaming, she rubbed her arm roughly against her face, the leather of her coat singeing with each swipe. Her stomach churned as acute pain rendered her senseless to the creature rearing on its hind legs to attack at her. Set was quick. Launching forward, he tackled the creature's torso, pinning it to the ground.

"Ash!" Set straddled the monster, its talons twisting unnaturally and digging into his wrists. He cursed and Ash jumped up, grabbing her sword handle from its side, still lodged in. It roared as she pulled it out. Set's arms strained as it buckled underneath him and he grit out, "Do it."

Ash moved to the monster's head. Its red eyes met hers and they stared, unblinking. It froze as Ash raised her blade. Before she could bring it down, it lurched forward, snapping its wide jaw with a ferocity that could only come before fighting off death. Ash slammed the blade down, both hands gripping its hilt. The blade pierced its eye, and it finally went still.

"Are you okay?" She reached out to grab Set's hand, but before she could attempt to help him up, pain lanced through her leg.

"Ash!" Set's cry was distant as her racing heart thumped in her ears.

She only had time to look at the claws spearing her leg before a monster larger than the dead beast at their feet hoisted her upward, so she dangled uselessly in the air. Swinging her blade, she hacked into the beast's hairy side, but it only shook her violently before roaring in her face. Putrid breath blasted her face and she gagged. The giant backhanded Set as he charged at it.

"Set!"

He sailed through the air and smashed into a tree. The giant barrelled through the woodland as Ash tried and failed to swipe at it with her sword. Blood rushed to her head as her vision blurred and she swung forward, crunching her abdomen long enough to ease the rush of blood flow. She could only hold it for a few minutes before dangling again as her capturer brought them through the trees and back to the shadowy line.

Upside down, the dark line appeared to stitch its way into the very fabric of the sky. She found herself unceremoniously dumped feet way from where the monster had first appeared. Gulping in deep breaths she willed her vision to return to normal as the giant shouldered the line, breaking into the mysterious barrier. The line fissured open and the beast disappeared once more into the void.

The rift sealed itself back together as though nothing out of the ordinary had occurred, leaving Ash kneeling on the forest floor, staring at the spot where the beast had vanished. Scrambling to her feet, she gripped her blade, readying herself for the giant's return. Where had it gone? What did that shadow seam lead to?

"Ash!" Set's voice rang through the woods, and she huffed out a relieved breath.

"Over here!" She stood facing the direction of his voice and Set broke through the last trees.

When he spotted her, his pace quickened, his eyes widening as he opened his mouth.

But there was no time. A whispering chasm of frigid air pounded into her back, her hair blinding her as a large hand gripped her midsection, yanking her painfully into the seam of shadows.

CHAPTER 61

MAEBH

"I'm running out of ways to miss you, Tier," Maebh whispered as she stared up at the stone statue.

Not a statue; Tiernan. The man who called her out on bullshit and excited her with his schemes even more outrageous than her own. The loss of him was a tangible thing that kept her company. In the long hours of the night, it kept vigil by her side.

If Bradan found out she revealed the truth to some of her clan . . . well, she didn't care. His son needed protection and she'd be damned if she didn't provide it.

The now-familiar heartbeat song of the guardians drowned out all else as she turned, shoulders and back stiff from hours standing and patrolling the cave. Her clan were stationed around the remaining petrified warriors. No matter how often she walked the entire cave, or that her father also stood frozen in stone feet away, her feet always led her back to Tiernan.

They'd stood watch for five hours without change. Dense shadows held fast where they stood, while scattered piles of rubble marked where statues had fallen. Tiernan, Aedan and the caillte remained untouched for now. But they had all been important to someone. Any of those lives lost was totally unacceptable.

"The next shift is on its way," Malachy said, standing before her own father's likeness.

She joined him silently.

"Gearoid was my best friend growing up." Malachy's throat bobbed. "He had his own demons to fight . . ."

"Yeah, her name was Imogen," Maebh interrupted, and grinned when Malachy shook his head, smiling in return.

"He loved you and Setanta." Malachy turned back to her father. "When you were born, I could see a change in him. He was less wild. Wanted to settle somewhere to raise you. But your mother was . . ."

"I know what she was," Maebh interrupted, a lump forming in her throat as she stared at her father. "Da always stood up for me. When she'd nitpick at everything I did, he was the one person she actually listened to."

"Gearoid wanted you to lead a happy life." Malachy squeezed her arm. "To live your life your way." Maebh only looked at him. He let go and smiled. "For what it's worth, your dad would be proud of you, taking this on when even the High King wouldn't."

"I don't have a choice." Maebh shrugged.

She felt her chest tighten as she spotted Conor and Orla deep in quiet conversation across the cavern. He had arrived bearing supplies while Breen warriors filed in to prepare for the watch changeover. Her eyes lingered on their ease with one another, the gentleness in Conor's manner as he handed Orla a waterskin.

The hollowness in Conor's eyes after they'd found him in the tunnel feet away from Imogen haunted Maebh still. And Orla's vacant face had only just found its way back to the fierce warrior she'd once been. Conor had fought through hell, and had dragged Orla out, too.

Part of Maebh was glad to see Orla comfortable with another, smiling even, after enduring so much. Yet she couldn't deny the familiar pangs of envy and loneliness their closeness stirred. Her eyes drifted to Tiernan and once again, her feet brought her before him.

All her feelings were tangled now with her title as matriarch. Duty weighed heavy as a millstone, distancing her even from those closest.

Even though the shadows had been silent, Maebh could feel their presence, knew they were not harmless. They were alive. Waiting. So many lives had been taken by the host of sluagh already. Turning, she faced what Tiernan could see, what his statue was stuck looking at. An uneven wall embedded with blue gemstones greeted her, while the cave entrance lay beyond reach, a taunt to those imprisoned in stone.

Maebh's attention snapped back to the wall. Shadows throbbed, subtly at first, but soon the cold, soulless hunger of the dark entities grew and her skin crawled.

"Warriors, get ready!" Maebh called, blade already in hand, her stare locked on the advancing sluagh.

Her heart pumped as wildly as the stone guardians' hearts behind her. She swallowed hard as she noted the shadow monsters stalking near. They were much too close, their path unwavering as the shadows grew. As Breens and McQuillans sprang into action, swiftly encircling the sarcophagus and statues, a piercing thought ran through Maebh's mind, cutting through her resolve like a sharpened dagger. Had she doomed them all?

The question thundered in her mind, echoing over and over until it filled every corner of her thoughts. Her stomach constricted with the weight of it, a dreadful realisation washing over her with every advancement of the shadows. Blood roaring in her ears, her pulse was a frantic drum begging for release of the tension that threaded through her veins.

"Maebh! Move out of the way!" Malachy shouted, but she shook her head.

Her eyes strayed to Tiernan. His silent form, motionless even now, when they'd clearly been freed from their state to surround Fionn Mac Cumhaill. She hadn't realised until now how much she wished he'd awaken, even in the stone form when he didn't seem to know who she was.

His vulnerable condition only cemented her resolve as she stubbornly rooted to the spot.

The sluagh's mere presence leeched the already muted light. One by one, the torches they'd brought snuffed out, flames guttering and dying, taking with it all warmth.

Maebh blinked, trying desperately to adjust to the dark.

The shadows surged forward in a horrific wave of menacing darkness, and she swung, meeting only air. Dreadful laughter filled her head as the shadows swirled, enveloping Maebh in their glacial grip. An anguished gasp ripped from her mouth as her sword clattered to the rocky ground, her body arching violently in the grasp of the shadow. A bitter chill seeped into her; an insidious coldness no fire could thaw crept into her bones, feasting and devouring her until it reached her soul.

A visceral silence filled her world, sight claimed by the all-consuming pain and terror of wherever the shadow touched her. Gritting her teeth against the excruciating pain, she sensed Tiernan's presence ebbing behind her, a faint beacon in the oppressive darkness.

She'd given him more time.

A tear sprang from her eye, but before it could trace a path of despair down her cheek, it was cruelly intercepted by the shadow's razored tongue, lapped up in its voracious hunger. The violation of her raw, honest emotion by the shadow clawed at the fringes of her sanity. Her heart shattered, the sharp fragments stabbing at her inside, escalating the pulsating agony in sync with her breath hitching in her chest.

As the darkness pulled her under, Maebh held fast to the memory of Tiernan's smile, brown eyes, and his long, elegant fingers. With one last painful breath, she surrendered to the shadows.

CHAPTER 62
TIERNAN

The woman with the golden hair saved him. He wished he could remember her name. He was stone. Cold. *Protect the High King.*

CHAPTER 63

AISLING

"Aisling!" Set's voice was muffled as if a thousand layers lay between them.

It was not rock or earth, but a veil of smoke and shadows. Intangible but impenetrable.

The giant's grip loosened, and Ash fell to her knees onto a dank, cold ground. It retreated, disappearing into the obsidian air and she jumped to her feet. Whirling around, she listened beyond the erratic pounding of her heart as screeching and growls echoed in the dark. Scrabbling desperately at the seam, it vanished at her touch.

"Shit!"

Looking down, she could barely see her hands, let alone what lurked in the mist surrounding her. Nothing attacked. The giant's footsteps grew faint, and she had no intention of following blindly when monstrous sounds worse than the ones it had made surrounded her. Inky black air pressed on her, seeping its way down her lungs with every ragged breath. She needed to calm down and focus. Most of all, she needed to get out of this hell.

"Set!" Ash called out as she spun to his next bellowing cry, but there was no door.

No rip in the veil. Nothing but darkness enveloped her, and she lost track of where the opening should have been. She'd turned too many times to the same view that her head spun and if she weren't standing on a solid ground, she wouldn't know what was up or down. If she thought too much and looked too closely, gravity wavered, and she feared she'd fall upwards like the cliff to get to Tiernan's prison.

A colourless talon appeared to her right, slashing at her arm before disappearing. Cursing at her ripped sleeve, she swung her blade blindly but only met the heavy air. Was she even breathing? Her lungs filled, her nose stinging with the substance she took in. Humans had to breathe oxygen, but whatever this was, was laced with something foul and wicked. Something latched on to her hair, dragging her to the ground, only releasing its vice-like grip upon impact. Before she could right herself, the world shifted and she was no longer lying down, but standing. The world had rotated. Disoriented, her stomach churned as another screech pierced the silence. A claw swiped at her, but this time she managed to jump back only to meet a solid mass. Crying out, she arced her blade upwards . . .

"Ash, it's me. I'm here." Set's voice was an anchor within this raging ocean.

Lowering her sword, she spun to face his shrouded, towering figure, leaning forward to make sure she hadn't imagined him.

"How?" Ash asked, clutching him close as the unseen monsters became distant. Had his presence scared them off? "How did you make it through to me?"

"I sifted." Set squeezed her before pushing her to arm's length, taking her in from head to toe.

Set tucked her in close to his side, his axe poised in one hand as he scanned their surroundings. But there was nothing but darkness, no light to show them what this place truly looked like. Perhaps it looked like nothing but shadows? Nothing was tangible, not even the shifting ground.

"Can you sift us out?"

Set held her close once more and she closed her eyes, waiting for the pull to take form. After several spluttering heartbeats, she squinted up at Set.

"I can't." Set cursed, shaking his spear, the lack of its sporadic glowing unsettling. "I don't know why, but I can't sift us out."

What if they couldn't make it out? Panic tore at her lungs as Ash took in one toxic breath after another. Set frowned at her, rubbing her arm gently as he spoke. He gripped her chin until she looked into his grey eyes. "We'll be fine."

"I don't know how you did it, but I'm glad you followed me to hell."

Set chuckled before kissing her forehead. "I willed my heart to find you. I would follow you anywhere, Breen, even the Underworld."

As if in confirmation, the creatures' noises echoed around them, and they stood back to back, ready for an attack. Flapping of what sounded like massive wings pounded stifling air above them, causing the shadow smoke to swirl erratically. Whatever was overhead sounded larger than any creature should be.

Ash squinted uselessly through the thickening mist, but nothing came at them. "Do you think this is the Underworld?"

"Yes."

A sudden chill curled its wintry fingers around Ash's spine at Set's response. The Underworld. The reality of their location hit her like a punch to the gut, anchoring them in a terrain of surreal horror. The palpable dread hung heavy in the pit of her stomach, an unwanted confirmation contorting her features into despair.

They stood waiting until Ash thought she'd go mad from the anticipation of it. These creatures were ancient, stuck in this forsaken realm, and they finally had food to play with.

"Look," Set's whisper may as well have been a shout as she jumped.

Turning, she gasped as a faint light floated toward them. It was only enough to illuminate a few feet ahead of them. There was nothing. No walls, no cave, no ceiling. Just black on black.

The light retreated a few paces and stopped.

"I think it wants us to follow," Ash said, tentatively. "Could it be a Will O'? The last time I followed one, I ended up being dragged underwater by merrow."

"The last time I followed one, I ended up finding you." Set intertwined their fingers, tugging her on. "What's the worst that could happen?"

"Death? Torture?"

"Bring it on," Set laughed, but she could see tension marring his features as he tugged her forward.

As they followed the tiny sprite, the muted growls quietened until the only sounds were their collective ragged breaths and footsteps.

"What do you know about the Underworld?" Ash said in an undertone, remembering lessons taught by the elders when she was a child.

"I came across some limited descriptions while researching . . ." Set paused, tightening his grip as if afraid she'd disappear.

Although the Will O' The Wisp was feet ahead, Ash's vision hadn't improved enough to see beyond her outstretched arm. She walked closer to Set, anticipating another claw to break their joined hands at any moment.

"The Fomorians' royals and their beasts were cast here a millennia ago, when the Tuatha Dé Danann defeated them," Ash said, licking her dry lips as they inched forward. "Some of the less threatening fae were left to the human realm, and none were allowed to remain in Tír na nÓg."

Remembering her encounters with the evil fae who stole human babies as changelings, she shivered. If that was less threatening . . . her hand cleaved to her weapon. Whatever lived here would be much worse. The giant had been gruesome and unbeatable. Was it just the start of what they would face?

"The Breen clan held weekly lessons with all the children; our elders taught us not to shed blood on Samhain because it could pierce the veil," Ash said, her brow creasing as she strained her ears for any signs of lurking monsters. "They didn't teach us a lot about the realm. But we were told that the same laws didn't apply here. Blood sacrifices won't work to pierce the veil between the Underworld and Tír na nÓg or the human realm. The worlds are divided by veils, but the one surrounding here is denser, foreboding. You can't just give blood; for this veil to pierce you must sacrifice part of your soul. Which I always thought was a relief . . ."

Set glanced at her, his features illuminated by the blue sprite. Finishing her sentence with a grim set to his jaw, he said, ". . . until now, because how will we get out?"

When she nodded, he pulled her in, kissing her forehead. "There was a tear in it to allow us entry, so if we find it, we can escape."

"Actually," Ash hesitated, looking up to meet Set's troubled countenance. "I had it within my grasp, but the moment I touched the seam, it disappeared."

He squeezed her hand before raising his axe. "Look, we're reaching something."

The ethereal glow of the Will O' guided them through their slow advance, gradually revealing a stone passageway. The walls seemed fashioned from eroded cobbles, stones worn smooth by the passage of forgotten eons, their surfaces hard and cold to the touch. The space constricted, forcing Ash to follow behind Set, his figure silhouetted in the blue light.

Anxiety caught in Ash's throat as the enclosure threatened to press too closely to pass through. Even now, she couldn't see anything other than Set's shadowed form, his lumbering frame blocking the sprite's light. The spectral glow of the Will O' nudged forward, disappearing for a tortuous heartbeat, before the constricting stone wall faltered, dissipating into nothingness as they plunged back into the churn of black mist.

"There's someone here," Ash said, her voice barely rising above a whisper.

Her fingers tightened instinctively around the grip of her sword. Almost involuntarily, her gift flared to life. Her forehead furrowed as she grappled with the convoluted aura of emotions emanating from an unseen figure up ahead. The smells were ambiguous, a myriad of fragrances that she couldn't quite identify, threads of the familiar interwoven with the distinctly foreign.

Unlike the simple aura of humans, she couldn't distinguish what exact emotions lay within, but it was a being more sophisticated than the lower level fae or giant which dragged her here.

The Will O' The Wisp pulsed and shimmered as a figure cut through the shadows, coming slowly into stark relief.

"Set," Ash warned, but it wasn't needed. Set was already poised, his axe raised as she aimed her sword. They held on tightly to each other's hands as the light disappeared, leaving them in darkness until a familiar voice spoke, her warm breath inches from Ash's face.

"Welcome to my realm," Ethne said, a hint of amusement in her tone.

Ash swung her blade forward just as Set jerked her backwards. She cursed before glaring at his shadowed face.

Ethne laughed softly in the darkness behind them, and Ash whirled. There was a snapping of fingers and then a faint glow filled the dense air. Ash blinked through the sudden light, finding the grey-gowned Fomorian standing at the narrow entranceway, her hands clasped behind her.

Glancing around, Ash let go of Set's grip, ensuring there were no monsters ready to attack behind them. The mist dissipated as if Ethne was finally allowing her to see the Underworld clearly. Ash hadn't known what to expect, but she surely hadn't thought it would look . . . familiar. Scorched white earth coated her boots and she could make out floating steam from hot springs behind Ethne. Bone white trees surrounded them.

"It's much more like the human realm than the Land of Eternal Youth," Ethne said, answering Ash's unspoken thoughts before she'd properly formed them in her mind.

She glared at the ancient female, who smiled sanguinely in response.

"You killed my mother," Ash hissed before lunging at Ethne who sifted to the right, just out of her reach. "You tortured Conor."

"Your mother abandoned you. She didn't allow your brother to seek you out. She gave you up before you were even out of the womb. *That* is your hero?"

Again, Ash sprang forward, but Ethne always disappeared and reappeared just out of reach.

"Ash," Set's tone was quiet, unreadable; she glared back at him.

"What?"

"Just . . . listen to her, please?"

Remembering his confession earlier, she stepped forward, hands shaking.

"Did you know we'd end up here?" The words tumbled out of Ash's mouth, but she wouldn't believe them. Couldn't. He wouldn't be that foolish.

"Of course not." Set shook his head, glaring at the Fomorian. He opened his mouth to speak but shut it, his face contorting as if in pain.

The smile on Ethne's face punched a hole in her gut. What had she done to him?

"Setanta did not know the full journey you must take."

Ash cursed at the female. "What did you do to Conor? How could you make him do those unforgivable things?"

"Interesting choice of words, Aisling. Do you not forgive him?"

"That's not what I meant." Ash gritted her teeth, the toxic air doing little to fill her with a calm she desperately needed.

"I can only influence a person so much. There must be intent already within. A part of Conor wanted to kill your mother." She sighed. "And in such a savage way."

Ash shrugged out of Set's reach when he approached. He winced but didn't touch her again. As she stared up at the bleak sky, she found an expanse of nothing. There were no stars, no moon, or sun. Not even clouds. Just ash-filled air with strikes of lighting to break up the otherwise bland expanse, illuminating winged beasts.

Their wings flapped rhythmically, cutting through the heavy air with formidable strength. Their vast bodies were hazy silhouettes interplaying with shadows of the sky. Spiked ridges arched down their spines, tapering off into tails as they flew in a horde. Scaled hides glistened against the forking light, illuminating their colossal size. A bellowing roar filled the sky. Despite their monstrous proportions, Ash found herself caught up in the deadly elegance of their forms.

"Oilliphéist."

Ash's attention snapped to the Fomorian. "I thought they only lived in the sea."

"Countless eons trapped within a realm teaches creatures how to evolve."

An uncanny proximity to humanity prickled Ash's senses, despite the dragons soaring high above. The unsettling realisation defied logic, and her head pounded with how effortlessly accessible this realm seemed to be, situated just a breath away from both Tír na nÓg and the human world.

Faint strands of emotions tugged at her senses, flirting with the edges of her gift. Elusive wafts infused the stale air. A bittersweet cocktail of dismay, longing and an occasional surge of joy drifted around her, but always out of reach. Human voices, muffled yet distinguishable, resonated around her ears. She could feel it. The veil.

The barrier that separated them from the voices, from the worlds teeming with life and warmth. It was as though thousands of inherent layers that were impenetrable moments ago were gradually depleting, thinning into a near translucent buffer. They were much closer to another reality than Ash had initially realised, the knowledge unsettling as it curled in her gut.

"What's happening here?" Ash asked.

"The same thing that is happening everywhere. We are at the cusp of its power. We are not only the readers of the story, but the heroes that will live it."

"Fomorian, why are we here?" Set's voice was low, a threat of violence rippling underneath.

For the first time since he came into her life, Ash thought he looked small. Like a normal man. His shoulders were hunched, his face furrowed into a tense glower. The man she'd have trusted with more than her life, the one she'd given her heart to even if he didn't realise it, had led them here.

She stepped closer to him but did not acknowledge his glances. She would let this play out for now. But as soon as she had a chance, she'd end the woman who took her mother's life and her brother's peace.

"My world is being spat into yours," Ethne said conversationally, inclining her head as she strode toward a grove of trees.

As soon as Ash and Set followed, the world shifted, and a sharp gust of air pulled them along until they were standing outside what looked like the Hill of Tara. There was no mound of grass covering it, nor the plains of undulating hills that were in the human realm, or anything resembling Tara Court. There was scorched earth and then the sudden jutting out of the ancient hills, the Lia Fáil a comforting sight in this alien realm.

Ash bent over, clutching her stomach as she willed herself to stay present. To not allow the dread to consume her. Ethne turned as if their sudden change in location was completely natural. Shadows broke free from the ground as monstrous sounds erupted from the direction of the hill that housed the tunnels and portals connecting the realms.

Ethne stood with clasped hands before her. Darkness crawled from all around, closing in on her until it seeped into her hands. Cupping the shadows, she pulled them apart to shoulder length. Though Ash couldn't detect anything at first, Ethne's hands stretched further as if weighed down. The shadowy matter thickened and formed until it took shape. A thin cylindrical tube emerged from the darkness, lightening until it turned to bronze metal.

"A hunting horn," Set said, stepping closer to inspect the ornate object Ethne outstretched toward him.

Ash gripped his arm, pulling him back.

"This is no ordinary horn, my children," Ethne said, offering it out and sighing when neither moved forward to take it. "This is the Dord Fiann."

"It can't be," Ash murmured, uncertainty souring her tongue as she swallowed her surprise.

She couldn't help noticing how Set's fingers twitched as if he wanted to hold it. "The hunting horn of the Fianna has been lost since Fionn Mac Cumhaill went to slumber."

"Not lost," Ethne mused, rotating the horn to turn in her hands. "Kept safe."

"You've had the horn this whole time?"

"No, but I did have to wait until you were ready. Don't you want to save Tiernan? That's why we're here, Setanta, isn't it?"

Ash turned to Set, who looked down on her with wide eyes. He reached out to her, but stopped before he touched her. "I know how much waking him up means to you and Maebh."

"And you won't just wake up your friend." Ethne took a step forward, placing the heavy-looking horn at her side. "The caillte will wake. Your fathers will no longer be lost."

"And so will Fionn Mac Cumhaill," Ash stated to which Ethne tilted her head. "Why do you want the first High King of Fianna to wake up so much?"

"The only way to leave the Underworld is to use the horn," Ethne replied, infuriatingly ignoring Ash's questions.

As if in response to a call only they could perceive, an unsettling chorus of monstrous voices began to reverberate through the thick air, preluding a horrific appearance of an army of grotesque beasts. Towering giants loomed close, their bulky stature rivalling neighbouring trees. Their faces were rugged landscapes of scars and coarse skin, eyes gleaming with malicious intent that made Ash's blood chill.

"Time is running out," Ethne pronounced, smiling at her new companions, before looking solemnly at Ash and Set. "The shadows have reached Tiernan. He'll be here soon. Once he reaches us, the Underworld will keep him. He will forever be made of stone."

"You're bluffing," Ash snarled, wishing her words to be true. "Everything you say is a lie to trick us into doing your bidding."

"So be it." Ethne threw the horn to the ground in the space between them. "Prepare yourself for more heartache by your own stubbornness."

The circling monsters stepped back, cowering in clusters, as if the forming shadows grouping beside Ethne were dangerous to them.

"Move back," Set cautioned as he pulled Ash toward him.

An ear-splitting scream tore through the space as the shadows grew from the ground up, forming a humanoid shape.

Gods, had she refused to do Ethne's bidding, only to leave Tiernan forever trapped? Ash was meant to save him, not condemn him to hell.

As the black shadows dissipated, the person within let out a slew of curses that, if Ash didn't immediately recognise as Maebh's, the creativity and sheer volume would have given it away.

Maebh fell to her knees, her head bowed as she heaved in breaths that sounded painful. Ash and Set lurched forward as Ethne laughed, but they didn't reach Maebh in time.

Her head whipped upwards at the sound of Ethne's mirth. "You bitch." She jumped to her feet, lunging for the ancient Fomorian. "This ends here."

CHAPTER 64

MAEBH

"You came for Tiernan!" Maebh reached Ethne as the woman continued to laugh, merriment shining through her grey eyes.

A wildfire erupted within Maebh's body, a molten surge which coursed through her veins, weaving ribbons of rage radiating from marrow to skin. She wrapped her hands around Ethne's neck, squeezing as her vision blurred. The fire within stoked a savage need of violence that clawed and gnashed at the confines of Maebh's physical form.

Let me out. A faint voice unfurled amongst the blaze, stirring the embers of her mind. It was feminine and strong, caressing her from inside. It was not hers, but through the threads of its voice was an intimate note of her own melody. It brushed against a wall Maebh hadn't known she'd had within, exploring the crevices, the shadowy corners, searching and prodding, seeking for any weakness to unleash her true fury. Her ríastrad.

Although Maebh's sword lay abandoned by Tiernan's feet, she had more blades in her belt, but her ríastrad was too close. She needed to feel Ethne's life leave her. There was no doubt that Ethne was causing the shadows. The how or why would have to wait, or never be discovered, as long as she ended this Fomorian.

Strong arms wrapped around her waist, but she didn't budge. Maebh ignored the slight pressure, pressing on Ethne's neck harder. The woman's eyes bulged, her mouth no longer curled up in a satisfied smile, but she did not lift her hands to claw at Maebh's.

"Mae, let go," Set grunted behind her, and she froze. Had he been eaten up by the shadows too?

"Maebh," Ash said, appearing at her side. "Don't give in to your ríastrad."

Maebh's eyes remained on Ethne's, her hands tightening further until she loosened them a fraction. "Why?" She turned sideways to look at her friend, ensuring it truly was her. Set's hands were still around her waist, but he didn't attempt to pull her further. They wanted her to release the monster before them. The cause of all their heartache. "Why should she live?"

"She's the only way we're getting out of here," Ash said, green eyes widening as she tracked Maebh's face, lowering as the seams of her coat tore.

Glaring at Ethne, who looked insufferably smug despite having no oxygen, Maebh debated. Ignoring the inner voice begging Maebh to open up to it, one finger at a time, she relinquished the Fomorian's neck, shoving her until she fell to the ground. Maebh watched with wicked delight as Ethne coughed and heaved in raw, gasping breaths.

Noises seeped in above the pounding of Maebh's heart and her attention was stolen by a ring of giants encircling them. They stepped forward, their feral growls growing. True titans of impossible proportion, their hulking forms loomed, powerful frames casting dreadful shadows that toyed with the feeble light. Their eyes were burning coals, holding a savage, primal glare that fixated on Maebh with an intensity that was nothing short of terrifying. These were creatures straight from hell.

A chill raced up Maebh's spine as she unsheathed two daggers. "We really need to get out of here."

"No shit," Ash muttered, coming to her side and Set to her other as they stared up at the beasts who stepped forward, footfalls snaking the ground beneath their monstrous might.

Ethne lifted her hand, and the surrounding group stopped, all noise muting simultaneously.

"You jumped in front of the shadows about to claim your friend." Ethne stood, smoothing out her long silken skirt. "How commendable."

"Why are you here?" Maebh asked her brother and Ash, ignoring Ethne, who only laughed gently as she rose to her feet.

"Set, care to tell Maebh why?" Ash asked in an accusatory tone, and Maebh's attention immediately pinned on her twin.

"What did you do?"

"She knows how to free Tiernan and our dads," Set began, holding his hands palms up as he shrugged. "I didn't realise we'd end up here, but she said she could help us."

"And I can." Ethne nodded to the ground where a long, bronze horn lay by Maebh's boots.

"What the fuck is that?"

"Blow it thrice with a blood sacrifice."

"Are you really rhyming your evil plans at us right now?" Maebh hunched closer to the horn.

"Don't touch it," Ash warned as Ethne kicked it closer. "It's the Dord Fiann."

Maebh cursed. This was the lost horn of Fianna. The horn that would awaken Fionn Mac Cumhaill. She cursed again. It would wake up Tiernan and the caillte. Her father. The man she'd left her world for to come and find. The parent who had loved her unconditionally, a feeling she had lost seven years ago.

"The only way you will leave this realm is through this horn," Ethne rasped to Maebh's smug delight. For once the fae didn't sound smooth. Ethne coughed, rubbing her neck. "You stopped my shadows this time, but I assure you, they will consume him next. If you don't, Tiernan will end up here in stone form, never to be freed. If you blow it, he'll be with you once more."

"You're not doing this out of the goodness of your wicked heart," Maebh shot back, but found her fingers reaching out, clasping the horn. A searing cold bit her skin. Recoiling instinctively, Maebh withdrew her hand, the residual sting of the freezing temperature smarting at her flesh. Grimacing, she inspected her fingertips; her normally warm skin had taken on a pallid hue, stinging to the point of numbness. Maebh glared at Ethne. "What does it matter to you if the first High King wakes up?"

"I don't like this," Ash said.

Set said simultaneously, "I don't see another way out."

"I'll take my chances." Maebh glared at the Fomorian. "Better the monsters we know than your manipulation."

Ethne's smile was soft. Motherly. "You were never meant for the shadows, child. You burn too brightly."

Set pitched forward, snatching the horn up, wincing upon contact before looking imploringly at them. "It's the only way."

"Wait," Ethne said, a wicked-looking dagger appearing in her hand. It was rusted in parts, but sharp. When Ethne saw the three stare at the blade, she explained. "I must use a pure iron blade or your wounds will heal too quickly."

"Because of your little experiment on us," Maebh retorted, crossing her arms.

"You are blood-blessed." Ethne slanted her head. "Your paths were decided upon while babes in your mothers' wombs. They agreed to it."

"You're lying."

"I am many things, but I am no liar. Your parents wanted you to be powerful Fianna. Elevated over all humans. And you are."

Raising the blade, Ethne waited expectantly.

"You've got to be kidding," Ash muttered, but Maebh and Set both offered their hands, palms up.

"All three must agree."

"Stop rhyming or I'll shove this horn so far up—"

"Okay, fine," Ash interjected, outstretching her palm and for the first time, Maebh noted Ash's dishevelled form and the many bloodied wounds her friend had.

She peered at her brother who looked equally worse for wear. What had happened to them?

Maebh winced as the blade sliced through her flesh, and she tried not to think of the dangers of her open wound being contaminated with both Set's and Ash's blood, let alone allowing a crazed Fomorian anywhere near her with a blade. As warm blood pooled in her palm, Ethne moved on to the others, slicing their palms too.

"Each of you blow through the Dord Fiann with your bloodied hand clasped around it," Ethne instructed.

Unease festered and bloomed within Maebh, but as she glanced at the others, she saw their resolve. It was too late to back out. Set blew first; the sound so loud Maebh swore the earth shook. He handed the horn to Ash, her hands shaking the instrument as she pressed her lips around the rim. This time, there was no doubt the world tilted as the noise pierced the putrid air.

The darkness itself held its breath as Maebh took the horn amidst a deathly silence louder than the sound of the horn itself. She cringed around the burning pain. It hummed now, the bloodied handprints of the others making it slippery and glowing in parts.

"Tiernan awaits you," Ethne purred, her voice soft.

Tiernan's face crept into Maebh's mind. The man who watched over them more than she'd ever truly understand. They'd become friends. They'd shared secrets and had explored what they could become to one another. His brown eyes, wise yet playful. Full of respect and a loyalty she wasn't sure how she'd gained. She pressed her lips to the horn and blew, and this time the world shattered into splinters.

CHAPTER 65

MAEBH

A flash of light blinded Maebh and when it dimmed, she found herself back in the cave. The ever-present sounds of stone heartbeats filled the cavern once more, gemstone walls pulsing with their faint blue glow. As if no time had passed, the warriors stood poised, ready for attack. Only the Fianna closest to where she'd been swallowed by shadows were shaken by her reappearance.

"Maebh!" Malachy reached her, sweat beading on his shaved head. "Where did you go?"

Set and Ash stirred beside her. Jumping to her feet, Maebh ignored Malachy's exclamations about their appearance, batting him away before reaching Tiernan. Her mind raced as cold, damp air filled her lungs. Tiernan's face remained frozen, his features engraved in perfect stone.

"She lied."

Tears sprang forth, but Maebh ignored them, fighting against the crack in her heart. She could hear it, the physical breaking.

"Look," Ash whispered beside her.

A spiderweb fissure appeared along Tiernan's cheek, splintering the once flawless granite. Maebh's eyes widened as another crack appeared, and then another. And another.

Gasping, she jumped back as the thundering heartbeats escalated.

Piece by piece, stone fell away, the cave filling with cries as the stone guardians awoke.

"Tiernan!" Maebh flung herself onto his rigid frame, but a shiver cut a brutal path down her spine from the bitter cold seeping through his clothes. A rising wave of panic bubbled up to her throat, threatening to choke her. When arms didn't encircle her, she leaned back, eyes darting as they searched his, to ensure he really had broken free. Beautiful liquid brown she'd missed stared back at her, but his brows furrowed as he grimaced. Retreating from him, she said, "We need to get you warmed up."

The stone had broken away, but his body was still hard, his familiar earthy scent now mingled with dust and stone.

A thunderous roar filled the chamber, startling Maebh from her shocked stupor. Tiernan moved her aside, his attention fixated on the sarcophagus at the far end of the cave. He moved carefully at first, as if unfamiliar with the constraints of flesh once more. With each step confidence returned until all guardians marched forward in perfect synchronisation, encircling Fionn's grave.

Ash and Set were by Maebh's side as they tried to push through, but they could gain no better view over the towering guard. A scraping and grinding of stone against stone filled the chamber. The heavy lid of the sarcophagus was lifted high by many hands before it was hurled against the cave wall, shattering into rubble.

Maebh's breath was laboured as her heart pounded in her head. Forced to retreat, Fionn's guardians marched backwards, separating into two even aisles, split in the centre.

"He's awake," Set breathed.

An unearthly hush fell over the once deafening cavern, every soul holding their breath as Fionn Mac Cumhaill climbed out of his grave, dressed in warrior finery far grander than Maebh had seen; leather and plaid with gleaming weapons slung on his belt. The first High King marched forward, rising to his full and formidable height. Dark eyes scanned his surroundings as he took his first steps after his long slumber. Silence reigned as the legend passed them, his face yielding nothing.

The cavern walls seemed far away, Maebh's body intangible. Only a hollow ringing filled her mind. She watched mutely as Tiernan marched after Fionn.

"Da!" Set called, but Gearoid and the other caillte continued their methodical steps, all the guardians following the first High King.

"They're in some kind of trance," Ash said wonderingly as the Breen and McQuillan clans surrounded them.

Maebh's mind floated as everything tilted. Thoughts scattered on unyielding winds, lost to an icy sea that held her heart. She stared after the retreating figures as they left the cave, conversations of their clans muted over the raging storm within her.

Only when Ash squeezed her shoulder did sensation rush back like a tidal surge.

"Maebh, it's okay," Ash consoled, holding the crook of her elbow as Maebh swayed, lungs gasping to fill.

Maebh only nodded before breaking into a jog, calling back to the others: "Come on! Let's see where they're going."

She and the others fell into line behind the procession as they made their way through the musty passageways. As they walked, Maebh took in Fionn's form before her once more. He towered head and shoulders above all others with his powerfully built physique. Long red-gold hair flowed freely in ringlets down his back and broad shoulders, swaying with each purposeful stride.

"He's taller than you, Setanta," Malachy muttered, and a few others sniggered, but Maebh couldn't join in.

In a blur, Ash took her hand as they left the tunnel, stepping into the bright light of Tara Court.

As Fionn crested the Hill of Tara, the Lia Fáil emitted a low vibration that Maebh felt in her bones. Most Fianna would be in the market and farmlands but the few that witnessed their emergence stopped and stared at their procession. As more Fianna gathered, Maebh caught stray words. "One of the Tuatha?" A few murmurs of "Fionn Mac Cumhaill!" wafted forward as the press of bodies at her back intensified.

Ahead, Fionn towered over the ancient Stone of Destiny, his guardians at his back.

As he laid his broad hand upon the ancient stone, the very air hummed with anticipatory power. The Lia Fáil shuddered violently beneath his legendary touch, trembling the earth.

Its cry shattered the still morning with primaeval force, a sound no mortal throat could emulate that shook Maebh to her soul. The holler rang out across the hills in waves, each echo multiplying in intensity until the earth rang with its otherworldly call. Pebbles and dirt jumped where Maebh stood as the bellow seemed to rend the bedrock underfoot.

Around her, Fianna clutched each other in awestruck terror, animals crying out from the farmlands from the bone-shaking note, birds taking flight in a symphony of shrieks. Maebh trembled in the roiling swell as she lay witness to the stone's claim of the rightful High King.

Panicked cries rose from below as people stampeded towards the hill in a disorganised frenzy. Maebh gripped Ash tightly, as Set and their clans encircled them, dodging flailing bodies in the press.

Fionn removed his hand and with it the world quieted. His guardians thumped their chests before bowing low. One by one. Every Fianna followed suit. Maebh lowered herself before the king as the air hummed with electricity.

Hooves sounded from the distance. Maebh glanced in time to see High King Bradan, flanked by a company of highguard, ride toward the hill. The guard called out for people to make way, and when Bradan drew closer Maebh tracked the alarmed expression on his face before he dismounted and was swallowed up by the growing crowd.

His highguard moved with a precision and unity that quickly parted the onlookers. Their formation was as flawless as their demeanour was stern, an impenetrable wall of strength and allegiance resonating around their king.

Bradan's face had transformed in those few steps, the calm assurance of a born leader radiating a quiet command. Behind the banner of his arrival, rumours caught the wind, creating ripple effects amongst the crowd as the king's presence imposed a hushed awe over the chaotic scene. His arrival was not merely an appearance; it was an assertion of power, of sovereignty, of unrivalled rule over his kingdom.

Maebh searched Bradan's calculating stare, waiting to see how he'd react to this challenge by the living legend. That stone had said it all. Fionn was the rightful king to Bradan's crown. But Bradan's countenance remained impassive as Fionn Mac Cumhaill turned from the vibrating Lia Fáil.

"People of Tír na nÓg, I am Fionn Mac Cumhaill." His rich baritone carried effortlessly over the stunned murmurs of the crowd. "Ireland has cried out for me to wake from my long dreaming."

"Great Fionn, returned at last!" a man cried out from behind Maebh, followed by more exclamations of his return.

Fionn continued with a wide smile. "I awoke to find our green island changed. I will speak with your current leaders to act against the darkness that threatens our land."

"That would be me, Fionn Mac Cumhaill," Bradan called before marching forward with highguard at his heel. "Bradan Cassidy, High King of the Fianna."

"Look, it's Aedan," Set breathed as Fionn's stone guardians barricaded Bradan's approach, the former High King included.

Aedan, Gearoid and Tiernan had stepped in front of Fionn. Bradan's steps faltered and Maebh's throat tightened as he took in his son's stony expression.

"Tiernan," Bradan stumbled forward but stopped when Tiernan unsheathed a sword, angling it between them.

"Hold firm, Tiernan," Fionn counselled, patting his shoulder.

Wordlessly the three guardians retreated, allowing Bradan access to the first High King who asked, "Did the Lia Fáil cry for you?"

Bradan remained mute, his face thunderous.

Fionn let the silence ring through the air for everyone lay witness to what that meant. "Rule as my advisor, Bradan Cassidy. This threat must be vanquished."

After a beat, Bradan clasped his arm, bowing his head. "It would be an honour to serve you . . . High King."

Lifting his voice, Fionn summoned. "All rígfénnid chieftains, attend me in counsel."

Tiernan strode forth with the others. His eyes met Maebh's but slid past; she saw unfamiliar, blank depths where a thoughtful and perceptive friend had once been.

"I have to go," Set said, a frown on his lips as he looked down at her and Ash. "I'll find out what's going on. What they remember."

Hands clenched numbly at Maebh's sides while ash swirled within her chest instead of breath or heartbeat. They'd woken Tiernan. But he was no longer the man she once knew.

CHAPTER 66

AISLING

The pounding of Ash's feet echoed off the gleaming stone corridors of the castle as she jogged toward the throne room. She knew she was running towards something, but she wished she was running away from everything. Tall arched windows were silent spectators to her hurried feet, letting in streams of sunlight which illuminated each gilded painting and armour display; yet where Ash passed, she overshadowed everything to a dull echo.

Her thoughts sprinted alongside her, a whirlwind feeding her journey toward another summoning between the rígfénnid, matriarchs and Fionn's guardians. Ever since the so-called 'Great Awakening', these gatherings were endless.

Ash cursed under her breath as she pushed her legs faster. She'd lost track of time with Conor at the satellite tree and she was still healing from the giant attack so her movements were more sluggish than she'd have liked. Checking in with her foster parents had been a frequent task on top of her never-ending to-do list. Her racing heart pounded in time with her footsteps, but she couldn't slow down, not when Fionn was sure to call upon her for an update on the human realm. Rounding the last corner, the towering oak doors stood open, and she poured on more speed.

Ash burst into the crowded chamber, panting heavily. Daring a glance at the congregated leaders, she nodded stiffly at Set before finding her place beside Maebh and Malachy. Her flushed skin prickled from Set's steady, questioning gaze. He had been in a deep conversation with the others, but he tracked her steps and continued to watch as the others conversed.

"I'm fine," she mouthed, leaning over to catch her breath.

She was anything but when it came to Setanta McQuillan. He'd told her he loved her, but he'd also been keeping secrets. She wasn't sure what to do about any of it, but she would not be distracted by him during this meeting.

"Cutting it short today," Maebh murmured, facing the throne as Fionn and his guard entered.

Ash's throat tightened at the sight of Tiernan and their fathers. She stole a glance at Maebh, who wore a face of utter boredom. But Ash knew her friend; she saw the tightening of her jaw and the grip of her clasped hands as the aloof men took their positions, facing them.

Fionn took his seat on the imposing throne that shrank in his presence. All chatter quieted as the High King spoke. "Matriarch Breen, report."

"Straight to it today, aren't we?" Maebh whispered, patting her on the back.

At the weight of everyone's attention Ash stood tall. "What we suspected is true, High King. The realms are now linked."

Murmurs filtered through and Fionn scratched his red beard as he processed the confirmation. "Ethne's curse has spread farther than we knew. The ritual she performed at Newgrange has linked Tír na nÓg and the human realm."

"What do you mean, High King?" someone exclaimed from behind.

"We are tied to the laws of man." Fionn paused, meeting each leader's eyes. "Time no longer jumps as it once did between the lands. Our realm and the human one flows as one, on the same unchanging course."

The room erupted in raised voices as Fianna came to terms with this news. Even though Ash had been the one to discover the revelation, her mind reeled at the implications, another piece that didn't slot into a puzzle she couldn't solve. Would the people in Tír na nÓg now age at the normal rate? Or were humans all gifted with longer lives from the magic within the Land of Eternal Youth?

"High King," Ash called over the multiple voices. When Fionn raised a hand, the room fell silent once more, and she continued. "Ireland is still cut off from the rest of the world. My people have reported that the Irish military has tried everything from aeroplanes, drones, and even a navy ship, but nothing gets through the new veil beyond the waters."

The veil seemed to have a mind of its own. Niamh said it was as if it were curiously intelligent and ruthlessly protective, allowing nothing to penetrate or escape out of the country. The aftermath always left baffled pilots landing right where they'd taken off, drones lost to the clouds, and ship crews left disorientated, with no memory of their fruitless encounter with the barrier.

When Fionn frowned, and Tiernan leaned forward, murmuring in his ear. The High King eventually nodded at Tiernan, who took his place behind him once more. "It is the hour to voice wisdom to the Taoiseach and align arm-in-arm with our human brethren. We must ready ourselves against any storm the Fomorian might brew. Both our realms, undeniably, stand on the precipice of exposure to peril."

Fionn's voice boomed around the room, his words bearing an ominous weight.

"What about the Cath, High King?" Bradan's voice cut through the silent tension gripping the room and glances volleyed from one king to the former.

The question wasn't unexpected, but the speaker was. Bradan, although now a mere advisor, stood with a discerning calm. The crown may have left his head, but the cunning ruler still danced within his steadfast expression.

"Our brethren of battle have journeyed vast lengths; 'tis not the hour to retreat from the Cath's call. Full well it is that our ranks should brim with only the finest warriors. We shall see this contest to its rightful end."

As Fionn gave instructions to the gathering on what to do in his absence, Ash's appraisal moved from Set to Tiernan. Set had more interaction with the stone guard. As rígfénnid, he attended even more meetings than the matriarchs. The bond between Fionn and the stone guard was impenetrable. Set said they often seemed to have conversations without speaking, linked together with an invisible bond. It would explain how they'd been so synchronised in their attacks when they'd first disturbed Fionn's resting place.

Ash's muscles spasmed as she rotated her shoulders, trying to ease the tension that had built. It was as useful as praying to the gods to bring those entrapped by stone back as they once had been. But none had returned as the people they'd once known.

"Everyone is dismissed, except you, Aisling Breen." Fionn raised a hand, calling for her to approach.

"I'll see you later," Maebh threw over her shoulder, already swallowed by the departing crowd.

Ash's brow furrowed as her eyes lingered on the back of Maebh's head exiting the throne room. Though they hadn't spoken about it, Maebh always seemed hellbent on leaving before there was any chance of interaction with Fionn's guard. Set passed Ash, catching her hand and giving a squeeze. She simply nodded, releasing his grip before facing forward, ignoring the scent of his anguish at her coldness.

They had argued over his secret arrangement with Ethne countless times since they'd blown the Dord Fiann, but it always ended with both seething that the other one wouldn't relent. With the bare responses he deigned to give, he could only see the end result. She had wanted to free Tiernan, and they had also managed to free the caillte and everyone else. But in doing so he had broken her trust.

Sighing, she approached the throne where the guardians remained stationary behind Fionn as if they were trapped in stone once more. The king's ancient gaze followed her as she stood before him, hands interlaced behind her back.

"Matriarch Breen, I have noticed your lone attendance at our gatherings. Your ally, Maebh McQuillan, has duly chosen a second in command upon her brother's elevation. Why are you without a right hand?"

Ash swallowed, unprepared for this question. "I lead my clan as best I can, High King."

Inevitably, her scrutiny alighted on Tiernan, who hadn't spoken to her since his freedom from the stone. Not from the want of trying, but he remained cocooned within his *new* clan, the guardians.

"A matriarch requires a second to offer counsel and bolster her responsibilities. Surely one among your clan is ready for such an honour?"

Ash's eyes remained on Tiernan, who stood impassively beside the others. "I do have a second, High King. Tiernan Cassidy was by my side before . . ."

Her voice trailed off as Tiernan finally looked at her, leaving her words dangling in the vast distance between them. Once her friend and confidante, his eyes were glacial, no spark of recognition peering back at her. A pang of anguish sparked in Ash, the burning in her throat threatening to travel upwards to form tears, but she blinked through his arctic contemplation, desperate to spread a warm path through her own.

Tiernan remained as aloof as the sculptures standing sentinel around the chamber, no hint of recognition reflecting back at her.

Fionn followed her eyes, his brows knitting thoughtfully. "Some deeds are as ripples upon the water, untraceable once set in motion. Our duty then, is to set our gaze forward, not back."

Ash could only offer a simple nod. Outwardly, she tried to don Maebh's mask of indifference though her raw heart thudded a sombre beat. She feared his words were true. Glimpsing her father's impassive expression along the line of guardians, she bit the inside of her cheek. He hadn't approached either her or Conor since he was freed. Did he even know their mother was dead?

The stone guardians were an impenetrable unit, with their imposing stature and inscrutable countenance; they answered only to Fionn. Ash had learned little about their time protecting Fionn's sarcophagus. Most had perished by the host of sluagh. The remaining were a mix of Fionn's original band of warriors, and Fianna who'd lost their way underneath the tunnels of Tara, keeping whatever secrets remained locked within.

In the new order, the highguard were no longer the elite warriors. That status now belonged to the guardians. So much so that competitiveness for winning the Cath had waned since the emergence of Fionn and his guard, but not other clans' brutality toward any unfortunate fae caught in Mide.

"You're dismissed, Matriarch," Fionn said, but not unkindly.

She bowed low as he rose, exiting the throne room to the side door. Digging her nails into her palm, she relished the sharp pinch of pain it provided. When she straightened, she didn't wait for the guard to leave. She approached her father. Ash remembered he had been quiet, but Lorcan was a shell now as he stared blankly ahead, detached from his surroundings. Silence was no longer an option.

"Conor is fine, by the way," Ash said, and when Lorcan didn't look at her, she stepped onto the platform until she was right in front of him.

But Lorcan gave no reply. He might not have heard her for all the acknowledgment he showed.

"And Cara is dead."

Finally, Lorcan met her eyes. "I know."

She blinked. And blinked again. "Is that all you have to say about your family? To your daughter?"

Lorcan turned on his heel, exiting the stage and marching with the others to follow after Fionn.

As the other guardians filed out, Tiernan paused in the doorway, turning his unreadable regard upon Ash once more. His towering form cut an imposing silhouette against the flickering torchlight from the corridor. Ash couldn't remember him looking so . . . formidable. Despite this, a flutter of anxious hope stirred in her chest. "Tiernan," Ash said, hiding her surprise when he nodded. "Can we talk?"

Something twisted inside her at the empty way he held himself, devoid of the kind man who'd once hacked into an entire realm. While the highguard favoured black, Fionn had dressed his stone guardians in a new uniform, distinguishing them above all others. Tiernan was clad in a breastplate of dark grey steel fitting to his muscular frame. His tunic and cloak were woven from sturdy fabrics of forest green and stone grey. Ash understood why Fionn had chosen these garments. The stone guardians belonged in an ancient folktale amongst the rocky terrain and moss-covered crags of the kingdom they guarded.

At his belt was a longsword, and a cloak clasp bearing a polished coat of arms gleamed on his breastplate. Within its divided quarters were symbols of Fionn's legendary past: a red lion, a tree, a salmon and a spear. The crest was a glaring reminder Tiernan no longer belonged to her clan.

When they were alone, she spoke, her soft words echoing around the vast room. "During my brief, you spoke with Fionn. What did you tell him?"

For a moment, Tiernan was silent, his posture giving nothing away. "I explained modern technology and the human world to him. About the tree I . . ."

He frowned, but Ash stepped closer. "The tree you rigged with Maebh. You remember that?"

A flush rose on his brown cheeks, but he didn't respond.

Ash's breath hitched. "Do you remember my mother ordering you to watch over me? That you saved us in that cave?" She dared another step. "That you are my second in command?"

"I am Fionn's guard."

But she refused to believe that. Digging further, she pressed. "And Conor? Do you remember him? He's been asking to see you."

When Tiernan didn't reply, she added, "He's my brother by blood, but he's yours by choice."

A flicker of emotion crossed Tiernan's chiselled features, there and gone in an instant. Ash stared at Tiernan, willing the man she knew to emerge from the impassive stranger before her. But all that greeted her pleading gaze was emptiness.

"He should be your second."

An aching hollowness spread through Ash's chest, her breaths coming short and painful. It wasn't supposed to be like this. After everything they had survived, she couldn't accept that her friend was truly lost.

"Please," she whispered, hating the tremor in her voice but powerless to contain it. "Don't do this. Don't let them take you from us, too."

Ash reached for Tiernan's hands, grasping them firmly in her own. His skin was cold as ice, yet she refused to let go, holding on with the last shreds of her desperate hope.

"I know you're still in there. You have to fight, Tiernan. For me, for Conor. For Maebh." Again, that flash of *something* shone through Tiernan's brown eyes. A struck matchstick before it was snuffed out by a silent breath. She talked through the burning in her throat. "For all of us who need you."

Her eyes bore into his, willing some further spark of recognition to answer her plea. Long moments dragged by in silence as Ash searched his unyielding face. Just when her strength was about to fail, the faintest of shadows seemed to cross Tiernan's eyes. His hands twitched faintly in hers before he broke free from her grasp.

Without turning, Tiernan left.

CHAPTER 67
SETANTA

Set woke as the morning sun filtered through the tall windows of his castle chambers. Stretching out on the plush feathery bed, his tendons and muscles popped and snapped from his unforgiving training routine the night before. It had never been that hard to exercise, finding only joy in pushing himself. But now . . . without his ríastrad. Set sighed at the fatigue in his limbs.

Running his hands along the soft furs, he swung his heavy legs over the side, relishing the cold stone floor seeping up from his soles. Looking down at his body, he hadn't appeared to have lost muscle, but a weight hung around his neck.

Rotating his shoulders, he took in the polished oak furniture, hanging tapestries, and fireplace ready to be lit. It was finer than anything he'd known growing up in a caravan. And yet as he willed his body to move from the soft bed, an emptiness lingered within these thick stone walls. The other rígfénnid were housed within the same corridor, but he avoided them as much as possible. As he glanced behind, he couldn't help imagining what it would feel like to wake up with Ash by his side.

This was not the home he'd grown up in, surrounded by his clan and sister. It was not the single bed he had shared with Ash, taking comfort in her warmth through the long night. Since becoming rígfénnid, duty and obligation kept him busy until exhaustion claimed him, but his sleep was still restless.

Fionn had brought the matriarchs and their seconds into his meetings, but they still slept within their clan campsites and Set had the distinct feeling Ash had been avoiding him. A punch of guilt hit him as he stood and approached his spear. Of course she was. He hadn't lied, but he also had not been honest with her. With the geas writhing on his tongue, Set fought even now in an empty room to say Ethne's name aloud. Nothing worked. He'd even tried writing her name down but was left with scrawling nonsense. Once, he'd persevered only to realise he'd written a crude poem. No doubt a sick joke from the cunning Fomorian.

Nightmares haunted him. Ash swallowed by the shadowy veil as her screams echoed endlessly in his mind as his heart strained with remorse. No matter how comfortable the bed or roaring the fire, true rest continued to evade him without her beside him, easing the turmoil within with her calm presence.

Running a hand along Lámfada, he waited. The spear hummed gently in response, offering reassurance. The familiar contours and engravings of the ancient spear anchored him despite the unravelling of his world. Tightening his fingers around the spear to the point of pain, the hum of might coursed up his arm, lending fresh energy to his tired muscles. The moment his grip relaxed, no sooner had the rush started, the strength ebbed away. The intimate surge of strength his ríastrad offered was as fleeting as a shooting star.

It didn't matter. No magical weapon could soothe the guilt still gnawing at him for deceiving Ash, leading her into danger through his own foolish desperation. The geas was a heavy burden and constant reminder of his tie to the ancient Fomorian. Set swallowed around it. Ethne had disappeared again. All that mattered was making things right with Ash.

He washed and dressed, strapping Lámfada to his back and slinging his father's axe into his belt. The familiar weight of the weapons comforted him as always, yet his hand lingered on the axe head a moment longer than usual.

The weapon had been in his family for generations. Gearoid had shown him how to wield it as a young boy, teaching him its balance and how to let it sing through the air. But his father had barely spoken to him or Maebh since awakening from the stone, acting as a mute sentinel in Fionn's guard.

It was clear their father was no longer the caring man he had once been. Set didn't blame him for that, but it pained him to see how Gearoid's detachment affected his usually indomitable twin. Maebh carried herself with her usual bravado, but he knew her well enough to see the cracks beneath the surface. Their father's absence, combined with the changes in Tiernan, had shaken her foundation in ways she'd never admit.

As Set marched through the long corridors, he pushed down that train of thought. His father was a problem for another day. Today was about making things right with Ash.

Nodding greetings to the servants and guards he passed, Set made a beeline for the main hall. At the rígfénnid table, the leaders were writing out assignments for the coming Cath. Fionn was still in the human realm with a small contingent of his guard along with Bradan. Standing over Deaglán Collins, who held a quill poised over fresh parchment, Set shook his head. "No, don't put the Breen clan on today."

Deaglán arched his brow, amused. "They are due a turn."

But something in Set's expression must have shown he would accept no argument. With a shrug, the Leinster rígfénnid nodded. "Done, but it'll be a favour you owe me."

Set shut out the unease at having made another deal with someone he didn't trust as he ignored the breakfast table and darted into the narrow steps that led to the kitchens. Half an hour later, and another favour owed to a kitchen maid, he walked down the stone steps laden with a wicker basket and tartan blanket slung over his shoulder.

Set made his way through the bustling lower bailey, keeping an eye out for a familiar head of ink black hair. Spying Ash near the towering outer wall where clan banners fluttered, he took a steadying breath and approached.

"Ash," he greeted with a nod, keeping his tone neutral even if his stomach was slithering with nerves. Her returning smile was strained, cautious eyes taking in the basket on his arm. An uncomfortable silence stretched before she spoke.

"I thought my clan would be called for duty today."

"That's a lucky coincidence," he said cheerily with a wink. "I'm off this morning too. Will you take a walk with me?"

Ash frowned and he closed his eyes, cringing. It seemed they both remembered the last time they'd gone for a walk, only to lead her to Ethne and the Underworld.

Clasping his hands around the wicker handles to resist the urge to reach for hers, Set said, "Please, Ash, come with me."

He raised the picnic basket, and she studied it as she asked, "Where?"

Biting the inside of his cheek, he failed miserably at hiding his reaction at her distrust. As surely as he could smell the tartness from her scent, she could tell what the burnt rubber wafting from him meant.

"It's not far, just in the farmlands. The apple orchard, to be specific."

Her eyes flicked to the basket and blanket again.

"I should train with my clan," Ash said quietly, and he stepped closer. Ash glanced toward the training yards, lips parting to refuse, but he hurried on.

"It's lucky you have a rígfénnid willing to cover for you."

Set held his breath, heart lifting as she sighed. Her smile was tight, but she nodded. "Okay, lead the way."

Managing a small smile in return, he turned to walk, letting out his breath in a whoosh. It was a start. Set led the way down winding paths until the towering castle walls were lost amongst groves of wild trees. He glanced back at Ash, gesturing ahead. "We're here."

Entering through a green-leafed arch, an idyllic orchard greeted them, heavy branches bowed low with ripe apples. Buttery sunlight dappled the long grass beneath the gently swaying trees, perfuming the air with sweetness. Bees droned lazily amongst the blossoms as birds sang overhead. White blossoms dusted the branches like snow, their petals falling lazily in drifts.

"This is beautiful," Ash whispered, as if afraid to speak too loudly and disturb the natural tranquillity.

Pale pink and crimson apples clustered upon the twigs. Some had already fallen, rolling amidst the grass in a burst of bright colour. A gentle breeze set the leaves to rustling like a sigh, sending more ripe fruits toppling.

"I can see this place from my bedroom window," Set said, biting on his lip to prevent him from inviting her to visit.

He picked a spot beneath the largest, most generous tree, and laid out the tartan blanket. Unsheathing his weapons first, he unpacked the picnic spread, laying out freshly baked scones, soft cheeses, cured meats and fruit.

"Wow, I haven't seen this much food for one meal in a long time," Ash said, sighing. "Living in the castle has its perks."

He hummed in response, carefully placing the travel teapot and cups on the blanket. Relief loosened the knot in Set's chest when Ash's eyes softened. Unsheathing her weapons, she knelt beside him, lavender mixing with the sweetness of their new haven. With no small measure of delight, he noticed the familiar etches of the sword he'd gifted her.

"I remember going to the orchard with Mary and Dom," she murmured, trailing her fingers along the smooth bark. "Mary would cram as many apples in her bags as she could to bake apple tarts and pastries for the cafe." Ash's pale hand reached across the blanket, plucking a fallen apple, rubbing it on her shirt before taking a bite. Juice ran down her chin and she grinned, holding the fruit out to Set. "Here, try."

Before taking it, he stroked the juice from her skin, sucking on his finger. Her eyes heated as they followed his movements, but she looked down at the contents of his haul.

Biting into the apple, Set leaned on his elbow, stretching his legs. He was content to simply enjoy Ash's company. For now, it was enough that she remained, giving him a chance to try and make things right once more.

"It's a good thing you have experience picking apples because that's exactly the payment I need for all of this," he said, motioning toward the spread before them. "A castle maid told me to fill as many barrels as I can carry back."

"We better get to eating all this food then, for energy," Ash allowed herself a small smile, loading the plate he offered.

They ate in silence, listening to the orchard's rhythms.

When Set finished his last bite of scone, he eyed Ash carefully, brushing crumbs from his fingers. "Ash, about . . . what happened."

She tensed at his hesitation, expression guarded. "What about it?"

Sighing, Set probed the geas, searching for any weakness to allow him to fully explain what had happened. "I needed help with my ríastrad. It was the only way you could be safe with me."

"And Ethne did that out of the goodness of her heart?"

"I don't know what . . . her plans are. But freeing the stone guardians was what everyone wanted, right?"

When she nodded stiffly, he pushed on. "And if I hadn't called on her, we wouldn't be any closer to freeing them."

"What does Ethne want from you in return?"

"Nothing I can't give." He pressed for more words, but it was all he could say. With a heavy sigh, he added, "I never meant to deceive you."

"You should have come to me," Ash said through tight lips, a bitter edge sharpening her tone. "We're supposed to face these threats together."

"I know. It was stupid and reckless." Guilt wormed through him as old arguments resurfaced. But then Lámfada began to glow warmly against his legs, thrumming softly on the soft grass. He took a breath as he gripped the spear. "You're right to be angry. I'm sorry, Ash. Truly."

Her glare softened marginally as she listened. "I just don't want any more secrets between us. We both want what's best for our people."

Releasing the spear, Set dared to reach for her hand, and waited for her to look at him. "No more tricks, I promise. What else can I do to regain your trust?"

Ash glanced at their joined fingers. "We need to get to the human world. We're connected now; if something else happens, my family will be affected." Her eyes lifted to his. "I don't want to travel through the tunnels and I don't have the ability to sift. Will you take me tonight?"

His thumb swept her knuckles gently. "Of course, I'll go with you. Didn't I follow you into the Underworld?"

When she glared at him, he titled his head. "Too soon for jokes?"

She rolled her eyes. "Much too soon, McQuillan."

"Noted." Leaning in, he waited for her to either accept or reject his invitation.

Ash met his lips with a softness he'd missed. Their mouths caressed, sweet as the apples perfuming the air around them.

"I've missed you," he murmured into her mouth.

Her only response was a smile before she crawled onto his lap, deepening their kiss.

The pealing of bells rang through the sweet air as Set wrapped his hands around her waist, drawing her closer still. Shouts sounded and Ash stilled. Pulling apart, her lips deliciously swollen, she glanced toward the tree's branches shielding the highwall.

"What do you think that's about?"

With a sigh, Set eased his hold, reaching out to help her up. Clasping her hand, he led them through the trees until the stone wall loomed into view. Fires sparked one by one along the top and a weight of dread sank to the pit of his stomach, tethering him to the fear that had painted the horizon red. His fingers closed tightly around his weapons. "We have to go. Now!"

Shouts were carried on the wind, the clamour in the distance increasing with every step they gained toward it. The bell tolled as the spreading fires along the battlement meant only one thing. Tara Court was under attack.

CHAPTER 68
SETANTA

S et and Ash ran as shouts rang out from the throngs of
Fianna entering the gate into Tara Court. As they neared
the wall, the ground shook.

"What the hell is that?" Ash outstretched her arms, gaining
her footing.

"I don't know. Come on," Set said, grabbing her hand
and pulling her up the steps of the highwall, following both
highguard and Fianna warriors.

They raced up to the turret, worn stone slippery underfoot,
air whipping at their exposed flesh and snatching strands of
loose hair. They climbed the last few steps and emerged onto
the battlements.

"Report," Set demand from a highguard, who held a bow
and arrow poised to strike.

"The trees are moving to the east."

Set scowled. "And?"

The guard licked his lips. "The trees then snap apart and fall."

"Something is coming toward us," another highguard said.
"Shaking the very earth."

Set peered over the edge, tracking the small figures of Fianna
pouring into the safety of the highwall before the gate shut.

The forest surrounded Tara Court on all sides, dense
woodland stretching as far as the eye could see. Sunlight filtered
through the canopy of leaves, dappling the undergrowth with

shadows. A creature hooted in the distance; a haunting call carried on the breeze.

Set and Ash gazed out at the peaceful vastness before them, the forest seeming timeless and eternal.

"Look. Over there," Ash said, pointing toward a cluster of trees.

From this height, the trees were like broccoli florets, and as if just as bendable, they swayed until snapping echoed to them and the trees fell apart.

Set frowned, squinting. "Do you see what's doing it?"

Thunderous footsteps approached. He didn't need anyone to answer as great trunks continued to snap and two monstrous heads came into view over the green.

"These are much larger than the ones we faced at the barrenland," Ash said and when Set turned to her, he couldn't help noticing how deathly pale she'd become. "There is no mistaking what breed of Fair One giants are."

"Fomorian," Set breathed as he gripped the battlements, the cold stone biting into his flesh.

Ash leaned into him, her warmth the only comfort in that moment. They knew what evil approached yet still they lingered a moment longer, sharing the fleeting peace before war. She disentangled herself first, nodding at him as the others waited, some watching him. With a start, he realised he was the highest-ranking official there.

"Everyone!" A hush fell as Set raised his voice; all eyes turning to their rígfénnid,all voices quietened. "We need to stop the giants before they reach the wall. Archers, light up and get ready."

As warriors along the battlements struck flint to tinder, the first rumbling footfalls shook the very stones beneath their feet. Emerging from the forest, a towering monstrosity broke into the gloom-shrouded clearing.

It stood the height of the surrounding trees, its boulder-like body covered in thick grey skin like a bloated, rotting sea corpse, pockmarked and sagging. Deep-set eyes the colour of spoiled milk scanned the wall, taking their measure with cunning intelligence. A jutting brow ridge creased as dripping jaws split in a grin, exposing foot-long tusks crusted with gore.

With fingers that ended in webbed hands, it snatched up a tree from the forest edge and hurled it at the wall. Stone shuddered and groaned under the impact.

Set swallowed a gag as a rank, river-bed stench rolled ahead of it, rot and brine and things long dead.

Ash cursed. "It's . . ."

Pus wept from torn flesh as it stalked, footfalls booming like a storm's approach.

". . . revolting," Set finished as the abomination drew closer. "Aim!" he commanded as another giant appeared. "Fire!"

A volley of arrows whistled skywards, blazing trails behind like shooting stars. Their fiery paths entwined until meeting their inevitable fall.

Ash gripped Set's hand as they watched, the leading giant tracking the arrows' descent with small, cruel eyes, bellowing tongueless laughter as they neared. Arrows struck true, sinking burning points into rocky flesh.

Howls shook the field as more missiles struck home in the hulking creature standing beside its companion, each blade embedding with sickening thunks. Liquid fire dripped down massive arms to sizzle upon the ground, and steaming flesh bubbled and blackened at each new crater.

Roaring its agony, the troll-like Fomorian tore free arrows stuck fast in its breast, brandishing the smoking shafts above its misshapen skull. Features twisted in promised vengeance as it bellowed a final time and charged.

Set looked down to the inner bailey where the other rígfénnid had gathered highguard, readying them to fight if the walls were breached. Fionn was still visiting the Irish leaders in the human realm, so it was left to them to defend Tara Court.

"Aim!" Set roared as Fianna shouted in alarm. "Fire!"

Arrows brightened the sky, but even though more hit their targets, the giants seemed impervious. Heavy strides devoured the distance, every footfall quaking the very world.

"It's not working, Set."

He didn't need to look at Ash to know how scared she was. These beasts would see the stone wall destroyed and the lives within crushed.

Set's fingers curled tighter around the shaft of his spear, the innate power of the weapon humming along his touch, an electrifying pulse that vibrated into his very bones. It seeped into his being, unfurling threads of strength within him, radiating comfort amidst the engulfing fear.

Let me out.

Set stilled, staring in horror at Lámfada.

Relinquish the spear and we'll be reunited once more.

His head snapped to Ash, who overlooked the edge of the battlement, worry lines heightened against the firelight. Her normally straight black hair was wild, whipping across her porcelain face. The flickering light caught in her eyes, and when the turned to him, he was floored by those deep emerald wells mirroring a resilience and inner strength he yearned for.

Could he release the monster? Be reunited with his ríastrad, unleash the raw primitive force that lurked within the cage of this spear? There was an undeniable seduction in its promise, tempting him with its tantalising whisper of unleashed strength when he needed it most.

Reality snapped him back from the precipice as another tree slammed into the side of the highwall. No. He needed the spear to stabilise the threat of his ríastrad. He could never let it slip from his grasp. Ethne had warned that if anyone touched it, they would be tainted by his monster. Looking at Ash, he would not allow that to happen.

Gritting his teeth, he squeezed the spear in a grip that would have easily broken it before. But not now. Not when he had the strength of only a man.

"What will we do?" Ash had retreated from the crenel, standing by his side.

Set released his grip, returning his spear to its harness at his back. He had lived for too long with the monster within; he had to learn to fight without it.

Set turned to her as the giant's fists shook the foundations; he found only strength in her gaze, the fire that drew him to her like a moth. They would fight together, as they were, side by side. "We fight as best we can."

Yet Ash stepped back, glancing toward the stairs leading down from the battlements. "I'm going to my clan. I need to be with them."

Set grabbed her hand, an argument to stay on his lips. But he stared at the unyielding determination on her face. She was a warrior, and a matriarch. With a solemn nod, he released her, allowing her hand to slip from his grasp all too soon. Set watched Ash descend the battlement stairs, each step taking her further from his side. An icy void opened within his chest as he flexed his fingers, missing the familiar pressure of her hand in his.

Watching her leave until another pounding shook the wall, he gritted his teeth, jaw clenching so hard his temples throbbed. He willed the rage and frustration away, focusing on the battle with a steely demeanour.

"Archers, step aside." He pointed toward the highguard heating oils. "Help them wheel the caldrons."

Grunting with the effort, Set and the others manoeuvred the iron cauldrons filled with scorching tar through the walkways.

"Hold until they're directly underneath," he ordered as both Fomorian monsters pounded the walls.

At his signal, cauldron lids were flung open, unleashing scalding liquid to gravity's domain. With a hiss, a torrential downpour of searing, vicious tar descended through the air like a waterfall of molten fury, glinting under the moonlight.

The cascade found its targets, clinging onto their rough skin with a cruel tenacity, a grotesque baptism of unholy water. As burning flesh mingled with the already rotting smell, inhuman roars filled the sky. Steam rose in blinding wafts. Set and the others backed away from the edge until it cleared.

"Did it work?" a guard asked.

Set stepped to the edge as silence filled the rotting air. A shake rattled the walls as the giants appeared through the steam once more. Bloodied and burned, but just as ferocious. Set cursed as he ordered for the archers to take position once more.

With a deafening crack and splitting groan, the leviathan creatures barrelled into the keep once more. Masonry that had withstood endless ages shuddered under the impact, relinquishing chunks of stonework that tumbled toward the lower bailey.

From where he stood on the parapet walkway, Set felt the trembling spread outward from the point of impact like ripples in a pond. The battlement swayed treacherously as the immense weight behind the blow took effect.

Great fissures zigzagged upward through the stone architecture, choking it with cracks as the integrity failed. Set's attention snapped to the stone underneath his boots as it bowed and sank where the beams below gave way.

"Retreat!" Set bellowed, as he ran toward the steps.

Motes of silt and grit flooded the air, stinging his lungs and eyes, but he could see his warning came too late as figures slipped through the widening gaps. Grabbing a flailing warrior, he hauled them back from the crumbling edge before turning to flee.

Behind, more catastrophic groans punctuated the giants' retreat as granite rained earthward. The uneven steps pitched and yawed beneath pounding boots as Set leapt down three at a time. Those lagging were tossed from the twisting stairs to smash on the stones below.

Set sprinted across the lower bailey, smoke burning his throat with each gasp. Turning, he surveyed the damage. A substantial portion of the highwall had crumbled, and the destruction had been fatal for many Fianna. Chunks of stone lay strewn amongst corpses and moaning wounded. Through swirling ash, the outer wall the width of a Tuatha Dé temple lay torn and trampled where it had stood for centuries. Over it all, the hulking Fomorians' roar was enough to signal this battle wasn't over; but they had already lost.

The giants would soon breach the highwall and there was nothing Set could do to stop them. The implosion of Newgrange would be nothing compared to the great highwall raining down on them.

Lungs burning, Set searched through the jagged rubble strewn like broken teeth. The warrior clans had gathered in tight, disciplined ranks across the inner walls alongside the highguard. Row upon row of ash-smeared figures stood with weapons grasped and eyes narrowed against the dusty sky. Set's throat bobbed as he spotted the McQuillans massed together in a bristling knot of leather and steel, with Maebh leading in the front, blue eyes flashing, fingertips white about her blade.

He ran toward them and spotted Ash and her clan next to them.

"Are you hurt?" Set asked, coughing through the smoke and dust that had filled his lungs.

Maebh smirked, but her lips were tight. "Only you would barely escape a wall collapsing and then ask if *we* are okay. Golden Boy."

She gripped his arms before embracing him tightly.

"Locals are within the castle," Maebh said, releasing him and jerking her head toward the towering keep silhouetted against roiling clouds.

Nodding briskly as they faced the wavering smokescreen that once held their fortress, as the giants' misshapen forms beat at the gaping hole with reckless abandon.

"What are they waiting for?" Ash stepped beside him. "The wall is breached."

Her words were a death knell that rang true. They were fighting off the inevitable. Should they retreat, and leave the castle while they still could? Set swallowed hard as he studied Ash and Maebh's grim expressions, his gaze trailing behind to his clan. There would be no place they could run to that these beasts couldn't find and destroy.

Before he could order a defence, the pounding at the walls intensified once more. Maebh drew her sword with a grim smile. "I guess it's time for us to have some action too."

"There are only two," remarked a familiar voice behind and they all turned.

Maebh's face coloured as Tiernan stood feet away, the rest of Fionn's guard behind him.

"Finally decided to show," she remarked coolly at no one in particular, but Set knew his sister as her eyes betrayed her, landing on Tiernan's impassive face more than anyone's.

"Is High King back?" Set asked, looking behind the rows of guardians, but not finding the imposing frame of Fionn.

Tiernan cocked his head to the side, his eyes glazing, but a heartbeat later, he answered. "They are returning soon. But we'll take care of the Fomorian problem now."

Without another word, the stone guard moved in synchronised steps toward the hole.

As the guardians passed, Set caught flickers of change sweeping through their forms like rippling shadows. Their skin thickened and paled to an iron-grey hue, hardening into stone-like plates across corded muscles.

Tiernan remained stationed, morphing the slowest, as if fighting the transformation. Yet beneath his flesh, stonework shifted and took shape.

"What's happening?" Ash asked, standing inches away from her former second.

Set went to her side, ready to pull her back if needed.

"He's changing into . . ." Maebh paused, peering into Tiernan's face as he gritted his teeth, closing his eyes.

Tiernan's jawline firmed to a sharp edge while his many tattoos etched deeper into newly-hewn planes of granite. He swelled in size, and Set gripped the women's arms, pulling them into a retreat.

"It's like my ríastrad," he warned, unsheathing his spear as it glowed brighter than ever.

Ash turned and gasped. "They've all transformed into . . ."

"Gargoyles?" Maebh frowned as shouts rang out amongst the warriors stationed behind them.

Tiernan's eyes opened, pinning on Maebh. Instead of stone eyes, Set noticed they were the familiar brown of the man they knew. His face was still his own but had morphed into a fierce creature, his high cheekbones and elegant features more prominent, sculpted into an intimidating sharpness.

As if in response to Maebh's question, an ear-splitting scraping followed, with pale leathery wings bursting from

Tiernan's back. Taut white membranes held the wings that were veined like marble and twice a man's height tip to tip.

Talons erupted from boot tips, curving and thickening into hooked claws. Tiernan's face was like marble, his expression akin to an avenging devil before he launched into the sky, blasting them with an unforgiving breeze. Set stood, immobile, unable to do anything but watch as Tiernan joined his other winged guard and launched an airborne attack on the colossal beasts.

CHAPTER 69
TIERNAN

White-hot pain seared every nerve, threatening to overwhelm Tiernan's mind. He clung desperately to his fraying hold on who he was, but the domination of stone was ever winning.

Fight.

Tiernan flexed his jaw as his wings snapped. His *wings.* Though he'd fought against it, instinct propelled him skyward as soon as the leathery appendages took form on his back.

It's not so bad being one of us now, is it?

Sinéad's distinct voice filtered through the hive mind, and he rolled his watering eyes. She chuckled, despite the reprimand brimming along their connection from the others. Gasps drifted on the wind and Tiernan observed the gathered Fianna below. Most stood stationary, watching their assent despite the giants literally banging on their doorstep.

Day by day, ever since they'd awoken from Fionn's enchanted cave, the stone guardians had transitioned from mindless chanting sentinels to a semblance of who they had once each been. It was still a battle, and for the first few weeks, Tiernan could barely hold on to his name, the awakening of so many voices connected to one hive mind: Fionn. The High King had ordered them to remain as one clan, separate from the other Fianna until Fionn determined who was friend and who was foe.

Whispers of pain from Tiernan's transformation spasmed throughout, stone clinging relentlessly over his flesh, but as the icy wind lashed at his face, he wondered at the logic of being covered in a layer of stone, of having damned wings, but the same magic couldn't allow for protection to their eyes against the unrelenting winds during flight.

Sinéad's trilling laughter tickled his consciousness.

Big baby, she shot at him as she came into view on his right, a wide grin on her face, showcasing the gap between her front teeth. Sinéad radiated vitality despite her stone imprisonment.

As he followed her petite figure, gliding on the same wind, he remembered all the times she'd broken through the stone enchantment to speak to him while underground. She had been the voice to name the stalking sluagh and had also given him back his name. Since the Great Awakening, Sinéad had been able to break through the haze of Fionn's stone enchantment more than anyone else, and the acidic burning of envy trailed along Tiernan's throat; he tried to shield that thought from slipping into the hive.

Enough, Nessa demanded through the hive. His attempt to shield his thoughts clearly hadn't worked as his mother took lead of attack. *Focus*.

The group formed into a tight V formation, Tiernan and Sinéad flanking Nessa, half a dozen guardians on each line. Below, the ogres' furious roars escalated as they circled into position.

Get ready, Nessa ordered as both giants continued their assault, smashing the wall, but not entering the gaping hole. Tiernan fixed his sight upon the bulbous head of his target, directing his stone body into a dive.

Protect. Fight.

The collective will of the guardians flowed into Tiernan, fortifying his resolve. He steeled himself, focusing on his individual purpose despite their mingled thoughts.

Like falling stars, the stone guard spiralled, smashing into the thick skin of the giants. Tiernan and Sinéad plunged together.

He threw himself into the goliath, but his blow glanced harmlessly off its thick, weathered hide. It kicked out, flinging Tiernan backwards through the air.

Stay.

Widening his wings, he used them as a parachute to slow his descent.

Regroup. We need more than our stone armour. Tiernan mentally gathered the guardians to him through their link. As one, they reformed their swirling flock and dove as an undulating grey tide against the giants, daggers and swords unsheathed.

The monster struck its webbed hand at Nessa. Time seemed to slow as Tiernan watched helplessly, unable to reach her in time. His stone fingers tightened around empty air, longing to shove her from harm's way. The crushing blow was mere inches from connecting when Nessa darted nimbly aside. Tiernan shuddered inwardly at how close fate had come to stealing his mother from this world once more.

Touching, Sinéad said, and he scowled as she flew beside him.

None of his thoughts were sacred anymore, even ones he wasn't sure he wholly believed in. Nessa had been the one to shove her hand through his chest, turning his heart and body into stone. His mother's snarl tore through the sky; at the attacking behemoth, or his thoughts, he wasn't sure.

Sinéad flew closer, ignoring his warning growl. *Focus.*

Tiernan and the other stone guardians swooped down upon the Fomorians in perfect unison. Their blades and talons rained blows upon the towering invaders, cleaving chunks of flesh as they attacked. Though taking hits that would kill any normal warrior, skin made of stone armour withstood each retaliation from the giants.

Sinéad battled fiercely beside Tiernan, raking her talons across a creature's misshapen face. It howled in rage and pain, swiping blindly at the agile guardian. But Sinéad smoothly evaded each blow. Tiernan redoubled his efforts, swiping his sword across its thick skin in fast, effective motions.

Sinéad followed his lead and together they swarmed around the attacker in a downward spiral, cutting and hacking at every chance. A bone-crunching impact echoed across the plains as their giant fell. The other creature roared, smashing and swiping until it reached its kin. Snarling up at the flying guard, it grabbed its fallen comrade, hauling it over its mountainous shoulder, fleeing from the castle wall.

Cheers rang out from the ground, but the stone guard remained airborne.

Do we chase it? Tiernan asked, but Nessa shook her head as Fionn's voice rang through the hive mind. His voice was faint because of the distance, but through their link Tiernan could tell he was almost back from the human realm.

Stay. Protect.

The stone guardians swept down from the skies, and when they struck the castle grounds, the earth splintered in an outward web around their feet. Clouds of gritty dust rose, shadowing them momentarily from the massed throngs of Fianna on the castle grounds.

How many perished before your arrival? Fionn asked, his voice a quiet command in Tiernan's mind.

Half a dozen fell from the damage caused by the highwall, Nessa answered. *It could have been worse.*

None should die by the hands of Fair Ones. Fionn's voice boomed through the link before cutting their connection.

Tiernan wasn't the only one who flinched. He contemplated his mother's stoic expression, but she simply nodded in agreement. As Tiernan and the others towered over the Fianna warriors in their stone forms, an expectant hush fell over the crowd.

I'd look at us like that too, Sinéad commented from her position, although no emotion was portrayed through her face. The stone guard remained aloof to their kin. No longer just Fianna. *Of my blood, but more.* Tiernan frowned at the phrase. It was like a half-forgotten dream that resurfaced occasionally.

His vision combed over the warriors facing them, soot-covered but unharmed, save for those that had lost their lives. He tracked the bodies lined by the fringes of the market square, sheets covering them, a veil of peace before they were given the funeral rites to move on. The number was small, but each shrouded figure represented a story cut short by the giants' brutal assault. Most of the residents had been hiding in the castle walls so the dead were made up of highguard and warriors.

Though victory had been won against the Fomorians, some warriors eyed the stone guardians warily. As the guard moved through the crowds towards the castle, a few warriors retreated nervously, reaching for weapons should danger still lurk before them. But most simply gazed up in awe and wonderment, taking in the stone sentinels with wings that took up more space than available in the confined area.

For a long moment, an uncertain stillness stretched out as guardians and warriors regarded each other across the divide between stone and flesh.

A lone whoop cut through the aftermath's silence, one warrior thumping a fist against his chest in Tiernan's direction and gesturing for the others to follow suit. Soon, a rousing cheer went up from the gathered clans, weapons clashing against shields in a deafening display of respect as the guard marched forward in an impromptu guard of honour.

Tiernan found himself within the eye of an unexpected storm as the cheers rose into a crescendo around him. As the back of his neck heated, he avoided all eyes to the glaring spotlight he hadn't sought.

Not so bad at all, Sinéad mused and Tiernan sent an eye roll through the hive, smiling despite her annoying jabs. Even though they had been strangers before his entrapment, he felt more like himself with her around.

As the victorious cheers heightened and the crowds gathered around them thickened, Tiernan couldn't help but feel the need to take flight once more. His hand clenched, fingers scraping against his palm, trying to rid himself of the prickling unease under the weight of their praise.

The fair-haired twins stood watching him closely, along with Aisling Breen, his former matriarch. All three studied his every nuanced expression that passed across his blank face. A spark flared deep within, a faint whisper of memory tugging at his consciousness and his eyes flickered to them before he realised what he'd done. For a moment, he saw glimpses of who he'd been. Laughing beside a fire with Aisling—Ash—and trading stories with Maebh beside a large oak tree.

Somewhere beneath the layers of rock, a part of him cried to grasp those flickering recollections, and the people who were in them. But another voice screamed in warning, and it wasn't the hive. To break free from his stone exterior and recall his past could shatter the cocoon that had kept him sane during his awakening. Despite the pull of his past, he knew that to reopen that chapter of his life could expose wounds still raw. For now, it was safest to remain where he was: one of the many voices within the hive, bonded with their High King against the threats of their world.

Knowing the threat was gone, Tiernan focused on the pain of transforming back into flesh once more. A ripple in the air surrounded him, as his colossal exterior cracked. Grey-white stone warmed as if under a blazing sun to the point the heat became unbearable, and he was on fire without flame. Gritting his teeth, he watched his stone clan undergo the same transition, each pair of eyes scowling in concentration.

His immense wings softened and shrank, retreating into his back. Each deeply etched furrow of his scowl smoothed into the gentler contours of a man. The rigid, rough stone converted into the canvas of flesh. His transformation was a symphony of suffering and rebirth, of stone breaking into particles before his body was flesh once more. Among the collective gasps of bystanders, the final fragments of stone dissolved, leaving Tiernan standing under the muted sky—a man reborn.

Following his clan, he barely nodded in acknowledgement to the three strangers standing before him. They had been a part of his old life. But he wasn't sure if they would remain in his new one.

CHAPTER 70
TIERNAN

Tiernan stood before the flames emblazoned with farewells, dread engulfing his lungs.

Dozens of pyres clawed the evening sky, their flames a haunting dance of goodbyes for the fallen Fianna who'd lost their lives mere days ago. Fionn's return brought with it the bitter command for the stone clan to ready and kindle the pyres. His order was a quiet accusation for their inaction. Their delay to join the fray had reaped an unspeakable cost, one that now sent columns of thick black smoke towards the sky.

Each flame was a story abruptly ended, each puff of smoke a sigh of parting, and while the warmth of the flames left no impressions on his stone body, the searing weight of regret left its stark imprint on his soul.

Fionn's departure for the human realm had been accompanied by a command: the stone guard were to remain distant, to abstain from intervening in the affairs of the Cath and the Fianna. His order was absolute to some of the stone guard, leaving them debating rather than acting sooner when the pair of Fomorian monstrosities had attacked.

A torrent of thoughts swirled within Tiernan, thrashing against the walls of his discipline. His heart clenched within its flinty cage, the weight of his duty crushing against his longing to act, but also to obey.

Tiernan's hard stare remained fixed on the flickering pyres long after the High King gave a final nod of respect and turned to make his way back to the castle. The clustered groups of warriors around the pyres began to disperse. Hushed voices replaced the sombre silence as Fianna spoke in muted tones to one another, sharing their farewells to the fallen before returning to their daily routines within the camp. Only then did Tiernan allow his stony facade to crack, quietly offering his apology.

"Come to The Raven with us to raise a drink to the fallen," a rumbling baritone cut through the haze of smoke and memories clouding Tiernan's mind. Turning, he found the towering figure of Setanta McQuillan had approached, powerfully built, like an oak tree in human form. Heavy brows framed grey eyes, currently crinkled in a smile as the Breen matriarch stood by his side. "First round is on me," he added.

Beside the warrior, Aisling Breen's dainty features held sorrow, though a spark remained in her emerald eyes when he glanced at her and for a heartbeat it seemed she knew his innermost thoughts. But he knew she couldn't; that ability lay with his stone clan and the High King.

Tiernan hesitated as he stared at Aisling, an unease weighing on his tongue, preventing him from refusing like he should. All the stone clan had retreated to the castle except one and he swallowed his sigh as Sinéad stepped forward, wild curls the colour of chestnuts haloing her face. Freckles danced across her features as a grin spread. "We will come. Thank you."

Even though she spoke quietly, a jolt of surprise ran through him. He sometimes forgot they had voices.

The matriarch's eyes widened, clearly expecting a different response, but Setanta nodded. "Great. We'll see you there."

"And you should invite the rest of your . . ." Aisling hesitated, her brows bunching together. "Companions?"

After a beat, Sinéad said, "We will."

Tiernan watched them leave, too slow to return the smile Aisling offered.

We do not mix with them, Nessa scolded, nowhere in sight but ever present in their mind.

Sinéad sighed dramatically, kicking at the grass at their feet. She was the youngest stone guardian. Although she'd somehow been able to shut out most of her mind from the hive, he'd gleaned she'd been entrapped by Fionn's enchantment not long before his mother and the rest of the caillte.

"We can't refuse a rígfénnid's offer of parting with coin," Sinéad said dismissively, smiling widely as the torrent of responses blared in their minds. Ignoring them, she grabbed Tiernan's elbow. "Come on, they're waiting; this will be good for you, Tier, my boy."

Steering him away from the pyres and through the gate to Tara Court, Tiernan tried to protest, but Sinéad simply tightened her grip until he trudged alongside her. The streets bustled with activity despite the ruins and aftermath of violence coating their backs. They zigzagged alleyways and lanes; the giants' attack hadn't affected this part of their stronghold. By the surrounding bustle, it was clear the people were determined to not allow it to take hold of them, either. A mix of celebration and unease hung heavy in the air and carried on the evening breeze.

Sinéad hummed a familiar tune, and he eyed the lean warrior as he tried to place it. It was an old pop song from an Irish band from over twenty years ago.

"What year did you get trapped by Fionn's guard?"

Her shorter steps made her bob alongside him even though he'd been walking at an ambling pace. Slowing further, he caught the wistful look, softening her already full cheeks and unlined face so she appeared even younger than she was.

"Two thousand and five." Her shoulders stiffened, but her smile never wavered. "I was eighteen and thought I knew it all."

Sinéad didn't offer any further information, and Tiernan didn't push. A splattering of chilly rain speckled the cobblestones as they continued in silence. She smiled and greeted passersby, ignoring the mental reprimands of the others through the hive mind. Tiernan watched in amusement. She'd been able to break through the oppression of Fionn's stone enchantment more than he had. He licked his lips, ready to ask, but of course she answered before he could.

"I heard you fighting against the enchantment." Sinéad's curly brown hair danced with every stride, bouncing with her jaunting steps. "Trying to keep hold of yourself before becoming one of us. You almost won."

His chest tightened at the word 'almost', but he let out a weary sigh. "I tried. How do you do it?"

She eyed him for a moment but didn't answer.

He tried to open the link into her mind and gritted his teeth with the effort. A black wall met him, and she smirked when he stared at her profile.

"You used to do that too, but since we woke up, you have kept your mind *wide* open."

Tiernan fixed his attention on her, studying the subtle signs that revealed her inner stillness despite the hyperactive awareness of the others within their shared connection. Closing his eyes, he focused inward. Swirling images and half-formed thoughts assaulted him from all sides, bleeding into a formless mass of colour.

You can do this. Sinéad's clear voice rose above the constant stream of noise, and he clung to that until a dark sheen like a beacon shone beyond her voice.

Peeling back veil-like wisps, the glimmer sharpened in a dark wall stretching endlessly in either direction. It pulsated with power, runes and symbols flickering to life underneath his gaze. He reached out through his mind with phantom hands. Upon his touch, energy surged up his arm in a heady rush until the wall rippled around him and he found himself standing in a void of nothingness. Silence embraced him, a sanctuary carved for a space in his mind that was solely his. A wide smile stretched across his face as his eyes popped. Sinéad returned his smile.

"Finally, I can take a break from your brooding for five minutes."

"Shut up," he said, but chuckled, surprising himself.

Soon they arrived at The Raven, its warm glow a welcome reprieve despite his reluctance. Sinéad dragged Tiernan inside and a pleasant-faced tavern wench greeted them as she wove through the packed room. Her yellow-flecked eyes widened when they landed on him.

"You're Tiernan."

"And I'm Sinéad," his companion said brightly. "Where's that ridiculously handsome rígfénnid and his promise of free alcohol?"

The woman angled her head, her eyes never leaving Tiernan's, and his skin tingled at her unnerving attention. "Setanta McQuillan and the others are over there."

The short woman pointed behind her before the tavern owner barked for her attention. Blinking rapidly, she excused herself before disappearing into the heaving crowds. Tiernan frowned in her direction. He could have sworn she'd had two sets of eyelids when she'd blinked. Sinéad tugged on his arm, forcing him to follow through the tightly packed tables.

"You made it!" Ash's face was flushed in the lantern-lit room, Setanta's arm casually slung around her shoulders. She smiled widely before looking behind them. Her attention came back to Tiernan. "Is it just the two of you?"

Sinéad answered for him, taking a vacant seat. "They might swing by in a bit."

Sit, she ordered through their shared mind when Tiernan stood awkwardly for a beat too long. They were introduced to the others at the table, and he nodded, greeting a few of them when pushed by Sinéad.

"Where's Conor?" he found himself asking before he knew why.

Aisling's smile was small as she gave him a look that he didn't quite like. Shifting in his seat, he bit the inside of his cheek to prevent himself from saying he'd changed his mind and didn't want to know. That would surely seem rude.

And it's also a lie, Sinéad mused while tapping her fingers on the wooden table. *You do want to know.*

Tiernan restrengthened his wall.

"Conor is with Orla Corrigan," Aisling replied with a sigh, a waft of aged paper filtering to him. With a start, Tiernan realised he was sensing her emotion.

"You're unsure of this match, Aisling?"

"Well," she said, tucking her midnight hair behind an ear and glancing sideways at Setanta, "it's not that. It's just . . . they've both been through a lot. Maybe it's too soon?"

Tiernan nodded, unsure what to say next.

"And, Tiernan," the matriarch said, leaning on the table. "It's Ash, remember?"

"I like that, it suits you," Sinéad said brightly, and Tiernan was grateful for her interruptions. His companion rapped on the table as if knocking on a door. "But what I'd like to know, Rígfénnid McDreamy, is where is my free drink?"

The group erupted in laughter as Maebh, carrying a tray of drinks, appeared from the throng of people. She placed it in the middle of the table with a thunderous bang.

"I swear, the service in The Raven is getting worse," she declared as she deftly handed out drinks. "But the mead is too good."

As the cheerful clamour of the tavern continued around him, Tiernan's gaze was unwittingly pulled to her as she thrust tankards into waiting hands. The matriarch hadn't acknowledged their arrival, and he brooded. Sinéad accepted her drink quickly, saluting before downing half the contents.

As the blonde matriarch passed behind his chair, an electric current flowed through his veins. Something stirred within until an overwhelming urge to flee warred with the will to stare at Maebh just to track her many facial expressions. He'd never encountered a woman who showed exactly how she felt on her face at every given moment. With a jolt, he realised he had. Tiernan had already met Maebh McQuillan, had got to know her, and found himself unable to think about anyone else. But that was before, and those feelings were gone.

Are you sure about that? Sinéad bumped his shoulder before joining in on a conversation with some of the Breens and McQuillans clanspeople at their table.

Stop forcing your way through. Tiernan clenched his jaw, but as Sinéad gulped her drink she shot back, *Try harder.*

Conversations swirled around him, but his jaw ticked as Maebh offered Tiernan a tankard without looking at him. The absence of her blue flaming eyes left him inexplicably cold. Clasping his fingers around the rim, he grazed his pinkie against her finger, partly to see if she would look at him, but also to verify if his memories of how soft her skin was were true.

She snatched her hand away as if bitten, those eyes pinning him like he'd hoped, sending a thrill to his stomach. For a moment, time suspended. His throat tightened as he held her gaze, the world blurring at the edges. Within her eyes lay a universe of stars, of stories that he should remember but didn't.

"Thought we'd join for one," a gruff voice said from behind and Maebh flinched before looking up at Gearoid McQuillan.

Tiernan studied Maebh's face as she observed every movement her father made. He and Lorcan Breen sat in the offered seats a warrior had hastily brought over for them. Ash mumbled something before departing from the table. With Maebh's eyes no longer on him, Tiernan sipped his mead. Honey and barley danced on his tongue, and he took another long drink, the months spent within a magical entrapment heightening the sensation of real taste.

We came to remind you of your station, Lorcan said through their bond. He accepted the drink Ash brough back for the two men, and she nodded tensely. From Ash's last encounter with her father, Tiernan was surprised she hadn't poured the drink over his head. He remembered the cool-headedness of his former matriarch. It was something he'd respected her for.

And we came here to drink, Sinéad shot back, calling to the tavern wench for another round.

Tiernan smirked as he leaned against the worn, wooden chair, nursing his tankard of ale as he observed their unlikely group. Conversations floated around him, and even as he marvelled at the attempts both Ash and Set made at conversing with their fathers, he couldn't think of how to take part. The stone guard were muted in his head, but the appearance of Lorcan and Gearoid had affected his ability to fight against the stone hold. Sinéad didn't seem to have that problem and had only grown more boisterous at their presence. Laughing inwardly, he imagined she'd been a nightmare for her parents.

You have no idea, she said through their bond, and the other two warriors scowled but didn't acknowledge their thoughts.

As the night wore on, with the Fianna saluting many drinks for their fallen comrades, the air grew thick with laughter, chatter, and the occasional off-key note from an outbreak of song. Maebh's eyes never found his again, but the night was still a welcome reprieve from the chaos that had consumed their lands.

A rowdy group burst into the tavern, their victorious shouts cutting through the din like a roaring storm.

"It's the Collins and McNeill clans," Setanta said, his hand going immediately to his axe slung on his belt.

The newly-arrived warriors only entered as far as the crowd could allow their gathering, faces smudged with dirt.

"The Cath ends tonight," a man shouted over the murmuring crowd.

Ash looked displeased, turning to the entranceway. "Says who?"

Deaglán, the Leinster rígfénnid, answered. "The province leaders held a vote to finish the Cath tonight and High King Fionn agreed. We need to react to the Fair Ones' attacks, not continue competing against each other for a glory no one will reap if we are all dead."

"I didn't get a vote," Set growled, standing, his chair scraping against the stone floor as everyone watched in muted anticipation.

Tiernan looked between his stone clan members, each with similar expressions. Fionn hadn't informed them of this decision either.

It is not for us to question the High King's decisions, lad. Gearoid's voice rang clear in his mind.

"Majority ruled," Deaglán said, shrugging. "You were nowhere to be found. And I took that favour you owed me to mean I cast your vote."

Tension rolled off Setanta, and another chair scraped along the dirt floor. Tiernan didn't know why, but he stood beside him.

"It doesn't matter," Maebh said, coming to her brother's other side and sneering at the rival clans. "We have the largest territory between us and the Breen clan."

"Not any more," a woman's voice called before the Collins warriors parted to reveal a dark-haired woman with the matriarch coat of arms on her jacket.

"What do you mean, Fiadh?" Ash asked, making her way to the stand-off as all eyes watched the tension build.

"We have taken the territories left unguarded during the giant attack," Fiadh said with a shrug, her voice echoing against the wooden beams of the tavern. "You lost."

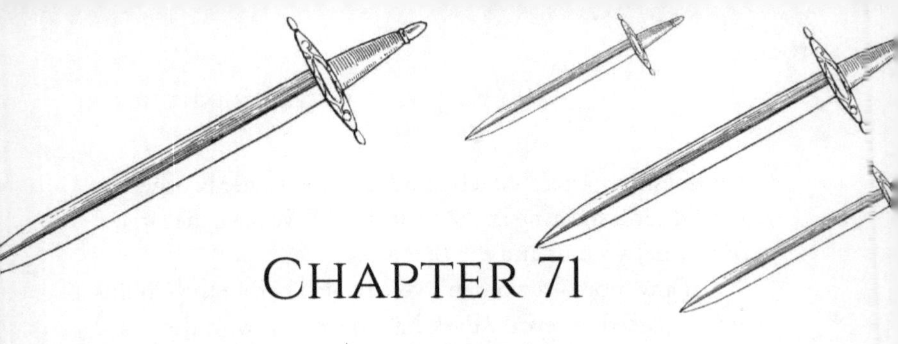

CHAPTER 71
AISLING

Ash ascended the hill in a haze, each step disconnected from her body while last night's revelations swirled in her mind. Through the morning fog, giant footprints marred the earth like jagged wounds where she could see through the hole in the highwall. Conor gripped her elbow gently, grounding her in their surreal reality.

The Cath had finished and they had lost. Fionn stood with the O'Neill and Collins clans on the hill summit, the Lia Fáil radiating with energy from the High King's close proximity. The Stone of Destiny still considered Fionn as the rightful king. Beneath celebratory cheers rose troubled scents from Ash's clan; bitter apprehension, sour regret. Had they truly lost all after so much struggle and sacrifice?

"People of the Fianna!" Fionn boomed. "For too long we have allowed the Tuatha Dé to rule over us, allowing the Fomorians to wreak havoc and misery upon humankind."

Murmurs of assent arose from the crowd and Ash invoked her gift, expanding it beyond the Breen clan. Unease tainted the air like spilled mead. While the people wished to be free of the Fair Ones' rule, had the declaration for their independence come at too high a sacrifice? Fionn continued, his voice rising.

"The Fair Ones think themselves above us, lording their power and magic over those they call 'lesser creatures'. They use humans as pawns in their eternal games, caring nothing for the lives they ruin."

A swell of agreement greeted his words, but Ash detected deeper undercurrents, the tang of metallic anger simmering at the violence just below the surface of the crowd's roars.

"No more!" Fionn's voice rang out across the plains, fist raised triumphantly. "We will allow no Tuatha Dé to set foot within the walls of Tara Court until humans are left in peace in the world they were meant to rule!"

The clans erupted into deafening cheers. Weapons beat against shields as warriors stamped their feet in support. Unease curled cold and heavy in Ash's stomach. While freedom was her deepest wish, Medb's fortress had revealed but a sliver of the Fair Ones' true strength.

Doubt needled her, though her gift detected no lies from Fionn, only his unshakable faith in their victory. But desires alone could never overcome such ancient powers. As the frenzied roars consumed the gathering, Ash found no solace in their call to battle. Only a mounting tension, like a tightening bowstring awaiting an arrow's release.

Fionn raised his hands, and the noise died down. "We were created to protect humankind from the Fair Ones and their malevolent ways. That is the sacred duty entrusted to us by Danu herself."

Ash glanced skyward as if the Tuatha Dé Danann goddess were watching them from above. She often wondered why Fianna worshipped the very gods that the Fair Ones descended from. They'd ruled every species, Danu being the mother of all. Did she truly want peace between humankind and Fair Ones? Or would the goddess demand humans serve the Tuatha Dé Danann like her descendants believed?

As Fionn addressed the crowd, Ash's focus was drawn inevitably to the tallest figure standing steadfast at the king's back. Even amongst the stone clan and highguard flanking the other leaders, Set's presence was all encompassing. Even at a distance, his palpable aura sent her pulse racing and breath quickening. Clad in his polished steel and black leather battle-suit, her eye traced the lines of powerful muscle beneath, memories of tracing similar paths across his heated skin bringing a flush to her own. His steel-like strength always enveloped her, yet was underlain with tenderness to match the stormy eyes now surveying the gathered clans.

"Our Cath has come to an end. Two great warrior clans will join the highguard. But you all have a role to play. Whether it be in Tír na nÓg or back in the human realm." Fionn clenched his fist. "The humans are unwilling to accept reality, so we will teach them."

Ash stilled. "What does he mean by that?"

Conor murmured, "I heard rumours that the Taoiseach didn't want to get involved with Fionn's plans against the fae. So Fionn plans to overrule the human leaders and take control of Ireland in this realm and in theirs."

Ash's stomach twisted as Fionn's booming voice carried on. "If the Fair Ones will not learn, then we shall teach them, by blade and blood and battle if need be!"

The clans erupted into shouts of approval, vowing to follow Fionn into war against the Tuatha Dé. Fionn's face remained impassive, but Ash saw the hunger for violence reflected in his eyes, one that seemed only satisfied by vengeance and bloodshed. A chill ran down her spine at the terrible light shining within her ancient king.

Foreboding snaked icy tendrils through her veins. She did not share his enthusiasm for vengeance. The humans needed their own leadership. There was a time where nobody could deny a war was coming, but to take away their right to rule? That was a step too far. War was never so black and white, the lines between right and wrong always blurring in the brutal chaos of the battlefield.

As Fionn congratulated the two winning clans, Ash noted several of them had worn their gruesome trophy necklaces made from killing fae, and bile rose in her throat at the tokens of butchery. The merrowspawn eggs flashed in her eyes, so vividly it was as if she were underwater once more; tiny, blackened claws pressing against translucent orbs. She'd almost killed those creatures. How was she any better? She'd hesitated, but had that been enough to align her with the clans delighting in tormenting the fae?

Gusting wind blew Ash's hair into her wary eyes. She whipped around as an ominous mass of flapping darkness passed overhead. The immense swarm blotted out the sun as cries resounded. In answer, ear-piercing caws filled the blackening sky. Ash ducked, shuddering at the discordant noise and flashes of cruel eyes within twisted forms of the writhing flock.

Drawing her sword, she slashed overhead but the swarm only pulsed around her blade before coursing toward the hill where Fionn and his men stood. Where Set and Tiernan stood.

"No," she gritted out, scrambling to her feet, blade raised.

Whatever the swarms were, they would not harm either of her men. Racing, her chest burned as her legs pumped harder than they'd ever before. Inhuman sounds erupted in the air as a lone dark shadow separated from the mass, and a beautiful, ethereal female stood beside Fionn.

"It's been a while, Fionn Mac Cumhaill." The Morrígan's multilayered voice amplified for the crowd to hear over her hovering mass of black birds.

Crows. They encircled high above, like predators before striking their prey. Ash's steps faltered as fear gripped her, rendering her frozen. Had they come back for her? Darkness formed in her vision until a familiar, cruel face materialised feet away.

"Tara," she croaked before he snatched her roughly and sifted to where The Morrígan stood.

A heartbeat later, Maebh was deposited beside her, followed by Tiernan and Set.

"These four are ours to take, Fionn Mac Cumhaill," the Morrígan declared.

Ash felt her blood turn to ice at the ominous proclamation.

"Not a chance, bitch," Maebh snarled.

"Macha," Fionn said, both hands wielding a sword and dagger as the stone guard transformed at his back.

With a sharp intake of breath, Tiernan's eyes widened, and in an instant, his body became rigid like stone. Leathery wings sprouted from his back, stretching outwards with a swift and graceful motion. Ash watched transfixed as he folded his mighty wings around their small group, creating a shield that enveloped them all. Shadows danced among the intricate patterns etched on his wings, casting an otherworldly glow as he stood tall like a statuesque guardian, ready to defend them.

"How interesting," Macha chuckled, her voice like tinkling glass, no longer layered with her sisters' voices.

Tiernan lowered his wings enough for Ash to see the fae stand before their High King. "We hear your toxic words on the wind. Claiming us as your enemy."

Stray feathers floated downward like the beginning of snowdrops in winter as the murder of crows continued their circular flight just above.

"Do you deny working against us?" Fionn demanded, his fearless gaze immovable against the might of the Tuatha Dé before them.

"Do you deny allowing a Fomorian to play around with your kind?" Macha countered, her sallow arm extended toward Ash and the others. "They hold our blood, therefore we shall keep them."

"You will take none of my kind," Fionn said, and in unison the stone guard encircled Macha and Tara.

Tara hissed, his eyes flashing with violent intent. But the Tuatha Dé phantom queen only smiled with cruel delight.

"Not yet, Tara," Macha said, dismissing the fae's fury. She leaned close to Ash, invading her space with mocking ease. Tiernan's wings snapped, causing the fae to retreat a few steps under his looming, silent warning.

"What do you want with us?" Ash demanded, inwardly recoiling from Macha's keen scrutiny.

A glimmer shone through the faerie's dark eyes, and then that dreadful echoing voice emerged from the Morrígan's full lips as she cocked her head. "Answers, young matriarch."

Beside Ash, Maebh tensed like a coiled viper, fingers tightening around her blade. Tiernan echoed her readiness, wings parting with a sound like fracturing stone. Maebh's voice was lethally quiet. "Well, we have none to give you, so fuck off."

Tara's face darkened with thunderous rage, but he did not approach. Above, the birds' caws rose to an unbearable shrieking crescendo. Ash glared skyward, noticing not only crows, but magpies writhing as if possessed within the roiling mass.

"One for sorrow, two for mirth," The Morrígan mused before transforming in a flash of feathers before her. Badb was the largest crow of all, flying toward her kin. Words came from its beak. "Three for a funeral, four for a birth."

Before Ash had time to process the old rhyme, they were engulfed in a murky whirlpool of claws, beaks and feathers.

Crying out, she flailed uselessly as the others attempted to free themselves too. She couldn't see beyond their feathery imprisonment as Badb continued her reciting in a sing-song voice. "Five for heaven. Six for hell."

Tara Court came into view once more as the swarms of magpies and crows rose higher, the biggest crow of all at its centre.

Badb's parting words rang through the air. "Seven for the devil, his own self."

The swarm rotated around Tara Court's highwall in a blur. Ash watched in horror as the crows and magpies swirled around the Morrígan in an ever-tightening vortex, their caws building to a deafening cacophony that drowned out all other sounds.

With a shrill screech, the Morrígan unleashed the birds upon the highwall. They descended like an obsidian tide, pecking and clawing relentlessly at the stone; chunks crumbled under the onslaught. The winged beasts crashed into the west wall, and as the inky swarm retreated, their impact left a gaping, smoking hole in the stone skyscraper.

"Archers, prepare and shoot!" Fionn bellowed and warriors sprang into action.

Arrows rained as the swarm advanced from the east, growing closer this time. When the arrows collided with the mass, she saw black winged bodies fall to the ground on impact.

"Take cover!" Ash shouted as arrows landed on the gathered crowd.

Tiernan shielded them with his wings, the thudding of arrows bouncing off his hardened exterior.

"They're killing themselves for this," Ash whispered, her voice a painful wheeze.

Inhuman sounds erupted in the air as the assault on the highwall rained chunks of stone upon them. Fianna ran for cover that was not there as the stone guard shielded who they could. The flock of birds swept toward the highwall again, claws latching onto the stone. The wall crumbled.

Warriors rushed to defend the wall, but the birds attacked in wave after wave, overwhelming anyone who approached. Their beaks and talons tore through armour and flesh with brutal efficiency.

The Morrígan smiled cruelly as she materialised before the High King once more in a flutter of robes. "This is but a taste of the power you seek to challenge, Fionn Mac Cumhaill. Know that we will not be banished so easily."

With a roar of anger, Fionn brandished his blade, but the phantom queen was already dissipating back into shadow, her parting words lingering on the wind as her laugh echoed across the ruined walls. A bone-chilling sound that plunged deeper than any blade, hollow and haunting, it held the promise of torment yet to come.

CHAPTER 72
MAEBH

The chandelier swayed on the ghost of a breeze, casting dancing prisms down the aged table crowded with the leaders of their kingdom. Maebh ignored curious eyes as she traced worn patterns in the wood, acutely aware of Ash and Tiernan sitting tall and steady on either side, and her twin to the left of the raven-haired matriarch. Heaving a weary sigh, she followed the gnarled whorls, finding the tangled threads easier to decipher than her turbulent thoughts.

The four had become objects of focus amongst the enclosing Fianna. Even the stone guardians who stood sentinel along the shadowed walls regarded them with inscrutable masks, a vague interest clinging in each veiled glance. One of their clan had once been human, then reborn in stone, and now revealed to share the Tuatha Dé bloodline with the misfit group of humankind.

Maebh wasn't sure she'd ever accept their mothers had sacrificed them for some dark experiment, unwilling subjects in a power game not of their own making. She glanced at Ash, Setanta and Tiernan: the only people who understood.

Despite the murmurs and distrust wafting from everyone else, her shoulders felt lighter. Deep down, a kernel of relief flared; their shared secret was no longer hidden within shadows. Their clanspeople could either accept or reject them, and

Maebh prepared for both scenarios as she glanced at their High King.

"Three Fianna mothers performed blood rituals with a Fair One. Such union of magic and mankind has granted the four seated amongst us with boons unique to faerie lineage." Fionn's voice vibrated in the air, delivering the truth about their unique abilities. "Though they be of humankind, gifted with Faerie Sight same as us, they bear gifts, privy to the emotional tide, possessors of the sifting skill, and a scarce few hold the rare ability of ríastrad."

His expression brightened on Setanta, and her twin fidgeted in his seat. Her brother's spear illuminated the dimly lit room and Setanta stroked it as if reassuring himself it was still by his side. Scanning him, Maebh looked for any signs of stress or anger. Usually, it was in these situations her brother would need to excuse himself in fear of his ríastrad, and this new calm Setanta was disconcerting.

Biting the inside of her cheek, she searched inward for that spark that whispered peril of her own ríastrad breaking through. Only silence responded and she breathed a sigh. With so much going on, she had tried to ignore the threat that she could transform into a mindless beast, but she'd seen how much pretending it didn't exist had worked for her twin. She could only avoid the inevitable for so long.

Nessa smiled faintly from where she stood, and Maebh had to bite her tongue as Tiernan's mother looked proud at having allowed the Fomorian near her unborn son. It took everything in Maebh to not reach for Tiernan in comfort. A glimpse of him had poked through at the tavern, but it had disappeared just as quickly, and the cold-hearted man had taken over once more.

Waves of empathic energy swelled around Maebh, lapping against her conscious thoughts. Disbelief, shock, then curiosity bloomed like early spring flowers, but it was winter that greeted them, and the frosted thoughts of man would snuff out anything as delicate as an open mind.

Murmurs continued as their emotions struck Maebh. Hints of citrus and flowers assaulted her senses, but there were tangs of vinegar. Eyeing the surrounding leaders, she sensed contempt wafting from Fiadh Collins, one of the victorious matriarchs who'd won the Cath. When their eyes met, the acidic scent intensified, so Maebh smiled smugly as the High King beamed at them.

Fionn's calculative perusal swept over each of the four, lingering with keen scrutiny as if to uncover any untold gifts. Maebh refrained from flinching, tension lashing like a whip beneath his penetrating gaze. She'd had enough of being used in someone else's game. Their High King saw them as weapons to hone, and now it was time to wield them.

Biróg rose from her seat, trailing her fair hands along the high-backed chairs until she stood behind them. Maebh's eyes watered from the incense clinging to the druid's billowing robes. "We must assess their gifts."

Fionn rapped the table. "These gifts will aid our defence against the Fair Ones. They seek to claim *our* people. We will not stand idly by whilst they think to claim governance."

The gathered leaders nodded in agreement, though Maebh noticed more than a few let their eyes dwell on her and the others with covetous intent, hunger for power evident in their appraisal. She glowered at Fionn, unwilling to just accept whatever plans he had in store, but it was her twin who voiced her concern.

"Do we have a say in this?" Set challenged, steadily meeting the High King's eyes.

"You came here to battle in the Cath for the honour of joining our highguard," Fionn stated, leaning back on his chair, scratching his bearded chin. "You have gained the role as rígfénnid due to your loyalty to Fianna. There is no greater calling."

"A greater calling?" Tiernan's deep voice sent a thrill through Maebh, but she refused to glance his way. She had waited so long to hear him speak once more, but she was constantly reminded he was not the same man he once was. Tiernan pressed on even when his mother glared at him. "Or are we a convenient tool for you use?"

A surprised huff of laughter escaped Maebh's lips as she allowed herself to turn in his direction. As ever, he sat tall, crow-black curls twisting around his golden-brown face much like a forest in autumn's waning glow. His cheekbones remained sharply carved as defiance lit within eyes too often locked behind a stoic mask.

Those long-fingered hands, which she knew could wield weapons with lethal grace or dismantle even the most sophisticated computer systems within moments, now lay interlaced upon the table. Tiernan turned his head, penetrating brown eyes finding hers between the small distance between them. A smile tugged at her lips, at the man she remembered gazing back, not just the stone sentinel. When his own lips quirked faintly, barely there but enough to crinkle the corners of his eyes, a thrill rushed through her like quicksilver, igniting other memories she'd tried to bury, but had never forgotten.

Murmurs teetered off as quickly as they started and Tiernan turned once more to their High King. Maebh studied Fionn's face hardening, his focus steady on Tiernan. She could see the calculation behind his eyes, the wheels of strategy already turning within his ancient mind. The room remained silent as everyone waited for his response.

"Your mother risked all to bestow to you these gifts," Fionn finally said. "She knew you would be a beam of hope in dark times."

Ash cleared her throat, pulling all eyes towards her. "We deserve to choose our own paths. And you need to respect that."

Lorcan stepped forward, breaking rank from the stone guard.

"My daughter has a point." He gestured towards the four of them, and Maebh noticed Ash gaped at her father as he continued. "I didn't agree when Cara allowed that witch near our unborn baby."

Bradan knocked on the wooden table, nodding as he looked sadly at his son. Nessa scoffed. Up until now, Maebh had thought the woman incapable of emotion other than mindlessly following Fionn's orders.

"It was a great honour," Nessa stated flatly, staring at her husband. "We chose to give our children the powers of both the gods and fighting men."

Tiernan stiffened beside Maebh, his arm grazing hers, and she dared another glance at him. His expression was a mask of calm, but she noted his bunched fist lowering to his lap.

"What's done is done," Gearoid said as he joined the saga unravelling between their parents. Maebh's chest constricted. He'd arrived at The Raven, but they hadn't spoken since breaking free from stone. And of course, he had to act flippantly about their magic in a room full of Fianna leaders and an ancient High King.

"Our gifts are our own," Maebh said, an angry flush heating her cheeks. "We are not weapons to be wielded."

"More than others, you see what comes to pass beyond these walls," Fionn said, sweeping his hand toward the stained-glass window overlooking Mide. "Your kin fights to shield the human realm, yet fails to prevail. The Taoiseach offers little aid to the fray. We fight for the self-same cause."

"The veil between worlds has vanished," Biróg said, taking her seat once more. "We need more Fianna to join the Druid Order to find ways to restore it."

"Who can join?" Conor asked, and Ash's hand spasmed within Maebh's grip.

"Any Fianna who chooses."

Conor simply nodded at the druid before addressing Fionn. "With your permission, High King, I'd like to join the order."

"Conor, no," Ash exclaimed, shaking her head at the king. "He's my second. I'm not losing another one."

Biróg said, "Aisling, we need to prepare . . ."

"What can't Conor prepare for here with me that he needs to join you for?"

Biróg stared into the distance, wearing an expression Maebh didn't like.

"Conor can aid Biróg in the final clash," Fionn said. "Between light and dark. Shadows and flame. The old gods against the new."

"We haven't agreed to allow you to use our gifts, High King," Ash pounded her fist on the table. "I will agree to whatever you want as long as Conor stays with me."

A shocked murmur rose from those gathered from Ash's bold defiance of the High King and as Maebh caught a dangerous gleam in Fionn's stare, a chill of worry clung to her like a blinding mist crawling across the sea.

Conor whirled to face his sister, leaning across Setanta, brown eyes flashing. "This is my chance to atone for what I've done, Aisling. Don't take this opportunity away from me."

"You haven't done anything of your own accord, Con," Ash's voice was a whispered plea. Maebh gripped Ash's hand tightly as the High King continued to stare at her friend.

Maebh tugged on Ash's hand until she looked at her. "We all have a part to play. If this is what your brother chooses, do you really want to stop him?"

Conor looked at Maebh with gratitude and Ash let out a heavy sigh before slipping her hand away.

"Your gifts were bestowed to serve this kingdom," Fionn's booming voice took control, demanding silence as he spoke. None would be foolish enough to deny him, not even Maebh, as his expression hardened on each of them. "You have no say in how that is achieved. As High King, my word is law."

As Fionn's voice rang out, the tension curling around Maebh tightened around her throat, rendering her speechless. Fionn's words carried unbendable steel, and she knew any defiance was useless.

Her fingers again found the grain of the table, pressing hard enough to leave crescents in the worn wood. When silence fell at the king's command, she noticed her nails had splintered in her grip. The others remained quiet which was as good as accepting the High King's decree.

Extracting her hands slowly, she found half-moons of blood welling from where she'd broken flesh. This was why she was here. What the High King wanted to use. Her blood. The metallic scent helped still the roiling in her gut, focusing her thoughts on pain instead of helplessness.

Thunder struck in the distance, met by a downpour pattering against the surrounding windows. A loud crack followed flashes of forked lightning, matching her mood perfectly.

Whatever was coming, it seemed even the gods themselves were unsure who would claim victory with the veil between realms pierced at last.

CHAPTER 73
AISLING

The Hill of Tara rose in inky shadows beneath a star-dusted sky, the town square shining with dancing orange and gold from the bonfires' scattered glow. The time had come for the Fianna warrior clans to bid farewell to the Land of Eternal Youth, and the High King had ordered a lavish celebratory feast be held at the market square.

Only the finest foods and casks of mead had been brought out for the clans to enjoy one final night together before returning to the human realm and the trials that would face them. Swallowing around a painful lump, Ash clutched her full tankard, unable to battle against the intrusive thought that their High King was merrily fattening the cattle before inevitable slaughter.

Ash's eyes alighted on her brother, who was smiling brightly, his arm slung around Orla's shoulder. The brunette was more subdued than Conor, her gloved hands twitching around his as if she, too, didn't want to let him go. A pang of worry swirled in Ash's gut as she wondered if it was Orla's emotions or her own racing in her heart.

"To new adventures," Ciarán said cheerily, raising his glass to Conor while their cousin embraced him.

The surrounding Breens echoed him as colour rose to Conor's cheeks. Ash couldn't deny the tentative hope within her brother since his decision to join the Druid Order. Taking a sip of her mead, she fought the tremor shaking her tankard. It didn't make it easier to say goodbye.

Market stalls lined the outer rings doing brisk trade in foods, spirits and trinkets, trying to sell their wares one last time to the visitors before their departure.

"Am I forgiven yet?" Maebh said from behind, and Ash turned to see her friend holding a wax paper parcel in an outstretched hand, with garlic and fried potato-infused steam filling the air between them.

Ash smiled, but said, "That depends on whether that food is for me or not."

Maebh angled the bag out of Ash's reach.

"I am not sharing a bag of these 'better than chipper chips' with you again. You scoffed most of them the last time." Maebh stepped forward with a grin before uncovering her other hand where an identical parcel was held. "But I got you one all to yourself."

"You're forgiven." Ash snatched it, inhaling the contents, ignoring the sting of her watering eyes from burying her face in the steaming bag. She followed Maebh to an unoccupied log, and they ate in silence as the sounds of the farewell festival floated around them. Taking hearty bites of the crisp potatoes, she washed the contents down with her remaining mead as she studied her clan, her eyes always finding their way to her brother.

"I wasn't mad at you for siding with Conor to leave," Ash eventually said, bumping Maebh's shoulder.

"Liar," Maebh chuckled around a mouthful of potato. "But I get it."

"We haven't had a proper chance to just be ourselves," Ash sighed, gesturing to their surroundings. "Conor is going all the way to Achill Island. Our clans are returning to the human world while we're expected to just stay here and let them test our gifts."

With every word, Ash's shoulders tensed until she could feel them pressing against her ears. Scrunching up the now empty wrapper, she willed her heart rate to slow down as frustration washed over her. "I don't want to be some lab rat. I want my family to stick together and for us to return to Mary and Dom and the rest of my clan."

Maebh scoffed, but when her eyes met her friend's, they shone with sadness. "I hate to be the one to tell you this, but life sucks and we have to do things we don't want to do all the time."

Ash stood, shaking out her hands, restlessness spasming her nerves into tight knots.

Maebh had a clan to get back to as well, but she didn't have people like Ash's foster parents to be her reason and desire to return. With Tiernan and Set both locked into this side of the veil, she knew she should also want to be here. That part of her heart was here. But she'd travelled between the worlds. She knew the demons they were facing on the other side. Her heart was so completely divided, but Ireland needed saviours.

"Let's go for a walk," Maebh suggested, taking their rubbish and discarding it before linking Ash's arm.

They strolled slowly around the grounds amidst the rubble of the fallen highwall. Staring out at the black sky and silhouetted woodland, Ash studied the newly unprotected Tara Court, no longer sheltered within walls. Although there had been a sense of security with the wall, Ash couldn't help but appreciate how open Tara Court seemed without it. Laughably, the gate still stood, nothing but rubble on either side.

"Where's Setanta?" Maebh asked a little too innocently and Ash bit down on her cheek.

"Don't you have that weird twin thing, so you know where each other are?" Maebh only rolled her eyes and Ash kicked at a loose stone. "He said he'd meet me here in a while."

"Are you two okay?" Maebh probed as they meandered toward the perimeter of the festival.

"Yes," Ash answered quickly, but sighed. "I don't know. We were great and then with everything going on . . ."

"Do you mean my stupid brother lying about Ethne and the Underworld thing?"

"No," Ash said, looking toward the castle with a frown. "We talked through that. Ever since the giants attacked, he's been distant."

"We're all a little stressed." Maebh said before shoving Ash playfully. "And I also thought I told you McQuillans are assholes."

"You might have mentioned that, yes."

Ash scanned the rowdy festival crowd, laughter and merriment flowing thanks to free-flowing ale. A commotion across the grounds drew her attention.

"Isn't that your . . . friend?" Ash pointed toward a short brunette tavern wench.

A group of men swarmed around her, their laughter a little too loud as they stood far too close to the púca. Maebh nodded as she glared at the group. Even at a distance, the barmaid's distress was palpable.

"She doesn't know how to fully behave like us yet," Maebh said, pulling Ash into a quick pace toward the group. "I've seen her glamour slip before."

"Why doesn't she leave?" Ash asked, as she picked up her pace. "If she's caught . . ."

Ash didn't need to finish her sentence. Exchanging a knowing look with Maebh, the two women broke into a jog, but a red-haired highguard bet them to it.

"Leave the girl alone, lads," he said as the women approached.

"We're just having fun with the wench!" a warrior slurred, saluting an empty tankard toward the púca.

"Sage doesn't look like she's having fun," Maebh said; her stare had an icy edge that threatened violence. "So, I'd listen to Michàel and back the fuck off."

The men did as ordered, but the mouthy one retorted. "She won't say where she's from or who her kin are."

Michàel smiled, showcasing a dimple. "It's your last night here. Don't end up in the dungeons for bothering a local."

With the men dispersing reluctantly, Sage's shoulders sagged, but the tray she held shook enough that empty tankards spilled from it.

"Let me help," Michàel said, hunkering to pick up the fallen cups.

Ash spotted a flash of gold in the barmaid's eyes as her glamour briefly slipped. Maebh stepped in between Michàel and the púca.

"I'll take that tray, Sage," Ash said, as Maebh grabbed the items from Michàel, who now stood, eyeing the púca.

Ash dared a glance and grimaced at the shadow of animal features painting her face in flashes.

"Who are your kin, Sage?" the highguard asked, ignoring Maebh's attempts at shooing him away.

"I . . ." the púca stammered, slitted eyes flashing to Maebh's.

"It doesn't matter," Maebh said through gritted teeth, pushing the tankards back into Michael's chest. "Make yourself useful and put these somewhere."

A crash sounded as Maebh released the empty cups and Michàel made no attempt at catching them. He stepped over them as the women moved away.

"She needs to come with me."

"Well, she's not," Maebh said, her hand going to her sword hilt.

The highguard didn't miss the motion. "Maebh . . ."

"Everything okay here?" Set's deep voice interrupted the highguard and Ash let out a sigh of relief.

"We're fine," Maebh said, her eyes never leaving the highguard's. "Micháel was just leaving."

He looked ready to protest when Maebh added, "Don't you have somewhere to be? There are dodgy places in this town that need patrolling."

Micháel glared at the matriarch, and they seemed to have a silent stand-off before he stepped away without answering.

"What was that about?" Set asked, taking the tray from Ash.

"Nothing," Maebh said, putting a protective arm around the shaking púca. "I'm going to take Sage home."

Set sighed as they watched the two disappear through the crowd. "If she's caught . . ."

"I know," Ash said, biting her lower lip. "Maebh says she sees this as her home, so she has nowhere else to go."

"Conor told me to tell you he's gone to bed."

When Ash arched an eyebrow, he smirked. "Orla left with him."

"That makes more sense. Little shit could have said goodnight though."

She contemplated following him, but they had a few days before he would leave for Achill Island. As Ash regarded the revelries unfolding, strains of tension took hold behind her eyes. The din of celebration rose to heights that became unbearable after the worries weighing on her throughout the gathering. She would scold Conor tomorrow.

"I have an early meeting tomorrow with Fionn before sunrise. It's the first time he's called on me personally."

"What do you think it's about?" Ash crossed her arms tight across her chest, drumming her fingers in a staccato beat as she weighed possibilities, but Set shrugged, not seeming too concerned.

"I'm sure it's something to do with me being rígfénnid but also 'blood-blessed'. Even though I have to leave early . . ." Set hesitated, clearing his throat and she stepped closer to peer up at his flushed face.

They stared at one another, unspoken words crackling in the space between them. As she looked up at Set, bathed in moonlight that highlighted his rugged features and intense grey eyes, she marvelled at his breathtaking beauty. Licking her lips, she whispered, "Remember, you can be yourself around me."

Set tucked a strand of hair behind her ear, his fingers lingering. "I'd love for you to stay with me tonight."

She shivered at his touch, and she leaned into him, pressing her face against his hard chest as she wound her arm around his waist.

"Take me to bed, Setanta McQuillan."

The night was a black vortex, swallowing the moon and stars as rows of caravans ignited in a booming symphony of destruction, fiery tongues lapping at the velvety sky. The air was thick with acrid smoke as flames licked at the metal homes, but Ash was frozen. Made from stone. Fighting against her imprisonment, she tracked dark shadows swarming the caravans, preventing anyone from escaping.

Screams filled the sky and Ash banged against the stone, unable to do anything but watch as her family burned. The world burned, and she welcomed the host of sluagh who swirled around her, ready to embrace the death they offered . . .

"I've come to warn you," a lilting voice said to her right before Ethne appeared.

Turning from stone to flesh once more, Ash still couldn't prise her eyes away from the flaming caravans as hands pounded on windows.

"Listen to me, Aisling." Ethne stood before her, and she gasped as warmth rushed to her limbs. Pushing the Fomorian out of the way, Ash stumbled, falling to her knees on the soot-covered ground. The caravans were no longer alight with flames, but carcasses of metal with no sign of life. Ash didn't need to investigate further to know that everyone was dead.

"Get out of my head," Ash croaked, glaring up at the female. "This is a nightmare."

"Just because you don't like what's happening, doesn't mean I'm lying." Ethne's face etched with lines that almost passed off as concern. "I helped you free Tiernan. I did that for you because he's part of your clan. I'm on your side whether you agree with my actions or not."

"You only do things for your own gain," Ash hissed, standing on shaking limbs.

"What my plans are have nothing to do with this." Ethne swept an arm toward the burnt-out caravans, grabbing Ash's shoulders and shaking her. "I want you on my side, and that won't happen if your family is dead."

"You killed my mother so why—"

"Conor killed your mother."

Ash reared back as if Ethne's words slapped her. Clenching her fists, she invaded the other woman's space. "You did it. You made him!"

Ethne's eyes turned skyward before her shoulders sagged. "We don't have time for this. Heed my warning or don't. Your foster parents will die this night."

Screams echoed in the surrounding wind, along with unearthly screeches and Ash bit down on a sob. "What is that?"

"When you blew on the Dord Fiann, the veils disintegrated, and Fomorians were freed once more. There are creatures from the very pits of the Underworld that even I can't control." Ethne swirled her hands until blackness formed; a bright light punctured the darkness until a long shaft formed. "You will need this in order to sift to the human realm."

"What?" Ash stared at Set's spear as Ethne ushered her closer to the caravans. But she dug her heels into the ruined earth, her boots digging up black soil. "I can ask Set to bring me."

"You may ask, Aisling, but if he says no and takes his spear, what will you do then? He may not be willing to leave Tara Court. Are you willing to take the risk?" Ethne only shook her head, her grey eyes wide as she licked her lips.

The surrounding air swirled once more until they were within Set's castle room.

Gasping, Ash stared at her sleeping form wrapped in Set's arms, their tangled forms illuminated by a dying fire. As she fought for a calmness that would not come, anger burned within her.

"Get out of my head." She needed to wake up.

"Not until you realise the truth." Ethne stood over Set, leaning down as if to stroke a wayward strand of hair from his peaceful face. Instead, she picked up the spear that had been leaning against the wall, always within his reach.

"Leave that alone," Ash demanded, storming over to the Fomorian.

Ethne was a manipulator, but as Ash stood before her, the smell of burnt metal seeped between them. Ethne whipped her head to the side as if she could hear something Ash could not. "They are here! Quick. Use the spear to save your family."

Ethne pressed it against Ash's chest, and they both stared down at the brightening tip. Screams filled the room and Ash sobbed as she heard the distinct voices of Mary and Dom, followed by the cries of children and her remaining Breen clan.

Her clan needed her. Even if they were safe, she needed to know. If Set's spear worked, she wouldn't need to wait for him to sift her to them. She looked at his sleeping form as she stood over the bed, arms tight around the sleeping version of herself. This had to be a dream, but why did it feel so real?

"Take it!" Ethne screamed, pressing it painfully into her chest.

A weight landed in her gut as she realised her hesitation could have already cost her family their lives. She snatched the spear.

Ash gasped at its coldness; so severe it burned, spreading from where her palms touched the steel, melding to her skin. Her vision blurred until she blinked, and Ethne had disappeared, along with her sleeping form beside Set. It had been a dream. And she was standing over Set with the spear she'd promised never to touch clasped in her grip.

A humming electricity sliced through her flesh, entering her veins to pump through her body as the spear came alive from her touch. Arching, she cried out, but no sound escaped as the rushing energy clawed and dug until it penetrated her soul. But it didn't stop there. Nausea churned her stomach as the energy began devouring her essence until she felt herself being altered into something . . . tainted.

An unearthly growl emanated from the bed, and Ash's eyes whipped to Set, his face a grotesque crimson as fury and betrayal filled his eyes.

"Set . . ."

No words found their way to her as finally, she was released from whatever force had taken hold. The spear clattered to the floor, rolling toward the bed. A crack formed from the tip and she watched in horror as the blue hue raced from the spear toward the man she loved —her feelings trapped behind unspoken words.

In one heartbeat, Set stared at her, and in the next his ríastrad rose from the bed, charging toward her.

She had no time to cry out as his hand swatted her away and she soared across the room before crashing against the opposite wall. Breath choked in her lungs as her head swam.

"Set!"

But she was too late. Set was no longer a man. The ríastrad had broken loose in the castle.

CHAPTER 74
TIERNAN

Tiernan hurried through the populated streets, keenly aware of the stone guardians' displeasure echoing through the hive mind. Nessa's scolding was the loudest, but he pushed her voice away, focusing his mind on navigating through Tara Court without talking to anyone.

Everyone he passed kept their distance. When he caught their gawking, most turned away apologising or pretended they hadn't been staring. Others openly kept eye contact, but they seemed to sense his emotions as much as he could theirs and they stayed out of his way.

The towering temples sprang up and it wasn't until he slowed his pace that he realised he'd entered a district he'd never intended on visiting. Incense and burnt offerings assaulted him and he climbed steep steps to a temple, not caring which Tuatha Dé god he was about to disturb.

He just needed peace. He couldn't find it with the incessant buzzing of the guardians, or the prying stares of Fianna waiting for him to turn to stone or sprout wings. Bunching his already stiff shoulders, he stuffed his hands deep into his pockets as he pushed open the tall wooden doors into an antechamber. The fragrance of damp, mossy stone walls greeted him as his eyes adjusted to the dim lighting, a subtle underlying sweetness of brine and musk as trickling water echoed from the next chamber.

Peering around the corner, he was greeted by a water fountain carved from limestone. A club jutted out from the centre of the cauldron-shaped base, water gushing from its tip. The glow of countless candles cast dancing shadows upon stony walls, and Tiernan sighed in relief when it became clear nobody else was there.

Sinking into the smooth stone seat adjoining the fountain, Tiernan smiled as faint mist caressed his weary skin. The constant gurgle of water soothed his frayed nerves, so he exhaled a long, drawn-out sigh, his hands resting on the moss-covered stone in a bid to feel the latent energy that resided there. Before he'd been trapped in Fionn's cave, he'd have argued over whether the Tuatha Dé gods existed, or what true magic was. He was no fool. Fianna knew of Fair Ones, of the power of a binding geas. But technology and science had been easy to understand. To explain away what he couldn't.

He took deep breaths, drawing in the earthen atmosphere, the lingering scent of the burning beeswax candles, the faint aroma of fresh harvest offerings in the air. He was no longer that scientific man and was now torn between a life he couldn't go back to and one he couldn't escape.

Each intake of air felt like an invitation to tranquillity, a soft note to let himself go, but he couldn't. Not yet. Letting his eyelids flutter shut, he focused on forming a shield around his mind, welcoming the darkness that promised a peaceful solitude from his stone clan. The chair was cold beneath him, but the atmosphere was not chilling; it was warm, like a comforting blanket on a winter's night.

The deep silence in the temple amplified every sound: the fall of water, the distant rustling of leaves outside, the whispering echoes of flame against wick. His eyes jolted open as the faint scrape of the heavy wooden door interrupted his pursuit of peace. The slight rhythmic crunch of gravel beneath boots indicated an arrival, but he knew that smell. A natural hint of jasmine mixed with the added perfume of myrrh and tonka bean she favoured.

Closing his eyes again, he listened to the familiar footsteps approach.

"You chose the Dagda's temple to hide out?" Maebh chuckled. "You know what they say about a man's club size?"

Tiernan's lips tugged into an amused smile and when he cracked one eye open, she was standing in front of the fountain, measuring the water club with her hands. He barked a laugh and surprised them both as she turned, her blue eyes wide as she scanned his face.

"I thought I'd never hear that sound again," she said after a beat.

He swallowed, nodding, his voice soft but steady. "Neither did I."

Slowly, day by day, he'd fought to gain a semblance of who he'd once been. Tiernan hadn't thought he cared to venture back into that life, but ever since he waited expectantly for Maebh to look at him at The Raven, frustration eating at him when she hadn't, Tiernan had decided that maybe he could try.

Her footsteps drew closer, her enticing woodsy evergreen perfume infusing the already potent air. Warmth radiated from her as she lowered herself onto the seat next to him. His stone clan filtered through for a heartbeat, but gritting his teeth, he slammed the shield into place, and profound silence pervaded his mind once more.

"Where do you go?" Maebh asked, her tone subdued as she studied him.

He momentarily averted his eyes to the fountain. His mother would reprimand him for this, but why did it matter if he shared the truth with Maebh? They were linked by Tuatha Dé blood.

There were far more secrets revealed about the four of them than the stone guardian clan had combined.

"We can communicate," Tiernan started, tapping his forehead until Maebh's eyes softened in understanding. "I've learned how to shut them out, but it can get overwhelming."

"And when you were trapped in stone?" she leaned closer, her eyes devouring him as if she feared that he would disappear once she looked away. Or perhaps she feared he would stop speaking.

He wasn't entirely sure why he *was* talking, but he opened his mouth once more. "I could hear and see you. But I would also lose myself to the stone call." He paused, looking for words to explain. "I'd black out and wake up, fighting to hold on to who I was. And I lost more times than I can count."

"Do you remember anything from before?" Maebh's voice was barely above a whisper, almost too hard to hear over the cascading water.

Somehow, they'd leaned closer, her warm breath on his face. Her tongue darted out to lick her bottom lip and his eyes homed in on the movement before being ensnared once more by her intense scrutiny.

"I remember . . . some things."

She smiled then and warmth spread to his cheeks, but it also pooled lower.

"You touched me," she said, before leaning away. "At The Raven. You touched my hand as if looking for a reaction. What did you hope would happen?"

"I don't know." He shrugged, leaning back against the cold stone. "I didn't like that you wouldn't look at me. So, I decided to make you."

"Tiernan . . ."

His name on her lips. Damn. He hadn't remembered how that made him feel. Lifting his hand, he traced her jaw, revelling in the hitch in her breath. When she didn't move away, he scooted closer, using his other hand to push back her curls to reveal more of her face.

"You're beautiful," he commented, gripping her chin to angle her face closer. "Can I kiss you?"

"I promised myself I'd wake you up," she whispered, enclosing her hands over the grip he held on her face. "I hated that we'd left things the way we had. But you're not the man you once were."

She pulled away, and he let his hands drop. She sighed as she looked at the fountain. "I don't think you want to kiss me. I think you only want to remember."

Tiernan cocked his head. "So, is that a no?"

She whipped her head back to him and he gripped her jacket lapels, bringing her close. He leaned in slowly, giving her time to pull away and smiled when she froze as still as a rabbit caught by a fox.

His lips brushed against hers lightly before he tugged on her bottom lip. When she made a delicious, startled moan, he moved his hands up to the nape of her neck, angling her so he could deepen their kiss.

A sharp tugging sensation seized Tiernan, an invisible force wrenching at the very core of his being. The boundaries between his consciousness and another's blurred into a disorienting dance. Flashes, like vivid lightning bolts, erupted before his eyes, each image carrying a weight that reverberated through his soul.

Red splattered across the walls like a grotesque painting, and a cry tore through the fabric of his consciousness. With a desperate jolt, Tiernan recoiled, tearing himself away from the haunting visions that were no longer his own, left breathless and haunted.

"Tiernan, what is it?" Maebh's panicked voice was distant. A thousand layers lay between her and where he'd been sucked into. He was no longer in his body, but within the minds of the stone guard.

"Something is wrong," he managed through gritted teeth.

The air grew heavy as Tiernan found himself thrust into the midst of emotions not his own, the echo of Nessa's anguish resonating in his chest. Gasping, his shield crumbled as the entire stone clan's devastation barricaded into him. Sharp claws slashed, blood spraying through the air.

"Come back to me!" Maebh's plea echoed through the recesses of Tiernan's consciousness like a distant cry, a desperate tether trying to pull him from the abyss.

Blinking, he found himself kneeling by the fountain, Maebh standing over him. Agony ripped through Tiernan's body as he fought for control over his limbs. He curled into a ball on the floor, battling waves of nausea and disorientation. Every muscle protested as he fought against the invisible currents, his mind a battleground where understanding and confusion waged war.

Agony, sharp and unrelenting, tore through Tiernan's body, but he stood.

"I need to get to the castle."

Maebh nodded and without hesitation, enveloped him in a tight embrace. His hands encircled her waist instinctively, but she wasn't trying to comfort him as a tingling sensation wracked his body.

The world outside their embrace faded into obscurity when a moment of all-consuming black descended, as if the universe itself had folded into an impenetrable void. In that breathless instance, time lost its grip, and the boundaries between them blurred.

He blinked and they were kneeling before Fionn's throne. Warm, sticky liquid coated his hands, and he looked down to see blood. Everywhere.

"What happened?" Maebh asked in a rushed tone and his head snapped upward to survey the surrounding room.

The stone guard circled them, blood and gore coating their terror-stricken faces. Piles of armour scattered the floor, and Tiernan stood on shaky legs, avoiding using his bloodied hands.

Nobody spoke and he took in the scattered bundles of clothing on the ground once more until he saw an unmistakable shape.

Horror tore through his entire body as he realised what he'd thought was abandoned armour and clothing were body parts. And feet away beside the bloodstained throne lay Fionn Mac Cumhaill's severed head.

CHAPTER 75

MAEBH

Maebh's ragged breath was all she could hear, standing alongside Tiernan as the stone guardians pieced Fionn back together on a stretcher. She stood motionless as Gearoid and Lorcan stayed beside the High King's remains, while some of the guard carried their ravaged burden to the men to put in order.

Biróg stood with other druids on the raised platform housing an empty throne, chanting solemn hymns. Their voices echoed melodies throughout the expansive room, sending prayers of safe passing to the heavens. Thick incense wafted from gold thuribles, spiralling in fragrant clouds alongside the iron tang of blood in the air. The acrid scents should have jarred Maebh, yet they only seemed to push her further adrift.

Sounds blurred together into white noise within the cocoon of detachment wrapping tightly around her thoughts.

"Oh, gods." Biting on her tongue, her lips twitched.

Shivers took control of her body, racking violently through her as muted conversations drifted around the room as they assembled the king.

"Why are you smiling?" Tiernan's voice broke through the fog, and her focus whipped to his face.

His brown skin was ashen, smudges of blood smeared where he'd unwittingly touched his face. Maebh's attention jolted to the place where she'd sifted them, their footsteps marred in red, tracking them to this spot.

She sucked in her lips. "I'm sorry."

She coughed before taking a deep breath and releasing it, the sound obnoxiously loud despite her efforts to contain it. Others turned her way, a mixture of baleful looks and scowls directed at her. Coughing again, she worded 'sorry' once more while Tiernan's dark eyes burned into her skin. With flushed cheeks, she dared another look at him.

"It's just . . . I can't help the rhyme going round in my head. And all the king's men couldn't put . . ."

A hysterical choke escaped her mouth and Tiernan gripped her arm, guiding her behind the throne. When a guard tried to stop him, he murmured something she couldn't hear as she fought to contain herself. What was wrong with her? Her throat constricted in a violent spasm; a burning sensation that refused to be quelled despite how hard she swallowed.

One hand flew to her mouth, failing to contain the ragged hacks being torn from deep within her chest. Tears sprang to her eyes from the rawness in her throat. Tiernan's blood-slicked hand gripped her tighter, dragging her through a curtained doorway.

The space was cool, with dimly-lit sconces illuminating the windowless room. Maebh hunched over, pressing into her sides as her heart burned. Gasping for breath, she followed Tiernan's movements as he opened another door, beckoning for someone and speaking quietly. Maebh willed her breath to steady, but an uncontrollable gasp broke loose, and she slumped to the floor until more tears sprung forth.

Visions of Fionn's dismembered body forced themselves through closed lids and she shuddered as bile crawled up her throat. Through watery eyes, Tiernan's face reappeared. He raised something close to her cheek, before murmuring, "May I?"

She didn't look away from his intense brown eyes, nodding as she finally quietened. A soft, warm cloth met her cheek, and she shivered as Tiernan swiped in gentle strokes.

"What do you see?" Tiernan asked, his voice a steady presence in the unfamiliar room.

"You," she breathed out, the word barely intelligible.

Tiernan's eyes met hers with steady care. Though shadowed by what they'd just faced, and the time spent underground, his face remained as angular and handsome as she'd remembered. Clean lines and tawny skin embraced full lips that curved gently now in a small, reassuring smile meant for her alone.

"Now, look behind me to the door at my back."

Frowning, she did. He spoke again. "To me and then back to the door. Keep going."

As her eyes darted in the pattern he instructed, Tiernan continued to wipe her face until he lifted a hand, swiping the cloth through her fingers before gently guiding it into a basin of warm water on the floor beside them.

Through the fitted fabric of his worn leathers, Maebh glimpsed lithe muscle shifting subtly with his graceful movements. Tiernan had always been strong, but as his coiled power rippled; it was clear he'd changed since turning into stone. Maebh bit her lip. The man had wings. She looked behind him once more, as if the thought of those wings would force them to sprout from his back again. Nothing but the cool air and shadowed doorway met her eyes.

"You're in shock." Tiernan rubbed in gentle circles, and she glanced down at the murky water, her heartbeat racing in her ears. "Keep looking behind me and back. Don't look at the water, Maebh."

Her name in his deep voice lifted her from the spiral she'd begun. Nodding, she concentrated on the repetitive action while Tiernan finished washing away evidence of what lay in the room behind. When he'd hastily cleaned his own hands and face, he sat cross-legged in front of her. There was nothing to be done with their clothes, and she shivered in revulsion at the cold patches of congealing blood on her knees.

"Thanks," she croaked, as shivers continued to travel around her body. "How are you so calm?"

"I'm not," he sighed before clasping his long fingers and resting his arms on his legs. "I'm linked in with the hive mind and we're helping each other remain focused right now."

Maebh nodded, swallowing painfully. She could really do with a drink. "What's happening in there? Is my dad okay?"

"He's fine. Like me, Gearoid is tapping into the collective calm we are providing each other. They've moved Fionn and have called the leaders to the throne room. They've cleaned up the blood as best they could."

Maebh shivered as the reality of what had happened kicked in. She jumped to her feet, the room turning stifling and the need to flee overwhelming. "Was anyone else hurt? Do they know who did it?"

"Aedan was killed and a few highguard." Tiernan angled his head before nodding, but it wasn't at her.

She cursed quietly, imagining the former High King who had been part of Tiernan's stone clan. The man who had told her that if he wanted her to bark like a dog, kiss his feet or sing him a song, then she'd do it; the man who had sent them in pursuit of a fairytale to suit his own selfish whims, holding them to ransom with the freedom of Conor and the caillte. His megalomaniac quest had led to Tiernan becoming trapped in Fionn's cave.

As she studied Tiernan, he didn't seem affected by the death of his clan member, someone he had called 'Uncle Aeden' as a child. She couldn't blame him for that. Nor could she take his expressions at face value anymore. His eyes focused again, and he stood. "Come on, they want us back in there."

When they entered the throne room, Maebh scanned the changes, searching through the crowded faces for a familiar one. Relief arrived when her feet carried her unerringly toward her father. His cold eyes landed on her, but there was a flicker she'd learned to look out for. A spark of recognition from the man who'd given her life.

She wordlessly embraced him, shivering at the chill emanating from his body. A few heartbeats later, strong arms wrapped around her shoulders, Gearoid's chin resting on her head. Withdrawing, she peered up to see his reassuring nod, the simple gesture calming her mounting fears. He was still in there. And so was Tiernan.

Maebh released him, turning to take in the rest of the room. No sign of Fionn's body or the destruction caused. Stains still marred the once pristine marble floors. Their High King hadn't been awake for long, but his ancient wisdom and assertive reactions to the threats they'd faced had been welcome to many Fianna. Maebh hadn't agreed with every decision, but he'd been a far better leader than Tiernan's father. Without Fionn's imposing presence, she'd never realised how small the throne room was.

"Ash!" Maebh's pace quickened at the sight of her friend, cringing at the squelching of blood-soaked boots with every step.

Drawing her into an embrace, Maebh was jarred at her rigidness, Ash barely returning her hug. It was unlike the strong matriarch to seem so diminished, emotions locked away where Maebh could find no purchase. Maebh searched her strained pale features. Something darker simmered underneath.

Breaking away, trepidation creeped into her tone at the hollow emptiness within Ash's eyes. "Are you okay?"

"It was him," Ash whispered, emerald eyes glistening as they finally met hers. Ash's limp touch turned vice-like as she pulled her friend closer still. Then Maebh noticed it: beneath mingled scents of the cleaning products used within the room, Ash emanated a cloying stench that assaulted Maebh's senses. The odour was acrid, like ashes left in the rain. "It was him."

Maebh didn't breathe as her attention darted to those assembled. Scanning the room twice to no hint of her brother, ice coated her insides as she pulled out of Ash's grip, shaking her head. "What are you saying? It was who?"

But Maebh knew who Ash was talking about. Knew the name that would stain her tongue.

"We caught the murderer!" Thunderous footsteps followed Deaglán Collins as he led his clan through the open doors.

A wide grin spread across his face as they marched to the front of the throne. Someone unseen struggled as men pulled a short figure along. A soft whimper escaped their prisoner before the warriors parted, revealing Sage, gagged and bound by iron manacles. Sage's face was contorted in pain and terror, her yellow slitted eyes widening into a plea as they found Maebh. Panic rent through Maebh's chest and a suffocating dread settled over her.

"What are you doing?" she demanded, pushing through the gathered crowd, but several hands gripped her, forcing her back.

She tried again, but a wall of men blocked her path. Maebh's eyes narrowed on the exposed skin where the púca was bound. It was singed and discoloured, welts forming where the iron touched her.

"Get those off her!"

"And have the púca shift back into the monster who tore our High King apart?" Deaglán sneered. He moved his clan aside to step face to face with her. They were the same height, but Maebh tilted her head to look down on him. He pushed a stray hair from her face and she lurched back, but his guard held her firmly in place as he cupped her chin painfully. "I recall seeing you several times with this creature. Either you're a stupid bitch who couldn't see through the monster's glamour, or you have been harbouring a Fair One in our kingdom. Which one is it?"

Maebh jerked her head, biting his sweaty fingers and clamping down when he tried to pull away. It took five guards to help him prise her mouth open and release their rígfénnid. With no little amount of satisfaction, she spat out Deaglán's blood on the ground between them. The rígfénnid charged toward her, but Ash stood in front, a dagger angled between them. Pressing it to his throat, she pivoted, eyes trained on his men until they released Maebh.

With her back hand, Maebh wiped his blood from her mouth, smearing it across her chin with a feral smile. "Touch me again without permission, and you'll lose those fingers."

"Enough," a soft voice spoke from the throne, and gasps echoed through the room.

Maebh didn't need to turn to know Ethne had appeared. Heart thundering in her ears, she shoved past the guards, willing her breath to remain even as she stared at her mother's murderer.

"Seize her," Ash demanded.

But nobody moved.

CHAPTER 76

MEABH

E thne chuckled. "That won't be necessary."

She wore a white dress that matched her skin so perfectly it appeared she wore nothing at all. Indeed, the fabric was sheer enough to display her colourful tattoos. She lounged on the throne, her legs dangling over an armrest as she surveyed the surrounding Fianna with a mirthful smile.

Motioning carelessly with her fingers, Set and the other rígfénnid strode out from the room Tiernan had taken Maebh to. Facing the crowd, Set's face was colder than ice as he clutched his spear.

"Setanta?" Maebh took a step forward and her twin's eyes narrowed in on her.

Pain emanated from him, but he shook his head. "Don't come any closer, Maebh." Set announced to the gathering, "The rígfénnid declare Ethne no longer an enemy to the Fianna."

"What the fuck are you talking about?" Maebh glared at Setanta, but he would not meet her eyes.

"The High King's wounds were not of this earth," Ethne announced, and the room fell silent, except for Sage who continued to whimper as they dragged her before the throne. "Only the touch of a Fair One could have inflicted such injuries."

"You're twisting the truth," Ash retorted, fury in her voice as she pushed through Deaglan's clan to stand with Maebh.

"I have no need," Ethne replied calmly, rotating in the royal seat to sit upright, commanding the attention of all as she motioned to the púca. "The evidence points to one culprit."

Maebh cut in, angrily. "Sage is no killer!"

Despite Ash's insinuation, she knew Sage didn't deserve to be blamed for this murder. There had to be another explanation. One that didn't involve Setanta or Sage.

Ethne kept her gaze steady. "The wounds match the claws of a shifting púca."

Maebh's hands trembled as she hunkered beside Sage, desperately searching for a solution to free her friend without the keys. Because that's what the Fair One had become. A creature from their enemies, but one of the few souls within this room she'd trust with her life. The púca's pitiful headshake sent a pang through Maebh as she fought against the gravity of their situation.

"It's no use," Sage whispered, her voice hoarse. "They've already decided my fate."

Ash came into view, blocking Sage from Ethne. "Your false 'justice' will only breed more chaos. We both know who killed Fionn."

A loud clatter of steel against marble echoed through the silent room and Maebh stared down at Set's spear rolling from the platform before it stopped by Ash's feet. Maebh tracked her twin's furious face as his eyes bored into Ash. He asked coldly, "And whose fault is it truly, Aisling?"

"Set," Ash said shakily. She stepped closer but stopped when Set glared at her, a rumbling snarl layered with the threat of violence filling the stifling air.

"Setanta," Maebh warned, but he ignored her.

Ash took another small step, raising her hands, palms up. "Set, it was an accident."

"Killing the High King is no accident, child," Ethne said firmly. "Order must be restored and the guilty punished."

Maebh met Ethne's eyes as she stood. "But Sage is innocent!"

Ethne arched an eyebrow. "You have evidence to prove this?"

"We don't need to hear any more," Deaglán said before plucking Sage up by her shirt and shoving her closer to the throne. "Let's get this over with."

Set looked to Ethne, who nodded at him, and Maebh's body turned to lead. Why was her brother following her orders? Why was everyone allowing the Fomorian to remain seated on the dead king's throne?

"Stop it, Setanta, *please!*" Maebh begged, but she couldn't move her limbs.

Her brother wasn't going to kill Sage. He couldn't.

Set's footsteps thudded against the steps as he inched closer to Sage, glowering down at her. Unbuckling his axe, Set's grip tightened around the hilt, but before he could raise it, Ash sprang forward, grabbing the discarded spear and the world slowed down so much so that Maebh noticed the tip of the spear had fractured as it swiped upward in a wide arc. Her beating heart decreased with time as she witnessed Ash's attack on her twin.

The broken tip grazed his skin.

Time shifted back in place once a curse left Set's lips and he stumbled back, a hand covering his left eye. Maebh cried out, rushing to his side, fear churning her stomach at the spreading crimson staining his fingers. Gently pulling his hand away, she gasped to find his eye intact, but the surrounding skin sliced, blood flowing freely from the wound.

Her fingers trembled as they cupped his cheek. "Setanta, are you okay?"

But he ignored her, wrenching out of her touch, his glare focused solely on Ash as he backed away. Whirling toward Ash, Maebh snarled. "Why the hell did you do that?"

Ash held Maebh's glare, green eyes brimming with anguished pleading before looking beyond her to the platform, spear quivering where it remained grasped in her white-knuckled hand. Her attention shifted back to Setanta as he dabbed at his wound.

Despite the growing murmurs from the gathering, Ash's voice rang loudly through the room. "Don't kill another innocent, Setanta. This isn't you. I know it isn't."

Her words were thrown between them, and Maebh couldn't help feeling the weight of them land.

A sickening slice filled the air, followed by a gasp and a thud. Maebh swivelled to find Sage lying on her side, blood pooling from her neck. Deaglán wiped his blade, looking down at the púca with a sneer, as if cleaning her blood from his sword was somehow the púca's fault. Every sense became painfully heightened, each minute detail etching itself into perfect clarity against the horror unfolding.

"Sage!" Maebh cried out, falling on her knees, scooping the fae's head into her lap. A cry out for help almost passed her lips, but as she looked at the surrounding hardened faces, she swallowed it down.

A shadow crossed over them and Maebh's eyes widened as she turned, only to find Tiernan standing above, his features etched with grim resignation.

"No," Maebh gasped, heart sinking as she turned to gently stroke the fae's hair away from her round face, desperate to shield her from this impending tragedy.

Sage lifted her bound hands weakly to the wound on her neck, staring up at Maebh with wide eyes as blood spilled over her quivering fingers. A sickening gurgling filled the air as her body spasmed. Maebh's heart shattered as she tasted tears at the back of her throat.

"It's going to be okay," Maebh whispered the lie in an attempt to paint over the harsh canvas of reality.

She implored the heavens silently while comforting the dying fae with soothing words. But the gods would not listen, no matter how much Maebh prayed, begged, or bargained. Her words were empty vessels, clanging in the space between them, their lack of meaning even more poignant.

The púca convulsed until her body stilled. Maebh jerked her hands away as Sage shifted, brown hair receding from her head only to cover her entire body as her true form took hold. Gold slitted eyes stared up at nothing, framed in coarse fur along her small body.

Strong hands rested gently on Maebh's shoulders, tugging her, but she shoved them off. Wrapping Sage into the clothing that no longer fit, she bundled her into her arms before letting Tiernan help her stand. Her body shuddered violently as she stared up at Ethne and then her brother.

Setanta swallowed, his jaw setting into a stubborn resolve that had always infuriated her. She swayed on her feet, the world blurring as shock and rage battered her from within like an unrelenting storm.

"And this is the monster you're all afraid of? This is the creature you say killed our High King?" She spun in a circle, glaring at the men and women staring in dismay at the bundle in her arms, small enough to be a toddler. When she faced her brother once more, she screamed. "How could you stand with her? Against me?"

Setanta's expression hardened as he lowered his hand, blood still trickling from the deep wound across his eye. He glared at the person who had scarred him. "It was Ash who betrayed me first."

"That's not a fucking answer. I'm your sister. Your twin!"

Maebh lunged forward, propelled by a surge of desperation that eclipsed reason, but Tiernan's grip was an immovable force against her frantic struggle. Panic crawled across her heated skin as she cursed and growled at him, the raw urgency in her voice not lost on her as she tightened her hold on Sage.

"Tiernan, damn it, let me go!" Maebh's voice quivered, the leash holding her rage weakening.

A spine-melting dread welled up from within as her ríastrad, too close to awakening, surfaced. Her restraint was not for the fear of what would befall her, but the dreadful anticipation of the havoc she was capable of wreaking if her shackles were cast away. The walls within wavered ominously, as if a battering ram pummelled against them.

"Maebh," Tiernan cautioned, his breath warm against her ear and she glared at him.

Her ríastrad clawed, gnashing its teeth at the bonds holding her true self captive, each snarl resonating within until a few broke through her throat. Sealing her lips, she looked down at the lifeless form cradled in her arms. This being, its innocence and curiosity, had kindled a spark in a secluded chamber of her heart, an area she never imagined could bear affection towards a creature of the fae.

"Maebh," Tiernan said again, more forcefully. His eyes pinned her before moving purposively to their surroundings. Maebh blinked, holding the heavy weight of Sage against her chest as she took in the many Fianna—highguard, stone clan and warrior—standing in defensive poses. Against them.

Maebh searched her father's expression. Even though he'd broken through before, the man before her was not her father.

"Tiernan. Come," Nessa commanded from her position.

Maebh swallowed her disgust at the woman when Tiernan spasmed before his face slackened and he marched to her side, his free will taken from him by the force of the hive mind.

Ash took up the space behind Maebh, her back a reassuring presence as they faced off the entire room. Maebh knelt long enough to place Sage's body on the ground, unsheathing her sword as she stood. She faced Setanta and Ethne as fire burned her from the inside. She couldn't look at her twin.

"There's no need for any more violence." Ethne stood from the throne with a weary sigh as Fianna swarmed Maebh and Ash.

Fuelled by a surge of defiant strength, Maebh lurched against the guard closest to her, swiping his blade away easily and disarming him with a swift, calculated strike. Beside her, Ash fought with equal ferocity, using Set's spear to carve against the many blades aimed in their direction.

As the guards closed in, Maebh and Ash fought back-to-back, their synchronised movements weaving a deadly game of steel and fury. A flicker of satisfaction crossed Maebh's face as she disarmed Fiadh Collins, the matriarch screeching as her clan pulled her out of harm's way. With a swift glance, she noticed the stone guard remained encircled around their fight, but none joined in. The throne room became a battleground of flashing blades, and Maebh's slashes grew deadlier with each strike; it was clear that neither side planned to lose.

The desperate muscles in her body refused to submit to their puppet strings, and as more guards encircled her, she fought with a primal rage, a kernel of that otherworldly strength awakening, but she would not release her ríastrad. Despite being outnumbered, Maebh fought on with a relentless resolve, but she felt herself tiring too soon as the onslaught against her blade never slowed.

The ancient force she had never tapped into stirred like a slumbering beast within, a dormant presence that now purred and stretched, a feline predator preparing to unleash its might. But her ríastrad waited for her. As Maebh fought, she felt its silent question. An invitation to sync into one and decimate their enemies.

Ash shouted at Maebh, and she turned to see her friend struggling against too many. Feeling her skin flush crimson, she debated succumbing and ending this fight. But that would make her a monster. Like her twin. With a sigh, she closed the link with her ríastrad.

It didn't take long for them to become overrun and unarmed. A sound tore from her throat, half-scream and half-snarl of defiance against their ruthless fate.

Ethne stood down from the platform, her slow steps clicking against the marble. "It may surprise you to know I don't enjoy the loss of innocent life."

"Are you High Queen now?" Maebh laughed; the sound empty as the female stood before her. "A Fomorian bitch to rule over us? We shouldn't see too much of a difference. Our High Kings have always been puppets and you're just like the Tuatha Dé."

Ethne's face contorted, her lips curling back over sharp teeth as she hissed in Maebh's face. "Never say that to me again."

Fury outweighed any sense of self preservation and Maebh headbutted her.

Ethne stumbled back, but Setanta caught her. Ash and Maebh were pushed forward; the guards holding Maebh in painful grips as they forced them to kneel before the steps leading to the empty throne. Soon after, the rígfénnid and matriarchs stepped forward, escorted by the stone guard to kneel alongside them.

Ethne nodded at Setanta, who strode to the side door, his steps heavy and mechanical.

Bradan appeared through the shadowed entranceway, a minn óir once again on his head. The golden crown was the only thing that gleamed in the room reeking of death.

"The throne is yours once more, High King." Ethne smiled before inclining her head. "As we agreed."

CHAPTER 77

AISLING

Ash knelt in the crowded throne room, growing unease swirling in her gut as Bradan took his seat on the throne, all leaders forced to kneel before their declared High King.

Beside her, Maebh shifted restlessly. A subtle brush of her friend's fingers steadied Ash's own jittery hands. Together they would face whatever came next. No matter how Ash tried, her eyes were irresistibly drawn to Set's imposing silhouette. Shadows painted harsh lines on his face as he stood beside Ethne and Bradan, no hint of the warmth once kindling his stormy eyes for her alone.

A jagged wound marred his handsome features above one brow, still seeping freely to paint half his face incarnadine. Guilt wriggled in her gut as the image seared itself upon her mind—this gash that would scar as tribute to choices cutting deeper than mere flesh.

Once Ash had traced gentle fingers over smooth skin, murmuring hopes for a future to share. Now only empty air separated their irreconcilable paths. Whatever Ethne had poisoned Set's mind with—to turn him against them—its roots ran deeper than the blood darkening his thunderous face.

Tendrils of remorse curled around Ash's heart, squeezing painfully. She couldn't blame Ethne alone. Her actions had caused this. Staring down at the spear discarded like rubbish on the ground between them, she fought against the urge to run to him. To explain why she'd considered using his spear. Her jaws ached from grinding them tightly. Set was not innocent in this. His ríastrad had taken control, but whatever actions had led to him standing side by side with Ethne was not on her.

Ash wrenched her eyes away, refusing to allow anguished tears to fall before their enemies. Set had carved this rift with his betrayal, no different than the blade marring him. She would get out of this without him. To where, she wasn't sure, but the truth that lay within this room was more painful than blades could ever scar.

"If anyone has an issue with me as their High King, let it be known." Draped in royal vestments beside a slyly smiling Ethne, Bradan's resonant voice reverberated off the lofty ceilings.

Muffled outbursts of shock rippled through the room as the weight of his betrayal struck home. A viper had lain hidden amongst them, slowly positioning its stranglehold upon the throne. He'd pretended to submit to Fionn, but his deception stood unveiled, an open challenge none could ignore.

Jaw locked, Ash met Bradan's stare unflinchingly before scanning the stone guard encircling the kneeling leaders. Whatever agreement had been laid in secret between them and Ethne, she would not cower. The truth was only the beginning.

Set stood like a pillar of muscle and fury between those on the throne and the leaders kneeling before it. Ash's heart broke into pieces as his wounded eye bypassed her as if she were a mere stranger. The cold dismissal cut deeper than any blade, reopening barely scabbed wounds with salt-laced fingers. He had chosen a woman who'd murdered their mothers.

Ash's breath caught as Nessa and the guardians stepped forward in unison, the alliance shift of the stone clan setting off a ripple of unease through the small assembly of leaders. She scanned their motionless faces desperately until Tiernan's features froze her heart mid-beat. Blinking back hot tears, she shut her eyes against the surge of loss and helplessness. He'd shown glimpses of the old Tiernan, yet an impossible chasm still severed her friend from truly breaking free.

When nobody spoke, Maebh tensed beside her, muttering, "Cowards."

"Do you have a problem, Matriarch?" Bradan asked, his face giving nothing away. "Alliances were formed for the elevation of all Fianna."

Maebh spat back. "Elevation? You are killing innocents without mercy!"

Ash shivered as she glanced toward the lone bundle by Maebh. Matted fur and pointed ears similar to a donkey poked through. The sight was disturbing and sad in the same breath. Maebh leaned forward, ignoring the stone guard who stepped closer to her. She picked Sage back into her arms, glaring up at their High King. Again, Ash's gaze landed on Set, who looked down on his sister with a tensed jaw as if he were physically restraining himself from going to his twin.

Bradan replied firmly. "Ethne ensured I took the throne. That is what matters."

Ash focused on him, inching forward on her knees, hands balled as she moved closer to where the spear lay between her and the throne. "You condemn innocent lives for power."

Bradan snapped. "I did what was necessary."

Ethne tapped on Bradan's shoulder, taking a step closer, addressing the line of Fianna kneeling. "Do you accept Bradan Cassidy as High King?"

Ethne's question dropped like a stone into still waters, sending anxious murmurs throughout the room. One by one, clan leaders voiced acceptance of the new regime, some more reluctant than others. Ash chanced a glance behind to Maebh, whose turmoil mirrored her own. Ash inched closer, the spear a solid presence against her knee. This choice could determine their clan's fate, for good or ill. When Maebh met her eyes, she nodded before glaring back toward the throne, face set in resolve.

The time for neutrality and half-measures had passed. Sacrifices must be made, and in that moment, Ash said goodbye to her clan, to her life. She was about to pay a price that neither she nor Maebh could afford. Their choice, for right or ruin, was made. Together they would face the fallout, come what may.

Slinking down, Ash swiped the spear as Maebh unsheathed the sword from the matriarch kneeling beside her. Fiadh Collins gasped in outrage, but it was too late.

Ethne cocked her head as both women raised their weapons in her direction, as if she were viewing two children squabbling over toys. Ash gritted her teeth as she glared at Bradan, angling the spear in his direction. "We do not recognise you as our king."

As if in response to her words, the spear thrummed, her sweat-slickened hand shaking with vibration.

"You are stripped of your titles of matriarch," Bradan answered quietly, each word laced with unbridled rage.

"High King…" Lorcan's eyes widened, and Ash's brows rose at her father's interference. She'd noticed how the stone clan had not engaged in overpowering Maebh or her, but they also hadn't come to their aid.

Gearoid gripped Lorcan's arm, pulling him back, but looking no less uncomfortable. Bradan continued as if uninterrupted.

"You are banished from the Kingdom of Mide, and you have thirty seconds to leave my sight before I condemn you to—"

"Do you remember your request of me?" Tiernan stepped forward, eyes blazing with unchecked emotion as he confronted the High King. Nessa tried to stop him, but he reared out of her grasp. "When I came to you asking for help when we searched for Fionn's resting place. You asked me to abandon my clan and rule at your side, long before catastrophe struck."

Murmurs rippled through the room at this revelation. The guardians' stoic ranks faltered in surprise at his outburst, but Lorcan and Gearoid flanked Tiernan, shielding him from the others.

Bradan nodded and Tiernan continued. "Do you still want me by your side?"

Bradan met his son's glare calmly. "Of course I do."

Tiernan turned then to face Ash and Maebh, a sad smile playing on his lips. "I'll join you on one condition: Maebh and Ash aren't banished, and they keep their titles."

"No, Tiernan!" Maebh cried, taking a step toward him but stopping when he raised his hand to stop her.

Ash's throat closed as she looked at Tiernan, the weight of his words settling heavily on her chest. Another sacrifice made to save them. Despite his claims at wanting his son by his side, Bradan's features hardened, shrewd calculation brewing behind his eyes.

The air in the room grew dense with strain, and Ash couldn't shake the knot in her stomach. She exchanged a quick, anguished look with Maebh; they both knew the heavy burden Tiernan offered to bear for their sake.

"No." Bradan leaned forward on the throne, the lines of authority etched deeper into his face. "I will not have disloyalty."

Ash let out a whoosh of relief, despite the predicament they were still under. Tiernan was not willingly walking from one prison into another for them.

"High King . . ." Ethne leaned close to Bradan, who went rigid at her closeness. His features contorted at whatever she said, a dance of conflicting emotions playing out on his face, too quickly for her to use her gift to determine what was transpiring between them. The air in the room crackled with tension as the silence stretched, Ash's anticipation growing with each passing moment.

After several long minutes that felt like an eternity, Bradan finally nodded, his jaw set in a hard line.

"So be it."

Ash almost let the spear drop with the weight of Tiernan's fate hanging on her shoulders.

"We don't want your titles," Ash spat at Bradan, turning pleading eyes on Tiernan. She whispered imploringly, "Don't agree to this, Tier. There's another way."

He simply shook his head. "You love your clans."

Maebh ate the distance between them and Tiernan, grabbing his arms, and he allowed her to tug him back to the centre where Ash remained. "You can't join him. Not after everything Ethne's done!"

Tiernan met her gaze sadly. "I have no choice, Mae."

Ash couldn't look away at their intimate moment. Tiernan was breaking free from the stone guard before her very eyes, only to be lost to them once more.

Maebh didn't let go. "Stay with me. We'll figure something out."

The spear thrummed again, and Ash's attention snagged on it. A pull formed in her gut, a sensation she'd felt before but never to this magnitude. When Nik had asked her if she could sift, she'd felt a barrier between her and the source allowing her to harness the gift that came so easily to Set. With the cold steel rod in her hand, she took a step closer to Tiernan and Maebh. Gripping Maebh's hand, she wrapped her arm around Tiernan, embracing them both as she thought about that tugging sensation.

"You don't have to join him," Ash whispered, remembering the weighted feeling she'd experienced behind enemy territory with a human stable-hand. Snatching that surge of power, she prayed she wasn't about to make the biggest mistake of her life.

CHAPTER 78
AISLING

Ash shut her eyes as cries from the throne room faded to silence, her world narrowing to linked bodies anchoring her against oblivion's pull. Icy wind screamed past, stealing breath and sound as finally, she succumbed. Reality warped sickeningly, spinning her into a black chasm.

All sensation bled away except the biting chill needling her exposed skin.

A bone-jarring wrench slammed her back into physical being. Gasping painfully, she collapsed to hands and knees upon solid ground once more. The disorientation ebbed slowly, sounds and muted light bleeding back in.

Ash blinked, vision swimming into focus. Twilight embraced unfamiliar woods, shadows creeping between gnarled trunks. The frosty night breeze kissed her cheeks, carrying the scent of pine and distant cookfires.

With a groan she pushed up from the carpet of fallen leaves and pine needles. Her limbs ached but no serious harm seemed done by their desperate flight.

Nearby, her friends sprawled likewise, faces bloodless from their journey.

"What the fuck did you do?" Maebh gasped, sitting upright with her sword still clutched in one hand.

Tiernan roused from where he'd sprawled amid the undergrowth. "She sifted."

"But to where?" Maebh asked, kicking at the leaf-strewn ground.

Together they took stock of their new surroundings. A sky full of stars greeted them, and a range of murky peaks loomed against the night, silhouetted teeth guarding hidden perils. Yet at the mountains' feet, lights beckoned from a village nestled in the sheltering forest.

"I've been here before," Ash managed through shallow breaths.

"Where did you sift us to?" Tiernan asked again.

Ash looked at the spear quivering in her hands, now silent as she willed her legs to move. Panic surged within, dread pressing against her chest like a suffocating weight. "We need to leave. Now."

Galloping hooves came from behind and she turned to see a black horse appearing from the trees.

"Croi Dubh?" Ash jumped at the sight of a hulking figure on his back. "Nik?"

"Why are you back here?" his gruff voice filled the air as he dismounted the horse. "You must flee!"

More hooves broke through the silence, thundering beats that shattered the uneasy stillness. Nik cursed under his breath as a legion of horses and riders broke through the shadowed woodland. The metallic jingle of armour and the rhythmic snorts from fae horses filled the air, drowning out the pounding in Ash's head.

The riders, their faces obscured by helmets and cloaks, formed an imposing circle around their small gathering. The glint of weapons and the undeniable essence that cemented them as Tuatha Dé Danann hung thick in their small clearing.

A blur of shadows flew past Ash before ice formed around her throat. Reaching up, her eyes doubled as her fingers brushed an alien metal. Clawing at her neck, both Tiernan and Maebh struggled against the collars that had been placed on them. When she met Nik's gaze, he shook his head solemnly. "I'm sorry, lass."

Gripping the spear, she lunged closer to Maebh and Tiernan. "We have to sift back!"

But the smell of iron filled her nostrils, taking over her ability to stand, let alone move through space. A hollowness consumed her insides until the only thing she could do was fall to her knees, both of her friends meeting her there.

"The collars," Tiernan choked, baring his teeth in pain. "They're magic repellents."

"Welcome back to Rathcroghan," a multi-layered voice said, before the Morrígan stepped into view. With a wide smile, her voice transformed to indicate only Macha was present in this moment. "And I see you brought company."

Ash froze, voice stolen as surely as breath, as the phantom queen's presence crushed her will like the dried leaves under her knees.

"Nik, see to it our guests have suitable accommodation." Macha's smile held no mirth, only ancient purpose as she beckoned her guards to hoist them from the ground. Ash couldn't resist, her limbs leaden from the iron collar. The weight of the magic bound within it pressed down on her, sapping her strength as the spear slipped from her limp fingers.

Training her focus on Maebh and Tiernan, muted panic set in at how immobile they were too. A weakness coated her body as she fought against the inexorable pull into unconsciousness, the edges of her vision blurring with each futile attempt to resist.

Noting Nik's bow at Macha, Ash watched in dismay as he galloped toward the ancient fortress shrouded in darkness without looking back. Dark spires reached for the heavens, clawing to snatch them in its grip.

"Your blood sings to our kind," Macha said, mounting her horse before training depthless eyes on her. The weight of her appraisal was an incantation, probing the depths of Ash's very soul. "Let's see how much Tuatha Dé is within."

Acknowledgements

Lovely reader, I hope you enjoyed the sequel to my debut series, *Fair Ones*. Once again, I've left my misfits in quite the predicament . . .

I dedicated this book to my stepdad, Brendan, who left this world far too soon. Brendan was the type of man who was the first person you called for anything. Whether it was to ask a question about the most random things, or to talk politics or world history. Brendan loved with all his heart, and he could fix anything that was broken. He's the inspiration behind my character, Dom. There aren't enough words to convey how devasting his passing was. Writing this book this year was both torture and catharises after losing someone so important to me.

Lee, you've been my rock. I'm so grateful for you and the kids and the weird and crazy bubble we live in. They are growing up too fast, and I'm blessed to have you by my side as we watch their beautiful souls shine every day.

Michaela and Mam, here's to taking on the world one sarcastic meme or gif at a time. Dad, thanks for being the one parent who actually reads my books.

Miranda, this book honestly wouldn't exist without you. Thanks so much for everything. Darby, thanks for all your support throughout the year. Here's to a better one ahead.

Thank you, lovely street team for being a part of my Fair Ones clan. I hope you've enjoyed this book!

Catherine, thanks for all your check-ins as I slowly turned into a recluse this year. I appreciate every single time you did.

Michelle, you have been a joy to work with. I'm so glad I found you as my editor! Your enthusiasm, encouragement, and attention to detail have been boundless. Rhys, thanks so much for the beautiful map you created. Taire, thank you so much for creating this stunning cover and for having boundless patience. I loved working on this with you!

Until next time, thanks for reading!

About the Author

Claire Wright is the author of the Irish fantasy series *Fair Ones*. She currently lives in Ireland with her husband, three children and one eccentric dog.

When she's not writing, she's usually listening to an audiobook while trying to juggle too many tasks.

Claire pulls her inspiration from the rolling mountains to her left, crashing waves of the sea to her right, and a small town steeped in lore.

Check out www.authorclairewright.com for extras and book merch.

Go Raibh Maith Agat

Enjoyed this book? Consider leaving a review! It helps other readers find new books to explore.

Follow Claire on her socials and check out her website www.authorclairewright.com for exclusive content and new releases.